About the Author

A teacher of English in international secondary schools for over 15 years, Debbie Duggan knows and understands the expat lifestyle. A keen observer of people and personalities, this novel reflects her fascination with the 'golden cage' fantasy fulfilment of the British expat experience and how it can change people.

Debbie Duggan

EXPAT

AUSTIN MACAULEY
PUBLISHERS LTD.

A CIP catalogue record for this title is available from the British Library.

ISBN 978 1 78554 171 1 (Paperback)
ISBN 978 1 78554 172 8 (Hardback)

www.austinmacauley.com

First Published (2015)
Austin Macauley Publishers Ltd.
25 Canada Square
Canary Wharf
London
E14 5LQ

Printed and bound in Great Britain

Prologue

Can you imagine how it feels to have everything you most want within your grasp? To know that fate has brought you to this pass, that destiny waits, coat in hand, while you make your decision? The minutes pass leaden-footed. The bright lights of the night-time traffic flicker by; outside the closed container of the car life goes on: trapped in this little metal box, this time capsule, there are just two of us. Two people who last week had no idea of the other's existence. The sound of waiting is palpable; my heart beats with thick strong strokes. There is no comprehension in my brain, only a beat like a ticking clock; a death watch beetle – but not for me. No comprehension of what this might mean and yet everything it would mean if I bring myself to say the word. He waits and in the harsh yellow light, his face is cold. He is a man of shadows and he hides from the light; he glances away and shifts in his seat. His coat smells of stale smoke; the leather squeaks uneasily under his weight. 'Well?' he asks, and his voice is dark, accented, redolent of the restless streets that are his territory.

And still I cannot answer. The breath sticks in my throat.

'Khelaas,' he says bluntly. The single word in Arabic is familiar: *enough.* He has had enough, he is making ready to go; his hand reaches for the door handle. The moment is here; it stands on tiptoe waiting to see what I will do.

'And there will be time, time to murder and create ...'

Carpe Diem.

'Yes', I say.

Part 1

The Meeting

For I have known them all already, known them all
Have known the evenings, mornings, afternoons,
I have measured out my life with coffee spoons ...

T S Eliot 'The Love Song of J Alfred Prufrock'

The first time I see her is, appropriately enough, spring, or what passes for spring in this desert corner of the world; the garden is basking in the late warm light of afternoon and the garden is abloom with a hundred fragrances and the red blaze of a tumbling bougainvillea, and I am sitting on the top step of the swimming pool contemplating the frangipani tree that stands at the other end of the pool. The day is like any other day, languid and warm, with the golden air dripping scents and a wonderful sense that there is nothing to be done that has to be done. It is a T. S. Eliot afternoon and indeed there will be time. But my peaceful vigil is interrupted.

The cat is on the wall again, hissing at the dog on the other side; that idiotic mutt leaps and barks quite pointlessly. But its noise has summoned next door's maid and I feel I should go and remove my offending feline; that would be neighbourly. I can hear the maid reprimanding the dog; the cat is now walking delicately along the wall, lifting its feet over the strands of bougainvillea and wearing the snootiest expression imaginable on its face. The dog, clearly immune to how foolish it looks, continues to leap and bark. As I walk towards the wall I can clearly hear the rhythmic thuds as it hits the ground, interspersed with the scrabble of its nails on the concrete. The maid's reprimands are clearly having no effect and I can hear a note of desperation creeping into her voice. I step up on the ledge behind the pond and make to scoop the cat off the wall, giving me a view of the other garden. A middle-aged Indian woman is trying to catch the dog and is poised at an angle – she looks up at me open-mouthed as I loom over the wall. I grab the cat and drop him without ceremony back into my own garden; immediately the dog ceases barking but it continues to scurry up and down the wall in case the enemy should once more heave into sight. It is a scruffy mutt of indeterminate breed, but clearly a dog of character. The maid straightens and smiles apologetically; my European face has clearly alerted her to the fact that I might take umbrage and words bubble to her lips, 'Madam, I am sorry, I hope your cat is not hurt.'

Hurt? That indolent creature that has deliberately put itself on top of the wall to cause trouble? Deliberate baiter of gullible canines?

'Heavens no,' I say airily. 'It's fine.'

She smiles with relief, and I am just about to step down off my ledge when a woman comes out on to the upstairs verandah of the house. Both of us turn to look up at her, the maid with a slight frown as if the fracas has disturbed her mistress's nap and she fears a telling off, me gawping at one of the most beautiful women I have ever seen. Seen close up, in the harsh light of a Dubai afternoon, she is almost flawless, and this in spite of clearly having risen from bed. Her blonde hair is tumbled, some concoction of lace and silk is dragged around her, but she still manages to look amazing. I have a vague impression of long, gloriously sun-washed limbs and a beautiful face.

'Hello,' I say foolishly. 'I'm so sorry; I think it was my cat that was causing the problem. Your dog was just responding as dogs do.'

At the appearance of its mistress, the dog has immediately fallen back on its haunches and gazes up at her with the kind of jaw-dropping foolishness on its face that I feel sure is reflected on the maid's and certainly on my own. We all stare at the vision on the verandah, waiting for the goddess to speak. She doesn't. She nods briefly in my direction, ignores the maid and the dog and goes back inside. The door slams shut and the maid, the dog and I look at each other.

'That,' says the maid in hushed tones, 'is my madam. I am afraid she sleeps in the afternoon and now we have awakened her.'

'I'm so sorry,' I say, also in a semi-whisper, as the maid collars the dog and makes to drag it indoors. 'Please apologise to her for me, my name is Sophie, Sophie Roberts. And you are? ...'

She bobs her head at me. 'Yes madam, I will. My name is Rosie. And that -' she gestures upstairs '- is Ms Natasha. We have only been living here a few weeks. The dog belongs to my madam's little boy, Alexei. He is not yet very well behaved. I am sorry, madam.'

I am about to say more, but she is on her way indoors, and now she and mutt disappear and all is quiet. I get down off my perch and retreat indoors; in my own living room the cat has curled up on the sofa and raises its head to give me a supercilious look. I look at it with pursed lips. 'Well,' I remark to it, 'It's an idiot dog but you didn't help. In fact, I suspect that was totally deliberate on your part.' The cat tucks its head under its tail and goes to sleep. I wander into the kitchen and muse on the little drama that had just unfolded over the wall. *Note to self*, I think, *go and introduce yourself*, but not, clearly, in the afternoon when madam is sleeping. I could perhaps be useful too; the dog could clearly do with some training and that's something I know about. I have seen a small thin boy coming and going, being delivered by a driver from, presumably, school each day; he looks to be about 9 years old. That must be Alexei. Interesting. I put it on my list of things to be done. The road itself is a united nations of different cultures and nationalities with whom, as yet, I have not become very friendly. Oddly, however, I feel drawn to the beautiful woman next door. It's the Libra thing, I know. Libras love beauty, and I'm totally a Libra. And she is totally beautiful. I wonder if she speaks English, what she does, if she works. Rosie did not mention a man, a husband or partner, and in my infrequent observations of the house next door I have seen no one who fits that old stereotyped description of the 'man of the house.'

This is of course unusual in this part of the world, as women rarely live alone; there is always a 'man in the case'. My own member of the male species, he who masquerades as sponsor and protector, keeper of the castle, as it were, is not here. He seldom is, as he is too busy exercising *son droit de seigneur* elsewhere. Unfortunately, in order that I may stay in this country, we have to maintain the pretence that we are still a 'happily' married couple; it's not so unusual, in fact I am frequently finding out how very common it is. Both parties put aside common differences and put on a public face to maintain the status quo; both have things that the other provides that they need. Hence both continue the farce as it plays both ways; for women, the benefits are largely economical, for men it permits the maintenance of an illusion of respectability which allows them to play around as much as they want. The patriarchal society is alive and well and living in Dubai.

I pour myself a glass of wine and, upon reflection, take it and the half-full bottle to my study upstairs and sit down at the desk, confronted by the usual pile of drafts and possible articles. I take out my red pen, but my eyes keep moving to the upstairs windows of the house next door that overlook my study. I am reading words without absorbing them, and the wine is going down along with the sunshine; an orange haze hangs over the garden speckled with mist as Ahmed sets the sprinkler system going. I can hear the TV going in the kitchen which means that Patti has begun supper. I don't know where Rick is but I do know he won't be ringing to tell me where he is either, nor can I be bothered to find out. But it is not fair that Patti should be cooking dinner for two people when only one slightly pissed and abandoned woman is staying in for dinner.

I pick up the empty wine glass and go downstairs.

Of course it wasn't always like this, and that note of cynical unconcern that I notice in myself more and more these days certainly was not part of my nature. It has grown, like all the other acquired attitudes with which we women make our way as wives and mothers, but seldom as individuals, in a society where we are largely valued by what our husband does or who he works for. The pecking order is fairly strictly established; the memsahibs of the Raj would certainly recognise this new type of colonialism. We arrived, bouncy and ignorant, following the leader of the pack and his new job in the Middle East. He came first and we followed; arriving full of excitement (and totally unsuitable clothing) desperate for the expat experience.

I cast my mind back to our arrival five years previously. Teenagers being monosyllabic, fortunately, they had tended to show their irritation rather than say it and whilst this was irritating, it was actually easier to deal with than whining. Their body language expressed very clearly exactly what they felt, but at least I did not have to hear it. We emerged from the cool streamlined terminal into heat which could only be compared to an oven, and which paused the attitudes in mid-twitch; now there was actually something genuine to register other than faux irritation. Just breathing was painful and I could feel my whole body breaking out in a sweat. I remember the vague grasping at impressions too; thousands of Indian workers, seriously elegant and beautiful women, both European and Emirati, tall good-looking Arabs in their long white dishdashas and head-dresses.

The growling noise on my left translated into 'There's dad', and sure enough, there was dad, my husband, Roderick, better known as Rick, waving and smiling in the boyish way that he has (he particularly cherishes his boyish charm and good looks and plays on them consistently). His mother named him Roderick Roberts as a joke, I believe; a kind of amusing alliteration but Rick Roberts works all right. Rod Roberts would be just too awful. He greeted us all with a bear hug and a kiss for Tash and me, although mine lands somewhere to the left of my ear as he is already gathering luggage and leading the way out. He looks well, tanned and happy. But then, compared to our British pastiness, most of the world looks tanned. Tash and I have clearly made the same note to self: *get a tan quickly!* My note would also read – *join the gym*. One does not want to look like a country bumpkin although I am staring like one at … the new car. Rick looks like a magician who has produced the required rabbit from the hat and we stand in admiring silence. It's a shining 4WD, basking sleekly in its bay, so new it almost has the wrappers still on it. I spare a thought for the elderly family Nissan that has just gone to a good home in the country. The well-worn seats, the windows much breathed and scribbled on by two excited children, the lack of suspension. So this is the future. We climb aboard and are driven away chattering excitedly; the car is so quiet and smooth it's like suddenly waking in a different century. I could be in 'Blade Runner' beside Harrison Ford!

Day two of my new life, and the most important part of the morning was the Meeting of the Maid. This, Rick explained, is positively commonplace; everyone has a maid. To a woman accustomed to doing her own housework for 20 years the idea of having a live-in maid is idyllic. I have a kind of Victoria Beckham view on life as I take a shower and abandon the heap of sheets, pillows and duvets that constitute the marital bed without a thought for its tidiness. 'Just leave everything,' says Rick, 'Patti does it all.'

Patti is introduced at breakfast. She is a short, plump Sri Lankan, very sweet and with a lovely smile. It is hard to tell her age, but she is probably in her early fifties. She looks very embarrassed at my proffered hand, and touches it only briefly. 'Welcome madam,' she says, and turns away hurriedly to dish up scrambled eggs on toast for our breakfast. We sit at the kitchen table to eat as the palatial dining room is too far away for early morning comfort.

Over coffee, as Rick goes off to his office, I pursue a conversation with Patti. She is hard to understand, being shy and not very good with English and my ear has not yet adjusted. I can see we will have to converse in a kind of pidgin English but I do manage to glean a few details. She has been in the Middle East for a long time, almost twenty years, in different countries. She is married to Paul who works in a factory as a line manager. She has a 14 year old daughter, who lives in Sri Lanka with Patti's mother and who has never been to Dubai. All the time we are talking, Patti is working. She cleans and washes up, stacks the dishwasher, puts things away while I sit in idle luxury, sipping my coffee. Our conversation sounds something like this:

'Patti, please don't call me Madam. I'm not a Madam. My name is Sophie.'

'Oh no madam, I like to call the madam, Madam. Always do this, all my houses.'

'Okay, if you prefer. It just sounds funny. I've never thought of myself as a Madam.'

At this point the children appear, and are introduced. They, like me, are gobsmacked at the thought of a maid, and sit in a kind of trance as Patti fusses round them, pouring cereal into their plates, adding milk, making tea, virtually putting the spoons into their hands. They say little, which is their usual morning behaviour, but there is a moment of altercation when Nick takes his plate to the dishwasher. He is intercepted by Patti who, moving at the speed of sound, smoothly whips the plate out of his hand and replaces it with a dish of scrambled eggs. Nick is steered firmly back to the table and settled into his chair once more with a startled 'thwump'. Patti smiles at him triumphantly, but her firm, pudgy hand on his shoulder brooks no opposition. Nick gets on with eating. Tash, always a quick learner, doesn't even try. As Patti brings her plate of eggs, she simply holds out her cereal bowl and takes the eggs in exchange. I can see we are going to have to change this system or my children are going to forget how to fend for themselves. But on the first day of their holiday, I will let them enjoy the fun of being waited on.

Carrying my coffee I decide to wander over my new estate. The villa, as it is known, is ridiculously large, really, for a family of four. The living room is massive and leads out onto a small square balcony which overlooks the garden. The air is much cooler than last night and the sky is blue. It is a beautiful morning in Dubai. I sink into a swing lounger, sip my coffee and wriggle my toes in delight. This is the life! Just as I am mid-stretch a small, wizened dark face suddenly appears between the pillars of the balcony, rising like a gnome and grinning widely. 'Morning Madam', says the face and now the rest of the body appears, tall and thin and clad in a slightly shabby long white shirt and pants. I am reminded that I am still wearing my pyjamas, which though perfectly respectable, are not perhaps what one should interview the gardener in. For this is who the gnome is; Ahmed, the gardener. 'Good morning, Ahmed', I respond, causing him to beam with delight and then disappear as he bends once more over the beds. I am pleased that I've remembered his name; something of Rick's briefing that stuck with me. I leave the sun lounger to resume my tour.

The dining room is another marble-floored and sizeable room which leads off the living room. It is graced by two small chandeliers that look vaguely ridiculous, but the living room has no fewer than four of the same. It all contributes to the palatial air that the place has. Back through the hall again, and the chandelier here is larger, with more layers of crystals. I turn it on for fun, and the hall is flooded with light. The stairs are wide, also marble-floored, with a shallow tread and a black wrought iron banister. As I ascend, I feel I should be wearing a ball-gown with a train flowing behind me. The landing is a wide central space called the 'majlis' apparently; it has been decorated with a rug and flat red cushions which form a sitting area. Rick has his study, a sunny room which makes up the fourth bedroom on this floor, and the stairs curve up again to the top floor and the roof, a huge flat space, *perfect for parties* I think, as I stand and gaze out at the view; nothing sensational, only houses and gardens, but there are some trees that are a credible size and the chattering of birds is surprising. I had thought it would be too hot for birds. I can see the neighbour's cat sitting on the patio, licking itself. The whole scene is surprisingly domesticated, and amazingly quiet. I can hear the hum of traffic away to the east, but we are in a quiet and suburban part of town and there is a gentle hum of activity as Ahmed trundles around the corner with his wheelbarrow, and the high sweet voices of the maids next door chatter as they hang out the washing on a line strung across the roof. They wave at me shyly and collapse with giggles when I wave back. I retire indoors once more and wander back down to my room. I have things to unpack.

So much has changed in five years. We have all changed and not necessarily for the better. Sometimes I wonder what went wrong; other times I think it was just the passage of time. Our marriage was almost on the rocks, as they say, when we came to Dubai; the move could have been the breath of life, sadly it has been the kiss of death. How ironic it is that in this land dominated by a strict and moral code of conduct, our lives have disintegrated and we maintain only an illusion of morality; my husband has a mistress, and me? Well, I have no-one. Occasionally I have my children, and I have my job. Mostly I just have myself. What I do have is an exotic place to live, a style of life that many would envy and the belief that it is worthwhile. I wonder where Sophie Roberts went to, sometimes. What became of lively, bubbly Sophie who was fun and sociable, cried like a child over old movies and adored her handsome clever husband and beautiful clever children? What changed the warm heart that that Sophie possessed into a block of ice? Why doesn't this Sophie cry over so much ruination? I don't know, but I keep on hoping every day that I'll find the answer, or at least a solution. My mother used to say "God never shuts a door but he opens a window" which was a wonderfully comforting thought that was fortified by a religious belief that I sadly don't share with my mother. But it lingers as parental advice often does, especially in forty-something adults, who are now parents themselves. But I am still looking for my window. And it's an awfully long time coming. Maybe God, like every other male in my life, has a warped sense of humour.

The note to self, as often is the case, did not make much difference; a week later as I swing into the carport, I notice a sleek black Mercedes parked next door, its engine purring imperceptibly. The windows are darkened, but it is waiting and, as I unpack myself from my own car, there is a click of heels and I catch a glimpse of my glamorous neighbour. She is dressed to kill, no doubt about that. As usual, there is only the briefest glance as she whisks into the car, door held open for her by a dark suited driver. I stand rather foolishly, arms full of groceries, as she is driven away and Patti comes out fussing that I have not called her and relieves me of the heaviest bags. A few moments later, Rosie appears to walk the dog accompanied by Alexei. I manage a brief greeting as dog and Rosie and Alexei dance away; the dog has clearly seen a cat and tows them off down the road at speed. I remind myself that I had intended to offer dog training lessons. I will leave a note on the door. I will do something! I also have an excuse to visit; there's an article that Wayne wants me to write about a maid's life in Dubai, so that will give me the opportunity to involve Rosie in my researches. There's no point asking Patti, she hates the idea of giving information and when I get out my pen and notebook a glazed look comes into her eyes and she gets completely tongue tied. Any question is met with 'yes madam' or 'no madam'. I try and tell her that it's just research but she is clearly terrified. So I'm thinking I'll try my luck with Rosie. She seems a good place to start.

There being no time like the present, I grab a cup of tea and keep an eye on the front window and presently I see Alexei's head whizz past followed by Rosie's moving more sedately. Clearly the dog has not been much tired by his walk round the park. I give them enough time to settle back and then trot round and knock on their front door. There is a volley of hysterical barking – *where to start?* I wonder – and Rosie opens the door a crack and peeps out. The dog, clearly being held by Alexei, sounds throttled somewhere behind her knees.

I briefly introduce the reason for my visit. Poor Rosie. You can see she's not too keen on any of this but she has the Indian maid's in-built respect for the white memsahib, and she can't think of a good reason not to let me in. Maybe, deep down, she's thinking *'oh let the madwoman help if she can'*! I slither through the crack in the door before she can change her mind.

Alexei is pale and thin; he has huge dark eyes and unruly dark hair and none of his mother's beauty, unless one counts his fine bone structure. I address myself to him and he listens with attention. Rosie has taken herself back to the kitchen and the dog (whose name I learn is Hector) is sitting panting quietly after welcoming me rapturously. Alexei and I sit on the floor, cross-legged, and he softly strokes the dog's head while telling me its history. His English is good and, typical of the international student, fairly un-accented; he has all the range of American slang one expects in a 9 year old and a rather sweetly endearing attitude. He comes across as a lonely little boy whose sole companion is the scruffy mutt who lies on the floor with his head in Alexei's lap. In between getting the lowdown on Hector (found on a rubbish tip as a puppy and brought back for Alexei by *'a friend of Mama's'*) my eyes wander all over the room. It is simply furnished in neutral colours and fairly screams "Ikea". There is little reference to personal items except for a couple of framed photographs on the sideboard; a middle-aged woman smiling with a handful of roses – Alexei's grandmother perhaps? – and the other one of a baby, presumably Alexei. The paintings on the wall are insignificant copies and, apart from a really beautiful display of flowers in the bowl on the dining table, the room has an unloved and unlived-in feel to it. Alexei continues to tell me of Hector's achievements and is fairly chronological in his discourse; we have proceeded from his adoption by Alexei and now advance through his first year, with anecdotes being added to confirm Hector's genius and superior character. The child gives the impression, even to such an amateur psychologist as me, of being starved of company and affection. It is clear that the dog is hugely important to him. He chats on until Rosie appears with glasses of lemonade for us both; beautiful homemade lemonade in a jug that clinks with ice cubes. Rosie is clearly a treasure. I seize the moment as Alexei downs his lemonade to butt in quickly with my ideas for Hector's rehabilitation.

'He's a lovely dog,' I begin, stroking Hector's head, 'and obviously very clever. Mixed breeds are the smartest you know.' Alexei's eyes are huge over the edge of his glass of lemonade. 'But it's important that we teach him some basic commands. It would be very useful for you if he was a bit more obedient wouldn't it?'

Alexei admits that sometimes Hector is a tad over-powering and Rosie and I exchange an amused look. I am beginning to like Rosie very much. I ask her to join us, and we sit and have a useful chat about Hector, ranging from what he eats and how he eats it through to a quick analysis of pack mentality. She listens with interest and her calm intelligent face reflects her commitment to what I am saying. Alexei listens too but takes time out to stroke and fondle Hector. It is clear that he finds constant reassurance in touching the animal, and it comforts him to have it there. After the lemonade is finished, we all adjourn to the kitchen. These houses are all alike and my house reflects this one like a mirror image. I explain about the need to be the dominant member of the pack and how to establish this through the feeding technique. Alexei and Rosie practice and there is a lot of giggling from Alex when he has to mime eating out of the dog's bowl to show Hector that master eats first and dog second. We leave Hector down the other end of the room snoozing in his basket as I don't want him to learn any of this before they have it pat. When that method has been mastered, we join Hector in the TV 'snug' area, and he sleeps peacefully, with Alexei once more established beside the basket, stroking him. I introduce the idea of 'positive training' using treats and explain how they should be administered. Rosie makes a note of what to buy. After a few more minutes, I judge that we've come to the end of the first lesson; no need to confuse them with too much on the first day.

Rosie excuses herself to make Alexei's tea, and I induce him to come and sit with me on the sofa and chat.

'There are lots of good dog training videos on the computer … do you have one so I can show you?' He brings his laptop and we go through a few, laughing at some of the antics and praising the clever dogs, especially one who brings beers from the fridge. Do I think Hector could learn to do that? Well, yes, I do, but that's rather an advanced trick. We will have to begin with the basics. He is rather a sweet little boy; shy initially but now snuggling up to me as he puts the laptop on my knee and leans into my arm as we look at the screen.

Rosie, ever mindful of my European need for constant nourishment, brings a cup of tea, which she places at my elbow. It is beautifully presented with a small biscuit on the side and a slim sachet of sugar. I smile my thanks at her.

Alexei's supper is now ready and dog wakes on cue, readying himself for scraps and looks most aggrieved when, true to my command, none are forthcoming. Alexei is clearly finding it hard not to feed his favourite friend, so Rosie and I sit with him at the table and distract him. When supper is finished, Alexei asks permission to leave the table (*'madam insists on good manners'* says Rosie) and is allowed to go next door and watch television in the snug. I give in and allow Hector to share the sofa with him; Rome was not built in a day after all. Rosie and I sit on at the table chatting. She is delightful and responds to my journalist-questioning with charm and dignity.

She has been with Ms Natasha ever since she came to Dubai, so that would be about 3 years. 'Alexei is so much better now; I would not believe he used to be so quiet and shy and very insecure. Madam was so worried about his wetting his bed and it was months before he would stop. But now, and especially since the arrival of Hector, he is a much happier little boy. He likes his school and although he has not a best friend, just yet, he is beginning to know some boys in the street and sometimes they invite him out to play. Of course he has not had an easy upbringing ... he was for a long time with his grandmother in Russia and when he came here he almost did not know his mother as he had never lived with her before and Madam is ... well, Madam is not easy. And she works very late hours and so much of the time it is necessary to be quiet so she can sleep, and she is often not here at night so Alexei is used to going to bed on his own and not seeing his mother sometimes for a few days.' I butt in to ask what Madam does for a living and Rosie's good natured, honest face reflects some unease with her answer, although it comes pat enough. 'Madam is a hostess for the palace; she organises events and is the hostess for them. And she speaks different languages too, and so when there are politicians present she will assist with translations.'

'So Madam is Russian?'

'Yes, and she also speaks English and French and some Arabic.'

'And what of Alexei's father?'

Here Rosie looks down sadly. 'I do not know, Madam. I have never asked but I have never heard anything of him. It is very sad for a boy not to know his father, but I have never asked. It is not my business after all.'

'And his grandmother in Russia?'

'I think she writes sometimes, Madam, but the letters are in Russian of course, and Alexei never talks about them'.

He must be very lonely, I venture to suggest. It seems odd that there are no cousins, no family who write to him.

'Yes Madam, it is very sad. I try to make up for it and give him as much love as I can but I am only the maid and I will not always be in his life. I try not to get too fond of him, but he is a child who needs me and I give him what I can.'

It is heart-wringing stuff and my hand automatically reaches out across the table to take hers. 'Rosie, I don't know you very well but I can see you are doing a fantastic job. And really, if I can help in any way, you must tell me.' She gives me a flash of that lovely warm-hearted smile. 'Thank you Madam. You are very kind. And this dog training is wonderful. Alexei will be so happy that Hector will begin to behave better. And maybe to do tricks!' We both laugh. I would love to sit and chat on with this lovely woman, but I realise that, even though I don't have anything to go home to, it is indeed the dinner hour for normal people, and I should make a move. We make a tentative arrangement for me to visit three days a week at around this time, and I pop my head round the corner to say *Dasvidaniya* to Alexei. He is engrossed in some awful cartoon programme but he calls out 'Goodbye' happily enough and Hector, re-established on the couch, grunts as the position of his head on Alexei's lap is disturbed. I thank Rosie again and show myself out.

The only time of the day when I feel almost happy is, contrarily enough, when I arrive at the office. Next morning, once seated in my swivel chair in our little glass box with '*Insider*' written boldly on the frosted glass door, life seems almost exciting.

This morning Wayne is there before me and is engaged in a phone conversation, his feet propped up on the desk in the manner of all aspiring editors. He waves and gestures towards a large box with Krispy Kreme emblazoned on the lid. "Dig in." he mouths.

Our Shazza is not in yet but has left me a couple of messages in the form of bright pink post-its with her scrawled signature in the corner. Alex is not here either; his is the third and most untidy desk in the corner of our little space.

I've often pondered on the composition of the *Insider* team and the fact that we're all misfits in different ways. Wayne is to the media born; he has come from a real job in London with the BBC and, for reasons which he fondly imagines to be inscrutable, is wasting his life away in this desert town on a magazine which, in spite of our combined good intentions, is really nothing more than the plaything of a spoiled princess. Literally. Our esteemed owner is a member – albeit somewhat minor – of the ruling royal family who cherishes the idea of a hard-hitting magazine that will expose the core, rotten or otherwise, of Dubai life. Unfortunately, she can never decide on exactly what she wants us to expose, and is consistently worried about offending one of her nearest and dearest so, in spite of our real talent and enthusiasm, we are really a magazine without a clear objective and all we manage to do is a couple of fairly serious articles drowned in a sea of fashion, make-up parades, mini-celebrities and advertising which serves no clear purpose. Frustrating, yes. And yet we stay … it is a paid job after all. PB (Princess Barbie) as Wayne calls her is generous to a fault, and fondly imagines we are all just as happy and as intellectually challenged as we would be under

Rupert Murdoch under her wide-eyed and eyeliner-heavy leadership. She attends an editorial meeting once a week with Wayne and sometimes Alex or me, which always follows the same pattern ... we put forward our ideas and she rejects them. Or modifies them. Or reduces them to bastard children that we would never own. Often it's just too much trouble to argue so we give in and go and report on the fashion show that she wants us to cover rather than the kind of hard-hitting investigative journalism that we are fretting about, for which there is actually so much material in this town. Unfortunately, we know in most cases that she's right. This is a benign dictatorship and all the lovely people who dance the night away, hang out in nightclubs, drink themselves legless at Friday brunches and patronise brothels have perhaps forgotten that they are here only on sufferance. The rule here is simple but unwritten; you can have what you want but you must never talk about it. Do that and you are out. 'Don't rock the boat' is the rule that will maintain the status quo. And that's what we all want – really. That's what my husband does. That's what all our friends do. That's what Wayne does. Wayne, with his live-in lover who is an air steward with Emirates; homosexuality is in no way tolerated here in Dubai but Wayne and Bertie live together and no one bats an eye. Why? Because it's easier to pretend that it doesn't happen. Wayne, darling, loveable, heart-on-his-sleeve Wayne who gave up the sort of journalistic career in London that I would sell my soul for, because Bertie doesn't want to leave Dubai and Emirates will not base him in London. The price of love, and he pays it every day.

The only one who's different is Alex. I would love to be like Alex. He is the real journalist among us and he has sources you wouldn't believe. Alex knows Dubai, knows it backwards and inside out; knows the dark alleys and the drug dealers, the peddlers of dope and child prostitutes, the inhabitants of the twilight world that is never suspected behind the glass towers and marble colonnades and designer labels. Alex has his finger on the pulse and a fascinating one it is too. He writes an editorial for quality broadsheets in London and New York –

using a nom de plume of course – but much of what he comments on is financial with the occasional foray into the social. Most of what Alex knows can never be told, but he knows it nonetheless. He says it's a kind of hunger, this nose for news, that can't be ignored; if he is out drinking a sundowner in some creek-side bar and sees someone he 'knows' he can't resist finding out why they're there. It may never do him any good – indeed we joke that his headless body will one day be washed up along the Gulf somewhere because the nose for news got in the way of somebody's need for privacy. So why is Alex here? Now that, I don't know. Escaping his past? He's certainly very reluctant to share the reasons why he's here but we have winkled a few facts out of him, mostly on certain drunken late night sprees when we all go out on the town and let our hair down. I know, for example, that he escaped from Moscow with no luggage and only a passport in his pocket having been tipped off that a certain newly-made billionaire – the exact origins of whose money Alex was investigating – had taken out a contract on him. Obviously he had got too close to the truth and a hitman was paid to silence him. But someone as smart as Alex has his reasons; I suspect he's here on a story and one day it will break and he will head back to the West and the land of the free press. He's Pulitzer prize-winning investigative journalism material through and through is Alex, and there's no way he's here just to enjoy the sunshine. Besides, as everyone knows, being a proper journalist in Dubai is an oxymoron. Not possible. Every piece of news is vetted; there are strict rules about what we can and can't write. But it's a deal that we enter into happily enough because we are all here for our own reasons, none of which, by themselves, bear delving into too deeply.

And then there's me. Sophie Roberts, nee Haddon, who once cherished the dream that she could write. And I could, once. Not now. Not really. I can write silly boring articles, with a minimum of research, about things that might interest our varied readership. I can do a few witty captions under pictures. I can edit and proofread but I've no nose for news and

I often feel overwhelmed by the futility of it all. The rubbish we write, the nonsensical glossy magazine that we produce and the idiots that we cater for. 'Be careful, darling', says Wayne, 'cynicism is the journalist's death knell.' But it's hard to remain positive and my career, like everything else in my life, is hitting the skids as well. Like all of us in this town, I pay a high price for the sunshine, the glamour, the glitz and the lifestyle. As Wayne says, we all sold our souls to Mammon a long time ago – in the form of gardeners, maids, manicurists, beauticians – the list goes on. The real world still beckons, but it is a siren call that can scarcely be made out above all the other distracting noises in this town. And I've lost my confidence, too. I can't imagine walking into an interview in London for a real job on a real newspaper. Sophie Roberts is 44 years old and she can never compete again with those intellectuals who are real journalists. Any newspaper worth its salt would laugh at my so called 'experience'. *I'm sorry Ms Haddon, but writing for a magazine in Dubai is not really at the cutting edge is it? Go back to your glamorous rag, Ms Haddon, and don't bother us. Go back to your fashion shows and your society pages and let us do the real work that proper investigative journalists do.'* No, I can never go back. I'm stuck here and I should be grateful. Unlike so many expat wives I do at least have a job. And there is, besides, the internal voice that tells me *Sophie Roberts is a dirty little coward.*

Now Wayne finally hangs up the phone – he's been trying to do so for a while – and peers into the donut box, pawing over its contents. 'Any idea where Shazza is?' he questions through a mouthful of Krispy Kreme. Wayne is struggling with the Dubai stone – those 16lbs that expats know so well, the product of the sedentary lifestyle we suddenly start leading and alcohol and donuts are a disastrous combination, as my darling colleague is just now discovering. Bertie, by contrast, keeps his slim Filipino good looks far more effortlessly, or maybe it's just rushing around planes up in the sky all day.

'I think she's gone to sort out a photoshoot for the new car showroom. PB's recommendation of course'.

Shazza is the really productive one in our team. She's a Liverpool lass with a mouth on her that, coupled with a sharp streetwise intellect and a restless passion to excel, makes her everyone's ideal employee. She can answer the phone, take a message, sell advertising space or organise a photoshoot with equal efficiency. When annoyed she will let fly with the most astounding swearing tirade you will ever hear but which, fortunately, no one other than a Liverpudlian native can interpret. Shazza looks the part, too. She is tall – but notwithstanding also wears outrageous platform shoes – with spiky blonde hair (she used to affect pink tips but has since dismissed that as 'cheap') and she dresses in the kind of eccentric and wacky outfits that only Shazza could pull off. We all love Shazza. She's awesome, intelligent, loveable and a serious achiever. One of these days she'll leave us because she'll get sick of having to see her best ideas dismissed and she'll go somewhere in the world where she will be recognised for the amazing qualities she has. Manhattan Avenue, perhaps. She really could sell ice to Eskimos could Shazza, although Alex always suggests it's because prospective advertisers are too scared to say no to Shazza. It is not something you would do lightly, it's true.

I direct a frown at Wayne. 'You know you shouldn't eat donuts.'

'I know, I know … it's just that they're sitting in front of me just begging to be eaten. I'm so weak. You know how weak I am!'

I shake an admonitory finger at him. 'Bertie will be cross if you put on weight. He told me so.'

He grins in his charming loveable gnome kind of way that he knows I can't resist. 'So don't tell him!'

'It's not a question of not telling him! He going to know there's more of you to squeeze!'

'Oh, that reminds me! Now are we talking about Rick or not – I mean is he a discussable subject?'

Immediately my lightened sense of happiness departs. 'What about Rick?'

'Oh help, she's got the thundercloud look … no darling, this is really funny.'

I try not to scowl. 'All right, well what is it?'

'Well you know that Bertie flies with *Herself*… so he had a flight with her last week. She's quite nice, he says. Quite friendly and efficient.'

'And I want to know this why?'

'Let me finish! Well … you'll never guess what her name actually is! It's Ophelia!'

I look up at that and raise an eyebrow. 'What …. As in *'get thee to a nunnery'* Ophelia?'

'The very same!'

I begin to grin and suddenly we both burst out laughing. Wayne rocks back in his chair and within seconds we are semi-hysterical, shrieking with laughter. I put my head down on the desk and try and keep the laughter from turning to tears. 'Oh!' gasps Wayne finally. 'As I said to Bertie, it's too perfect. You know what bizarre names some of these Filipinos have. I mean you only have to look at Bertie.'

That makes me look up, mopping my eyes. 'What?'

'His parents named him Egbert, darling! As in Saxon, Ethelred the Unready and all that.'

'Good God. No wonder he's switched to Bertie.'

'Anyway,' says Wayne, wiping the last crumbs of Krispy Kreme off his moustache, 'I just thought you'd appreciate that. Not that it means that we hate her any less!'

'I don't hate her,' I say carefully. 'I don't ever think about them. It's an arrangement and I have what I want out of it. No one cares, not me, not the kids – if they even know. I've never told them.'

'Methinks the lady doth protest too much! I don't care what you say; it has to hurt at some level. Everyone needs love, darling – especially you. We will have to find you a nice lover!'

Wayne's phone buzzes briefly and he glances down at it and loses his light bantering tone immediately, which I appreciate. Wayne and I are best friends, but I can't really talk about Rick to anyone. And I don't. No one knows. They may guess, but they don't hear it from me.

'PB is on her way. Since Shazza is God knows where, can you be an angel and get some coffee brewing? Fortunately I've saved a pink-iced KK for PB.'

I get up and go to work out the idiosyncrasies of the coffee machine. 'She won't have one,' I tell Wayne. 'Not looking the way she does – you can't eat donuts and look like that. Have we got an agenda for the meeting?'

'Oh I've scratched a few items on a piece of paper. But she'll have lots of ideas which we'll have to wade through of course. Your idea of a story on dogs in Dubai – I don't know. Going against the cultural grain on that one, I think. But no doubt seriously edited. But she was happy with last month's issue. Of course.'

'Oh please!' I fill up the machine and switch it on. 'She interviewed Paris Hilton on her visit to Dubai and the up and coming series. Of course she loved it. It was all about her.'

Wayne is putting chairs around our small round table and setting out his papers. 'Now don't be mean. She doesn't write badly.'

'Oh come on! It was mostly all images with captions and a bit of infill. I thought Shazza wrote most of it.'

'Mmm,' Wayne will never argue, only change the subject. He opens his drawer, whips out three bottles of water and places them in a neat line at the back of the table. 'So what's your slant on the dog article then?'

'Oh just the rise in the numbers of dogs in Dubai, interesting in a Muslim country where – as you know, they are about as popular culturally as pigs – numbers of vets now in town, increasing numbers of shops selling pet-related items,

29

almost exclusively in some cases. And it's not just expats. And the K9 unit with the Abu Dhabi police – that might come here too, German-trained German Shepherds with a variety of roles.'

'Oh, sweet!' Wayne puts a box of tissues centre-table and boyishly swings himself round in the swivel chair. 'And how do our good Arabic policemen deal with the German-speaking German Shepherds?'

'I believe the handlers have to acquire a few basic German commands. But there's the dog show here now, of course, big family event, and the police put the dogs through their paces. They're a very popular act.'

'Hmm, an interesting dilemma has presented itself,' says Wayne, leaning back in his chair and steepling his fingers. 'The existence of crime is always denied in this country, so why do they need police dogs to track criminals?'

'Probably just for the professional image,' I say distractedly, as the machine froths and gurgles, and I try to direct it towards my mug without scalding myself. The machine is elderly and bad-tempered and really responds only to Shazza's knowing touch. 'I guess that's the sort of thing I'll be finding out. I met my first expat Dubai dog trainer the other night and the resemblance to Barbara Woodhouse was uncanny!'

At this moment there is the sound of feet on the stairs and one of the princess's bodyguards appears and opens the door for her. A few moments later PB herself arrives in the elevator. The guards have to be sure that all ways are safe, of course. It was Wayne who began calling her Princess, which is not strictly correct, but never mind, she loves it and we always try and keep on her good side. Now he jumps to his feet and nods, beaming, as PB sweeps into the room. Always beautifully dressed, she looks taller today due, I see presently, to the several inch-high platforms on her Jimmy Choos. Her abaya and hijab glitter with crystals and her hands with jewels. Her watch is only one of several, but is my favourite, its large circular face embedded with pink diamonds. She is heavily made-up, as the Arab women are, but it is, as always, flawless. I imagine she has a whole bevy of beauticians waiting on her hand and foot. Nice life if you can get it, or are born to it.

We sit down. I serve coffee in our best white china cups with gold borders, and the princess, as I guessed, refuses a Krispy Kreme. Wayne goes through the next issue in detail; she asks pertinent questions and makes suggestions and I sit stirring my coffee absently, idly wondering how many pounds sterling are represented in her jewellery. Finally we get to my piece and Wayne gives me my cue. I sketch out the article – show her a few photographs, outline the interviews. She likes it. She gives me the name of the Chief Vet at the Ministry who will be able to assist me and, to give her credit, she does have the inside track so essential for a good story. She does not, however, have friends that we can interview who own lapdogs, an indication that this is still very much expat territory and cultural traditions die hard. Dogs and Islam don't go together and despite the Hollywood glamour that so many rich Muslim women adopt, it seems that this partnership is still taboo. Interesting. She does, however, know a store about to open which stocks lapdog jewellery and accessories. I jot down the names and numbers and try not to catch Wayne's sardonic eye. I can tell too that she's happy that we are not dirtying our hands with stories about building contractors and workers or enslaved maids. Dubai has a big carpet for sweeping such stories under and we know what we'll get away with. I do have an idea for a story about maids, but it's more slanted towards the expats and will be a dull tale of rules and regulations that apply if a European family wants to hire a maid. She gives me a little lecture on 'no silly stories of abuse or anything like that' and will look over it herself before it goes to publication, but essentially I can rough something up. But she has something else she wants me to do first. The Sheikh Mohammed Centre for Cultural Understanding is now sending representatives into schools who will, through discussion with students and staff, create more respect and understanding for the Islamic Culture. She gives me the name of a woman who is one of these representatives; I need to interview her and also interview some teachers from one of the visited schools in order to find out how effective the programme is and how it is bridging the cultural awareness gap. Wayne makes enthusiastic noises and I jot down all the details. I can see it would be a good article; the princess waxes lyrical in praise of the scheme and says I will 'love' these Emirati cultural ambassadors, male and female, who are "Young and beautiful, very open-minded, open-hearted and wonderful speakers". I promise this will be my key task and she smiles very graciously upon me.

Throughout the meeting both the princess's phones buzz or ring continuously; she visually checks the messages but the calls go to voicemail, presumably. The bodyguard, something of a gorilla if truth be told, stands with legs apart facing the door and when she rises to go, he steps forward to take the massive designer tote bag she hands him in order that she may walk unencumbered; the better to concentrate on those preposterous heels. I have worn an abaya myself on occasion and they are hellishly difficult to manage; the hem trails and you feel in imminent danger of tumbling over your feet. Well at least I do, but PB is born to it. She departs, swishing regally, steps into the elevator and is gone. Wayne sinks back into his chair, wiping his brow, and drinks off a whole bottle of water.

'I'm thinking dogs and Emirati cultural ambassadors in the same issue? Maybe not,' he says with a laugh.

At this moment, the door flies open and Shazza appears with a couple of young Emiratis in dishdashes in tow – her new photography duo – Abdul and Mohammed. Neither has serious talent, but both are anxious to learn and both, of course, are related to PB. Never mind, they are charming lads, the pair of them are wonderfully naïve; to them it's the equivalent of my working for Vanity Fair. And when Shazza says jump, they say 'how high?' She has them very well trained already. The office is so small there is hardly room for them, but they pour themselves coffee and take the vacated conference table chairs while Shazza tells us about her morning at top volume with frequent use of the F word. Abdul and Mohammed's vocabulary will be coming along in leaps and bounds, especially their knowledge of the vernacular and cruder byways of the English language. They polish off the remaining Krispy Kremes with no difficulty whatsoever.

'Was that PB's car just pulling away when we came in?' queries Shazza. 'Did I miss anything?'

'Not a thing, darling,' says Wayne smoothly. 'I'm roughing up the schedule for next month and as soon as it looks halfway promising, we'll all go over it together.'

After we have heard all about Shazza's car showroom photoshoot, she takes over the conference table and she and the lads go through their shots and start planning the piece. Both are vying for Shazza's approval; it's really quite funny to observe. She is strictly fair and impartial in her choices, and invites Wayne over to look at one or two and make the final judgment. True to form, Shazza, though not really 'up' on cars has, in the course of the morning, now got all the jargon at her fingertips, heavily assisted by the lads who, as true Emiratis, are car mad. The leather-seated Maserati has really taken their attention and they have hundreds of images to prove it. When they start enthusing about what goes on under the bonnet, Wayne looks glazed and retreats to his own desk.

Finally, they're done and the lads go home for their siesta, while Shazza retreats to the other desk and starts tapping away on her laptop. Silence descends while we all concentrate on our screens.

The afternoon wears on and lunch comes and goes. Alex has still not appeared yet but has sent me a text message explaining that he is 'checking something out' which is the kind of bland statement that could mean anything. Wayne comes back from lunch and falls asleep in his chair, only to be woken as I embark on a list of phone calls, setting up interviews and making appointments to see people. Shazza departs breezily, promising to see us in the morning. I follow her at around 4pm. Such is our day.

Next morning – sometimes the days seem to run in a continuous blur like the way we used to peel apples, maintaining the rind falling in a continuous circling motion – I can sleep in a bit later as my first appointment is not until 10am and, the traffic, being what it is, means going to the office first is pointless. I have a half-commitment to join Tracey walking her dog round the park, but given a vague hangover from being out drinking with 'the girls' the night before, it doesn't take much time to decide to pass on that. I don't have close friends here in Dubai – just acquaintances really that I've made in various places; the tennis club from the days when Rick and I were quite a good doubles pair, the hotel gym I used to use, etc. We are all so superficial it's alarming really – modern day Dubai plastic Stepford Wives, if truth be told. Yvonne and I are the only ones who work; the others are two of the most elegant kind of Jumeirah Janes – rich expat women who spend their time in a busy bubble of visits to the gym, the manicurist, the salon – anything and everything just to pass the time and make them look as good as possible. They all have maids (and sometimes I am appalled by the way they treat them), so they don't have to bother about housework; beautiful cars, beautiful houses and husbands who keep them in the lifestyle to which we've all so easily become accustomed. The husbands are, of course, the linchpin to the whole operation. If hubby loses his job, the whole beautiful Cinderella dream will be gone quicker than you can say 'pumpkin coach'. In the meantime we eat, drink and are merry for tomorrow we may die (as metaphorically, many would, if the dream should die). Interestingly, both my friends are well-educated women who used to, in their youth, have careers; Marisa was a lawyer and Kirstie a landscape gardener. But the Dubai dream has scuppered all that and now they party endlessly to stave off boredom and to maintain the illusion that they are 'busy'. Like me their children have returned to the UK to university and they live, as I do, for the visits back home or for the university holidays when planeloads of expatriate kids land in Dubai and the pallid, sun-starved occupants fall gratefully back into the bosom of their families for a few weeks of fun and fantasy. For all of us the real world is just around the corner, waiting in the wings.

I like these women and they like me, but only in the superficial way that we all 'like' each other in Dubai. We kiss each other with great enthusiasm in the two-kiss approach (some go for the Arabic three but not me), call each other 'darling', gossip and admire each other's clothes, new jewellery, new haircut, new whatever. The rule here is if you have it – flaunt it. Marisa has a sapphire ring that Jack has given her for their wedding anniversary; it's a huge stone of amazing depth and colour and she has a new manicure to set it off. Personally I wouldn't fancy Jack for a shedload of sapphires, but what's that to purpose? I maintain the fiction that Rick and I are still a happily-married couple and throw his name carelessly into the conversation once in a while to allay any suspicions. The talk is all of a certain Ball that is coming up in a couple of months; Kirstie is on the committee and has us all down for a table, with husbands of course. I accept airily and there is much excitement and chatter about the theme for the evening. 'There was so much discussion,' Kirstie tells us, 'and so heated! All the ladies had their own pet theme and were quite bitchy about others' ideas. Finally we settled on the black and white – that satisfied everyone.' I promise we will send a photographer and coordinate a lovely social-page spread of who was there and what they wore. We almost always have one of these social occasion 'centrefold' issues; the Upper Ten Thousand love to see themselves in print and to show off to others where they've been.

The evening is of a wonderful temperature; the kerosene burners flicker, the white sofas are soft and hugely reclinable and the voices of the fortunate fill the air. That's what we are, of course – the chosen people. We sit in our short silk dresses, wearing our beautiful jewellery and are absorbed by the beauty of our manicured hands and glittering rings displayed to advantage on the cocktail glasses. The chatter is desultory but full of important detail; Marcellino (the Filipino darling of the hairdressing world – Dubai's answer to Vidal Sassoon) may be leaving town! Why? All eyes are on me as the doyenne of the gossip column. What do I know? Is it true that he gave a gay party that the police raided? I don't know anything. I am 'so disappointing!' They were 'counting on me to know!' Fortunately Jackie is able to report that mutual friend Julia, who is all of 44, is currently screwing a 28-year-old banker in his expensive and elegant apartment most lunchtimes. 'It won't last, of course,' Jackie says smugly. 'Not when he realises how much available ass there is in town. But Julia says she can't believe how good the sex is and I must say she looks amazing!' We titter collectively and toast Julia's concupiscence. Lucky Julia. Yvonne reports on two new children in her class whose parents have come to live in Dubai after scooping the UK lottery fund of 13 million pounds. 'They're common as muck,' she says. We all agree there is no justice in the world.

Down on the beach under the barasti palm shelters the younger age group are gathered, blonde twenty-something party goers. The sight of all those short dresses and tanned legs reminds me of my mysterious neighbour. Up here feels like Cougar Town and I can only stand so much of it.

When happy hour is finished – the hour is a misnomer as they go on for several hours – we debate the idea of dinner but I cry off with the excuse of having to be up early for an interview. Not true, but I've had enough of tinkling gossip and posturing and take my miserable self off home. It seems – unless I've misread all the body language and not-so-subtle hints – that Kirstie is getting rather too friendly with her gym trainer, but why am I surprised? Such affairs are commonplace here; the devil, as my mother used to cite, will always find use for idle hands and Shaitan, as the Muslims call him, certainly thrives in this town as there are idle hands aplenty.

Lying in my expansive – and expensive – super king size double bed all alone, I am able to ponder two things that occur to me; one is why Natasha has never appeared (or at least to my knowledge) in any of the social page spreads I am so used to seeing or even compiling. That one is relatively easy to answer; we don't have anything to do with Palace events, being limited entirely to expatriate shindigs. It is very rare that we photograph any eminent Emiratis unless the occasion is a launch of some public company or new project. And, secondly, her job. What job entitles one to be sleeping at home all day? But then, I think, that's not fair; after all she might just have finished some big project and has been taking time off. I wonder who employs her at the Palace. In fact, the more I think about her, the more I want to meet her. Finally I get up, get dressed and sally forth to visit, of all exciting places, the vet.

On the way out of my front door I meet my errant husband who is on his way in. We both stop and stare as he opens the front door to find me standing on the other side of it. There is a little awkward moment when he flashes the charming (he thinks) Rick Roberts smile and then remembers that it doesn't work with me. 'Hello, darling,' he says, a shade too heartily, aiming a kiss in the direction of my ear. 'You look lovely! Just off out?'

'Yes,' I respond with a frosty look which clearly says *'don't 'darling' me, you bastard.'*

'I've just popped in for some shirts,' he says, calling for Patti as he walks off down the hallway. I acknowledge a sneaking awareness that he's looking quite good; he's lost a bit of weight and has had a haircut. I have to remind myself not to think about it; it's key to my equilibrium to remember that I don't care.

I step outside and shut the front door with the slightest suspicion of a slam and am just about to get into the car when I remember the conversation last night and the upcoming Ball. I have to reserve Rick for that, unfortunately; it is necessary to appear as a couple in public once in a while and foster the togetherness scenario. He has gone upstairs and there's a suitcase on the bed which he's packing full of shirts and suits – clearing out the cupboard, in fact. He looks up, surprised; he thought he'd seen the last of me for today.

I glance at the suitcase but forbear to comment. 'Rick, there's a Ball coming up in a month; Kirstie was telling me last night. It's a big one with lots of people we know there and we should go together. So can you remember the date please – the 20th of May? I can send you a text to confirm too if you want.'

'Uh huh, good idea,' says my husband brightly. 'Do I still have a DJ?'

'Should do,' I snap, 'unless you've packed it.'

'Don't snarl, darling. It doesn't become you. If you can find it and have it dry-cleaned or whatever, then yes, I'll call for you and we'll go together.' He turns back to the wardrobe and continues to ferret through it. More things get flung into the case.

There's nothing else to say. I turn on my heel and walk away, the sharpness of my clicking heels on the marble echoing the words *'Don't cry, don't cry'*. How good a stiletto would look plunged into his cheating heart. I get into my own car, slamming the door to relieve my feelings somewhat and ignoring the thought of how rejuvenating it would feel to reverse into his gleaming Mercedes sports.

I drive off down the road, gnawing at the inside of my lip. The sun is particularly bright this morning and my eyes sting with tears while I tell myself roughly, *'Stop it, stop it! This is what you want ... this is what you agreed to ... and you don't care ... you DON'T CARE!'* But what was with the packing? The suitcase? Is he moving out for good? *Why didn't you ask? Because Sophie Roberts is a dirty little coward.* I put on my dark shades and blot my eyes at the next set of traffic lights.

Fortunately the vet's clinic is not particularly crowded and anyway, I have an appointment. I get out the laptop and we have a quick chat before she directs me to her office manager who has facts and figures at her fingertips. I am concentrating quite well on the whole, but when she goes off to fetch me a glass of water, I can still see Rick's face and the suitcase on the bed. For months now we have had an unspoken agreement that, although he's with Ophelia *(Jesus wept, what a misnomer)* he still comes home for the odd meal and a quick touch-base. So do I assume that's over now? He's moving in with her full time? Surely not. Perhaps they've taken a bigger place together? *No*, I muse, chewing the inside of my mouth, that's unlikely; Rick is not that well paid and keeping the villa takes most of his spare cash; not to mention the Mercedes and all those smart clothes and accessories he thinks he needs. I can't quite work it out but when the woman comes back with the water I throw a couple of headache pills down my throat as well just for good measure. *It probably should be Prozac,* I think savagely as the interview goes on. Fortunately I've jotted down all my questions so it's quite a seamless give and take question and answer session and if I was in a better mood, it would be interesting. She's an intelligent woman *(would she put up with her husband cheating on her?)* and has some thoughtful perspectives to offer.

From there, it's fortunately only a step to the Posh Pets store where I don't have an appointment but am welcomed by the Indian manager, who flashes his gold-filled teeth in a wide white smile which becomes even broader when he realises that he could be in for some free publicity. I am shown around the shop; there are puppies in cages and kittens which, in my present mood, cause my emotional pendulum to begin to swing once more. Poor little caged animals. Their mewing and yapping, their clawing attempts to scale the wire perfectly echoes my own state of mind. It's difficult to make Mr Patel answer my questions as he is constantly distracted by the need to show me some revolutionary new pet resource that has just arrived. Finally I give in and take his photo squatting next to a cage of kittens, their jaws open in silent appeal. I jot down his answers on my pad and manage to isolate the most important trends; yes, more people are buying pets, the pet accessory and pet-food markets have really taken off and that must be so because the supermarkets are now getting in on the act too. Yes, there are more pet shops in Dubai and therefore more competition for him, and yes, they all make a good living. But he has been long established in Dubai and he gets his pets from unimpeachable sources … his father came to Dubai in 1976 and set up this shop and …

'Well thank you so much, Mr Patel. You've been most helpful.'

'Thank you, madam, thank you, and thank you for visiting my shop. Please tell your friends I have so many beautiful pets, all very healthy, and so many beautiful pet toys ...'

I pass over my card to distract his fulsome explanations. 'Yes, it's a wonderful shop. So this is my magazine – here – and when the article is published we'll send you a copy of the issue. It could be several months though, so don't hold your breath.'

He presses the card to his breast, opens the door for me and I am bowed out of the shop with smiles and much waving. Well, at least I've brought pleasure to somebody's day.

My headache has really set in by this time; it is very hot and even my short walk back to the car makes me dizzy. I have not been drinking enough so I take ten minutes to drink off a bottle of water and recline my seat, but the moment I close my eyes, the image of Rick returns, gazing at me quizzically across an open suitcase and I feel the tears stinging again. 'Oh, bugger it!' I say violently, yanking the seat back into its upright position and slamming the bottle into the dashboard. 'I really think you must be menopausal, Sophie! Pull yourself together!'

Looking at my schedule, I can see that the next interview is the pet grooming parlour, just across the Umm Suquiem Road and on a quiet back street where there are several takeaway places, one of which does the most perfect deep-fried samosas. Just what I feel like. I can almost taste the oily delights of deep-fried comfort eating. Thank God for some small pleasures left in the world. I fix my eye make-up which is, like me, wilting in the heat, and reverse out into the road.

Allie Macpherson is a middle-aged Scot who came to Dubai as a nurse and got into the pet-grooming business about ten years ago. She is charming, tough, red-haired and successful. I have met her before, but not professionally, and as I walk through the door I am at once charmed by and respectful of her little empire. The relatively small space is divided into four areas; in one, small pampered pooches are being washed, in another they're being clipped and in the third they're being blow-dried and brushed. Their assorted small faces reflect nothing but the deepest satisfaction and joy, eyes closed, noses pointed skywards. I have a moment of amusement imagining Hector in these scented surroundings. Allie's assistants are walking around in their pink trouser suits; one or two European girls but the majority are Filipina. The fourth area is Allie's office where I am invited to sit and drink a glass of cold water with mint leaves and ice brought to me by a beautiful Filipina girl who is slim and young, with skin like a pale lily. *Ophelia. The clawing of pain is like a paper cut; deep and sharp and unexpected.* There is a glass runner around the top of the area which allows Allie to see what's going on but cuts out some of the noise of running water, trimmers and hair-dryers. I force myself to concentrate and produce pen, notebook and camera, and summon an expression which reflects nothing but professional focus.

We get down to business. Allie has already expanded the business to three salons across town and is about to go into partnership with another Scot who deals with pet relocation; filling in the paperwork required to move pets from country to country. Yes, business is booming. No, it's mostly entirely expat; she can't think of any Emirati family who use her services. Now, of course, with the pet passport scheme being established in Dubai, more families are bringing their pets with them, and taking them when they leave. During my interview time, the phone rings constantly as the receptionist takes bookings and small, pampered dogs are dropped off and retrieved by their owners, no doubt just out of spas themselves. What a town we live in! Allie tells me that dog grooming parlours are on the rise worldwide, but it's only the preponderance of expats living here that make it so popular. Yes, competition is opening up but she has eight or nine years' head start on everyone else and she's kept ahead of trends. Any cats? Not really, it's just the specific breeds of Persians, Chihuahuas etc. that need to be clipped for the summer. A small side-line only. I skip around and take a few photos and the girls smile charmingly as they wield brushes and blowers. Several of the dogs look as if they're permanently smiling with their wide-mouthed grins; I do a close up of two rather cute Pekes whose bulging eyes reflect total inner contentment and harmony. It's a far cry from the mewings and whinings of poor Mr Patel's trapped-pet shop.

Back in the street, I realise that if I skip across town now to the office, I can miss some of the worst of the lunchtime traffic. I am equidistant between home and office, but the office wins out as it always cheers me up. I set off.

Shazza has left me a note stuck to the computer screen which reads **'Got you an appointment today with Jason Knight at JCE – he says turn up at 2.30. Sounds HOT!'** and from this missive I deduce that I have an appointment with the teacher who is in charge of the Cultural Centre programme at his school. As I am stuffing my face with the remainder of the samosas, Alex appears and nicks my last samosa. 'These are yummy!' he says, through a mouthful. 'Where did you get them?'

'Fab little takeaway behind Mall of the Emirates – they're to die for, aren't they?'

'Mmm. Without doubt. I suppose you've scoffed the lot have you?'

'Yep,' I say cheerfully. I love Alex. He's one of the kindest, smartest and most trustworthy people you could ever imagine. He isn't much to look at, as he himself admits, being tall and rather gangly, with thick dark hair and a thin clever face. But he is an angel, a darling and a genius all rolled into one.

'Oh lord, I'm exhausted,' I say stretching with loud noises over the back of my chair. 'I've been driving around all day on this pet story and I'm worn out. I don't suppose there's any coffee is there?'

'Not a drop. Shazza thinks the machine might finally have given up the ghost and has gone out to buy us a new one.'

'And Wayne?'

'Oh, gone home to get some beauty sleep. He's going out tonight and wants to look his peachy best.'

I grin at him. 'Good thing the workers are still hard at it then, eh?'

'Well certainly *you* are. Shazza was tickled pink by Mr Charm who she's booked you an appointment with later today. Sounds as if your pet story has finally produced a real pet!'

'Oh very witty. Wish it wasn't today though. I'm bushed.'

'A rabid reporter like you? Don't believe it!'

'So what are you working on? I haven't seen you for days.'

Alex is one of the most secretive journalists alive but mostly that's because he's got the lead on some amazing story or other which will never see the light of day. So his answers are always vague when you tackle him on what he's doing. 'I'm doing my by-line for the New York Times actually. You know, bread and butter stuff.'

'Yeah, yeah,' I say, shaking out the last remaining crumbs of samosa by tipping the bag over my nose. 'You don't fool me. So what's the dirt? What's new in town?'

Curiously, for a moment Alex looks almost anxious. Then he comes back with 'Nothing that would do you any good to know. And nothing that can ever be printed.'

'Oh go on, *do* tell. You know I have no excitement in my life!'

'Well nothing you don't know really. I mean it's common knowledge that HM pays off Al Qaeda to keep them out of Dubai and hold their citizen bombing exercises somewhere else. It's just interesting that there happens to be some rather fascinating characters in town …. And if you put two and two together, you might come up with six and a half!'

I can feel an ulcer coming up in my mouth where I am constantly biting the inside of my cheek. I worry it with my tongue and Alex laughs. 'I can tell from your preoccupied expression that you're hanging on my every word!'

'Mmm, sorry, no, I have an ulcer coming. Really? So who's in town? Al Qaeda operatives?'

Alex shakes his finger at me. 'You stick to your samosas and pet stories, young Sophie! It's by far the safest option.'

'Actually, no,' I say, throwing the oily samosa bag in the trash can and getting up. 'I'm going to check out Mr Charm Personified at JCE. If I go now I might just miss the school rush.' I push everything back in my handbag, blow a kiss to Alex and head to the lift via the Ladies.

'Make sure you take explicit notes!' Alex calls after me. 'Shazza will want all the details!'

By the time I fight my way through the rush hour school traffic, and find myself parked outside the elegant new glass and wood campus which is a leading expatriate high school in Dubai, I am beginning to feel tired and hungry and the samosa is but a distant memory. A quick glance in the car mirror reassures me that I am not looking my best; my dark bob is greasy around the hairline and most of my make-up has come off. Still I'm not trying to impress anyone, least of all the unknown Mr Knight, charmer or not, so a quick comb through and a dab of lipstick is all I can be bothered with.

The receptionist, bless her, gives me coffee and biscuits which rally me somewhat and I sit sifting through my notes and trying to work out the story angle. The glass door next to Reception gives a quick woosh and I look up. A young man (to me), probably mid-thirties, smiles down at me, stretches out his hand and introduces himself as Jason Knight. He has a lovely smile and a pleasant slightly mid-country British accent; a welcome change after the cut-glass accents of most of our circle. The British still define themselves through accent, and it's as marked here as anywhere.

I follow this attractive being up the stairs and along several corridors; there are a few students still wandering around and once or twice he stops to have a word with them while I have a quick look around. Finally after another corridor or two, and some more steps, we arrive in his classroom, a large room with windows that overlook the sports field, and its walls decorated with all the paraphernalia that teachers have been using since time immemorial.

He pulls up a chair for me in front of his desk and sits opposite me; not behind the desk, I notice, and approve his good manners.

'Ok,' he begins with a smile. 'Now, I'm not sure what you want to know, so do you want to tell me what you need, or shall I just talk you through the programme, and you can interrupt with questions?'

He has soft blue eyes and attractive, clean-cut features. He reminds me of someone; I can't think who. I gaze for a moment longer, taking in the short-back-and-sides fair hair, and trying to jog my memory. He smiles a little hesitantly. I pull myself together and sit up straight, pen in hand.

'That'd be great. You just talk me through what you do, initially anyway. We're looking really to spread the good word about the Cultural Centre, so I just need to know how it works for this school, how you got involved, etc.'

'Right. Well, it's a fantastic idea, you know. Works brilliantly. The kids love it. It started with a visit from two of the ambassadors from the Centre; they came just before Ramadan last year and we started with them talking first to the staff. A lot of teachers are new here, to the Middle East that is, and they had lots of questions. The two Emirati representatives were fantastic – they emphasised early on that no question would offend them and they were happy to discuss any subject. People didn't expect that and, initially, it was a bit quiet, but after a few brave souls had broken the ice, things really hotted up. We talked for about an hour, I suppose, and then some more helpers arrived with lots of cooking pots which they spread out all over the floor, with plates and knives, and we all had a good old nosh up. Fantastic food, and they explained all about the choices, why they ate those foods for Iftar, etc.' He smiles boyishly at the memory. 'It was great fun.'

'Anyway, after that, the same two reps came back to talk to our senior classes and brought an Imam with them. They were a little less relaxed with the students than they'd been with us, and the old boy didn't have any English, so he spoke in Arabic.'

'But some of your students speak Arabic?' I interrupt.

'Oh yes, quite a few. And quite a number of them are Muslim, too. But the Culture Centre reps translated for him anyway. He spoke about Ramadan, its role in the Muslim faith, that sort of thing. It was fascinating. The kids were quiet as mice and hanging on his every word. And he totally looked the part, marvellous long patriarchal beard!' He laughs again, and then looks as if he might have been caught out in a moment of cultural inadequacy and darts a hasty look at me to check I am not offended. I gaze back blandly. He goes on. 'Anyway, then the kids were encouraged to ask questions, some did, and then the Cultural Centre reps finished off by talking about the Centre and what Sheikh Mohammed hoped to accomplish by setting it up. It wasn't quite as relaxed as when they spoke to us, but probably more appropriate to the students of course.'

'So this was, what, the introduction to the programme? Did they visit again?'

'Actually, no, they haven't been back but I'm assuming that's probably because they've got a lot of other schools in Dubai they have to visit and I'm not sure how the Centre is organised, how many reps they've got, things like that. Those two were particularly good, with excellent English and totally brilliant with any audience. I imagine it must be hard to recruit people as good as that.'

'Yes, I see. So it's not an annual event?'

He leans back in his chair, 'Sadly, no. Well not yet, anyway. I believe, though, that there's some sort of workshop coming up which I think I have an invitation for somewhere …' He skids the chair on its wheels over to his desk and skims through a pile of paperwork. I can begin to see what Shazza was talking about; this young man has a genuine friendly charm that is very appealing. He keeps his blue eyes fixed on me when he talks and gives the impression of a sincere level of interest and enthusiasm in the conversation. It's such a relief to meet someone who's not totally self-involved, not trying to make an impression. He has, I can't define it, a kind of pleasant *happiness;* he strikes you as someone who takes pleasure in his life. I don't know any teachers; maybe they're all like this.

I make some notes in my book while he searches and, just as I open my mouth to speak, the door flies open and a woman bursts in. She doesn't come into the room, just hangs on the door handle, flicking a hostile glance at me, but speaking (or shouting) directly at him. 'For God's sake, Jason! I said two thirty and it's almost three. I'm sick and tired of waiting for you! If you don't come *right now* I'm taking Jack home and you can get a lift with Sally! OK?' She doesn't wait for an answer but slams the door shut and we can hear her steps pounding away along the corridor. I look at him in some alarm.

'I'm awfully sorry,' I say with a nervous smile. 'I hope I haven't made you late.'

He is looking somewhat stunned. 'No, um, not at all. I'm sorry, that was my wife... no, don't worry, it's not a problem. She'll take the car and I'll get a lift home. We do it quite a lot – I'm always running late.' He grins rather ruefully. 'And I'm always getting into trouble!'

Gosh, what a shrew, I'm thinking but he goes on looking for his paper calmly enough. Clearly he's used to it. 'OK, here it is. Yes, see ... they're doing an Evening Introduction to the Cultural Awareness programme ... 14th May, that's next month. Why don't you go? I'm sure you'd find it very interesting.'

Since he shows no signs of wanting to rush off, I go on with my questions. He gets up and digs around in his filing cabinet for photographs that I request to borrow and possibly use? No problem. We chat on, until I begin to wonder if the ubiquitous Sally has also perhaps gone, and I worry about the possibility of Mr Knight getting home at all. He seems alerted, finally, by the gentle clink of buckets and the chatter of the Indian cleaners approaching down the corridor.

I get to my feet and thank him once again for his time. He gives me that rather charming boyish smile *(eat your heart out, Rick Roberts, for a genuine smile like that, with dimples)* and says he'll see me downstairs. He grabs an old and rather

47

battered briefcase from behind the desk, and holds the door open for me. We wander off down the corridor and he calls out to the cleaners 'Thanks guys!' as we go past. *Nice,* I think, most of our crowd simply ignore the manual labourers as if they're not there. I've decided I rather like Jason Knight, even though I can't for the life of me figure out who it is he reminds me of.

'I'm so glad you're escorting me downstairs,' I say as we negotiate yet another set of stairs and corridor. 'This place is a maze. I'd be totally lost.'

'I'm a geographer,' he laughs. 'Goes with the territory!'

'Oh, I see, that's why you've been put in charge of the cultural programme? Social geography?'

He grins over his shoulder. 'Well that's a very good reason, but I'm just the mug who couldn't say no. But it is interesting. Watch your heels on this bit – the tiles are uneven.'

We finally make the car park. 'I do hope your lift is still here,' I say awkwardly.

He holds out his hand. 'Yeah, no problem. Anyway, great to meet you, Sophie, and hope the story goes well.' His dimple pops out again. 'And give my love to that charming Liverpudlian lass who made the appointment. She sounds great!'

'She is!' His hand is firm and warm and I release it only to fumble in my bag for my card and pass it over with my usual little speech about the magazine, print date, free issue etc.

'Yeah, brilliant. Look forward to it. And no rush to return those photographs!'

A slightly built woman comes out of a door on the other side of the quadrangle and hails him. 'Jason! I'm ready to go!'

We both look at each other and grin. 'All set then?' he enquires. I thank him again and walk away to the gates and the security guard who comes out to open them for me. I glance back and am surprised to see Jason Knight still standing in the middle of the quadrangle, looking after me and suddenly I am glad that I wore my new skirt and heels, although my feet are hot and uncomfortable. At that moment, suddenly, ridiculously, I remember who he reminds me of.

'Oh my God,' I say to myself on a giggle. 'I just met Kester Woodseaves!'

That little amusement puts me in the right frame of mind to negotiate the traffic and I arrive home amazingly unfrazzled after such a long day. Patti is surprised to see me in the kitchen, making a large cheese sandwich, and even more surprised to be greeted through it. Patti has such good manners, I'm sure she thinks we are a race of barbarians. She greets me with the news that Alexei from next door has been over, enquiring if I will be giving another "dog lesson" as he calls it, tonight, and there is a note from my husband waiting for me on my dressing table. That knocks the smile off my face pretty fast; I had forgotten Rick. She says she has made me a tuna salad for my dinner because, 'Madam, if you permit, I would like to go and see my friend tonight.'

'Of course, Patti, and thank you.'

'You will find the salad in the fridge, Madam, but I have not put mayonnaise on it yet.' 'Thank you Patti. You go out and have a nice evening.' She vanishes to her own room, and I pour a large glass of wine and wander reluctantly upstairs to see what bombshell my darling husband has left for me.

It's a model of brevity, actually:

'Soph – I am moving most of my stuff to Lia's for obvious reasons. If you want anything just call me. I haven't mentioned anything to the kids but you can if you think they need to know. I'll be in touch about the Ball. Rick.'

I sit down on the bed and puzzle over it. What, pray, are the 'obvious reasons'? He's playing for keeps, he's in love with her, or simply that it's easier if her maid irons his shirts. 'Bloody hell,' I say out loud. 'You're such a wanker, Roberts, you can't even write a bloody note that makes sense!' And I can 'tell the kids' if I think they 'need to know.' Need to know what, exactly? That their father has moved out to live with a

Filipina air hostess half his age? Yes, that would improve their opinion of him. Well, I am not going to be the one to whistle blow, it's too demeaning. He can do his own dirty work. And this piece of information is not shareable, at least not yet, and certainly not with my children. Let them stay in ignorance a bit longer.

I fall back on my pillows and sip the wine. If only I could ring my mother and talk with her. But I can't. *She's dead*; I remind myself coldly and shake away the tears. It's hard sometimes, not to feel abandoned, but once I start I won't be able to stop, so I get up quickly and grab my copy of Mary Webb's "Precious Bane" off the bookshelf and flick through it. Yes, there is Kester Woodseaves, in a rather beautiful watercolour illustration, gazing meaningfully at the "hare-shotton" heroine and he is, as I surmised, our Mr Knight to a T. The same warm smile, blond hair, and blue eyes. He is dressed, of course, in the style of a well-to-do working man (he is, after all, the weaver) of the early 19th century, and I can just imagine Jason Knight in a green velvet coat, fawn buckskin breeches and Wellington boots. The illustration perfectly reflects the romanticism of the story; a budding Shropshire spring, with a ray of light just catching Kester's golden locks. As a shy, quiet, only child, late-developer and hopeless romantic, Kester Woodseaves was for me, for years, the epitome of the romantic hero. Not for me were disordered Byronic locks or the Heyer heroes with their titles and their wicked secrets. Kester Woodseaves with his clean cut good looks and golden smile was the one who saw beyond Prue Sarn's deformity and loved her for what she really was. But I never found my Kester Woodseaves. I found instead the good-looking, exciting and totally selfish Roderick Roberts, who exchanged a doting mother for a wife who couldn't believe her good luck and treated him every day like the wonder that she thought he was; who was putty in his hands and clay under his feet. I take a final look at Kester and slam the book shut. But I am aware of a little quirky smile playing around my lips. Who would believe that Kester Woodseaves was alive and well and living in Dubai? *Well*, I say to myself, (this talking to myself is getting to be a troubling habit but there's no one else to say it to) I don't think he's found *his* Prue Sarn. The bad-tempered shrewish blonde of the classroom would not seem to fit that image at all. Poor man; another one trapped in an unhappy marriage. What was it that Thoreau said? *'Most men lead lives of quiet desperation and go to the grave with the song still in them.'* Most women too, I think. I knock back my wine, put Kester back in the bookshelf, and change into my jeans. Alexei and Hector await. Time to get back to things that really matter.

I enter, as they say in romantic novels, on the echo of my knock, and find, surprisingly, that there is a thin trail of smoke arising from the living room couch which is in direct eye line with the front door. The goddess herself reclines in a Madame Recamier pose, arms over her head and long legs stretched along the sofa. She cocks a questioning eyebrow at me as I burst through her front door, but doesn't move as I go awkwardly across the hall and stand in the archway looking at her. The smoke skeins up towards the ceiling and no one speaks.

'Um,' I begin at last, unaccountably tongue-tied. Another skein goes up and disintegrates. I give myself a mental shake but, truth to tell, I am mesmerised by the shimmering beauty of the woman in front of me. Seen close up she is almost flawless; the golden hair tumbles artlessly, the arms stretched nonchalantly above her head are as perfectly moulded as a Greek statue's and her legs, stretching down the sofa towards me, seem endless. For more than five heartbeats we stare at one another, then suddenly I stumble, bounced from behind, as Hector leaps up on me followed a second later by Alexei's bear hug which almost topples me over. The goddess snaps a single word in Russian and both boy and dog stop, almost comically still, suspended in mid-air. She raises her eyes and looks at me directly through the smoke. Her eyes are almost turquoise and the chilly stare is one I remember from a few days back. She does not look particularly pleased that I have burst into her house and disturbed her peaceful evening. Then suddenly, smoothly, time clicks over and the moment moves on. Rosie appears with the by now almost customary glass of lemonade, Alexei and Hector slink back to the kitchen, and the goddess, accepting her own glass without comment, surveys me head to toe, taking a long drag on her cigarette (but how elegant is the movement!). Finally she speaks and her voice is deep-toned with just the faintest softest hint of a Russian accent.

'So – you are the mystery lady from next door that my son is so crazy about. Tell me, why would you come just to teach a mongrel dog how to behave? I have heard you English are obsessed with animals. Is that true? Is that why you are here?'

I can't read her; is she friendly or antagonistic? There is nothing in her tone of voice to indicate either stance clearly.

Clutching my lemonade, I sit awkwardly on the edge of a chair facing her. It feels like an interview except it's not me who is asking the questions. 'Yes, I'm Sophie Roberts from next door. It's nice to meet you at last.'

The phrases fall heavily into the quiet room and they sound so foolish I am embarrassed. She says nothing, just blows another skein of smoke ceiling-wards, and continues to regard me. I bumble on with my explanation. 'It's true we are a bit nutty about animals I expect, and me about dogs particularly. I lost my own dog quite recently and I really miss him. So when I saw Alexei and Rosie and the trouble they were having with Hector, I thought I should help.' I try a smile for effect. She doesn't smile back. On I plod, holding my lemonade for moral support. 'I know a bit about dog training, and Alexei is such a good owner and so keen to improve Hector, I'm enjoying sharing what I know with him.'

She sips her lemonade, the other hand maintaining the cigarette still held in the hand behind her head. 'How did you lose your dog?' she asks presently, catching me off balance.

'Oh, in an accident I'm afraid. He ran out of the door when it was left open and was killed on the road by a 4 Wheel Drive. I was terribly upset. You grow to love them so much.' *At least I can talk about it now without welling up with tears. Simba's loss was far more painful than losing Rick.*

She continues to gaze at me with that measuring look but doesn't comment. The pause goes on, then suddenly she sits up, puts the lemonade on the table and stubs out the cigarette butt in the ashtray. 'I am not, as you would say, a dog lover,' she says, 'but you will see that Alexei is. It is kind of you to come and help.'

She stands up then, her willowy figure topping me by almost a head, and walks off down the hall to the kitchen. I follow nervously. Alexei and Hector are sitting in the snug, watching TV, but she walks in and turns it off and both boy and dog sit to attention as she stands looking at them. 'So,' she says, 'here is Sophie come to teach you some more dog management, Alexei. Let us see what she has to show you. So, Sophie ...' she pushes dog and boy off the couch and sits down herself, 'How do you plan to improve Hector's manners today?'

I seize the initiative and ask Alexei to repeat what I taught him yesterday, interposing with questions as to why certain behaviour has to be established, and asking him how things have gone today with Hector. Hector sits at the boy's feet and his intelligent eyes look first up at his master and then at me. At the goddess, he does not look at all. Maybe he does not dare. Rosie, I notice, is busying herself at the sink end of the kitchen and does not interfere. The goddess is in charge, it seems. She lounges at her ease and her chill blue eyes follow her son with no perceptible warmth; she occasionally moves her gaze to me and it makes me as awkward as a schoolgirl in the principal's study, called in to explain some questionable behaviour.

The little lesson comes to an end and I seize the opportunity to suggest that we walk Hector in order to stop him pulling on the leash. Rosie steps quietly forward with the tiny bag of treats and Hector's eyes fasten greedily on them; he has already learned what those are for. He starts to whine and jump as we fix his lead and with a sudden and unexpected move, the goddess rises gracefully from the sofa and walks out of the room on her long-toed, red-nailed feet, effacing herself from the fracas of our panting departure. Unfortunately she is not quit of us yet; one of my strategies is to teach Hector that 'not every departure means a walk' and for this purpose he must be led out and back in several times in order to dampen his enthusiasm. Out of the corner of my eye, as this performance is repeated with varying degrees of panting, huffing, resistance and excited barks, I see that she has retreated to the sofa once again with cigarette smoke curling towards the ceiling, her long limbs stretched out and that curious expression of blank calm on her face, impervious to our junketings in her doorway. Her detachment is extraordinary; she takes no interest in her son, she is not at all distracted or annoyed by the dog's behaviour, she does not react at all to my quiet comments to Rosie or the child's voluble enthusiasm. She is completely distanced from us. A phrase slips into my mind (oh the distractions of a classical literary education) *icily regular, splendidly null.*

Hector gets the idea very quickly and, although there are a few lapses, on the whole we walk him with pleasure as he matches his strides to ours. Finally he is so calm that Alexei can hold him by himself and his face is alight with the pleasure of being in charge and the giving out of treats. We walk as far as the large man-made lake, round the green and back home. Alexei is pink with pleasure; Rosie and I are actually able to enjoy our walk and exchange comments in the manner of two people at ease with one another and moving from acquaintance to friendship. Rosie has the same quiet self-effacing dignity that Patti possesses but she is also well-informed, easy to talk to and has a rather dry sense of humour which is delightful and engaging.

Although I wonder if I should barge into the goddess's temple once again, I yield to Rosie and Alexei's entreaties for lemonade and discussion and after all, what is waiting for me at home? Only one tuna salad, mayonnaise to be added at will. We enter through the back door, discreetly, and Hector goes straight to his water bowl as Alexei runs through to his mother telling her something in Russian which, judging from his tone of voice is akin to 'Mamma! I walked Hector all by myself!'

Rosie hands out lemonade in a tall glass filled to the brim with clinking ice cubes and I relax with my back against the bench just as Alexei comes back and tells me 'Mamma would like to see you. Please go in.'

She is still in the same position as before and I take the same chair as before. Principal's office, take two. She turns her head and looks closely at me; the look is almost intimidating and something in me rises to the challenge. I am just about to speak when she does.

'So, Sophie, who is waiting for you at home? Your children? Your husband? What is it about my house that you find so pleasurable?'

I snap out an answer, my nerves tautened by her attitude. 'My children are in England at University. And my husband doesn't live with me any more. He's left me for a Filipina air hostess half his age.'

There, Ms Natasha. You're not the only one who can do straight-talking.

The beautiful eyebrows arch delicately in surprise and her lips curl into a half smile. She looks at me totally differently now; there is respect in her blue gaze and a little less chill. She props herself on one elbow and reaches idly for another cigarette, tapping it out of the packet with long elegant fingers, carmine-tipped. The smile develops and widens and her eyes hold mine as she lights the cigarette.

'You shouldn't smoke,' I say.

That makes her chuckle and she stretches back into position, arms above her head, a skein of smoke drifting up from her lips.

'Don't worry, Sophie. Smoking is one of the better things I do.'

She wriggles up the cushion and looks at me directly. 'All men are cheats and bastards,' she says clearly. 'You have to turn a man's weakness to your advantage.'

Well, this I did not expect. I look down at my glass.

'Life is full of disappointments, Sophie. You can only rely on yourself. That's the only person you can trust completely.'

I give a little shrug. 'I didn't expect to find you a philosopher,' I say, concentrating on tapping my thumbnail against the glass.

'Do you hate him?' Her voice is soft, caring.

'No ... I don't think so. I probably should, but I try not to think about it. We ... have an arrangement ... I stay here, in Dubai, in the house ... and we pretend that we're still a couple. I know it sounds weird but that's what people do in Dubai, they make adjustments. How would it benefit me to have to go back home and live on a pittance as a divorced wife? No, this works, I ... just have trouble getting used to it sometimes.'

'Ah yes,' she says, an edge of sarcasm in her voice. 'That's what we all do in Dubai ... we make adjustments.' She exhales. 'What did you expect?'

I look up. 'What?'

'You said you didn't expect to find me a philosopher. What did you expect?'

There's something about her which makes me want to be honest. 'A blonde bimbo,' I say, with a laugh. She laughs too and all I can think is how beautiful she is when she smiles. Perfectly beautiful. Her mouth is wide and beautifully curved with a full bottom lip setting off California-white teeth.

'So what do you do all day, Sophie? Are you one of the ladies who lunch? The Jumeirah Janes, the trophy wives?'

'Of course not! I'm a journalist ... of sorts,' I add lamely. 'You can't really be a proper journalist here in Dubai, but I work on a magazine. It's not much really, but it's a job and I like it.'

'Ah ha,' another puff of smoke to the ceiling. 'What is the magazine?'

'It's called *Insider.* We don't have a clear theme really, just a bit of everything. It's a bit of a rag if truth be told but, as I said, it's a job.'

'I know *Insider,*' she says, 'It's the princess's plaything, is it not?'

That makes me look up in surprise, until I remember her job; of course she will know PB if she moves in Palace circles. 'Yes, we call her Princess Barbie, PB for short.'

She gives a short laugh. 'That fits. But Sophie, why do you write as Sophie Roberts? That is not who you are, is it?'

I gaze at her blankly. 'You've read my pieces?'

'Some of them, yes, but who is the real Sophie? You are not your husband's possession, so why do you use his name?'

I think my mouth has fallen open; I've never met anyone like this woman. She goes straight for the jugular and I can only say in a voice that has all the resonance of a piece of damp cardboard, 'You're right. Why don't I write as Sophie Haddon? That's who I am.'

The goddess leans over and stubs out her cigarette butt. 'Ok,' she says, and there is a real amusement in her voice. 'I think we are making progress. And now, Sophie Haddon and Roberts no longer, I am sorry, but I have to get dressed to go out.'

'What? Oh yes, of course. Thank you.' She swings her long legs off the sofa. 'Goodbye Sophie Haddon,' she says and walks out past me. I hear her steps going off up the stairs and I continue to sit there, shell-shocked. From the kitchen comes the muted sound of Alexei's cartoon show and the clatter of dishes as Rosie serves dinner. I feel drained in a bizarre way but at the same time curiously rejuvenated. I let myself out quietly and go home. Unbelievably I sleep like a log.

Shazza is, as usual, full of bounce, efficiency and curiosity the next morning, and very short on her usual piss and vinegar (but then it *is* early in the day). She greets me with a smile and a pink polka dot bow in her blonde spikes as she washes the coffee cups in our small corner sink. She has already roughed up the car article and wants my opinion on the copy which she has emailed me. The new coffee machine, resplendent in shining chrome with pink enamel stripes is bubbling in its corner with a wonderful smell *(of course it would be pink, if it was chosen by Shazza)* and I notice she has dressed to match it with an amazing fake-lizard jacket with black and pink stripes, black leggings and shocking pink shoes. 'Nice outfit, Shaz,' I murmur, 'You have, of course ...'

'Themed my outfit to match the machine, friggin' hell yeah,' she finishes the sentence. 'New coffee machine day is a big day.'

'Well,' I admit, 'it is pretty spectacular. I think you blew the budget on that one.'

'Pretty much,' she admits, 'but then how often do we get a new coffee machine? And, you will have noticed, it is perfectly in tune with the spirit of our founding mother, Princess Barbie!'

We chat companionably over our coffee; there is no sign of Wayne, unsurprisingly, or Alex, and 'Shazza's lads' do not usually arrive until late morning. They are not, by any stretch of the imagination, early risers.

Shazza is, of course, keen to hear about my interview with the charming Mr Knight whom she has taken quite a shine to – albeit aurally. I am happy to give her all the details but have to say that I don't think that straight-back-and-sides Mr Knight is really going to interest our Shazza, although she is tickled to know that he thought her "charming" and sent his love. She is intrigued to hear about the shrewish wife and we agree that it is one of life's great puzzles why the nicest men often have the meanest wives. We debate this at some length and finally agree that most of them are victims of their own kind natures and probably end up married because they are too afraid to say no. Shazza has a hilarious tale of a male friend who, pursued by a woman of this paranoid and possessive ilk, took a trip to South America and forgot to come home. I remember the 'Friends' episode where Chandler leaves for Yemen; we giggle over our coffee like a couple of schoolgirls, enjoying the sun shining through the window, the peace of our little oasis and the delicious coffee. *Small pleasures,* as Nancy says in 'Oliver', *who would deny us these?*

Suddenly I remember the May Ball and get up to pencil it in on the large wall planner. I talk it over with Shazza, who will schedule the lads to attend for an hour or so and take photos. She herself is going with a young man called Gary and is thrilled to have my inside track on the 'black and white' theme. She wanders off to flick through a recent copy of 'Vanity Fair' to see what outfit she would fancy wearing, while I start earning my keep and get down to some serious writing.

Wayne staggers in around 10am and certainly looks amazingly peaky. The hair of the dog notwithstanding, Shazza makes coffee for him and he manages to keep it down. There is an editorial meeting planned for 11; at a quarter to, the lads slam their way into the office. Wayne winces and Shazza hushes them hurriedly. We all take our places at the board table and spread out pages and mock-ups, waiting for Wayne to be able to make it the few feet from his chair to the table.

We begin. Half way through Alex rocks up and joins us. It looks like being a good month and the planning is tight. There is not much of a synchronised theme, but when was there ever? Shazza has had a great idea of putting up what she calls the 'Eye on Dubai' photo once a month which is simply an image that captures the extremes of the fantasy/workplace that we live in. This month's is fabulous and the honour goes to Mohammed who captured the photo in the Mall. It pictures, simply, an Emirati woman (on the phone) as she powers her way along the Mall, followed closely by three gaunt and undersized Indian maids strung out in a line like fishing boats following a liner. One carries the son and heir, a child of about 4 years old; the second maid lugs a solid female toddler about twice her size, and the third bears aloft, shimmering like a magic relic, The Handbag – an outsized monster in leather and chrome. We absolutely love it and praise Mohammed until he is almost as red as the bag and Wayne calls us to order – not because he fears too much praise will damage Mohammed's ego – but because our noise is hurting his head. We agree dates and times for final copy. Wayne, duty done, takes himself off home, the lads go out on a shoot with Shazza, and Alex and I decide to go to lunch.

There's a nice sushi bar down from us where the food comes past on a conveyor belt and we decide that would be a good choice for a healthy lunch, although Alex comments, fairly, as we wander down the dusty road, that he will probably be ready for a hamburger come 4 o'clock, sushi tending to wear off quickly and leave one quite peckish a few hours later. The bar is quite busy but we find a couple of high seats and order green tea. I love going out with Alex because he makes me feel like a genuine journalist; the aura of Fleet Street that hangs about him allows me to bask in his reflected glory and he has a way of making me feel like he's genuinely interested in my professional development by giving me little titbits and tests. Now over teriyaki salmon we chat about nothing in particular and I find myself telling him about my mysterious neighbour – she who reads *Insider,* knows the Princess, has the inside track, as it were, on Palace life through her job there. Alex listens with attention, sipping his tea.

'Did you ask her what she did at the Palace?' he asks finally, after I have burbled on but am now temporarily silenced by a hot tempura prawn.

'No, we never talked about work at all. Only Rosie – that's her maid – told me.'

'She said she was a hostess for the Palace and a translator?'

'Yes, and that she organised events. Although what events she didn't say.'

'Hmm,' Alex has a martial light in his eye; he loves any sort of mystery and won't rest until he gets to the bottom of it. Now he stirs his tea and ponders while I finish off my prawns and whip another aubergine and ginger pancake off the conveyor while I wait for his brain to do its Sherlock Holmes thing and come up with a conclusion.

'Sophie,' he says finally, 'let me give you the facts and then you give me your conclusion. Here, in Dubai, where single women are a rarity anyway, a very beautiful – and clearly very talented – Russian woman in her late twenties is employed by a palace that is organised, occupied and administered by men. How likely is this? Would they not be more likely to find and employ a male interpreter – and preferably a Muslim male – for their male-dominated events? Would not the administration department – and it is a huge one, and, again male-dominated – organise and administer their own in-house events which are, if not political, always guarded and are in-house affairs?'

'Um,' I say foolishly, fiddling with my pancake; 'Well, possibly. But what's your point? What do you think she does?'

He ignores the question. 'And, furthermore,' he goes on, 'this lady goes out every evening, dressed most glamorously, returning home late and sleeping all day. She has a car at her disposal, and a driver, and clearly mixes in illustrious circles.'

'Well, yes ... but – well, what's your conclusion?'

Alex's thin clever face has a weasly quality about it. 'Uh uh,' he says, shaking a chopstick at me, and reaching across to cut off a piece of my pancake and pop it into his own mouth. 'I said you had to reach a conclusion. What do *you* think she does?'

This game is annoying me, as is Alex's habit of always taking food off my plate. 'Stop it, you gannet!' I say sharply. 'Why should she not be exactly what she says she is? Isn't it possible that this male-dominated palace has a women's section; in fact you know it does! Why couldn't she be employed on the female side of the palace?' I finish triumphantly, pushing the rest of the pancake into my mouth before he can poach it.

'Because, my darling, your naïveté is causing you to miss the point. The ladies of the palace are relatively few and far between although you are right that they have their own administrators and supervisors. But they are not, I promise you, going to be stunning Russian girls. No, Sophie, think again.'

I have no idea what he's getting at and it's making me cross. I like Natasha (although, as yet, I can hardly say I know her) and I don't like it when Alex pulls my stories apart and makes me feel gullible and childish. But, equally, I can't stamp my foot and refuse to play.

'Walk it through, Sophie,' he says calmly but with the weasly expression even more pronounced. 'You're not considering the facts; you're letting sentiment cloud your rational judgment.'

The waitress appears and Alex orders more green tea, while I sit cogitating, examining the facts and suddenly I see what he's driving at. 'Oh, I've got it,' I say, 'you think she's there for very nefarious purposes. What, you think she's a prostitute, just another Russian hooker who happens to have done rather well for herself? One they trot out at parties for whoever fancies a shag?'

'Good lord, no!' Alex looks genuinely shocked. 'Not a hooker, dear me no! A far more desirable article altogether; nothing less, I believe, than a *courtesan de marque.*'

'A what?'

'A very old and very tough French title, my dear. We are talking of the mistresses of great men who play the game of love and politics with a great deal of skill. The Madame du Pompadours of this world. Women with real power, bought in the bedroom.'

'Really?' My face reflects my scepticism. 'Now it's my turn to scoff. In a Muslim country, would the several-times-married ruler of Dubai keep a Russian mistress? I think not.'

'Ah but the sheikh is not the only male resident of the palace. There are a number of very powerful relatives – any of them could be her keeper. And don't allow the religious aspect to confuse you. Men are men and when you can buy anything you want, you will naturally buy the best.'

I am still not entirely sure I believe him. 'So,' I say slowly, 'You think she's an exclusive mistress to one of the princes? But surely it doesn't fit. The Pompadour sold her favours to the king, did she not? People paid her to drop a word into Louis' ear, to change his mind. She was paid for her influence; for her political role. That's not going to happen here.'

Alex pours himself another cup of tea, watching as the pale green liquid arches elegantly out of the spout. 'A few years back,' he says absently, 'I was staying in a high quality hotel in Moscow. I went downstairs to the lobby to meet my contact, and the whole place was full of single women. Every single one of them was slim, gorgeous, blonde and had legs – as they say – up to her armpits. There wasn't a man to be seen, only women, and not one over 25. My contact told me they were Russian prostitutes and that for a single girl with any pretensions to good looks and a good figure, prostitution was the only way out of a factory job in a dead end town. Earning money in the world's oldest profession. And for some, it's extremely lucrative. If they play their cards right and find a rich Middle Eastern prince, there's no end to what power and riches can be achieved. It won't last forever, but in five years, with luck, someone like your friend can make more money than you or I will see in a lifetime.'

'Wow,' I say finally. 'Well, I suppose you could be right.'

'We're not talking someone who's been kidnapped from Moldavia and sold into the sex trade at 13,' he said. 'These girls, if they're lucky, and especially if they're streetwise and educated, get to manage themselves, no pimp, no middleman. Getting established is the tough part, but once they've found a keeper, it becomes semi-permanent. They normally live in their own house, all expenses paid, and visit when required. That keeps everyone happy. All hush-hush and swept under the silk carpet, and nothing disrupts the status quo.'

'How do you always know so much, Alex?'

He laughs. 'Ah, a misspent youth, my child! And a permanent inability to keep my nose out of anyone else's business!'

'Well, that I believe!'

'I wonder if I'm right,' he muses. 'Any chance you could find out?'

'Of course not!' I splutter. 'I don't know her at all, and goodness knows, she's intimidating enough without my barging in and enquiring which prince is keeping her and how much she gets paid!'

'Shame. I'd love to know. Any chance you could introduce us? God, what a brilliant source she'd make. What secret dealings must she have seen and known! She'd probably be able to answer all my questions on who's in and what's up.'

'I don't think so,' I retort somewhat waspishly. 'She's not the type to cosy up and chat on the sofa. She'd put you in your place in no time flat.'

He cocks an eyebrow over his glasses. 'I can be very charming when I want,' he says primly, making me laugh.

'Well, could you be very charming and pay the bill?'

'No indeed! You failed the quiz and are not, on this occasion, deemed an appropriate person to have in MI5!'

'Excuse me, I did not! You were completely wrong about the *courtesan de marque* angle; no woman here is selling that type of influence with one of the royals!'

Alex purses his lips. 'And how do you know?' he asks sweetly.

'Well, I don't *know* but it just seems very unlikely. I just can't see business being done that way here. Women selling influence in a country where women are second class citizens?'

Alex signals the waitress with his credit card. 'Uh huh, but may I suggest, young Sophie, just because you can't see it doesn't mean it isn't happening. People are bought and sold every day and in stranger ways than you can imagine. There are a great many factions who would pay someone to use their influence here with the powers that be. I can think of five at least.'

'I wish you wouldn't call me young Sophie,' I say crossly. 'I am 44 and I'm not a rookie reporter. I do know a few things about this town. And I'll do the tip if you like,' I add as he hands his card to the waitress.

He laughs and ruffles my hair. 'I meant only young in the ways of the world. You are, you know, but it's a charming quality. Keep your innocence my dear, you don't want to become old and jaded like yours truly.'

I decide to forgive him, but only because I know he's right. 'But wouldn't that be dangerous?' I ask as we stroll harmoniously back to the office. 'Taking money, I mean ... when an outcome couldn't be guaranteed. I can see it happening in the court of Louis XIV, but here? Baksheesh is time-honoured currency; why not just pay the wazeer, or whoever, to drop a good word in for a certain contractor. Wouldn't it be very suspicious coming from a woman?'

Alex bursts out laughing. 'Whoops, we just went from France to the Ottoman Empire! I would argue most strenuously that the favourite wife or mistress of the Sultan had far more interest with him than the Wicked Wazeer!'

I always get rattled in conversations like this. I never went to university, and all my knowledge of history has been gained from reading, mostly novels I admit, and is therefore patchy. Arguing with Alex never lasts long because he's too damned clever. Or maybe, and far more probably, because I'm too stupid.

The next day, around six, just as I am contemplating another glass of wine before dinner and have asked the cat, very seriously, if he thinks I am becoming an alcoholic, there is a ring at the door and, on opening it, I am surprised to see my willowy neighbour, hair tied back, dressed in running attire. As usual, she does not beat about the bush.

'Sophie,' she greets me, 'I am going to my kick boxing class and I have decided you should come too. Go and put on some sports gear and we will go together.'

I gape at her then say feebly, my eyes running over her long limbs to which black lycra clings as if it were moulded to them, 'Um … I don't have anything that would be suitable, I don't think.'

'What?' she steps through the doorway and heads towards the staircase. 'I don't believe it. You must have something. Don't you go running, go to a gym class?'

I follow her up my stairs and into my bedroom, mumbling a pathetic string of excuses as to why I don't go to the gym. She ignores my protests and stands centre bedroom. 'Show me what you have,' she commands.

I start hauling things out of drawers, T-shirts, shorts, but no Lycra anywhere, only some old tracksuit bottoms that I used to wear to walk the dog. 'As you can see,' I say, as she paws through the stuff that I've tossed onto the bed, 'I am not a lycra person. It shows off too many bulges.'

She gives me a look that indicates I am being foolish. 'Wait,' she says, pulling out a tatty pair of stretchy black three-quarter length pants I used to wear when Rick and I had gym membership about a hundred years ago. 'This will do and that pink T-shirt. It is old but it's okay. Do you have socks and trainers?'

'Yes, but … a kick boxing class sounds very hectic. You know I'm not in very good shape; I'd be absolutely useless.'

'Change!' she commands airily, walking out of the room, and, calling back to me as she goes downstairs, 'I'll wait for you outside in the car, and bring some water.'

I scramble into the pants – not too tight, thank goodness – and pull the T-shirt on. It doesn't look so good; it pulls across the bust and has clearly seen too many washes. I dive into the wardrobe and pull out my trainers which, fortunately, have socks stuffed inside them (not too smelly, I establish with a quick sniff) and whizz downstairs quickly to grab a bottle of water out of the fridge. Outside the sleek black Mercedes that I recognise is waiting kerbside, its engine purring quietly. The back door opens mysteriously and I step in.

The gym is not far and Natasha doesn't speak. Neither do I. Neither does the driver. When the car swishes to a stop she gets out and I scramble out of my side and follow her. Those long legs cover the ground so efficiently I am almost trotting to keep up. At this point I remember I've brought no money, and I also notice that she has a gym bag with her and I have nothing, so I trot a bit harder to get abreast of her but she is through the glass door and up the stairs and into the studio, moving as lithely as a cheetah. I halt on the threshold, rather shocked at the bevy of young matrons who are grouped artlessly in front of me, all beautifully attired in matching outfits, all greyhound slim and fit, and all staring at me with varying degrees of, thank God, snooty disinterest. Natasha goes to the front and I scuttle in her wake. *Oh God*, I'm thinking, *this is an absolute nightmare! Not the front!* The trainer is a Natasha lookalike, also tall, blonde and Russian, but she looks as if she were trained in the KGB. Her hair is scraped back, and her face is hard and sculpted, as is her body; her Lycra one-piece looks as if it were sprayed on to a body as deeply muscled as a porpoise. They exchange a quick word in Russian, and the trainer looks at me and nods. She adjusts her head microphone and suddenly her voice booms out 'Welcome ladies! Let's start with a quick warm up!' The class shuffles into a phalanx of intensity; the trainer (Anna) at the front, nearest the mirror, Natasha away on the right wing, and me on the left. I pin my eyes on Anna and try and mirror her movements. The techno music begins thumping and we are off! The next hour is nothing short of torture but it's impossible to stop or think or even do more than concentrate fiercely as we move (I, stumbling, everyone else transitioning seamlessly) into a full-on cardio and kick-boxing class. Within the first twenty minutes (*oh God, is it a full hour – is there a clock on the wall I can see?*) I am pouring sweat and only realise this when we have a one-minute break for water and everyone else whips out their bar-sized towels and I drip helplessly. Anna glares at me and hands me two paper towels which, I realise as the first one tears, must only be used to blot the sweat. There's also an unpleasant odour arising from my old pink T-shirt which, I now remember too late, has a tendency to smell no matter how many washes it has. The class escalates into full scale kick-boxing movements and, looking hopelessly into the mirror, I see that whereas Anna's and Natasha's extended kicks are long, straight and high, mine closely resemble that of a dog cocking its leg against a fire hydrant. The torture goes on. I am amazed at these women's resilience and stamina. In spite of their perfect appearance and matched outfits they are seriously fit. But, of course, I reason (as I gasp for breath in the second water break), this is Dubai and probably the majority of these glamorous young things will be spending much of their free time in the gym. It is part of the expat 'regime': the school run, the gym run, the supermarket or Mall run and the home run. And in spite of her smoking, Natasha is totally focused on the class, eyes like slits as she kicks out savagely at an imaginary opponent, feet dancing like a boxer, arms hard and muscled and her breathing relatively normal, not like me, puffing like an old billy. Well, I reason, she can probably give me ten years but now my muscles are aching so much I can't think much beyond the pain. Only a fear of looking a complete loser keeps me hard at it. Now, thankfully, we are into the 'cooling down' period which only involves several hundred sit ups and some more torment of screaming muscles, but this time at least I can lie on the floor between takes. Finally, thank God, Anna says 'It's a wrap, ladies!' and there is a little spatter of applause. The women all rise gracefully from the floor, whereas I have to stumble up first to my knees and then finally to my feet. Forget the applause; I can hardly lift my arms, let alone coordinate my hands to clap. There is a little flurry of goodbyes as everyone drifts off, thanking Anna who doesn't pay them any attention as she is having a chat with Natasha. I fill up my water bottle and laugh at the sight of myself in the mirror. I am soaked in sweat; my hair is slicked to my head, and the pink T-shirt is emanating waves of BO. I wait patiently by the door, panting quietly, and finally Natasha is ready to go. She says nothing but cocks an amused eye at me and my dishevelment. Several of the young women are still in the car park, chatting, and eye us with interest as we head towards the purring black Mercedes. They are probably wondering how such a scruffy Cinderella merits such a glamorous carriage. As we are whisked smoothly away, Natasha wrinkles her nose delicately. 'Sophie,' she says, and there is a quiver of amusement in her voice, 'I think it is you that I can smell!'

I blush. 'I'm sorry, I forgot I meant to throw out this T-shirt because the moment it gets hot it starts smelling. I promise I'll throw it out the minute I get home.'

'Please do.'

I look down at myself in distaste. 'God, I look such a mess! How do you manage to stay so cool?'

She gives me a sideways smile. 'I can see you're surprised and disappointed. Surely a smoker should be far less fit. Am I right?'

'Well you are superbly fit. I can't quite understand it.'

She looks out the window. 'I like to be fit,' she says distantly. 'I am what they call obsessive. And also, I enjoy the physical effort of kick boxing. It releases lots of stresses.'

I laugh. 'Yes, I could see your eyes and you were scarily focused. Who were you kicking the hell out of?'

She puts that chill blue gaze straight on me. 'Men,' she says clearly.

I am a little taken aback but respond in kind. 'You know,' I say with a laugh, 'I should have been kicking the shit out of my cheating husband but do you know, all I could think about was getting my leg higher and coordinating my movements. I think I need a little more practice.'

Her chill look thaws a little; she softens. 'You did well Sophie,' she says. 'I was proud of you.'

Her words make me feel ridiculously chuffed. 'Aww shucks,' I say and those delicate eyebrows lift.

'What does that mean?'

'Silly American expression. But, seriously, did you see the height of my leg? I felt ridiculous! Honestly, I've seen Hector lift his leg higher!'

That makes her laugh. 'So will you come again Sophie? Do you dare?'

'Who dares wins!' I say boldly.

Late the next afternoon there is a knock at the door and Patti goes to answer it as I am lying prone on the couch, complaining, as I have all day, that there is not one single part of me that doesn't ache appallingly. She comes back carrying a parcel and gives it to me. I have no idea what it can be but I struggle to sit up and open it with some excitement. No one sends me presents! Silky black Lycra drops into my lap with lime green inserts down the legs and across the bodice of a matching top and pants set, made by a leading sportswear manufacturer. And the surprise continues. Lime socks followed by brand new state-of-the-art trainers in white with matching lime green slashes and laces complete the themed attire. I have seldom seen anything so pretty, let alone owned such an outfit. Patti smiles at my pleasure as I hobble upstairs, wincing at each step, as excited as a five year old, to try on my new gear. It all fits perfectly and, intriguingly, the stripes are so placed that they define my body shape so that I look leaner and taller. I am entranced with my new silhouette and on a sudden thought want to run next door to show it off to Natasha, who has surely sent it. *What a friend*, I think excitedly, as I limp down the path and step carefully over the half-metre hedge between our properties. *What a kind thing to do*. I tap on the front door and open it, half expecting to see the skein of smoke that announces she is within but there is nothing, only Rosie calling out a 'Hello!' from the kitchen. We meet mid-hallway and she smiles at me with her gentle kind smile. 'Oh madam!' she says with a little clap of her hands, 'How nice you look! Ms Natasha said she guessed you would be coming over in the new sportswear and I was to tell you that she hopes you like it.'

I give her a little twirl. 'I do,' I say with a bright smile. 'I love it! Is she not in?'

'No madam, I am afraid she has gone to work. But I will tell her that you are very satisfied!'

'Very satisfied, but very stiff from yesterday,' I add, 'Make sure you tell her that!'

She smiles and nods. 'I do not understand quite what you girls get out of all this running and kicking. I am sure it wouldn't suit me!'

I am grinning with delight, both at the sight of myself in Natasha's full length hallway mirror and amusement at being called a 'girl'. But I do feel girlish, I decide, as I peer at my back view and discover, to my continuing pleasure, two tiny green lines that define my waist. There is a little bit of a muffin top, no doubt about that, but I am now determined to do away with it. *What's a little pain?* I ask myself. I thank Patti, send regards to Alexei and Hector and more thanks to Natasha, and take my leave. Totally irrationally, I decide to jump the hedge and manage it, although it's hardly hurdling height and the pain of my stretched muscles makes me gasp. I hobble back inside full of a burgeoning sense of direction. Sophie is going to get fit!

The next day the pain is already wearing off, assisted by several long hot baths, and I am childishly keen to get into my new outfit and back into the gym. Shazza is a bit of a gym bunny herself and has lots of advice on classes that would suit me. She is seriously impressed that I managed to survive a kick-boxing class, cold, with Anna, whom, it seems, has a reputation throughout Dubai as being 'one tough mother' (Shazza's words). She clearly wants to say that she didn't think I had it in me, but confines herself instead to remarking that toning up before wearing an awesome new outfit to the May Ball can only be a good thing. So that afternoon, as I make my way home, I stop off at the gym and sign myself up for a six month stint of classes and frequent user time. It virtually cleans out my bank account but is, I reason, worth it. On my way out, as I descend the stairs, I see a young man coming up them towards me and realise it is he – Kester Woodseaves! He smiles up at me with that easy smile of his, blue eyes crinkled up in that appealing way that he has and I feel myself lighting up in return. 'Hello!' he says with enthusiasm, 'fancy meeting you here!' managing to make the old cliché sound charming. I grin at him. 'Yes, I'm shaping up for the summer. Just signed up for six months!'

'Well done you! What a pity you've missed the Marathon. Still, there's always next year.'

'Oh I don't think I'm quite up to Marathons,' I say, as we stand in the sunlight on the stairs and I notice, with pleasure, how a beam is lighting up his fair hair, just as in the illustration in the novel. 'I'm really not much of a runner.'

'Well you've got plenty of time to practice. We're always looking for new recruits to our team, so I can sign you up any time.'

The thought makes me laugh. I, who have barely survived a class, albeit with the fearsome Anna, running 26 miles! 'Thanks,' I say lightly, 'but I think at this point I'll just stick to shaping up to get into my dress for the May Ball.'

'Oh are you going to that?' he asks, blue eyes alight. 'Perhaps I'll see you there. We can have a dance.'

I feel a blush coming on at the thought of dancing cheek to cheek with Kester Woodseaves and my heart is racing uncomfortably fast. 'That would be fun,' I manage finally. Really, he is very cute. There's something almost teddy-bearish about him; a quality that makes you want to cuddle him. I blunder on to cover my confusion. 'Unfortunately I'm not much of a dancer either.'

'Oh me neither,' he says lightly. 'I can't offer to fox-trot you round the floor, but I think I could manage a slow number.' His blue eyes look into mine and my heart picks up the pace a bit. Oh God, Kester Woodseaves is flirting with me!

I fumble with my bag and look away. 'Well lovely to see you again. I must go,' and he steps aside to let me pass. Unaccountably, or perhaps not, we both step the same way and end up bumping into each other. His hand steadies me as I stumble, 'You're not very good on stairs are you?' he says almost in my ear, and I laugh breathlessly remembering the school stairs that he steered me down on our first meeting. 'Watch out for those heels!'

I clutch on to the railing and look down at my feet. 'Well they're not killer heels but I guess dangerous enough.'

He still has his hand on my shoulder. 'I think they're very pretty.' His voice has dropped and his eyes are only inches away from mine as he looks down at me. He adds softly, so softly I wonder if I've dreamt it, 'as are you!'

Then, smoothly, he steps away from me and moves on up the staircase. He looks back from the top, with a smile and the shadow of a wink; the door wooshes shut and he is gone. I totter on down the stairs, clinging to the handrail, my heart doing somersaults and my knees feeling weak. Did Kester Woodseaves actually say I was pretty? Did he? *Did he*? I wander dazedly round the car park for a few circuits before I locate the car and my hand is shaking so much I can hardly find the keys which, as always, are right at the bottom of my handbag. I get out my water bottle and gulp down several mouthfuls. Then I flick down the mirror and look at myself and I see sparking hazel eyes and a big smile – not the usual doleful Sophie look at all. I wriggle my foot around and admire my shoe myself; it is one of my favourites, in black and white patent with a plaid toe-bow. 'Yes, you are very pretty', I tell it with a giggle, 'As am I! *As am I!*'

Buoyed up on this new wave of surprising happiness, I am actually waiting for Natasha two evenings later when we are to have our next kick-boxing class. But sadly, she does not come; there is no black Mercedes anywhere to be seen so I assume that she must be working and take my own car to the leisure centre. Anna looks surprised to see me back and properly – not to mention stylishly – attired. This time I have all the necessary accoutrements – the bottle of water, the sweat towel, the bag. I look the part. And I can maintain a similar haughty cast of countenance to the rest of the willowy young mums; after all Kester Woodseaves told me I was pretty!

Although I am suffering the next day and creeping around like a spider, Shazza tells me it's perfectly normal and recommends a new salad bar for lunch. It's been a while since Shazza and I have done lunch, so we leave a note for Alex or Wayne or whoever should wonder where we are and wander off to fill ourselves up on a collection of small-portion high-price salad in some glitzy little local eatery in the company of other 'ladies who lunch'; *'Jumeirah fucking Janes'* Shazza calls it and eyes them with derision. Over lunch, Shazza sketches out her dress for the Ball, which she is currently in the process of buying fabric for. It is, in Shazza style, truly spectacular. I pity the poor Indian tailor who will be making it, however. It has a bodice cut on the bias, stripes, polka dots, tulle and lace – and that's just the bit I can see. Shazza wants to know what I will be wearing and is appalled that I don't know.

'Jeez, Soph,' she tells me, 'you gotta get cracking. Every tailor in town will be chokka with orders and then where will you be? Or are you planning to buy it off the peg – or even online? My friend got a smashing outfit from some American prom queen website. You should look around. But what's your basic idea?'

'Probably strapless,' I ponder, pretty much making it up as I go along. 'A close-fitting bodice suits me best.'

'Yeah,' twinkles Shazza, 'It's coz you got little boobs. Now with me ...' she looks down at her own very respectable sized breasts and pats them fondly, 'and these bad boys, I gotta have *support!'*

'Indeed you do!' I laugh because I know how much Shazza loves her underwear and how much she spends on it. 'You are the queen of uplift!'

We order more drinks and chat on. After all, the afternoon is relatively empty; there is no dash for anything to be done and the men are not even in the office. After another hour or so has gone by we have pretty much sketched out outfits for the pair of us. Shazza has abandoned the tulle overskirt and has gone with a plain satin drape that will cling to her hourglass shape; I know what suits me and have an outline of something fitting, probably floor-length, strapless with some kind of ruching or gathered feature at the waist. Clearly there is a weekend of mall-trawl to be encountered in pursuit of this gown. Fortunately the shoes that Jason Knight admired, being black and white, should be fine to wear as they are a good height and comfortable. A black lizard clutch-bag, bought in Hong Kong years ago, will complete this, as yet not quite accomplished, ensemble. 'Jewellery,' ponders Shazza. 'Now you gotta have something strong round your neck; loads of bling, you know, rock-sized diamonds.'

'Haven't exactly got anything that would suit,' I say, adding 'necklace' to my shopping list. 'I got loads,' says Shazza with a confident wink. 'I'll sort through them and find something for you.'

'*Help!*' I think, keeping my expression neutral. Shazza's taste, although spectacular and representative of her larger-than-life, in-your-face personality, is not really mine, but it would be rude to decline. And I might be surprised; it is true I am very conservative in my taste when it comes to jewellery. Not that I have much to choose from; Rick was never a buyer of jewellery, for me anyway. He preferred to spend the money on himself, Rolex watches and the like. My mother left me very little and what there is are mostly old-fashioned settings and small stones. But we are not talking real stones of course; costume jewellery and bling is what is required here.

On our way back to the office I pop into a stationers and buy a card to say thank you to Natasha. Looking at the vast array of designs makes me recognise how little I know her or her tastes. Flowers don't look right so, in the end, I opt for one depicting 'The Kiss' in the painting by Gustav Klimt for no better reason than I like it. When I get home I write a brief message in it, thanking her for the gym outfit. It's curious that, where I know her so little, she seems to understand me very well. How did she know, for example, that Roberts was my married name? It almost implies that she knew about me before we met. Yet how would that be possible? And as regarding the gym gear, well, that's another mystery. I have very little spare cash; the job pays only enough to keep me in a basic style of comfort and, if Rick did not pay for Patti and the villa, there is no way I could afford such a lifestyle on my tiny salary. In fact, given the strain that such expenditure must put on him – he is only averagely well paid after all – I am constantly expecting him to suggest that Patti should go and the villa along with her. Although I would balk at it, it's quite frankly amazing that he has not suggested I move to a smaller apartment to cut his hefty overheads. I can only think that it's because he prefers to keep the status quo as it is for the moment. There may be several reasons for this, none of which I've explored with him, but only surmised, as I don't want to raise the question and get the answer I don't want to hear. So, in fact, I don't buy much at all; nothing now for the house and very little for myself. Fortunately, I've always had a good wardrobe and now I'm appreciating that fact as well as classic brands that can be trotted out season after season. But a brand new leisure outfit would have been an expenditure that I could not have afforded all at once, but how Natasha should know, or even guess at this, is a mystery. The likeliest answer is that she was just being kind, although she doesn't initially strike one as being of a kind and caring disposition. Another suggestion, but I shrink from it, is that she was embarrassed by my appearance and bought me the outfit to make sure the next time I looked presentable in her presence anyway. The Ball dress presents another such dilemma but at least I have time to solve that; I have more than a month to find something either new or second hand and, given that Patti has a sewing machine she will lend me if needs be, I should be fairly respectably turned out. The thought, however, that Jason Knight will be doing a slow dance with me makes a spectacularly sexy outfit almost imperative. I hum as I drive home. Now 'sexy' is not an adjective I've used in connection with myself for a long time; it is not an adjective associated with women whose husbands have left them. After all, society reasons, husbands need sex and if they're not getting it at home they go elsewhere, hence, ergo, I can't be judged to be sexy by that definition. I put the car away and aim a defiant kick at the rubbish bin, connecting smoothly with its black plastic middle. 'Take that for society!' I tell it.

I get into my T-shirt and old jeans in order to wander across and see if Alexei and Hector are up for another lesson, having scribbled a brief, but heartfelt, thank you into the card and popping it into an envelope. I tap lightly and enter and am pleased to see the familiar skein of smoke arising from the couch. Natasha is at home.

'Hi,' I say with a smile, popping my head round the corner of the door. 'May I come in?'

Her face reflects nothing but polite interest but I am fast becoming used to the fact that Natasha does not, as the saying goes, wear her heart on her sleeve. I proffer the card. 'I can't tell you how lovely it was to get a present,' I say enthusiastically. 'The outfit is absolutely gorgeous, I love it! And I went yesterday, all by myself; I must say Anna looked most relieved that I was dressed properly. Thanks so much! It was so kind of you.'

She looks tired and pale although no less beautiful. She flicks open the envelope with a long red nail, and extracts the card. Reading it, she smiles, then turns it over and looks long at the illustration. 'This is very you, Sophie,' she comments at last. 'Beautiful idealized golden love.'

'Oh no,' I say earnestly. 'People think that's not what Klimt intended. Look at the women's head and the way her lips are turned away from the man. In spite of the flowers and the golden couch and all the wealth and beauty, he is not The One.'

She looks at it a little more closely now. 'How appropriate,' she says softly. She tosses the card onto the table and looks up at me.

I burble on. 'So now, I'm so enthusiastic about wearing my lovely outfit, I've signed on at the gym for a full six months and, even though I am sore after Anna's class yesterday, I kept up pretty well, and I'm full of determination now to get fit and keep that way. I think I was becoming very lazy and I'm really grateful to you for getting me back on track!'

She continues to gaze at me. 'No,' she says at length. 'There's something else. Something else has put a light in your smile.' She raises a quizzical eyebrow.

'Oh nothing,' I say sheepishly, but with a rising blush I can't hide. 'I just got a nice compliment yesterday from a rather cute young man and it's put me in a good mood. I don't know how you get to be so perceptive!'

'Young man?'

'Oh well not exactly *young',* I counter foolishly. 'Only younger than me. A bit. Maybe...' (I cast my mind back to Jason Knight's blond good looks – how old would he be exactly?) 'Six or seven years perhaps. But very cute. Like a lovely teddy-bear. Anyway, we met at the gym and he told me I was pretty. I know it's stupid to get excited about it, but I get so few compliments, I value the ones I do get!'

A very slow smile shapes her mouth. 'What a child you are, Sophie,' she says softly. 'And in spite of your cheating husband how very obvious it is that you still believe in true love.' She points at the card.

'No, it's just ... well ... it's Kester Woodseaves, you see!'

She cocks her head. 'Is that his name?'

I perch on the edge of the chair and explain the Kester Woodseaves connection. She listens, looking more cynical by the minute. Finally, she laughs lightly. 'I stick by what I said earlier. You are a child, in love with a character from a child's storybook.'

I feel I have to defend myself. 'It's a classic love story,' I say hotly. Kester is the only one who loves Prue Sarn for who she is. Everyone else just uses her. Oh! I'm going to make you read the book! You can't understand unless you do! I'm going to get it right now!' I stamp out of the house and am back in five minutes with 'Precious Bane' in my hand which I put down on her coffee table with the faintest suspicion of a slam.

'All right,' she concedes. 'I will read it.'

'And see here,' I take up the book and flick to the watercolour at the front. 'Kester Woodseaves. And Jason Knight looks just like him! It's such a coincidence, don't you think?'

'It would seem so, yes. So what is wrong with this Prue Sarn? Why do they think she's a witch?' She peers at the picture.

'Because she's 'hare shotton' as they call it – we would say she had a 'hare lip'. In the old days it was thought that a child was marked like that if a hare, or a witch, had crossed the mother's path in pregnancy. It's not only Russia that has the old folk beliefs you know. Even in England, the land that you assume is all milk and honey, we have our dark legends too.'

She counters quickly. 'This is in the countryside,' she says, reading the blurb on the back cover. 'The peasants always have these legends which explain natural events. Yes,' she goes on, 'We understand witches very well in Russia.'

'I know,' I add with a mock shudder. 'I read Russian fairy tales as a child and they scared the life out of me! Anyway,' I add on a different note. 'Is Alexei in? I thought he and I might do a bit of dog training.'

She lies back again, the book on her chest. 'No,' she says absently. 'He has had to stay late at school for some reason and Rosie has gone to collect him.'

I'm suddenly aware that I may have interrupted her hard-earned, presumably, rest. Looking at her, and thinking back to Alex's words, I continue to be mystified by the woman before me. Who is she? What does she do? And why do I feel that, in spite of that glacial exterior, she does like me?

'I'm sorry,' I say, 'I just realise I think I woke you up didn't I?'

She yawns. 'No, I was just dozing. But I think I will go upstairs now and sleep.' She unfolds herself from the sofa, book in hand. 'I will send Alexei over when he returns or rather, I will leave a note for Rosie. And … I will read this.' She drifts out of the room and towards the stairs. 'I am pleased you like the clothes,' she throws back over her shoulder.

'I really did. It was a wonderful present. Thank you again!'

Her footsteps go on upstairs and presently a door closes. Hoping that Kester is in safe hands, I go home.

My phone is ringing as I go in and I am surprised to hear Tasha's rather hard clipped little English voice.

'Mummy?'

'Hello darling!'

Tasha never has long gossipy conversations such as one dreams of with one's daughter. It's all part of Tasha's tough, no-nonsense, get on with it personality; she selects her conversation depending on who she's talking to and I don't rate more than the minimum. She is, and always was, very much Rick's daughter. I always felt Tasha had me sussed at about three months old and played me masterfully; she and Rick, by contrast, were always totally *en rapport* and the original father and daughter team. They had their own jokes, references and secrets; very early on they had a lovely secret club of two from which 'silly old mummy' was always excluded. I remember once coming upon them playing hideout in a huge cardboard fort Rick had built in the playroom and Tasha, aged 3, raising her head, saying to me coldly 'Go away. We don't want you. This is our game.' And Rick, sitting by, laughing at her, regardless of how it hurt me. Later they played tennis doubles which I had enjoyed but never excelled at; everyone could see how Rick loved tall pretty Tasha as his doubles partner, their twinned competitive spirit and steely-eyed determination to win and the strong thread of intuitive understanding that ran, fine-spun, between the two of them. But, inevitably, there had been fallings out, inevitable between two people as totally self-absorbed as these two. Tasha is exactly like Rick, vain, selfish and somewhat cruel. People see only her beauty initially; later they find out, too late, about her strong will and determination to have her own way. But when she left, a little piece of Rick's heart went too; it was at that point I believe that he began to think about replacing me.

'Mummy, you know it's Easter vacation. Daddy's sent me a ticket to Dubai so I'll be arriving on Saturday morning but just for a week. I'll send you details; can one of you collect me from the airport?'

I am caught wrong-footed on this one. Rick sent her an airfare, but why? I know nothing about this. Where is she staying, what does she know?

'Yes, darling, of course; daddy didn't tell me any of this. I'll have to find out what he has in mind.'

'Oh I don't need entertainment. I have a load of people to see, and I desperately need clothes. You can take me shopping if you want.'

Um, no, I don't think so, not with my bank balance! 'Of course, darling, that would be lovely.'

'And daddy's taking me out somewhere for a day, I don't know where. Early birthday present, he says.'

'Oh,' I say feebly. 'That sounds nice.'

'All right,' she says decisively. 'I'll send you details. Don't forget!' And she rings off.

I look at the phone pensively. 'Oh bother,' I say to Puss, 'Now what's going on there? Do you think I have to ring her wretched father to find out what that's all about?' Puss meows in response which I take as a yes, so I text Rick's mobile. I don't want to have to speak with him especially with *her* listening.

The next week is busy; I have an appointment with the Chief Vet, a delightful man who gives me more than enough information to finish my article and, after a few afternoons' hard work I have one of the best pieces I've written in a long time and worthy of the new me: Sophie Haddon. I use some of Jason Knight's photographs to flesh out the article about the Cultural Centre, and just as I am rounding this off, I remember the meeting he told me about which must be coming up in a few days. I am literally pawing through my cluttered desk trying to find the notes I made when Shazza answers the phone and waves to get my attention. I have no idea what she's on about but there is much signalling and pointing so finally I stand up to see what all the fuss is about. Shazza is giggling and flirting with whoever is at the other end of the line; finally she puts me out of my misery and says 'Yeah, she's right here …. Yeah, good to talk to *you!'* and passes the phone to me. 'He sounds so fucking *hot!*' she says in a stage whisper. 'Jason Knight, from the school.'

I feel a rush of blood to my cheeks as I take the phone but opt for a breezy approach, partly to throw Shazza off the scent.

'Hello!' I say with enthusiasm, 'this is such a coincidence! I was just searching for the flier you gave me for the Cultural Centre function. I know it's very soon.'

'Hello,' he responds, and my tummy does a butterfly flip at the sound of his voice. God, he sounds even cuter on the phone than in the flesh, if that's possible. Shazza is nodding and smiling encouragement at me and mouthing kissy noises which I know are deliberate to make me laugh. 'Funnily enough, I was ringing you about that. It's this Thursday night, at 7.30pm. I didn't want you to miss it, because I think it will fill in the bits I missed.'

'That's so thoughtful! I'll just get my secretary to write this down …' That nearly convulses Shazza who nearly throws the pen at me and I scribble down the details. 'Fucking cheeky cow,' she says, sotto voce.

'I would have liked to have gone too,' he goes on, 'but unfortunately I'm tied up that night with a Parents' Evening. '

I am conscious of a moment's disappointment. An evening with Jason Knight, even listening to a boring lecture, would still be about the most fun I could have just now.

'Never mind,' I say in my I'm-such-a-professional – journalist voice. 'It's so kind of you to ring. I really appreciate it.'

'No problem,' he responds. 'I'll hope to see you at the Ball instead.'

'Absolutely!' I say in a nicely neutral tone. '*Oh absolutely*,' mimes Shazza beside me, in a terribly put-on accent. I ignore her. 'Well, thanks again, and see you then.'

'Looking forward to it,' he says and hangs up. I put down the receiver and frown at Shazza. 'What are you taking the mickey for? Next time you're on the phone to one of your advertisers I'm going to try and make you laugh!'

'Children!' barks Wayne, 'can we have some hush please? I can't concentrate with you two screeching like cockatoos!'

I go off to finish my article, leaving space for any information forthcoming from the meeting, and Shazza gives Wayne a mouthful for using gender-biased language.

This conversation does, however, prompt me to get cracking with sorting out my dress for the Ball. After a couple of fruitless weekend mall trawls, my patience is rewarded by a find in a surprisingly tatty shop; a Ball dress in my size and pretty much what I had in mind. It is a strapless black satin floor length dress, which fits snugly enough, the waist being emphasised by a broad sash of pale cream satin which ties in a huge bow to one side. The satin is not perhaps the thickest quality, and could crease badly, but once on it looks really very becoming. I turn and twist in front of the mirror and decide that I won't do any better than this at a price I can afford. Once home I try on the whole outfit complete with shoes and bag and feel that wonderful *frisson* of excitement that accompanies buying new clothes and also some excitement because of the Ball. It is so long since I went out to a function like this that I find I am really looking forward to it. Rick, in spite of our fallings out, is always a handsome, if not hugely attentive, partner; indeed he adores these occasions which give him occasion to show off the famous charm. How many times have women commented to me after such affairs how lucky I am in my husband? How many times have I sat by while Rick held the floor, dominating the table with the telling of a joke, cigarette in one hand, glass of wine in the other, his eyes flirting with all the women who are gazing at him, wide-eyed, hanging on his every word? There is a curious sense of displacement in such moments; it is like being trapped in a bubble. Everyone is part of something that you are not; I glance round and see that they are enthralled by my husband with his good looks, flirtatious eyes and sexy voice. All except me. Not that anyone ever looks at me, but if they did they would see a woman who is trying not to yawn because I've seen it all before, heard all the jokes, even walked into rooms after a long dinner or a function and seen Rick unhanding himself from the clutches of some deluded woman. For Rick, flirting is as natural as breathing. He thinks it's a desirable quality and prides himself on his ability to attract women; I suspect he used to think it made him more attractive as a husband. He used to hope I would be jealous. Maybe I was – once. However, in spite of this, or maybe because of it, he is an attentive date if only because he wants other women to be envious of the attention he gives to his lucky wife.

On taking off the dress I can see the difference that the gym classes have made to me. My arms are looking very toned and my waist is tighter and slimmer. I admire the slight arch in my thighs too as I walk around the room in underwear and high heels. *Looking good enough for Kester*, I tell the mirror.

A week or so before the Ball, Shazza comes over with a bag full of assorted jewellery and we spent an amusing evening upstairs, glass of wine in hand to aid creativity, working out which piece suits the dress best, deciding, finally, on a piece that is wonderful, sparkly made-in-China fake diamonds in a thick band with a diamond-shaped pendant. It brings the dress to life and I like the matching long earrings which have a beguiling shimmer when I shake my head. Shazza pronounces me to be 'Fucking gorgeous' and I find myself thinking that I hope Jason Knight thinks the same. Of Rick I do not think at all, so it is a bit of a shock when he rings that night and says he'd like to come for supper before the Ball because he wants to talk to me about a few things.

Of course Natasha has been hearing about the dress and the night before the Ball I put it on, with the jewellery, and go over to show her how it looks. She smiles that slow lazy smile as I pirouette around and I can tell she's thinking – again – what a child I am. She has 'Precious Bane' on the coffee table, I am pleased to see, and it has a bookmark stuck in it halfway through, so I assume she's making progress with Prue and Kester. Annoyingly, though, she doesn't mention it. However, she approves of my outfit, as do Patti and Alexei – and Hector by default. She frowns, though, at my Chinese jewellery. 'I do not like that at all,' she says. 'Why do you wear it?'

I explain the difficulty; I don't have much jewellery, or nothing like what is required for this. 'It's just fake rubbish,' I admit, 'but it's the fashion. No one will be wearing anything else.'

Natasha looks down her nose and flicks me a look when I call her a snob. 'Of course,' she says lazily, shrugging her shoulders.

'So will the man of your dreams be there?' she asks me with a raised eyebrow. 'Kester Woodseaves of the golden hair and blue eyes?'

I sit on the edge of a chair and fiddle with my bow, retying the satin so the ends are longer. 'Yes, I think so,' I say with careful nonchalance. I have not seen Jason Knight at the gym again, except for a quick wave as I went to a class, and saw him cycling away in a corner. I don't think he saw me as he was intent on what he was doing. His wife I've never seen at all; I don't even know if she belongs to the gym.

'And you're hoping for a dance?'

I keep my head down and concentrate on the bow. 'Well, that would be nice. He said he'd ask me for a dance on the day I met him at the gym.'

'The day he said you were pretty?'

'Yes,'

'Well I hope he remembers!' she says lightly.

I finish the bow and lift my head. 'Unfortunately Rick is coming to supper tomorrow night and I have a bad feeling about it. He says he wants to talk to me about 'things' which I'm afraid means that he's running out of money and wants me to either give up Patti or the house – or both.'

Rosie brings me a drink and a napkin, bless her, in case I spill any on the dress. Natasha asks,

'And you will do what?'

'Nothing. What can I do? I don't have an income to speak of. If Rick says I have to go, then go I must.'

Natasha frowns. 'You are so passive, Sophie, so obliging. This husband cheats on you, leaves you and you say 'I will do whatever you want'? Throw me out of my house and I will understand and go willingly?'

'No, no,' I say with a flush rising to my cheeks. 'But that was our agreement, you see. I would stay here, in the house if possible, because Rick couldn't afford a divorce and I didn't want to leave anyway. I have nothing to go back to in England, so I might as well stay here. And we do have two expensive children and they're my children too, so I have to make allowances.'

'You are the most accommodating cheated-on wife I have ever met!' she says lightly. 'Me, I would stab him!'

I sip my drink and giggle, 'Yes, you would! But I really don't want to move although the villa is probably too large for me on my own, so I hope it's not that.'

Unfortunately, it is. The next night Rick, looking handsome and debonair in his DJ, sits down to a very light supper opposite me and tells me, 'Sorry, Sophie, there just isn't the money to maintain the house, the gardener and the maid as well as pay university fees and living expenses for two very expensive children. I'm afraid I'm running out of money and something has got to give.'

'And I don't suppose it could be the Mercedes sports?'

He smiles winningly. 'That would help for a while, of course, but I'm talking of long term expenses. I don't suppose you're likely to be getting a pay rise any time soon?'

There's a sting in that one. 'No,' I say shortly.

'No,' he repeats, 'what a pity you're not trained to do a real job.'

'What,' I snap, 'like air-hostessing?'

His blue eyes sparkle because he's got a rise out of me; he sips his wine and goes back to the subject. 'I had thought of getting rid of Ahmed and Patti initially. I am sure you could water the garden occasionally, it's just a question of turning on the sprinkler really. The pool guy is paid for until June but after that, I'm not sure. But Patti is an on-going expense and really, we don't need her. I am sure you could vacuum once a week and do the washing. You used to manage it well enough back home when there were four of us.'

I am still stinging over the 'real job' jibe. It always hurts when I think of my early marriage, early children, and the loss of those university years that so many of my peers had. But Rick knows all my weak spots; he knows how to target me and does it with finesse and the unerring facility of long practice. And also because he enjoys it.

'All right,' I mutter. But I can see what's coming. This is a stay of execution really; the thin edge of the wedge. Ahmed and Patti are nothing in the real scheme of events. Rick probably does genuinely have financial concerns but he wants me out. Already he's going back on the deal we had and there's nothing I can do about it. And, as always, I have no argument, no response. I just accept it and hate myself for doing so. 'I suppose you want me to tell Patti?'

'If you could.' Now I get the warm treacle treatment because he's got his own way so easily. 'I'll pay her for this month and she can leave at the end. That will give her four weeks' notice almost, if you tell her tomorrow. I'll ring the landscapers tomorrow about Ahmed'.

'Tasha rang me,' I say baldly. 'She said you've sent her a ticket, also that you propose to take her out and have a chat about something. Are you going to be telling her about ...' I falter, 'our new living arrangements? Is she staying with you or with me?'

'She's a grown up,' he says casually. 'Yes, I'll tell her; she will understand better than most. She'll have to stay with you, of course, but I don't mind collecting her from the airport. And the ticket is a case in point. These things are expensive and you can't pay for them. I can't afford for Tash and Nick to come home every holiday. Not if you are living here. That's another thing I have to talk to her about. Things are going to have to change.'

I ignore all the gibes in that remark. 'You could have told her not to come.'

He gives me a cold look that seems to indicate that I am not a proper mother. 'She's my daughter. Of course I want to see her. I would have thought you did too. Not that there's much love lost between you two.'

It's pointless even rising to that old chestnut; Rick always has to reinforce the point that he, and only he, understands Tasha. Nick is different. For years Rick tried to mould Nick into the kind of son he wanted, only to be frustrated by a personality and a behaviour he couldn't fathom. So it became my fault. Nick was a 'mummy's boy', I had 'spoiled him' 'ruined him'; 'Tasha was worth twenty of him.' For years Nick referred to Tasha as 'my daughter' and Nick as 'your son'. The inference was plain. How Nick came through all of this I am not sure, but he did. He grew not to hate his father but to vaguely despise him. He is smarter in every way than Rick, and he knows it. So finally Rick took the only road left; publicly he boasted of his clever son, privately he feared his intelligence and, where he could, undermined his self-confidence and emotional security. People like Rick can't bear to be seen through and hate those who find out their secret that, under all the showiness and the charm, there is actually nothing worthwhile. Nick was always my son, and if Tasha and Rick had their cosy club, so, in a way, did we. But only very quietly, and when no one was watching. Tasha always bullied Nick and vaunted her position as daddy's girl; unfortunately when Nick walked off with the school academic prizes under her nose she, like Rick, felt the humiliation keenly. Nick, it may be said, has had the last laugh. On the day he packed up his things to go off to university, it was clear that he, at least, would not be coming back to Dubai for shopping trips. He and I had a last heart to heart and he told me, 'I'm always there for you, Mum. But you have got to be stronger. Don't allow dad to dominate you any more; you've got the opportunity now to break out a bit. I don't want to have to worry about you.' I haven't told Nick about our domestic changes because he'd be angry for me; my plan was to tell him when I was able to do so calmly and represent it as a step forward for me. I think, thanks to Natasha, I am almost at that point.

I fold up my napkin and finish off the wine and am just about to get up when there's a faint knock at the door. Rick goes to answer it. It is Natasha. She steps in without so much as a sideways look at Rick and comes straight to me. Rick looks her up and down as if he can't believe his eyes. She is, herself, dressed to go out and has on the most marvellous pale gold Grecian-drape dress with a gold belt and gold high heeled shoes. Her make-up is immaculate, as is her hair, which is tonight up in a French roll, pinned with diamond clips. She looks, as always, stunning and also, as always, totally unaware of herself.

Rick comes forward with his hand held out. 'Good evening,' he purrs in his most seductive voice. 'We haven't met. I'm Rick.'

She turns her head on that long neck and gives him the most glorious drop-dead look from those chill turquoise blue eyes. I can see him take a step back and blink and suddenly I'm shaking with suppressed laughter. Rick has seldom had such a set down in his life. He stands there, hand still extended, while Natasha ignores him and turns back to me.

'Sophie,' she says, 'come upstairs, I have something for you.'

I get up and follow her upstairs as she walks into the bedroom, turns on the light, and puts a box on my dressing table. 'Turn around,' she says briefly, and I turn with my back to her. I have no idea what she's up to until I feel the cheap Chinese necklace being taken off my neck and, in its place, a heavy chain being put on instead. I can't see it but when it's fastened I turn and look in the mirror and gasp. Around my neck is the most amazing necklace of square cut diamonds interspersed with baguette-cut stones from which is suspended a massive square-cut sapphire. I am still gaping at myself when Natasha removes the earrings from my ears and puts on two long and heavy diamond and sapphire drops instead. 'Oh my God,' I mutter as the light catches the gems and they twinkle with a wicked, and very genuine, glitter. 'Is this real?'

She laughs in my ear as she adjusts the earrings. 'I hope so,' she murmurs. 'It's my pension.'

I look at her in the mirror, then back at myself, then her again. 'But I couldn't possibly wear this, it must be worth a fortune.'

She stands back and looks at me critically. 'Yes,' she says with satisfaction, 'that looks very nice. Of course you are wearing it! You're not going to lose it are you?'

I put my hands up and pat the stones. 'My God,' I mutter again. 'Is this the frigging Star of the Sea out of Titanic?'

She ignores me. 'Where's your eye shadow?' she says, walking into the bathroom, and coming out with the box and a brush. She fixes my eyelids and then steps back again. 'Yes,' she says, putting the things back on the dressing table. She comes close and laughs in my ear again. 'I hope that you get your dance with Kester. And tomorrow, come and bring my jewels back and tell me all about it. And now, I must go.'

She turns and I hear her heels going off down the stairs. I hear a hurried something from Rick but there is no answer and the door slams and I grin to myself. There's absolutely no doubt what Natasha thinks about Rick and I love her loyalty. I take one last look at myself in the mirror, noting how her knowledgeable touch has made my eyes bigger and more exotic, grab my shawl, and go downstairs gracefully. Rick is still at the table, looking sulky. 'What was that all about?' he asks.

'Nothing,' I say airily. There's little chance he'll notice the change of jewellery; Rick is always far too concerned with how he looks than with what I'm wearing. Besides, he's already paid me a compliment tonight when he arrived and it wouldn't do to waste another one. 'Shall we go?' I collect up the tickets and my bag and head for the door, Rick taking a last long look at himself in the mirror before we step outside.

The ballroom looks fabulous and our table is almost full as we arrive. Five couples, four of whom we know fairly well. There is much kissing and exclamation as we all admire each other's dresses and tell Kirstie how well she's done. The committee has really excelled itself; the room is a poem of black and white and the theme is faithfully repeated in every detail down to the single white lily floral arrangement in the middle of the table. While Kirstie tells us, breathlessly, of all the near misses and disasters that have brought us to tonight's triumph, my neighbour, Jack, turns to me and fills up my champagne glass. 'Haven't seen you for ages, Sophie,' he says cheerily, 'how are things?'

'Oh, very well,' I say lightly. Jack has put on weight, I notice, and looks rather squeezed into his jacket. 'The magazine has got a couple of photographers here tonight, but fortunately I don't have to look after them.' Jack looks slightly blank for a moment then slots into place that I am talking about my *job*. Heaven forbid, the woman has a job. Oh, but not a very serious one; never fear, Jack. I'm looking around for Shazza, secure in the knowledge that she'll be coordinating the two *Insider* camera men somewhere. You never have to worry about Shazza, but I'm also dying to see her outfit.

'You're looking well,' he says now, 'I suppose you manage to find some time to spend in the gym. Lucky girl!'

'Yes,' I say, smiling charmingly, 'I can see that you don't.'

Wham – that one hits him between the eyes, but he rallies. 'Fighting the 40's flab, I confess,' he says a shade too cheerily, making me feel mean, suddenly. I take pity on him and go on to ask him about his job and the children. Poor Jack is not Rick.

Rick, on my other side, is doing what he does best and already his neighbour, Julia, (I wonder briefly if she is still indulging in her banker-bonking lunchtime affair), is flirting with him as he fills her champagne glass and flatters her in that convincing looking-into-your-eyes way that he does so well. On Julia's other side is the cuckolded husband (*does he know it – does he care?*) Chris, plump and sleek in his black satin jacket, chatting to Mimi – who I don't know at all yet, but who sounds a bit Essex for our little elite circle and fits the bill by being blonde and buxom. She is flanked by her as-yet-unnamed husband, and then there's Marisa who is chattering nineteen to the dozen to Kirstie while her husband, Martin, gazes skywards absently. *What a collection of perfection*, I think, still smarting from my supper time conversation, but I remind myself to be on best form tonight ... no cynicism, after all, the night is full of promise.

The evening rattles on; the champagne flows like water and the band tunes up for a quick dance before dinner. I look around for Jason Knight, but can't see him among the throng. Shazza bustles up looking amazing in clinging black satin and bunches of white tulle and assures me – and Kirstie, who is clamouring slightly on the subject – that the lads are on their way and she just hopes that people won't be too drunk to take a good photo. Then she notices the necklace swap. 'Fucking hell!' she says forcefully, 'what the fuck is that?' I mutter hastily that I'll explain later as I don't want to have to tell the whole table; Jack stares wistfully after Shazza's retreating form that he had been admiring as she was leaning over my shoulder. 'Marvellous boobs,' he says sadly. The band tunes up for a quick before dinner dance, and Rick and Julia (both consummate exhibitionists) seize the opportunity to get up and show off their moves. Mimi leans over the table and introduces herself. 'I sort of agree with your friend,' she says with a laugh, 'that necklace is absolutely gorgeous. What on earth is it worth?'

'Oh, thousands,' I say with a smile, 'if it were real, which it's not, of course.'

'Oh shame!' she says brightly. 'It's absolutely fabulous though.'

She introduces her husband, Dom, and we chat. They are relatively new arrivals in Dubai and I recognise it all. I recognise myself in her round, excited eyes, the sense of elation, the feeling of having 'arrived'; her slightly breathless absorption of the glamorous surroundings, the dresses, the drinks, the heady display of wealth and privilege. She will learn, as we all do, that there is a price to be paid for all this beauty and elegance. *And I have known them, known them all* ...

Dinner is a glorious summation of the art of the chef; there are wonderful combinations on gleaming platters, glistening meats, architectural wonders of puddings. More champagne and the evening is getting somewhat raucous. Rick has the whole table in fits over dinner with a couple of his favourite stories and is flushed with success and also, I surmise, the presence of Julia's hand on his thigh. But he manages to be very attentive to his oh-so-lucky wife; he helps me with my plate at the buffet, tops up my glass assiduously, references me once or twice and throws in the odd 'darling' for good measure. That should throw anybody off the scent. Abdul and Mohammed from *Insider* have finally put in an appearance (just as Kirstie is just about to throw hysterics) and everyone seems to be able to hold a fairly steady smile as they circle the tables, snapping. It seems like a good time to sneak off to the toilets.

The Ladies is enjoying a momentary lull which is probably due to the fact that the band has just struck up and everyone is heading for the dance floor. I find a cubicle and have just gathered up all my satin skirts when I hear a couple of women come in and within seconds discover that it's Kirstie and Marisa. One heads for a cubicle and the other is clearly standing in front of the mirror; their shouted conversation is very audible.

'I see Rick Roberts is up to his old tricks tonight,' this is Kirstie, who sounds as if she is in the cubicle next door to me. 'He really does think he's Mr Irresistible doesn't he? Although I suppose he is quite cute.'

'Ah huh,' Marisa sounds as if she's inspecting her teeth. 'You mean having Julia grope him? I'm not sure he was entirely responsible for that. You know what a ho Julia is.'

I stifle a giggle as the toilet roll next door goes round rapidly and Kirstie laughs. 'That's true! But what about this rumour that he's left Sophie and gone to live with a Filipina air hostess? I was looking to see what the atmosphere was like between him and Sophie tonight, to see if it was true, but she looked exactly as she always does.'

I bite my lip. So much for the well-kept secret that nobody knew. I sit in shock as Kirstie, with much rustling, sorts out her dress and flushes the toilet. Marisa dives into the vacated cubicle, and slams the door. 'Why don't you ask her?' she calls out.

'Oh no, I couldn't,' this from Kirstie. 'But I've heard it from several people. He seems to be living with her quite openly.'

'Maybe Sophie doesn't know,' suggests Marisa. 'Jack hasn't said anything to me about it and he and Rick play tennis quite a bit.'

'Oh, don't be stupid!' says Kirstie with some feeling and I have to say I agree with her. How stupid do they think I am?

Marisa mutters that the floor is wet and there is more rustling as I sit, frozen into immobility. Then the toilet flushes noisily and she joins Kirstie at the basins.

'Well I wouldn't be surprised if it is true,' on goes Kirstie. 'I mean I love Sophie but she is *so* boring. Now the kids are off their hands, he's probably decided to go too.'

I almost gasp aloud. This from my so–called friend!

'Rubbish!' says Marisa, clicking the towel dispenser violently. 'Rick Roberts is a spoilt little boy and Sophie's probably had enough of mothering him and he's gone off to find it somewhere else. I wouldn't put up with him for five minutes!'

Thank you Marisa! Their heels click across the floor and then the door wooshes shut and I am able to get up at last, my back stiff with tension. I stand in front of the mirror looking at myself in the mirror as women come in and out; washing my hands under cold water revives me somewhat but when I put on more lipstick it is with shaking hands. I can't believe that my friends would talk like this about me; but then, I think, of course, I believe it. I wander out, finally, into the foyer, and stop dead. There, in front of me, a deus ex machina, is Jason Knight, and my jaw drops. He has chosen, tonight, to eschew the black and white DJ and has gone instead for an all-white Top Gun uniform complete with gold epaulettes. He looks drop dead gorgeous and, judging from the admiring looks being flung in his direction, I am not the only one who thinks so.

'Oh my goodness,' I say eventually, re-aligning my jaw. 'You look wonderful.'

'Thanks,' he says with his usual cheeky grin. 'You look gorgeous too. Got my favourite shoes on I see!'

I laugh and lift one of my feet for inspection. 'I was waiting for you,' he says artlessly. 'Do you remember we were going to have a dance?'

This is a night of extremes; from betrayal to bliss in all of five minutes. 'Yes, of course I remember,' I say, 'I just hadn't seen you.'

He offers me his arm with old-fashioned courtesy and as we walk back down the foyer as I say suddenly, 'Please don't tell me you have the cap to go with that uniform. That would be too much!'

He flashes a smile at me and raises his eyebrows. 'I do indeed and it made quite an entrance!'

Oh God, I think, *in the whole ensemble he would be altogether too divine.* 'How does your wife keep her hands off you?' I say and then suddenly hear what I've said. 'I'm so sorry,' I apologise on a giggle, 'I think I've had too much champagne!'

He sweeps me into his arms and onto the dance floor and I feel quite unlike myself, a real femme fatale with thousands of dollars' worth of jewellery around my neck, dancing with a man for whom I feel not just a spark of attraction, but a heart-stopping, knee-weakening infusion of sheer lust. My childhood dream has come true and I am dancing with Kester Woodseaves! He holds me closely and strongly; his eyes are very soft and are looking into mine and I feel as if I am in the middle of a whirling cosmos where his firm body is the only fixed spot and I have to hold on to him to avoid being swept away into the outer darkness. My nerve ends are on fire with the chemistry and the closeness; my body seems to be so light, almost melted into sinuous chocolate, so that I want to mould myself to him. It seems he feels it too; he adjusts his hands and holds me more closely so that we move, as one, to the music. Words march across my consciousness, springing appropriately out of nowhere, Kester's words to Prue: '*I've chosen my bit of Paradise. 'Tis on your breast my dear acquaintance.'* Then the band, God damn them, moves on to something more jazzy but he seems reluctant to let go of me; glancing over his shoulder I am momentarily shocked to see Rick and Julia, circling slowly, and as they turn in the movement of the dance, I can see Rick's hand is clamped firmly on Julia's bottom. For a moment I stare, then I laugh. Jason Knight arches a look at me. 'Sorry, am I holding you too tight?'

I adjust my arm around his neck. 'Not at all,' I say softly. 'I just saw my husband groping my friend, but hey ... no surprises there!'

He looks slightly shocked. 'Maybe he's had a little too much champagne.'

I am fighting the urge to press my breasts into his chest. 'No,' I say airily, 'just acting totally true to form. You know he's left me for a Filipina air hostess?'

Now he really does stare at me and I feel like staring myself. What have I said? Jason Knight's pity is the last thing I want. I want him to like me, desire me, but not pity me.

And I think I've ruined the moment anyway; he withdraws slightly and says, awkwardly. 'Really, I'm so sorry. Why would he do that?'

'Oh I think he's just bored with me; we got married very young, and the excitement goes out of marriage after a few years doesn't it?'

He looks grim all of a sudden. 'It certainly does,' he says, and I think of the bad-tempered blonde of the classroom and wonder if perhaps Jason Knight is also a lonely soul. I think he is. He's not a self-publicist like Rick in search of a conquest, with a range of compliments that he trots out for effect. There's a core of boyish sparkle in Jason Knight, but it's genuine and wells up from a happy character and a desire to please.

He loosens me slightly and lifts his arm to whirl me around; then he does something totally unexpected. He pulls me backwards into his arms and holds me tight round the waist; his breath is warm on my neck and I can feel him moving against my bum. My breath is almost stuck in my throat and my heart is pounding. He breathes softly in my ear and the words have a mocking edge. 'Your heart is going like a rabbit's'.

I can't speak for lust, shock and breathlessness, all tied into one. I feel I have ceased to become dull Sophie but have morphed instead into a creature of sinuous attraction. The feeling of him pressing against my back makes my pulses quiver and I feel a trickle of moisture running down my thighs. I arch my head back so that he is nuzzling my ear; I think I say 'Are you surprised?' but it's possible I don't say anything because I can hardly draw breath. The music changes; he swings me out again, and back, holding me breast to breast and I can only think to say, (oh how feebly), 'You said you couldn't dance.'

He grins. 'I lied. And you are lovely to dance with.'

I swing out again and am caught back in the same position. Our mouths are only inches apart, and he says, very softly, exactly what I'm thinking. 'I want to kiss you.'

And then, just when time needs to be suspended, the band swings into some rocking foot-stamping 90's number and my opportunity is lost. He loosens me – how reluctantly I can't tell – but the moment is gone, fleet-footed when it should have been heavy as lead. But something has changed in that brief encounter; we don't know it but nothing will ever be the same again. He looks and smiles but now we are far apart; as the music moves to its final stamping close, he pulls me close and says into my ear, his words punctuated by the heavy bass beat, 'I have to go back to my table. But meet me outside on the verandah in twenty minutes? If you want ...' he adds with the little boy dimple flashing out.

The sapphire on my breast is heaving as I force my way through the swirling couples back to my own table; I toss off a glass of gin and tonic in the mistaken belief that it is sparkling water and then drink down another one that is. I am shaking and breathless but with such a curious new feeling pulsing through my veins, almost as if my blood has turned to champagne. Mimi staggers up now and falls into a chair opposite me; we look at each other and burst out laughing. 'Help!' she says, 'It's fast and furious out there.' She too gulps back some water and I glance at my watch. Twenty minutes to an assignation. *Oh God. Will I kiss him? Will I?* There is the distinct possibility that nerves will mean that I can't actually get out of my chair in twenty minutes. Mimi chats idly, throwing me the odd line that I can hardly hear above the music; I see Rick and Julia clamped together as they dance and can only think she is welcome to him! I am fidgeting and clock-watching like crazy; hardly the sophisticated and languorous seductress I aspire to be; after ten minutes I can't bear it any longer and excuse myself to go out into the foyer and head for the long verandah that runs along the side of the hotel, overlooking pools and gardens. There are a few people out here already; couples, and plenty of dark corners.

I flutter nervously along to the end where the verandah curves slightly and lean on the parapet, breathing in the heady scent of cream and gold frangipanis and trembling in spite of the heat of the night. I hope I am visible. The sapphire is proving to be a very useful fidget stone as I glance up and away and then suddenly his white outfit gleams in the doorway and he walks along the verandah towards me. He reaches out as he comes level and takes my hand; with a twirl I am out of the light and pressed up against the stone. Curiously, though, he doesn't kiss my lips but, in a gesture that makes my whole body quiver, he gently sweeps the hair away from my neck, his lips brushing as softly as a moth's wings, trailing his mouth down to my collar bone. The sensuality of it is staggering; it is pure eroticism as if he had all the time in the world, and I register it as a shiver that flickers down my spine to my toes. Finally, his mouth finds mine with a gentleness that is deliciously vulnerable and at the same time the summit of all my wildest dreams. This isn't, this cannot be, quiet Sophie, in the arms of a handsome stranger; I feel I am outside my body looking at a girl and a man kissing on a hot moonlit night but at the same time I feel it so intensely; my arms are round his neck and I feel as if I am drowning but oh – to die at such a moment would be perfect! Later I will add up impressions and relive that moment of trembling ecstasy, but now I am aware that already he is drawing back and smiling at me. 'Can I see you again?'

'Yes,' the word is merely a breath because I want him to kiss me again. But he doesn't. He catches my hand as it slides off his shoulder and kisses it instead. 'I'll be in touch,' he says and walks away.

And that, as they say, is that. After a while I too prowl back to the ballroom and, sitting down once more beside my husband, I have a fleeting moment of perfect comprehension of Rick. Is this how it feels to cheat? This wonderful feeling of being totally alive and fulfilled and yet craving more fulfilment? Curiously, we are closer tonight than we have ever been. I watch his handsome head bent to hear Mimi's words and see his smile and for the first time in years, perhaps ever, I understand my own husband. And Julia? Maybe I have been too judgmental of Julia. This is the headiest feeling I have ever had; no wonder women actively seek it. Ingénue Sophie.

When I prepare, the following day, to take Natasha's jewellery back to her, returned to its beautiful velvet-lined Garrards box, I am aware of a curious little smile that has played about my lips all day. It began last night and travelled home with me quietly in the darkness of the taxi; it accompanied me to bed and played through my dreams all night; it gets up this morning and has coffee and bathes in the swimming pool as I swim leisurely up and down, glancing up at Natasha's window wondering when she will be awake. I move to the swing lounger and Puss joins me as we move in quiet reflection. The smile was not disturbed by Rick's kiss on the cheek, 'lovely to see you Sophie' farewell or by the fact that yesterday was a dream and today is reality. The Sophie who went to the Ball is not the same one who came home because this is a Sophie who dared; she dared to keep an assignation with a man on a moonlit balcony and in so doing realised her dream. For the briefest of brief moments in time Kester Woodseaves was in my arms and he was mine and, in a curious way, I feel rejuvenated, given back my youth, almost as if Rick had never been. Swinging this morning with Puss I feel seventeen, untouched, with all the pain of growing up yet to come, as if Rick and our life together are still a distant goal to be realised. I feel washed clean and ready to begin again.

Natasha's curtains do not move until well into early afternoon when I am still in my nightie, drinking tea and pottering. I have a shower, get dressed and wander over, and she smiles when she sees me and calls Rosie to make tea and bring it outside. She lies on her sun lounger, smoking, and looks up at me. 'Well, Sophie, you are not jumping for joy. Did your evening not go as you wished?'

I recline on the matching lounger and swing gently. 'Actually, it was even better than I'd hoped.'

She laughs. 'Ah, now you are being enigmatic!'

I wait as Rosie appears with tea and goes inside again. Alexei and Hector have been in the pool most of the morning and are now draped over each other, exhausted, indoors in front of the television. The garden is sun-dappled and peaceful. 'Yes,' I say finally, 'I got a dance *and* a kiss.'

We swing in silent contemplation for a moment before she gets up and pours the tea. 'Tell me all,' she commands, so I do. She listens without comment and I compare her composure to the kind of interchanges I was part of last night; the bursts of animated disconnected conversation, the shrieks of laughter, the defining tags of the chattering classes. Natasha is – I search for the term – so *grown up.*

'So, my Sophie,' she says finally, and I feel a little thrill of pleasure at the pronoun. 'So now Kester Woodseaves has kissed you and wants to see you again. And what do you want?'

'I don't know. In a way the kiss was almost a completion in itself. I feel quite different today, like I finally grew up. As if I'm ready now for life. It's the strangest feeling, I can't really explain it.'

She nods quite seriously. 'And are you ready for an affair with a married man? I am not sure I would recommend such a course of action to someone who is as emotionally vulnerable as you.'

One can never accuse Natasha of saying anything less than what she really thinks. I swing and sip. 'You're right, of course. I shouldn't consider it on all sorts of grounds. But the truth is I do want more. Last night I began to see just how incredibly exciting the whole thing is, can be ... I actually had sympathy for Rick! I haven't felt so alive for... well I can't remember how long for, maybe never. And it wasn't just because it was the fulfilment of the romantic Kester dream. I was kissing a real flesh and blood man who I am incredibly attracted to. And who seems to want me. And seems to want an affair,' I finish vaguely. I think back to the dance and relive the moment of warm melting bliss as he pulled me backwards into his arms. I sit up straight at the memory. 'Oh!' I say, 'I think I just worked it out. Last night I told him that Rick had left me. Maybe he thought it was deliberate; that I was indicating I was available!'

'Maybe,' says Natasha.

I blunder on, trying to explain how I feel to myself as much as to her. 'So, maybe, he thought it was all right to kiss me and tell me he'd call. He was sounding me out!' I feel I should be shocked by this, but somehow I'm not, although it does make the whole thing sound more calculating, especially considered in the cold light of day. 'But nibbling the forbidden fruit was so damned good, I want more! And, you know, I feel I *deserve* more. I feel like everyone else is having a good time and I want to know what it's like! I want to be loved, I want to be desired, I want Jason Knight ... and, strangely, all the reasons I shouldn't have him don't seem to matter. And I'm not doing it to get back at Rick. I'm doing it because I want to *for me!'*

Natasha lights up another cigarette and takes a deep lungful. 'I think, my Sophie, that there is very little I can say to change your mind. You know my philosophy, be true to yourself, so I am not exactly going to be the one who discourages you. I think you do deserve love, however you construe it. All I am counselling is to remember that you are the most soft-hearted woman I know and not someone who can be used and then discarded. It will break your heart. But as long as you know that, then go out and take it.'

I am not really listening, lost as I am in a daze of warm and fuzzy hopefulness, but I do vaguely register those two words 'used' and 'discarded'. I can't somehow associate them with Jason Knight, ridiculous of course because I hardly know him, but I feel instinctively they don't seem to fit with his schoolboy grin and easy charm. Somehow it never occurs to me that the grin and the charm may not be genuine. It just seems impossible that he is not what he appears to be – and besides, Kester Woodseaves would never let me down. I ponder it all day and finally, as my head hits the pillow, I think I have the answer. Jason Knight is lost and lonely and so am I. Drawn together by an unfathomable chemistry, we are drifting towards a sexual conclusion that we both desire. Beyond that I cannot see because the present is too blinding. And it fills me with an absurd happiness that wakes me the next morning with a smile on my face and a feeling that life, at last, is going to start paying me a dividend.

It is just as well I feel buoyed up because, within days, my daughter arrives and my world is once again put back on its accustomed tracks. Rick picks her up from the airport and when I get home, I see the Mercedes parked in the drive and on walking into the living room, am confronted by a stormy-faced Tasha and Rick wearing his most long-suffering expression. I know I'm in trouble when I am refused a daughterly kiss and Patti, looking slightly askance, brings tea. Patti has taken the news of her redundancy with all the calm and dignity one would expect from her; truth to tell I don't think she was very surprised. She could see the writing on the wall; she knew the Babylonians were at the gate.

Tasha sulks very obviously as tea is poured; I try and rally a conversation but it's clear that Tasha has been told the news and she is furious – although with whom, it is not quite certain until Rick departs, with promises of an outing tomorrow, and I am left alone with Tasha who wastes no time saying exactly what she thinks.

'Mummy! How could you just stand there and let this happen! I can't believe it! I am absolutely furious with you!'

'With me? Tasha, why me? I'm not the one who's run off with a Filipina air hostess who's practically your age!'

'I know and I've told daddy I'm absolutely *disgusted* with him but I know why this has happened. You allowed this to happen! It's because you give in to daddy all the time; if you had *put your foot down* it never would have got this far! I'm furious with you Mummy! I hold you entirely responsible!'

The old Sophie would have been trembling with full eyes at the injustice of it all by now; the new one simply laughs. 'Darling, I promise you I am *not* entirely responsible for your father's behaviour. He is someone who needs constant admiration and I am afraid this is what's known as the male menopause. Your father feels younger because he's got a younger woman to play with. It's pretty standard behaviour I'm afraid. He's at a dangerous age.'

Tasha is so angry she's choking on her tea. 'Oh don't give me that psycho-crap! Daddy would've stayed home if you ever gave him any encouragement. But you... you're such a fucking doormat!' she bursts out. 'Why would he ever stay with someone who's so fucking boring?'

'Darling …' I begin but, with a sob, Tasha dashes out of the room and runs upstairs where a door slams violently. I refrain from going after her and drink my tea calmly enough. After all, there's worse to come. How will Tasha take to being told that her shopping spree may be slightly under-funded and that the home for her holidays, that she so takes for granted, may not be so freely available any more? Things are going to change for Tasha and they may, at bottom, be worse than having to admit that her father has the morals of an alley cat and pretty much the sense of one too. I can't deny that there is a sense of come-uppance in this which is not altogether displeasing to me. I pour another cup of tea and ruminate. Sophie Ingénue to Sophie Bitch in less than a week. Not bad.

Surprisingly, the next morning I encounter my daughter at breakfast and am not immediately shrivelled by the harpy quality of her gaze. She has calmed down. She is drinking her coffee politely so I take the opportunity to introduce the subject of forthcoming economic restraints. She takes it pretty well actually; maybe she sees that I am not completely without personal inconvenience in the matter. I explain that the house is now on the market and that we are hoping a buyer will turn up soon. If and when, that happens, Madam Tasha's lifestyle will be back on the rails and I will be moving to a smaller, cheaper place, probably an apartment in one of the complexes that are springing up all over the city.

'Just as well we haven't got a dog any more then,' she offers gloomily. 'Can't see Puss enjoying it much either.'

'I don't think either of us are going to like it,' I agree, 'but unfortunately there just isn't enough money to go around and we have to cut and paste to make it all work. You and Nick are our priorities of course, at least until you've finished university and can find a job. But in the meantime, it's going to be hard on all of us.'

Tasha has a mulish look around the mouth as she rips a croissant into bits. 'Except daddy,' she mutters, 'I don't see that he's suffering too much!'

I am trying to keep it calm so I say obliquely, 'Well daddy is the linchpin in this whole operation you know, Tash. I don't earn very much so we're all reliant on one income really, and it's not even a very big one. Your father has decided to leave me, but I want to stay in Dubai. I love my job and I want to keep it. Things have changed, certainly, but I took the offer your father made me and I'm happy to stick with it. So I guess I have to be obliging if I want to stay here. I've agreed he can sell the house. There's nothing for me in England, let alone a job or an income, just life in a freezing bedsit.'

'Ha,' says Tasha, slopping jam on her croissant. 'No, that's what I have to put up with!'

I laugh indulgently. 'Hardly, darling, your accommodation is very comfortable.'

Tasha isn't used to admitting to being wrong so at first I don't understand what the muttering represents, but finally I get that she's trying to apologise for last night and for shouting at me. 'That's all right, darling.' I say reassuringly. 'I realise you were very upset. It's not a nice thing to have to confront. I guess I've just got used to it, so I've calmed down a bit.'

Tasha looks at me with welling eyes. 'Honestly, mummy, how can you stand it? I would never be able to bear the *shame* ... I mean, how can you? How can you just calmly accept it? I just don't understand!'

For almost the first time in my life I am sorry for my daughter. Beautiful trusting Tasha has just had her world fall apart and the god at the centre of her universe has now revealed himself as a clay idol, fallen into the dust and broken into pieces. And, even harder, the woman she has known all her life as 'silly old Mummy' is now actually acting like a grown up, and Tash can hardly stand it. The roles have been reversed and poor Tasha is watching her world spin violently out of control, and she finds herself struggling to gain a foothold in this new and frightening universe. Suddenly, without warning, she throws herself into my arms and, for the next ten minutes or so, I have to deal with a wildly sobbing girl and, even while I listen and pat and mop, I am thinking never, never, never has this ever happened before. Tasha and Sophie as a pair united in the face of adversity; mother giving advice to daughter who never needed or asked for it before. Tasha is taking Rick's desertion personally, as if he has left her and I suppose, in effect, he has.

In the middle of all the chaos, just as we are embarking on tissue box number two, I hear the front door click open and Natasha strolls into the kitchen and stands surveying the scene with some amusement. Anybody else would apologise for intruding and beat a swift retreat, but Natasha has come for a purpose and it would take more than a hysterical teenager to deflect her. She pours herself a cup of coffee and joins us at the table; her appearance has all the effect of a jug of cold water emptied over Tasha, although whether she is stunned by my neighbour's looks or has just finally run out of tears, it is hard to tell.

Natasha pretty much ignores her anyway, and comes straight to the point.

'Sophie,' she says with her usual calm direction, 'I have decided to buy your house. Then your husband can have his money and you can stay here. It seems a good plan to me, but I thought I should ask you. Would you be happy to stay here? Would you want to do that?'

Tasha and I are now united in quite another emotion – shock. 'What?' I counter feebly. 'You want to buy the house? Can you do that?'

She smiles in that cocked-eyebrow-amused way that she has. 'Of course.'

Tasha and I look at each other in amazement. After all, one does not expect a fairy godmother to waltz into one's kitchen and, with a wave of her wand, sort out all one's problems. Judging by Tash's bemused expression, however, I can tell that she thinks that's exactly what Natasha is.

'Of course, that would be wonderful. I want to stay here; I love this house … and having you as my neighbour.' She nods to acknowledge the compliment. 'But how much rent would you want? I don't know how much I can afford to pay. I'd have to ask Rick.'

She frowns. 'No,' she says decisively. 'I am not doing this for Rick. He is nothing to me. I am doing it for you. I want you to stay here, so I will buy the house for you.'

Tasha looks at me with huge eyes. 'Mummy,' she breathes.

'Natasha,' I begin, 'I can't let you do that. Buy the house as an investment by all means, but you can't let me stay rent-free. It will be your house and I would want to pay you something for allowing me to live in it.'

She makes an impatient gesture and lights up a cigarette. 'No,' she repeats. 'You can keep it tidy, have a gardener and the pool man still, pay for them if you like, you can improve my investment. We can, perhaps, share Rosie. But I don't want rent. You are my friend and I want you to be living here.'

She looks at Tasha. 'What's not to like?' she asks in schoolgirl jargon.

Tasha clearly thinks she's marvellous. The hair, the designer clothes and the natural beauty will have had a lot to do with it, but what's she just done is to wave a magic wand and our world, or Tash's world anyway, has just righted itself. 'Oh my God,' breathes Tasha. 'This is amazing. I don't know who you are, but you've just … solved all our problems. Just like that!'

'So, Sophie?' A straight look and the hint of a smile. 'Do we have a deal?'

'I don't know what to say,' I begin.

'Just say yes, mummy!' urges Tasha.

I give in. 'Natasha,' I say, 'meet your namesake. This is my daughter, Tasha.'

Natasha gives her usual slightly chill smile and receives the hug that Tash runs round the table to give, with cool calm. She waits 'til Tash gets back to her own chair, and has poured herself another coffee, before she says, 'Remember this day, Tasha. Men will hurt you and let you down, even those you love best. But put your trust in women and you will not be disappointed.'

Tasha looks slightly wide-eyed over this. 'It's true, mummy,' she says, 'daddy has let us down.'

Tash accusing Rick of letting 'us' down! I sit rather stunned. It is extraordinary that Rick's plan should be so overset and by the one woman he had thought would be on his side. He had reckoned without Tasha's jealous streak; 'silly old mummy' was never a rival but now her father has admitted to loving someone else and Tasha is furious, humiliated, jealous and lost all in one, and, for the first time in her life, she is turning on her father. 'He has totally lost all my respect,' she tells Natasha in serious tones. 'How can you respect a man who has abandoned his family and is living with such a little *slut!*' Tasha is warming to her theme; she is not one who usually indulges in dramatics. I wonder what her attitude will be when Rick turns up to take her shopping or out to dinner; will she give in and forgive him, or will she maintain the moral high ground? It's hard to tell but listening to her talking, I can see that she's deeply hurt and shocked. The tears and hysterics were genuine after all; given that tears and hysterics are usually foreign to Tasha's nature.

Natasha gets up to go and I get up too, to hug her. It's the first time I've ever done so; she is not a woman who invites embraces. But today I owe her so much. 'Thank you, my dearest friend,' I tell her, as she laughs lightly. 'It's totally selfish of me,' she says, 'I want you to continue as my neighbour! Besides, who will train Hector if you are not here? I will get my man of business to ring the agent about the house. Do not worry, my Sophie...'

As the door closes, Tash is full of questions. I answer as many as I can, truthfully, but I won't give Natasha away, not even to Tash, so I let her surmise, which she does without any assistance concluding that Natasha must be a top model and be earning 'serious bucks' if she can afford to buy the villa outright. I caution her not to say anything to Rick; I don't want him to know who the buyer is, or not yet anyway. 'That was a funny speech she gave me about sisterhood. Is she a lesbian, do you think?' Tasha ponders.

'I don't think so,' I say seriously, 'but men have not treated her kindly, and women have. But I wouldn't want you to be too cynical about men. They're not all liars and cheats you know!'

'Ha!' says Tash, 'Just the ones in our family!'

'Oh no,' I protest, 'Nick would never be! And your father is ... well, he's just going through a difficult time. Men panic about growing older; it's a mid-life crisis thing.'

'Mummy!' says Tasha with a stern look. 'You know this isn't the first time daddy has cheated on you – not by a long shot. But it's the first time he's ever let you know about it. Or moved out,' she adds.

'I didn't know you knew.'

'And I didn't know if you knew! He used to laugh about it with me so I knew it was never serious. He liked the idea that women found him irresistible. And I guess I did too in a weird way. It was fun to have a dad that all my girlfriends fancied. Oh mummy,' for a moment she looks stricken. 'Do you think I *encouraged* him?'

'No, darling, I don't. Your father needs women to adore him and always has. His mother did, I did, and he just moved on from there.'

'And I did too,' says Tasha pensively. 'But not any more!'

I feel myself drawn to take Rick's side, which is typical of my 'Soppy Soapy' attitude, as my daughter used to charmingly phrase it. 'He does love you,' I say, 'perhaps more than anyone else. Always has. But this is about *self-love,* Tasha, do you see? This little air hostess is a pretty little accessory which proves, in Rick's mind, that he still has what it takes to pull a girl that other men fancy. It's all about ego as in *you're only as old as the woman you feel.* But don't hate him; it's not worth it.'

'Oh,' responds Tash airily. 'I don't hate him! I'm just *sorry* for him! It's so pathetic. And I'm disappointed too, that daddy doesn't see how sad it is.'

I chuckle. 'To quote Alex, he's thinking with his little head, not his big head.'

Tasha giggles. 'Mummy!' she says reprovingly. 'That's a bit risqué for you!'

'Actually, I feel that this whole thing has been quite a journey for me. When it first happened, I was stunned, and went through the usual stages of feeling abandoned, rejected – and terribly angry with him. Then I realised, slowly, that it wasn't about me at all; it was just that Rick is afraid of growing older and this is a last desperate attempt to stave it off. I don't think he loves this girl, but I don't actually care if he does. I feel curiously liberated … I can't expect you to understand, but in a way I feel as if finally I am free to live my own life. Before, I always felt I was living the life daddy wanted me to live and always as an accessory to him; someone who was kept on merely to showcase him. So although I am staying here, and now thanks to Natasha I can, I am not doing it because he wants me to but because I want to, because it suits me. I think I've finally grown up and realised I don't need your father anymore. I'm even writing under my own name – Sophie Haddon.'

Tasha looks at me as if she's never seen me before. 'Wow, mummy,' she says at last. 'I think you *have* grown up! This doesn't sound like you at all. How ironic – daddy has reverted to being a teenager but you've actually become your own woman!'

So, by the time Tasha goes back, we have actually become friends, and I am aware that my daughter *respects* me, and values who I have become. It is indeed ironic that Rick believed that by bringing on board his staunchest ally, he would win the battle for hearts and minds. Instead he has lost the war. Of course, he doesn't see if that way, but I am becoming more of a convert to Natasha's theory that men are often obtuse. Rick pockets a cheque for the villa and never thinks to inquire from whence it came; it is then with a certain smugness that I tell him that my neighbour has bought the villa and is allowing me to live on at a peppercorn rent because we are friends and I am training her dog. He gives me a blank blue-eyed stare as if he can't quite fathom that (a) anybody would do this and (b) I might have friends.

'What neighbour?' he asks tersely. 'Not the stunning blonde?'

'The very same.'

'Christ. Are you two having an affair or something?'

'No Rick, I have not become a lesbian just because you abandoned me.'

He raises an eyebrow as if to indicate that there can be no other explanation. 'But the payment came from a London property company,' he says. 'I don't see the connection.'

'So what?' I counter. 'I only know what she told me.'

'Hmmm,' he ponders. 'Well, it's not important. It's sold, which is all that matters and at least I can pay off some of my expenses. It costs an arm and a leg to keep those two at university you know.'

I yawn. 'I'm sure it can't be *my* fault that we have clever children,' I say with a guileless smile and catch him off-guard. There's nothing more to say so he takes himself off, relieving me of both his presence and a case of wine under the stairs, which is more annoying since I thought he'd forgotten it.

The next saga to present itself is Patti's departure which is a sad day but she has found a good job with a kind family so I have no doubt that she will be happy. She leaves with all the dignity one would expect; it's me who has to choke back the tears. 'I wish you well, madam,' she says, as she puts her things into the new family's 4WD. 'Thank you for five happy years.'

I hug her. Impossible to thank Patti for everything she's done for us, but the two months' bonus salary will help, although it will all be sent home to Sri Lanka as her money has always been. One day, perhaps, she will go too.

The new plan that Natasha and I have discussed is that Rosie will come and clean for me and Rosie, when approached, is in favour of it. I suspect Natasha may be paying her more, but she denies it completely; my role is simply to pay for pool and garden maintenance, which is something even I can easily afford. I ponder, occasionally, why Natasha, the cool elegant goddess who has no other friends except me, would do such a thing and why she values my friendship so much. But, curiously, although we are friends it is not on a level that many would recognise as friendship and sometimes her coolness makes me nervous. I often feel childish and undisciplined in her presence, like a chattering toddler who is cautioned to silence by adults. But she never criticizes, never judges, and whilst she does not deliberately deny me knowledge, she is adept at concealment; at the end of six months of friendship I wonder, sometimes, if I know much more about her than I did on that first afternoon when I walked into her house. I don't know what she does, where she works, who pays for the wonderful wardrobe, the fabulous jewellery (I've seen more of it and am astonished at the carelessness with which she treats it). I have never seen a single piece of correspondence, have never heard her phone ring, have never heard her chat to anyone but me. At the gym she does her exercise, talks briefly with Anna; she is not involved with any of Alexei's school events and, as far as I am aware, has little interest in his schooling generally. She comes home in the small hours of the morning, she ignores the rest of the street, she lives a solitary existence with Alexei, Rosie and now, me. And I still don't understand any of it. She is one of the most intensely private people I've ever met which is refreshing in an age when everyone assumes that you want to know fairly intimate details of their lives within hours of meeting them.

One rare night in (for Natasha) we are lounging on the twin sofas watching an agonising documentary about two young Russian girls who were kidnapped and held as sex slaves for four years in a cellar under the garage in a Russian town but who, freed, are relating their story. It is heart-wrenching stuff, hearing this tale of consistent rape and abuse from the lips of a teenager who was 14 when she was captured. The older girl had two babies as a result of the rapes but the children were adopted out by her captor and she never knew what had happened to them. But what is almost unbelievable is that these two girls have since thrown off the shadow of those four dark years and are now married and leading happy lives. After the documentary is finished Natasha and I discuss the events. The fact that I find most extraordinary is that these girls could emerge almost unscathed from such trauma, and this after no psychological intervention. They had been to a state psychiatrist only once and he had offered them sleeping pills; they had quite rightly dismissed him as useless and had not gone back again. They had, all on their own, decided to put the horrific events from the past behind them, and move on. Natasha scoffs at what she calls my 'Western sentimentality'.

'You English are so absurd. What can you know of the Russian psyche? Do you not know the history of Russia? The capacity to endure, to overcome, is part of the blood of my people. We do not need the intervention of these idiots who think they can heal the mind. The only way of healing is to be what these girls are; strong and independent and refusing to see themselves as victims. You Westerners are all the same – sentimental, lacking in self-confidence and independence, always depending on others to tell you what to think or do.'

'But Natasha ... be fair ... this is an extraordinary level of abuse over four years, kept in a dark cellar and raped almost every day, having children for God's sake. One can't dismiss that ... there must be mental trauma that may not surface for years. But no one can *forget* that.'

'Did you not hear what the girl said?' Natasha queries. 'She said *'it was like it happened to someone else.'*

'But it didn't happen to someone else!' I protest. 'It happened to her! I can't believe that one could just forget that ... obliterate it from memory ... and go on to live a perfectly normal life. I'm not sure that's possible!'

Natasha tops up her wine glass and reaches over to top up mine. Then she sits back on her sofa and curls her long legs under her. The TV has been turned off; the lights are low and the hour late. It is the time of the night when the heart is perhaps encouraged to share its secrets.

'I knew a girl once,' she says softly, 'in the town where I grew up. She was pretty and bright and she was an only child so her father loved and spoiled her. She was his princess and every night he would take her on his knee and read to her of the Russian legends, and talk about what it meant to be Russian. He was a tall good-looking man and he meant everything in the world to her. She worked hard at school so he would be proud of her and, as she grew older, he took her out into the countryside, on shooting trips in the winter, and in the summer they would bike through the long light evenings and he would buy her ice cream and they would talk and talk. Her mother never came; she was a fool. She had been pretty once, a long time before, but now she was fat and she hated her daughter because she was everything that she was not.

And then things changed. Russia changed. The father no longer had a secure job at the factory and he began to drink heavily because he could not adjust to the new way of life. He was too old to adapt to capitalist ways. He had always been a Party man and he could not conceive of a Russia where there was free enterprise. He drank and he got into debt; finally the people who had loaned him the money came looking for him and insisted that he pay them. If they did not, they would kill him. So the father borrowed the money from his friend, who had a taxi business that was doing quite well. He paid back the money but now he had a new debt – to his friend. And finally the friend came to demand that the debt was paid. The father had no money … but the friend had a solution. He admired the man's beautiful daughter and he said if he could have her, the debt would be wiped out. So the father went to the daughter and told her that, to save him, she must marry the taxi driver. She was stunned. The taxi driver was her father's age with a big belly and a rough, coarse manner; he came over that night and looked at her with lust, fondled and squeezed her and laughed with the father about how he would treat her; how she would be his princess now.

So that night, when the house was quiet, the girl packed her bag and left her home forever. She took nothing with her because there was nothing to take – only a few clothes. No mementos. Nothing to remind her of that town or of the betrayal. She left and she never looked back. The memory was wiped out; she had been betrayed by the person she had loved most and she had learned the lesson that you can only ever rely on yourself.'

My throat is aching and my lip is trembling. So this is her story – Natasha's story. I don't know what to say. The house is very quiet and she sits, with her head bowed. But the tears are mine; they spill over and run down my cheeks and my heart aches for that beautiful betrayed girl.

Finally she looks up. 'You are crying, Sophie?'

I blow my nose and nod silently.

'Why?'

I answer carefully. 'Because I think that was your story, wasn't it?'

'It is the story of hundreds of girls in Russia, Sophie. Maybe thousands. You English, you live in your little warm houses, in your secure well-lit cities, with your well-paid parents and you have time to be sentimental. You have time to weep. You have time to waste on making everyone happy, time to lie on psychiatrist's couches while he tells you that it's not your fault. But the rest of the world is not like that.'

'Sometimes I feel you despise me for my Englishness.'

'No,' she says softly. 'But I will teach you a better way. I will teach you to trust in yourself, Sophie. I will make you stronger, so that you are the one who defines your life and does not wait for someone else to define it for you.'

'I don't think I'm very promising material,' I say. 'After all I have that legacy of the safe secure environment in the safe well-lit city … I don't have your hungry fighting spirit.'

'You may not see it, Sophie, but you are very changed from that lonely woman who came in the spring to teach my son's dog.'

My eyes flicker towards the framed pictures on the sideboard. 'So that's not Alexei's grandmother then? I thought perhaps it was.'

'No,' she says shortly. 'It's just a woman who was kind to me. Someday I will tell you about her perhaps, but not now.'

'And the other one is Alexei? As a baby?'

'Yes,' she says, and adds, as an afterthought, 'he was not a pretty baby.'

There is silence. I am thinking over her words and it's true, I realise. I am a very changed woman. I am able to see Rick as a rather foolish man who has gotten away with his bad behaviour because of the patriarchal society that we are forced to live in. Those feelings of anger and rejection and hurt have, over time, broken down into nothing more than complete disinterest. I simply don't care any more. Rick and his mistress are nothing to me; I would be more interested in a television

116

soap opera than I am in their lives. And the thought of Jason Knight, always latently on the rim of my consciousness, flashes into my mind. I remember his warm kiss on the night of the Ball, and the chemistry between us. And I realise that this Sophie has experienced a kind of rebirth at Natasha's hands; a rebirth of courage and self-belief. Maybe this Sophie is now strong enough to go out and get what she wants. And I start thinking about what I do want – and I realise it's him.

Part II

The Liaison

Time for you and time for me
And time yet for a hundred indecisions
And for a hundred visions and revisions
Before the taking of a toast and tea.

As the heat of summer approaches, I am, most appropriately, pondering how my relationship with Jason Knight is going to develop. I am aware that the holiday season is almost upon us when the schools close and half the expatriate population of Dubai departs as mothers and offspring, largely, flee the intense heat of July and August and revisit the motherland for a quick dose of family and culture. There they boast of their lifestyle and, having alienated most of their relatives with tales of tax-free earnings and hedonistic doings, finally return to school in late August and life in the gilded cage resumes its usual predictable pattern. *Insider* itself has a very limited summer issue as the Princess is away at her villa in the Mediterranean, and most of the staff have also departed to far-flung destinations. I am the exception here as, apart from a few weeks in England staying with my aunt, I will be here most of the time, suffering no doubt from the cabin fever that accompanies the intense heat of the summer months and the onset of Ramadan. Nick and Tash are both away on summer jobs; Tash is working on a golf resort in Scotland with a college friend and Nick has gone south to New Zealand on a university rugby trip, funded by the university for the boys of its First Fifteen division.

Natasha, as is her wont, has not yet said anything about her summer plans, but I am fairly certain that she will be away somewhere too and Rosie will no doubt be left in charge of two houses and one small boy. I feel it is unlikely that Alexei will be taken anywhere. One cannot help but feel for him, and if it were not for Rosie, I would probably be concerned for his welfare and the fairly complete lack of attention he gets from his mother. However, Alexei has Hector, has Rosie, and is not my business.

Following the Ball I have waited with some anxiety to hear from Jason Knight but as days and then weeks go by, nothing has been forthcoming. I am disappointed, no doubt, about that, and have toyed on more than one occasion with the idea of picking up the phone and calling him. The kiss has, on occasion, haunted my dreams and sometimes, when lying in the bath for example, I have relived its magic and felt the warmth of lust creeping through my veins and igniting my senses. On one occasion, as we are coming back from the gym, Natasha asks if I have heard from him; she senses, perhaps, my disappointment as I say no. She says nothing further but perhaps is speculating that he was not, after all, serious. But I am disappointed on a more emotional level because I had trusted him and believed that the kiss was a pact; it had seemed a natural conclusion to his flirtatious remarks at the gym and the feeling of attraction that I had hoped we shared. Once more I face the fact that naïve and romantic Sophie has misread the situation and attributed feelings to another that are, in fact, predominantly my own. But now I am not content to let things ride; I am determined to find out, before the summer break, just what he has in mind. If it is nothing then I will at least know and possibilities will stop leaping out at me from dark corners. At bottom, there is a hint of self-blame, too, for telling him about Rick's leaving me. I am sure that he might see me as a desperate housewife, over-sexed, deprived, irrational; the sort of woman who would, I imagine in my ignorance, scare any normal man off.

So I set up a plan. Alexei and Hector would benefit, I am sure, from a walk on a bare tract of land some way behind our compound; it is earmarked for development but has not yet been built on and at the weekends it is deserted and therefore ideal for dogs to run and play. Rosie has found out about it from one of the Maid Mafia; I had investigated it one Friday morning, early. The mornings, which, although hot, are rather beautiful and there is pleasure in seeing Alexei and Hector run their hearts out. I leave a message on Jason Knight's original school number that I have called and ask him to call my mobile; then I have to wait with some trepidation for him to return my call. When he finally does, I put forward my plan with as much airiness as I can manage for a wildly beating heart. He says he has no dog, but his son loves dogs and yes, it sounds fun. He likes to be up early on Fridays and do something before the heat is too intense. I give him careful instructions and then only have to wait; Thursday night I check my alarm several times to ensure that I don't oversleep. Friday dawn sees me up and pacing at 5am; minimally made up and looking casually sexy (I hope). I knock quietly at Alexei's door and we all pile into the car and set off.

Hector is unstoppable on a Friday morning (as if he knows he has a whole weekend of Alexei ahead) so I let them run and am just wondering if Jason will actually turn up when a metallic blue Jeep comes bowling along the dust road and swings in beside me. It is Jason, in T-shirt and shorts, accompanied by a small blond-haired blue-eyed boy, aged, saints be praised, about 7 or 8 and roughly the same dimensions as Alexei who is small for his age. Introductions are performed and the children, as children do, race away with dog over the dunes, fast friends in fifteen minutes, while the ubiquitous Mr Knight and I follow at a more leisurely pace. I had expected to be nervous, and I am; and he, it seems, is too for he is tending to talk rather fast and inconsequentially, feeling perhaps guilty that he has not called as he said he would. On the other hand, I am grown-up enough to know that it might have been the kiss and the champagne, and he might never have intended anything to develop. Maybe he thought that to say he would call would be a more socially acceptable palliative than just walking away from a kiss on a moonlit verandah. It was only a kiss, after all; I must remember not to read too much into it. On the other hand, he could easily have decided not to meet me today. The fact that he is here must mean something.

Anyway, as we walk and talk the atmosphere eases and the relaxed ambience of our first meeting emerges and I remember how much I like this man's company, apart from fancying the pants off him. He tells me about Jack, his son, and why his allergy means they can't have a dog. We laugh over Hector's antics as we stand, comfortably close atop a small dune and watch the children running and laughing. The sun is getting hotter and I notice the boys are becoming an interesting shade of puce; Hector too is panting and exhausted, so we head back to the cars and the bottles of juice and water. Jason slants a look at me; 'This is a great place, Sophie. It was good of you to include us. Jack's having a marvellous time.'

I glance up from under my hat brim and green eyes look deep into blue. I say daringly, 'Well, if I can't have a kiss, I guess a dog walk is the next best thing!'

He looks flushed but it might just be the heat of the sun. 'I wouldn't want to disappoint you,' he says quietly.

'Disappoint me how? Your kiss certainly didn't disappoint.'

He turns to see where his son is, as if checking we can't be overheard. 'The thing is,' he says awkwardly, 'I am not at all a free agent. I probably shouldn't have said or done those things at the Ball, but I was a bit carried away because my wife wasn't there and because I do think you're gorgeous. But I wouldn't want you to get the wrong idea.'

'So what is the wrong idea?'

He flushes again. 'I'm not sure what you want,' he says obliquely.

Well at least we're being honest. 'I don't know,' I say fairly, 'but I liked very much what I got and I hoped there was more of it. You know my situation. Maybe you aren't interested in a woman whose husband has left her for someone else.'

'Well, I can't understand it,' he says frankly, with a grin. 'I think you're a cracker!'

That makes me laugh. 'But seriously, I want you to know that I do really like you, fancy you, and I thought you were interested in something more than just a kiss under the stars.' Curiously I feel I can say these things to this man; I like him, I trust him and it seems possible to say exactly what I think. Besides, the chemistry is electric and I find myself wanting to stroke him and my eyes keep drifting to his mouth. I am hot and sweaty and it's not entirely due to the weather.

The kids run past, shrieking, with Hector in mad pursuit, and Jason Knight takes the keys out of his pocket ready to unlock his car. 'Yes,' he says softly, 'I am. I just don't know how to do it.'

I unlock my own car and put out Hector's water bowl and fill it. Alexei, chattering at a great rate, snatches his drink out of the seat pocket and he and Jack stand panting, giggling as Hector gulps his water noisily. I am unmanned by Jason Knight's words; his boyish uncertainty makes me feel like the one in charge – not a feeling I'm used to. Within a few minutes the kids are off again, although we remonstrate, but feebly. Jack is a small version of his father, and full of energy; he and Alexei throw the ball for Hector and dash off over the dune in pursuit. Jason Knight stands looking at me and I think how much I'd like to kiss him. Even in cap and shorts he still looks drop dead gorgeous.

'There's a tree up there,' he says, 'let's go and sit where we can keep an eye on the kids.' He takes the water bottle and sets off as I follow. The tree is question is a thorny acacia, but there is a fallen branch underneath it that makes a good place to perch and we can see the kids as they lug bits of wood around, making, it seems, some kind of fort. 'Boys,' he says with a grin. 'Always on the go.'

'I'm all alone,' I say softly. 'And I'm lonely, as, I suspect, are you. Am I right?'

He looks at me and his left hand moves along the branch and touches my hand. 'Oh yes,' he says. 'But I'm not at all a free agent. I don't know what I could promise you.'

'So you already said,' I counter. 'And I don't want promises. I'd like to see you. I have a house and I'm all alone. Could you manage to come and see me?' I can't believe this is me, doing all the planning. It's coming across pretty clearly that Jason Knight is either scared stiff of his wife or else he doesn't know what he wants. He's certainly a lot less forthcoming than he was at the Ball.

'Maybe,' he sips water. 'I'm sorry this is sounding awfully pathetic. It's just that I have a very suspicious wife and I am on a very short lead. That's a fact, not an excuse. I would love to see you, kiss you for a very long time,' he slants a look at me, 'and more … but it may not be possible. I just want you to know how things stand. If you were prepared to work with that … well, I would love to be with you.'

'Your wife doesn't come to the gym with you?' I query.

'Sometimes, but not usually. She's not into fitness in the same way I am.'

The T-shirt and shorts disguise what I know is a toned body, and the fingers stroking mine are proof that Mr Knight likes physical contact. I can feel my nerve ends thrilling at his light touch. I remember the uninhibited sensuousness of his kiss on the night of the ball and my gut feeling is that Mr Knight is a very sensuous being, perhaps even the lover with the slow hands that every woman dreams of. My heart rate begins to rise at the thought of what I'd like to do to him, very slowly, in my over-sized double bed.

'You do look fit,' I say softly, letting the double meaning of the word stand. 'And my house is very close to the gym. You could certainly drop by before or after. Will you remember the address?' and he repeats it after me. Sophie Seductress is a new role for me but I'm enjoying it.

'I have to go,' he says now, standing up. 'Jack is over-doing it. He thinks he's tougher than he is.' He strides off down the slope, calling to the boys who come, reluctantly, with Hector, who is pretty much staggering by now. I wander back to the car and pour more water into Hector's bowl and pull another bottle of water out of the portable icebox for Alexei. It is getting hot; the sun is blazing down and the heat is shimmering off the sand. Both children look pretty done in actually; we give them water and turn on the car engines so the a/c kicks in. Jason Knight thanks me and prompts Jack to do the same; he hopes 'we can do it again soon.' No promises. As I watch his car nosing out onto the dirt road, I'm not sure quite what progress has been made here except that I now know that I'm up against a suspicious wife and a man who clearly fears what he stands to lose if he is found out. Not that I'm surprised; the bossy blonde of the classroom looks like a bunny boiler. At any rate, I said what I came to say and there is some satisfaction in that. Whatever happens now is in the lap of the gods.

Natasha, however, is frankly sceptical when, the following day, I wander in for a cup of tea and a chat. She doesn't say much as I go through what happened; she just listens and, when I have finished, says briefly, 'You sound disappointed, my Sophie.'

I admit I am. 'He was different, somehow, subdued … at the gym and at the Ball he was bouncy, happy, prepared to flirt, whereas yesterday he was rather dampened, like something had happened. And he kept stressing that he wasn't a free agent … which, obviously, I knew he wasn't. It's just irritating me really, that there were so many mixed messages going on. But at least I said what I wanted to say. The ball is now in his court.'

'I cannot respect a man who apologises for not having courage,' she says decisively. 'He sounds too passive, maybe too much under the thumb of his wife.'

'Mmm. Well, possibly. She looks like a bunny boiler.'

Natasha lifts one perfectly groomed eyebrow. 'What is that?'

'A bunny boiler? Oh it's from a great old movie called 'Fatal Attraction'. Glenn Close plays a woman who's obsessed with Michael Douglas and, just to show she means business, she steals his child's rabbit and they come home to find it cooking on the stove.'

Natasha wrinkles her nose and laughs. 'So this is now meaning an obsessive woman. Ah yes, bunny boiler ... I like it. Anyway, Sophie, now you will have to be patient and see what happens. I suspect your Kester Woodseaves is showing his flaws; we will have to see how brave he is and if he will escape the bunny boiler.'

'Yes,' I say, with a sigh. 'I suppose so.'

'I have now finished the book,' she says, 'and yes, I see why you like it.'

We enter into a spirited discussion of 'Precious Bane' and I can see Natasha is playing devil's advocate because she knows it's my favourite; I also suspect she's trying to take my mind off the disappointment of my real-life Kester. But she's impressively introspective in her analysis and I can't catch her out either, considering how well I know the novel. Natasha is an astute reader and an intellectual adversary; I certainly don't rate myself as an intellectual but I know one when I see it and I respect her even more if that's possible, as we argue our way in friendly debate through the classic. She admits she has found the Shropshire dialect and the lyricism of the prose tough going, but she finds a Russian element in the setting and the characters that appeal to her. Afterwards I wonder why I am surprised by her insight and analysis; women like Natasha do not succeed in the world she inhabits unless they are intelligent and astute.

I do try to follow her advice and put him out of my head but it's easier said than done. I admit to a certain cocking of the ear when a car stops outside late in an afternoon and always leave the French doors open when I am in the garden or the pool so I can hear the doorbell. I berate myself for being stupid and, as the days go by and the end of the school term approaches, I know I am doomed to disappointment.

Late one afternoon, after we have walked Hector, and he has wowed us with his obedience at coming when called, Alexei and I are back in Rosie's kitchen talking and I ask her, softly, what plans are in the pipeline for his summer holiday? After all, at some point Rosie herself has to take a break, and I wonder if I should offer to have him for a few weeks. I am not particularly adept at entertaining children, but there are shows and films on and I am more mobile than Rosie, who does not drive. Rosie reports that Alexei has, recently, been asked out more to play dates locally, which indicates that he is making school friends who live in the neighbourhood, but more than that, neither of us know. She has not heard, either, of Natasha's plans but that is fairly typical. Natasha plays her cards very close to her chest. For example, this very morning she has breezed into my house and informed me that later today a man will be coming to fit a small wall safe. When I look questioning, she laughs that it is not for me but for her. 'This is my second house,' she says with a smile, 'and I think I may want to keep some of my jewellery in a different safe. How do you say? Something about eggs and baskets?'

I am, therefore, even while talking to Rosie, keeping a weather eye out for the safe fitter's white van. 'Madam is upstairs, getting dressed,' says Rosie. 'Why don't you go up? It might be good to know what plans are made for Alexei. The school holidays are almost here after all.'

So I wander upstairs, and find Natasha in front of her dressing table, with her favourite silk robe (one that is ablaze with birds and flowers hand-embroidered on a bright turquoise background) hanging open as she does her face in front of the mirror. She indicates that I should sit, so I perch on the edge of the bed and broach the Alexei subject; she listens but continues to do her make-up with a steady hand.

'So,' I conclude, 'I was wondering if you'd be happy if I took him out a few times to the cinema or whatever, if you're away. After all, it's easier for me than Rosie, and I do owe you so much.'

'Not at all, Sophie,' she says, curling her eyelashes.

'Are you kidding? I wouldn't even still be living next door if it wasn't for you! I'd be in some small poky flat in some tower block downtown.'

She swaps the curler to the other eye and smiles her distant smile. 'De rien,' she says softly. She finishes her eyelashes and turns to face me. 'I think I will be here for some weeks yet,' she says carefully. 'After that I am not sure. There is some talk of a yacht in the Mediterranean but nothing is yet resolved.'

I laugh. 'Really? Wow! I wouldn't mind cruising off Monte Carlo … it certainly beats two weeks in the rain in Worcester!'

'Alexei will be here,' she continues, 'if you want to take him out, please do, but do not feel under any obligation. I am sure he is quite content with Rosie and Hector.'

I feel obliged to voice a small criticism; after all, I am a mother and I know how important it is for children to have a break, especially as the days of high summer are long and hot, and full of frustration when one is trapped inside to escape temperatures in the high forties. Already we can only walk Hector in the late afternoons when the full strength of the sun has subsided.

'Is there nowhere you can send him?' I ask now. 'What about relatives in Russia? He should be out of here for a couple of weeks anyway, and have a change of scenery.'

She gives me a chill blue look. 'There is nowhere and no one,' she says shortly. I feel I am about to be told to mind my own business, but continue anyway.

'Have you considered a summer camp? We used to send our two to camp holidays for two weeks in the summer – in England, and when they were bigger, in America – and they had a brilliant time.'

'Alexei does well enough,' she says shortly.

I feel annoyed; Alexei does not, in my opinion, do well enough. He is a solitary child, whose best friends are a maid and a dog; his mother does not, to my fairly certain knowledge, ever attend school functions and I have already seen his year-end report tossed carelessly on a pile of unopened mail as I came through the hallway. Sometimes Natasha's attitude towards her son annoys me; she can be cold to everyone else but it seems unnatural to be so uncaring towards a child of 9 years old. 'I saw his school report downstairs,' I say, 'were you pleased with it? How is he doing?'

She goes to the wardrobe and, after some deliberation, takes out a long evening dress of emerald green and lays it on the bed. 'Why do you want to know, Sophie?' she asks. 'What is Alexei's progress to you?'

'I'm interested because I care for him,' I say hotly. 'I think he's a great kid and I worry because he has so few friends and sometimes you seem so ...' I search for an inoffensive word, 'distant towards him. I mean, after all, Natasha, he is your son and he would seem to warrant a little more involvement, I think.'

'No,' she says shortly, taking gold shoes out of the wardrobe, 'he isn't'.

'Isn't what?'

'Alexei is not my son,' she says clearly, turning back to the wardrobe.

I stare stupidly. 'What?'

She throws off the silk robe and steps easily into the long green dress. 'Can you zip me up?' she asks, and then repeats the request as I continue to sit on the bed, trying to take in what she's said. 'Did you adopt him?' I ask finally.

She is putting on her earrings now. 'I suppose so,' she says, 'but unofficially. He was left on my hands, more or less.'

'But who is he? A friend or relation's child? How come he was left with you?'

She gives her chill smile. 'That's a very good question,' she says ruefully. 'I don't even like children.'

'Natasha!' I say severely, sitting up straight. 'This is serious. You are in charge of Alexei. Even if you took him for the wrong reasons you owe it to him to be his mother.'

She spreads her hands to check her nails. 'Oh Sophie, but we don't live in the world of black and white where you are so happy because all the moves are defined. I took him because no one else would have him and my friend begged me; she was dying and I could not refuse her. Often I have been tempted to leave him somewhere. I feel so little towards him, but in common decency I have looked after him, given him a home and security. He has so much in many ways; so much that I never had. And you ask me to give him more?'

'But don't you love him? He's a sweet little boy ...' I think of all the times Alexei has flung himself into my arms in welcome, the times he has looked up from cuddling Hector, his eyes bright with pride over something the dog has done. I remember his cuddling up beside me on the sofa, poring over something on his laptop with me; he lacks the confidence and pushiness of many of his peers but he is an intelligent and not unattractive child. I find him hugely endearing on occasion.

She slips on her shoes and ties the high straps. 'I am not like you, Sophie. I don't fall in love with the world. Besides, I know his story. You would not love him if you knew where he comes from.'

'Of course I would,' I say hotly. 'A child is an innocent victim, no matter what. Whatever Alexei's story is it wouldn't matter because we are not our parents, we are ourselves.' I pause. 'Does Alexei know he's not your son?'

She has gone back to the dressing table. 'No,' she says shortly. 'It is not something he would wish to know. He has asked, sometimes, about the past, but I say nothing.'

I am tense and cross at her coldness; this is, I know, all part of her keeping the world at bay policy, but it infuriates me that an innocent child should also be the victim of it. 'He should know something,' I begin hotly, when Rosie calls up from downstairs that the safe installation man has arrived and is knocking at my door. I have to go; she says nothing and I bounce out of the room in some dudgeon and go swiftly home. The safe-fitter goes about his business and the air is full of the high-pitched whine of a drill slammed into concrete and there is dust everywhere. I shut the door of the master bedroom and leave him to it; the noise is ear-splitting and so I take Puss – who has retreated under the sofa in fright – out into the garden and swing quietly whilst I sip wine and brew on what Natasha has told me. I do have a tendency to be up in arms to defend the defenceless; it's another aspect of my Libran love of justice. But I do really feel for Alexei now and find myself frowning over the fact that he has been told nothing of his past, which seems cruel. Every child needs to know where they come from. I consider Natasha's words again and realise that I am judging the situation from my middle-class, middle-English viewpoint; there is a cruel and violent world in the East that Natasha has escaped from, and Alexei too. I think of Romanian orphanages and the awful parade of images of malnourished children, tumbledown buildings and a depth of suffering only to be guessed at, that the press has used to guilt-fix the Western world. Maybe it is from this hellish environment that Alexei has been saved; maybe I have judged too harshly. I may be innocent but not, after all, completely ignorant, just perhaps slightly over-emotive. I resolve I will find out more about him and think that, whatever I learn, I will not love him any less, but maybe even more than I do already. My husband and children always used to mock my tender heart and emotive response to sick or hurt animals or children. I wonder now if this is part of my response to and the appeal of Jason Knight; the need I sense in him to be loved, his shyness which spells vulnerability to me and yet is not consistent with his moments of boldness. Rick never needed to be rescued; for years I was his herald, his sounding board and his support network. The way that Jason makes me feel is a new Sophie, a shield maiden, who can ask for what she wants, and that level of trust and fine-spun understanding is new to me and immensely appealing, giving strength and confidence if this relationship should ever develop, which I have to admit at the moment does not seem likely.

By the next day when Natasha comes over with jewellery to put in the safe, I have quite recovered my equilibrium and she can see it as I offer tea and biscuits (I have made her favourite ginger crunch) and she laughs at what she calls my 'obviousness'. 'So you have forgiven me today, Sophie?' she asks as she cuts her crunch evenly into dice and eats each one slowly.

'Yes,' I admit, stirring my tea. 'I did over-react a bit about Alexei when I know, of course, that it's entirely your own business. But I still stick with my argument that he needs to get out of here in the summer. I have a plan which I'd like to put to you.'

'And what is your plan?'

'When I go back to England I could take Alexei with me and enrol him in one of the day camps near to my aunt's house. They're wonderful places, and he could strike up some friendships and he'd have a great time with kids his own age; they do lots of sports and have a huge amount of fun. I think it would be very good for him, and I'm sure you can afford it.'

She slants a look at me which I respond to with a wink. After all, I have just helped her put thousands of dollars' worth of jewellery into the new wall safe and I am sitting in a house which she has, essentially, bought for me. Money is not the issue, whatever else is.

She laughs. 'All right, you are very persuasive, my Sophie, and Alexei is lucky to have you as his advocate. You organise it, and I will give you the money. And now … I suppose you want me to tell you his story, do you?'

'I would like to know it, yes, but I will always love him, no matter where he comes from.'

She lights a cigarette and I refill her cup. 'Alexei is the product of a rape,' she says coolly. 'When we were leaving Russia I had met a girl, and she and I were travelling in a truck with some refugees. They were barbarians and pigs. She was unlucky; she could not defend herself. Me, they did not touch.'

I blink at her, but I can almost see the images behind her chill words; tall strong Natasha would defend herself at the point of a gun or a knife and would not scruple to use it. You only have to look into those chill turquoise eyes to know that she does not bluff. 'She became pregnant and, in spite of all that our *babushka* did to abort it, Alexei was finally born. Poor girl, the birth killed her, as well it might; we were in the back streets of Warsaw and there were no facilities. I hardly knew her but she begged me to have her baby and to look after it. I was on my own and I had no wish to saddle myself with a child but I said yes to calm her. *Babushka* kept him for a while but when I became settled here, she sent him to me. I did not want him, but when he arrived on my doorstep I was forced to accept him. Since then I have done what I have to do but no more. Alexei already has more than either I or his mother ever had and I consider that I have kept my promise. At least he will grow into a decent man, unlike his pig of a father.'

I digest Alexei's history which is pretty much along the lines I had imagined. 'Who was Babushka?' I ask finally.

'The woman in the photograph,' says Natasha shortly. 'She was a madam of a brothel in Poland but she was a kind woman and, for some reason, she took to me. I was like the daughter she never had, she used to say. She saved me; thanks to her I never had to take the road that so many other girls from my country do. I was fortunate, and for that reason I had to do what I had said I would do and take Alexei. And so,' she reaches for another slice of ginger crunch, 'now you know, Sophie, and you may judge me if you choose.'

'I think you're even braver and stronger than I first thought,' I say with warmth, and watch her smile at my earnest tone. 'I am sorry I was cross with you; I didn't understand. You are doing the best you can for Alexei and now it is my turn to do something for him too, because you are my friend and I want to help both of you. I will book him into a wonderful summer camp and he will flourish. Alexei has a chance to live the life his mother never had and I want to be part of that!' I get up and go around the table to hug her; it is not something I do normally, and something that I know she does not respond well to, but I want to somehow impart my depth of feeling to her, for her to feel that I love her and admire what she has done. She is a totally admirable human being, is Natasha, and I want her to know it.

Buoyed up on a new wave of energy and enthusiasm I book Alexei on the same flight as me as well as ten days at the nearby summer day camp, which is obviously divinely meant as there is a last-minute cancellation which I seize with delight. Alexei himself, when given the news, cannot determine whether to laugh or cry. He is thrilled on one level, but on another cannot deal with the fact that he must be away from his beloved Hector and Rosie for two whole weeks. He is a little scared at the prospect of travelling to England (even with me), and going to a camp (he looks askance at the pictures on the camp's website of children indulging in thrilling activities) but Rosie begins a gentle programme of soft-focus integration and within a few days he is babbling excitedly of archery and swimming and wondering if his soccer skills will be superior to those of the 'English children.' I promise weekend treats of visiting castles and theme parks and Natasha gives Rosie money to buy him new clothes and we have a couple of amusing days out at the mall outfitting one increasingly excited little boy. All of us are infected with the pleasure of the moment and Rosie, no doubt, is also looking forward to having two whole weeks of rest and relaxation, with only Hector to keep an eye on.

The summer is now upon us in good earnest, and I have time on my hands as the magazine has closed for the month. After a cleaning out of cupboards and sorting of clothes and shoes I decide on a complete refurbishment of the master bedroom; it seems appropriate now that Rick has gone that I should spend my summer bonus on giving myself a new look. I pore over magazines and go on the internet looking at interior design schemes; after some pondering and deliberation and rather fruitless conversations with Natasha who has no interest in anything to do with house decoration, albeit of her own property, I decide on a lovely neutral base called 'linen' with grey and lavender silk curtains and matching bed set with a few throw cushions in a deep purple silk. Natasha cannot believe I intend to do it myself, and hopes (with an indolent smile) that I will not be asking her to climb up ladders, but Alexei is full of excitement and proposes that he should also have a change of bedroom décor. I leave him and Rosie looking at various themed bedrooms on the internet, and with a rueful glance at Natasha, and her softly spoken ironic, 'thank you Sophie, for starting this', I go home and start cleaning walls and rubbing down skirting boards, laying dust sheets and prepping paint rollers in my self-declared painting outfit of very brief old shorts and skimpy top with my hair tied off my face with an old scarf. Halfway through the morning, just as I am in the middle of rollering a large section of wall, the doorbell rings, and I descend grumbling from my ladder, certain it is Alexei come to show me some radical designer bedroom interior he has set his heart on. It isn't. It is Jason Knight standing there, smiling his boyish grin at me and my dishevelled appearance, with my bare feet, hair tied up, and paint on my arms and hands.

'Oh!' I gasp. 'I thought you'd left town.'

'Next week,' he confirms. 'Can I come in?'

I can't believe that he should turn up on today of all days, catching me totally unprepared. 'You look very cute,' he says as he steps inside. 'The paint on the nose is particularly becoming.'

We stand awkwardly looking at each other; I think he would have kissed me but I step back as my hands are held away from my sides and covered in paint, and now I have wrong-footed him. 'I think it's time for a tea break,' I say, 'come into the kitchen while I wash off this paint.'

I precede him into the kitchen and he leans against the bench as I frantically wash my arms and hands, aware that I am shaking, and fill the kettle. My heart is beating like a drum at the sight and sense of him in such close proximity, yet I am aware that I am delaying the moment of contact. I am towelling myself rather feverishly when it is taken from me and he slides his hands around my waist and pulls me towards him. I yield and everything is forgotten as I fall – there is no other word for it – into something that can only be described as mindless rapture. I have no sense of anything other than the sweetness of what is occurring; the taste and softness of his mouth and tongue and the feverishness of the total need for each other as our pulses pound in unison and the space between us is electric with unspoken desire. Lust consumes us;

my bra-less nipples are hard and aroused; my knees are weak and my body quivering, the pulse between my legs jumping; moisture is trickling down the insides of my thighs and I long for nothing except to be totally absorbed, to be held up against the wall even, and taken in a violent consummation which is what I desire above everything else. But I am to be disappointed. He pulls away finally, and I tighten my arms round his neck to pull him back into another kiss. Indeed, I can hardly bear to let him go. He is saying something, but I kiss him again and the words are lost in the rising passion of the incredible chemistry between us. I will think later that I have never experienced anything like this reaction; Rick considers himself a lover without peer, but I cannot remember ever feeling like this before. He pulls away finally and, with a smile, lifts my hands from around his neck. 'I have to go,' he says as I gawp at him in surprise.

'You have to go?' I repeat stupidly.

'Yes, I'm sorry, Sophie.'

'But why did you come?' I query rather pathetically.

'I couldn't stop thinking about you,' he says with his little-boy smile which makes me forgive him anything. 'I had to see you before I left. But I'm gone now 'til the end of August. When I come back I'll come and see you for longer and... we can talk about things.'

I can't help slipping my arms around his neck again. 'I don't want to talk,' I say kissing him lightly.

'Me neither. I want to be naked with you for a very long time,' he says rubbing what is presumably a spot of paint off my nose with his finger and making me purr like a cat at the gentle intimacy of his touch coupled with the spurt of pleasure his words have given me. 'But it can't be today. I'm sorry,' he repeats edging towards the door. I follow him down the hallway rather dismally but there is nothing I can do to stop him going. He gives me a last long kiss and then opens the door. 'Have a lovely summer,' he says, and then is gone, and all that is left is the trembling of my body to reassure me that this is real.

Natasha, coming over later with (I gawp at the sight of them) small gold bars to put in the safe, admires my work in the bedroom but looks down her aristocratic nose at the story of Jason Knight's all too brief visit. 'He came to kiss you? That was all he came for?'

I stir my tea and sniff rather miserably. 'I'm afraid so, yes. But he did say that he will come back and hinted at much more to come … and he said he couldn't stop thinking about me, so I guess there are a few bright spots in the gloom.'

'And you think this is romantic?'

I don't want to incur her scorn but have to answer honestly, 'Well, in a way, yes. He could have just as easily stayed away. And he does kiss like a dream.' I sigh wistfully at the memory and she laughs shortly. 'Well, my Sophie, at least now you have memories to keep you warm at night. When you pleasure yourself you can think of him.'

I look blank. 'When I do what?'

'Pleasure yourself. Masturbate – though not a word I like.'

I blush and look embarrassed and she laughs again. 'Don't tell me you don't do it.'

I pick at a spot of colour on my teacup and keep my eyes down. 'No,' I admit, 'it's not something I've ever done. I know nothing at all of vibrators or anything like that.'

She relaxes in her chair, totally at ease. 'Sophie,' she says quietly, 'we women have few pleasures, goodness knows, and men we are with seldom give us orgasms although we pretend that they do, to massage the male ego. But women are sensuous beings and we need release just as men do; it does not have to be a vibrator. You have fingers and lavender oil and now you also have lovely memories of a man who kisses you and evokes passion in that naïve little heart of yours.' I glance up at that, but her smile has no edge at all. 'Take my advice, Sophie, you have a loving passionate nature and it does not need a man to develop it. Pleasuring yourself will relax and soothe you; and when you do, finally,' she laughs, 'get into bed with the elusive Mr Knight, you will be a beautiful and finely-tuned instrument that will respond to his every touch.'

'Instead of a clunky old piano do you mean?' I laugh as I look up.

'Babushka used to tell us of the ladies of the harem of the old sultans of Turkey; so many beautiful and highly-sexed women trapped together with only other women for company. So they developed the arts of the concubine by caressing other women and being caressed in their turn. This way they understood their own needs, and developed their arts of allurement.'

I imagine all those beautiful houris and sinuous silk-clad forms moving with the grace of magnificent cats; much of that exists already in Natasha, I realise. She never hurries, never rushes anywhere, but has an almost sinister prowling grace of movement that is flowing and elegant but hints at a controlled restraint. I never thought of it as being a deliberately cultivated style; the movements are fluid and natural and fit her rather chill exterior, her cool smile and hard turquoise eyes. She is, as they say, all of a piece. By contrast I am sentimental, emotionally childlike, passionate and foolish and I have never dissembled in my life. But perhaps I can adopt something of that sinuous grace of movement which is so attractive. It is, after all, immensely seductive and that is what I decide I want to be. In order to change the somewhat embarrassing subject of masturbation, I comment now on the gold bars she has put in the safe. It is the first time I've ever seen a gold bar, let alone housed one.

'It's nothing,' she says lightly. 'You buy them in the gold souk. It is better than banks, which I mistrust.'

'I can see that!' I say with a laugh. 'You must have thousands of pounds worth of jewellery alone in that safe and now gold bars too! I feel like a bank myself with all that sleeping next to me.'

'It is my danger money,' she says, and I feel she's totally serious. 'There is cash too, of course, but that I keep separately.' She looks up now and her eyes are cold. 'Sophie,' she says carefully, 'you never ask me what I do, where all the money comes from. Why not? Why are you so incurious?'

'It's none of my business,' I respond readily enough. 'And I don't need to know.'

'An odd attitude,' she muses, 'for a journalist.'

'I suppose so, yes. But I know how you guard your privacy and, as your friend, I wouldn't want to probe and upset you.'

She seems inclined to reminisce, which is not typical of Natasha. 'The first day I met you,' she says slowly, 'I was sure you were some pushy woman come to find out about me. I knew who you were. I'd seen your photograph often enough and I assumed the journalist next door couldn't resist sniffing after a story.'

'Well I'm flattered that you knew who I was. I suppose there are lots of copies of *Insider* lying around the palace.'

'Dozens,' she says, 'the princess is very proud of her creation. It was a long time, however, before I felt I could trust you. I'd never met anyone like you, Sophie, so innocent and naïve and forgiving; almost as if we didn't inhabit the same world.'

She smiles, but those turquoise eyes are still bleak and cold. 'Sophie,' she continues, 'listen carefully to me now because one day you may need to know these things. I am, as I think you may have guessed, kept by a prince of the house of al Maktoum. I am his mistress and to that end I have clothes and jewels, a house and a driver, so that I may maintain the position and reflect his honour. But no relationship is static, especially ones that are founded on such principles, and there will come a day when all this comes to an end. But these things are mine and I have worked hard for them and I don't intend to give them up. That is why I am guarding my investment. No one knows that I own this house and I want it to remain that way. In this situation secrecy is important.' Now she gives me a genuine smile. 'You see Sophie, how I trust you.'

It seems strange to hear her speak of her life after all these months of guarded comment and surmise. All these things I have imagined but have avoided speaking of because, as the months have passed, I have come to realise that the role Natasha plays, what she does, is not who she is. Her career choice, as it were, is not important because Natasha is a very rare human being. She has survived an extraordinary amount of trauma in her life and still retained her humanity. She has utilized her considerable assets and works hard for her economic success. Whatever she does, it does not alter the fact that I love and admire her.

'You can trust me,' I assure her.

'I know that,' she says, 'if it were not so, I would not tell you.'

We twinkle at one another. I do not need to tell her how I respect her and value her confidence in me. She knows. Now the journalist in me takes over. 'Do you feel that you have to hide your jewellery? Do you feel you are not safe?'

'I trust nobody,' she says shortly, 'and I try to anticipate. I know it is possible that one day I may fall foul of the palace. And I must be prepared for that day.'

'Put not your trust in princes,' I murmur.

She smiles. 'Ah yes, Shakespeare I think?'

'The only man with all the answers,' I confirm.

'I have covered most of my bases,' she goes on. 'The property company in London is my major investor and the most profitable. It is also hidden. I have never gone with off-shore investments or with banks for the obvious reason that such investments can be traced and perhaps tampered with. Jewellery and gold is portable and also, of course, I need the jewellery here so I can wear it.'

'You are very cautious,' I say. 'One could almost say paranoid. Who would tamper with your investments? Why should your money not be as safe as anyone else's?'

She pauses and looks down at her hands for a minute, considering her smooth red nails. 'Ah Sophie,' she says softly, 'I know too much.'

'What do you know?'

'Things that I ought not.'

I consider her words and Alex's comments flicker across my mind: *'what secret dealings she must have seen and known'*. 'But things that you would never tell?'

'Ah,' she responds, 'but telling them is not the point. Knowing them is the problem.'

I lean my elbows on the table. 'My colleague at *Insider,* Alex, is the only real journalist amongst us and he hints there are plenty of dark dealings going on in this town. But I never thought it would be dangerous to know it. Saying it yes, publishing it never. But just knowing it?'

She twists her ring round on her finger and this little movement betrays her nervousness. Natasha is not used to sharing secrets, but perhaps too, I wonder if I am witnessing anxiety. She is not comfortable, that much is obvious, but now I wonder if she is not even afraid.

'What does your colleague do with his knowledge?' she asks.

'Oh just sits on it, but no doubt he's planning some scoop or other; he's insatiable when it comes to raking up dirt but, to be fair, he's an investigative journalist of the highest quality. He has some interesting contacts and probably knows more than is good for him. But, if it all remains unsaid, then I can't see that it would be dangerous.'

'Politics is a dirty game,' she responds. 'And when you are perhaps the foremost Islamic society in the world, you guard your reputation very carefully.'

'Ah yes,' I say, turning to one of Alex's favourite quotations. 'Wheels within wheels and fires within fires'.

Her eyes flick up. 'Shakespeare again?'

'No, Arthur Miller, actually. 'The Crucible.''

'I don't know it, but it fits the situation here very exactly. And I see and know a lot of it … and I am a woman and therefore … dispensable, perhaps even disposable.'

There's an awkward silence because I can almost feel her fear as the words drop softly. 'Are you afraid?' I whisper.

She sighs. 'Sometimes.'

'Can I help?'

She looks up and smiles. 'You are helping, Sophie, by what you do. And also by your friendship. I never had a woman friend before who cared so much for me; no one I could trust in such a long time.'

I feel my throat beginning to ache. Natasha has this effect on me because she's so strong and beautiful and brave, and yet so vulnerable. She makes me want to put my arms around her and hug her and tell her everything will be all right but instead I reach my hand across the table and take hers, squeezing it hard. 'I'll look after you,' I promise, 'I can be a tigress in defence of those I love!'

She laughs, but ruefully. 'Yes, Sophie, you are my contingency plan. If anyone should wonder who owns this house, it has been bought by a London property company; if anyone should seek to know more I would counsel that you say you don't know any more.'

'Um,' I say, biting lip, 'actually Rick knows it was you who bought it. I might have said something … sorry.'

'He is not important,' she says, 'and you were not to know. Anyway, we should not worry. Nothing will happen.'

I say nothing, but I am thinking that Rick has a lot to hide and a man with a secret will be happy to divulge other people's secrets in the hope that his own will be overlooked. After she goes, I ponder on wondering if perhaps I should do as Alex has long wanted and bring the two of them together. Maybe Natasha would be safer if it were made clear that whatever information she possesses that is burdensome has been leaked, effectively, to the press and, should anything happen to her, that information would be made public. Then I think that

142

perhaps I have watched too many movies, read too many thrillers. But perhaps a word with Alex would be beneficial. He does, after all, know the dark side of this town which I definitively don't. Unfortunately Alex is away for the summer, gone to visit friends in New York, but I anticipate his whiskers twitching with delight if Natasha should agree to an interview with him. It does vaguely nag at me, though, that Natasha, always so cool and self-possessed, should be so clearly anxious. It seems so out of character that I cannot help wondering what has happened to upset her. Clearly I have not been told the whole story, but I cannot probe for more. All I need to know is that the jewellery and the gold bars in my safe, are in my house (which is not my house) for safekeeping, and are presumably mine, should anybody ask. That seems patently ridiculous, but I suspect that Natasha is effectively hiding them with me, although why she should feel she needs to is again, unclear. I definitely need Alex's clear logical brain to work through this with me.

However, no more is said on the matter. The bedroom is finished and I am ridiculously pleased with it, partly because it is my scheme from start to finish, and therefore a first, as Rick always made interior design decisions because he was, apparently, 'a designer'; he believed he had an inspired eye for colour and design choice and the first I knew about anything was the day it happened. Having lived in a green and white bedroom for years – a colour I despise – my new pale grey and lavender bedroom pleases me no end. Alexei is wooed away from his bedroom scheme by the excitement of the forthcoming English trip, and since Natasha is indeed off to the South of France, Rosie is kept busy packing.

Alexei and I arrive in England on a bright summer's day and everything is thrilling to a nine year old boy who has never been out of a desert city in his life, or at least not that he can remember. The plane ride is quite challenging for me as a newly minted foster mother as I had forgotten the exhausting processes that children go through on aircraft of sampling every device and bringing all outcomes to adult attention. Fortunately for my sanity, and my continued good relationship with Alexei, there is another small boy seated across the aisle, and they continue the sampling exercise together, thus leaving me free to down a couple of V&Ts and wonder if I am up to two weeks of this. One contributing factor to Alexei's effervescent happiness is, I feel sure, the fact that Natasha actually allowed him to hug her before we left, a circumstance so unusual that Alexei could not quite believe his luck. I wonder if she has taken my advice on board about being less distant with a child who believes that she is his mother or whether the hug was permitted as she will be without him for three whole weeks. At least Rosie's hugs were genuine and the excitement of the journey has prevented Alexei from worrying about Hector, whose woebegone face still lingers in my memory.

My idea of a seamless transition from Heathrow airport to the Underground is also overturned as the train is hugely exciting and Alexei has to be hustled through what is, to him, a continual parade of delights and fascinations; by the time we reach the mainline station for the last stage of the journey on a high speed train, I am exhausted and ready to fall in to my seat and drink a strong coffee. At no time, however, am I cross with Alexei; it would be like being cross with an over-excited puppy that cannot help the size of its paws or the shrillness of its bark.

Introducing Alexei to my aunt at Worcester, I can see that she too has fallen for his particular brand of innocent appeal. Everything is wonderful to him and he cannot wait to explore; the high-walled garden with its beautifully maintained floral borders, the tortoiseshell cat sunning itself, the half dozen free range chickens that are running around, the striped bedroom under the eaves that Jessie has allocated to him and from which, joy of joys, an old windmill can be spied across the fields. The first few days we can only laugh at Alexei's sheer delight in exploring as words bubble from his lips and he is on the go from morning to night. The sun blazes down from a sky the colour of forget-me-nots and Jessie takes us on a picnic down by the river where swans and moorhens paddle at leisure, and Alexei is himself as bright and exuberant as the flashing kingfisher that we spy under a dipping willow. In the slow unwinding loveliness of an English summer's day it seems impossible to remember the darkness from which Alexei has been redeemed and, as I share his story with Jessie, we can only rejoice that he is one who has been saved and revel in his wide-eyed smile and palpable happiness as he holds hands with us or runs ahead, dancing like a sunbeam along the edge of a field of blowing barley. And so my concern for him on entering the summer camp is also allayed; everyone is, after all, a newcomer, and Alexei is immediately scooped up by a gorgeous blonde pony-tailed teenager called Katrina who, it seems, will be his team leader. Alexei departs with never a backward look at me and, that evening, when Jessie and I collect him, he is so excited that he babbles all the way home, through dinner and bath time, and is still babbling as I tuck him into bed.

And so the two weeks pass happily for both of us. I am close to my aunt, my mother's only sister after all, and although she is initially shocked by my reports of Rick's behaviour, she is sensible enough to realise that my life does not have to be negatively impacted by what he has done and that I can stay in Dubai and find happiness in the satisfaction of my work and contacts. Of Jason Knight, however, I do not speak at all; some things are too precious to be discussed and besides, wonderful and accepting and understanding as my aunt is, adultery is not something with which she could deal easily, or at least not my planned adultery. Sophie Seductress is best kept under wraps and I am not unhappy to keep my dark side hidden; Jason Knight is a secret that I think of as I lie in my single bed and watch the moon trace a trail across the sapphire summer sky. I think, too, of what Natasha has said and I find her advice to be sound here too; orgasm produces such a feeling of relaxation in me that I fall asleep with his name on my lips and a belief that the future is full of optimism and will bring me everything I desire.

The crowning glory of Alexei's summer camp is the Awards Ceremony, which I film with all the pride of a foster mother as he walks away with the Most Promising Footballer trophy. The passionate excitement on his face, alight with joy, brings tears to my eyes, as do the farewells he exchanges with all the children he has got to know over the course of two weeks, as well as a hug from gorgeous blonde Katrina who tells him he is 'awesome' and that she can't wait to see him again next year. I am like a dog with two tails over the success of the summer camp; Alexei has been transformed from a rather severe little boy who was shy in the presence of his peers to a buoyant and friendly lad who is self-confident and assured. I feel a corner has been turned and when Alexei gets back to school he will find making friends far easier.

Arriving back to the searing heat of Dubai requires a moment or two of adjustment but Rosie and Hector are waiting and both look rested and rejuvenated and thrilled to have us back, although Hector's joy is rather more extravagant and physical than Rosie's quiet pleasure as she makes tea for me and a large sandwich for Alexei. Finally I take my suitcase and go home; my house is as bright and shining as a new pin and I send up a silent thank you for Rosie's care. My new bedroom has lost none of its charm in my absence, the garden is clipped and slumbering in the late summer heat and the pool twinkles invitingly. I fling my case on the bed and decide that I am glad to be back. The weeks ahead no longer fill me with the dread of loneliness but are shot through with a golden thread of excitement; I will see Jason Knight again and perhaps I will at last achieve what I now desire above all else.

Natasha is not back for another week but finally she too arrives and our small family is once again complete. She is bronzed and looks amazing; her eyes gleaming turquoise in her tanned face and, it seems to me, a slightly softer approach. She admires Alexei's footballer trophy and watches my video footage of the presentation; she listens with a half-smile to all of five minutes' worth of Alexei's adventures before moving, but she herself places the trophy on the sideboard and this small act means the world to Alexei. At last he has his mother's approval and his world is complete. I invite them all to dinner at my house, the first time I have done so, and this small dinner party is a real family occasion; full of friendliness, happiness and warmth. I take a photo of us all at the table; a moment of shared laughter, frozen forever in time. After dinner Rosie takes Alexei home while Natasha and I take our coffee into the garden and swing in compatible silence, breathing in the scents of the garden and enjoying the quiet warmth of a Dubai night, although it is, as yet, a little humid for comfort. She seems disinclined to share her holiday stories; she has heard Alexei's and my adventures, but apart from saying a little about the yacht itself, as usual she has little else to share.

'So,' I say finally, as I reach for the coffee pot. 'Where did you actually sail to? Any gaming in Monte Carlo?'

She flicks a half smile at me. 'That would have been very civilized. No. We went further afield.'

'Really? Round the Med?'

'No. Through Suez and the Red Sea.'

'Oh amazing! Through the Suez Canal?'

She smiles at my enthusiasm. 'It is not so amazing, Sophie. There are a lot of Arabs who holiday on the Red Sea. I did not go ashore much. I did some diving. It was interesting.'

We chat on, or rather I do. Natasha sips her coffee and listens to my prattling. After a moment or two she says, suddenly, apropos of nothing, 'Is there anything you really hate, Sophie?'

I don't see the connection and look puzzled. 'Really hate?'

'Yes.'

'What sort of thing? Children dying, wars do you mean?'

She looks serious. 'No, personally. Any people you really hate?'

I laugh at such an unlikely question. 'I don't think so! I don't really know that many people and most of them I like, love even.' I try to think laterally. 'I suppose I would hate a drug dealer, or a mass murderer, but I'm not likely ever to meet one I hope!'

'I think you can sometimes hate someone you feel is intrinsically evil,' she muses. 'I've met a few over the years but this time I met one who made my blood run cold.'

'Oh horrible,' I offer. 'There's a great line from an Alistair Maclean novel about someone like that; *'I looked into his eyes and could almost smell the earth of a freshly dug grave.'*

She doesn't answer me directly. 'I could see my death in his eyes,' she says remotely. 'He was as black as night, with robes of the purest white, and his eyes were full of death.'

The description is so graphically sinister that it stops me in my tracks; it is no time for flippant remarks. 'Who was he?' I ask quietly.

She refocuses on me. 'A bringer of death and destruction,' she says clearly and her eyes are bleak and cold. 'A fanatic.'

I have no idea what she's talking about, but this conversation has echoes of the last one we had before she went away and it reminds me that the twilight and half-hidden world in which she lives is a dangerous one. Even a simpleton such as I can see that, and I wonder again if Alex can help her. 'I've had an idea,' I begin. 'You know my colleague Alex, the one who's a real investigative journalist; I wonder if he could help you.'

'Help me how?' She looks up and I am struck that her eyes are so full of sadness.

'You said before that you knew too much and it was dangerous. If, perhaps, someone else, like Alex, knew it too, and was prepared to publish it if ever anything happened to you, would that keep you safe do you think?'

She frowns. 'I don't know. I don't trust journalists.'

'Oh you could trust Alex. He's immensely clever and professional. He would never betray you, and he might even have a better suggestion. Would you like me to ask him?'

She muses. 'Perhaps,' she says but I can tell she's thinking it over. 'Yes, perhaps. Ask him to meet me; but I promise nothing.' She gets up to go and I get up to kiss her.

'Goodnight, my dear friend. Sleep well and don't worry. I will keep you safe.'

She laughs then and flicks my nose with her finger. 'You, Sophie? You couldn't keep a mouse safe!'

'Indeed I could!' I say laughing. 'I am a tigress – I told you!'

Dubai is slowly easing back into post-summer mode. The roads are filling up, the planes bring back mothers and children from long summer sojourns, work begins again. I feel a sense of suppressed excitement that Jason Knight will be back in town but, more important even than that is the need to accost Alex; I leave message after message on his answerphone but it is not until a week later that he finally calls me back. The office has been open for three days but only Shazza and I have put in an appearance; Shazza blonder than ever after a summer trekking through the Basque country. Wayne's return is delayed; his mother is ill. Of Alex there is no word until one evening the phone rings and it is he. 'My dear child,' he greets me, 'what is all this besieging of my phone with messages? Such impatience!' but the languid tone is soon replaced when he hears my news. I can almost see his ears pricking up and his nose moving into newshound twitch. 'Really?' he breathes. 'The dazzling neighbour, the courtesan de marque? She wants to talk to me?'

'Can't tell you anymore over the phone,' I say mysteriously. Really, it is fun to whet his appetite; a little bit of payback for the Sophie cub-reporter way he treats me. Now I have a scoop for Alex; one that he could not have got on his own. There is a definite sense of smugness in the way I arrange a rendezvous.

The next afternoon Alex arrives panting on my doorstep; I pacify him with a vodka and tonic as we wait for Natasha to come in. She has agreed to talk to him on the condition that everything she tells him is in strictest confidence and will never be revealed unless it is under the terms she will arrange with him. She arrives dressed in her evening finery and, accustomed as I am to her stunning outfits, I pay little attention, but Alex's mouth drops open as he encounters Natasha's chill beauty for the first time. She is dressed in a long gown of sapphire blue silk, that colour so flattering to blondes, with lace inserts in the bodice and the long sleeves. The V-shaped neckline reveals the Star of the Sea sapphire, the same one she lent to me, and the earrings glitter seductively from under the upsweep of hair into the French roll she frequently favours. She walks into my sitting room and requests a fizzy water to drink; Alex tosses back his vodka and gets down to business. I bring back her water and perch on the edge of a chair but, to my dismay, she directs a chill look at me and tells me, 'Sophie, this is not for your ears. It is enough that I am sharing this with Alex, but to have you know it too would be irresponsible of me and might place you in danger unnecessarily. Go out now and shut the door behind you.'

There is nothing I can say and to remonstrate will, I know, do no good, so I do as she asks. I wander upstairs and tidy my office, putting books away on the shelves and things away in the drawers. Below me, faintly, I can hear the hum of voices, but no individual words penetrate upstairs. I move to the window just in time to see the long black Mercedes draw up; below I hear movement as Natasha realises that the car has arrived and that she must be going. She calls goodbye as she leaves and I trot downstairs to see how Alex has fared. He is sitting in his chair still, his notebook lying open and unheeded on his lap, and his small recording device on the table beside him. He looks, frankly, stunned, but at the same time exhilarated. He turns to me and his eyes are alight with excitement.

'Get me another drink, young Sophie,' he says, 'and make it a strong one. Then come and sit yourself down.'

I do so, making one for myself as well, and then wriggle into a chair opposite him. 'Well?' I say.

Alex gulps his drink and shakes his head. 'I feel like the Queen of Sheba visiting Solomon,' he says, 'where the half had not been told her. Much I suspected but this … it's huge … and to think that I am bound to secrecy!' He takes another gulp. 'I really think this could be the crowning moment of my career, and I am not allowed to publish! Could anything be more ironic?'

'I don't suppose you can share any of it?' I ask wistfully. Cub reporter though I am, it's hard not to want to know the secret that Natasha believes could kill her.

He shakes his head. 'You wouldn't believe most of it,' he says with a sigh. 'What she has seen, and knows! No wonder she's afraid.'

His words chill me. If Alex recognizes Natasha's fear has such a solid foundation, then I am convinced that it must be true. 'Do you think she's in danger?'

'She thinks she is and she's a highly intelligent woman,' he says thoughtfully, putting the empty glass on the table and flicking through his notes. 'This may help to keep her safe but, unfortunately, when it's known that she has created this insurance policy, as it were, it will only prove that she's aware of the danger she's in and perhaps, in this case, ignorance might be the safest route. I don't know.' He looks tired suddenly, rubbing his brow which, it seems, has good cause to ache. 'No, Sophie, it's safest that you know nothing because you, I fear, may be suspected. After all, you're the friend and you're a journalist and unfortunately,' he gives a sudden little bark of laughter, 'they don't know that you're a complete babe in the woods in this affair.'

'Who are 'they' Alex? Is it Al Qaeda?'

He looks grim. 'Worse. Al Shabaab.'

'Who's Al Shabaab?' I query, confirming his assertion that I am totally ignorant of these matters.

He takes a deep breath. 'We don't know much about them,' he begins, 'except that they are of course from one of the most lawless places on earth, and so far they've seized the world's attention by hijacking ships off the coast of Somalia and holding them to ransom to raise funds for, amongst other things, terrorism. But how far they're connected with Al Qaeda in the Arabian Peninsula I don't know yet. And what they're planning here I can only guess.' He sees me opening my mouth and jumps in quickly to say, 'No Sophie, I'm not going to tell you anything more. It's a complete hornet's nest and you're best out of it.' He looks at my disappointed face and says gently, 'continue to do what you do my sweet; be the friend and supporter and leave the rest to me.'

With that I have to be content. I do some little research of my own into Al Shabaab, and try and make things add up in my own head but without much success. The desperate state of shattered Somalia and the rise of the fundamentalists and warlords make depressing reading, and after a while I tire of it. I, unlike Alex, cannot see a link between the rabid fanatics of a war-torn country and the elegant Islamic empire of Dubai. Wayne comes back and we gird up our loins for another year of doing what we do at *Insider*. The princess arrives for our first meeting and everything slips back into its accustomed groove. I decide to follow Alex's advice and leave him to pursue the terrorists while I get on with my job writing about what makes Dubai tick and wondering when Jason Knight will call me.

It's about three weeks actually before he turns up on my doorstep and I am on the point of setting out on a walk with Hector and Alexei, who instantly corners Jason and asks about Jack and when we can go off to the wadi again. Jason's eyes meet mine over his head; he can see that it will be impossible to talk to me now or to distract Alexei from his walk, so he agrees that yes, this Friday would be great and we should meet at the wadi. So that is what we decide to do and I am forced to watch him drive away with only the promise of a Friday morning walk in the company of two small boys. But the excitement that I feel when I see him thrills me with the pleasure of anticipation, and to Alexei's astonishment I run with him and Hector, shouting and laughing like a twelve-year-old about to have a treat.

The following Friday, reckoning that I may as well look the part of seductress, I put on my new English shorts in white linen which make my legs look very brown and a rather saucy top in deep turquoise which gives a hint that there are bare boobs underneath and more than a hint of cleavage. The gleam of approval in Jason Knight's eyes when he gets out of his car and sees me more than proves my choice right. Jack and Alexei, complete with Hector and football, set off immediately for their fort. Jason unpacks the water bottles and we wander up the small dune to sit under the tree and converse. The first thing he says is 'love your tits in that top' which makes me giggle and after that it's easy; we chat with all the interest and pleasure of old acquaintances but there is a delicious *frisson* of suspended pleasure, an undercurrent of sexual tension in our conversation. Every little touch has a charge like a live cable; our words and phrases are full of double entendres; the moment of consummation is drawing closer and we both desperately desire it. Indeed I am like a text book of arousal with hard nipples, hammering heartbeat and a clitoris that feels twice its normal size.

After we've briefly discussed our respective holidays, he moves over slightly on the tree trunk and says softly, 'My wife is away on a school camp next week. I wondered if your offer of checking out your newly decorated bedroom is still on?'

I can't resist touching him and my hand slides slowly over his thigh as I lean closer. 'Of course,' I say breathily, looking into his blue eyes. He lifts my hand carefully back on the branch but keeps his own over it as if to mask the rejection of the movement. I see his eyes glance over to make sure his son is not watching and am aware, once again, of his instincts for self-preservation. 'Which night?'

He laughs softly. 'Sunday, Monday, Tuesday, Wednesday?'

I gasp with surprise and pleasure. 'What? All of them?'

'Maybe. It's such a lovely feeling to be a free agent and the maid will babysit Jack of course.'

'Come to dinner,' I say, 'and you can have me as dessert. Come every night.'

He says softly, his eyes on me, 'I can come just by thinking about you.'

It's a corny old double meaning but it has new charms for me and I giggle appreciatively. I feel a veritable Eve in this Garden of Eden; the apple of knowledge is far too appetising for me to resist and I don't even speculate on any soul-searching that may lie ahead, being able to envisage nothing more than the here and now and an overwhelming desire to have sex with this man. Maybe I should be made wary by his caution but I am not. I am a single woman again, answerable to no one, and besides, Sophie is never cautious. Sophie blunders in where angels fear to tread every time.

Sunday I am in a fret all day; I can't decide whether he really means to have dinner with me or if we should just immediately retire to bed with a bottle of champagne and a platter of strawberries. On the other hand, he might really be hungry. My stomach has been flipping and plunging all day on a roller coaster of apprehension; I am certainly not hungry, just tense with a desperate excitement. In the end I buy scallops and chorizo sausage and a couple of avocados; this will take only minutes to prepare and a large bowl of hulled strawberries for dessert. If Jason Knight wants to eat them off my stomach that's fine by me. I send a brief note to Natasha in the morning, giving her a quick outline of events, and in the afternoon a florist's delivery van pulls up outside and an Indian lad with a beautiful smile delivers a huge bouquet of red roses into my hands. For one crazy minute I think they're from Jason Knight, then I read the note and laugh. **'To make your evening perfect in case he doesn't. N.'**

What to wear is, of course, an all-consuming question and, after taking a long shower where I wash every part of myself with care and make sure everything is trimmed or razored to perfection, I put on my new red silk bra and knickers (bought, I kidded myself at the time, with no particular person in mind) and examine the contents of my wardrobe. This, however, only after I have admired myself from every angle in the long mirror and decide that the goods ain't half bad. Exercise is the key to my new muscle development but, truth to tell, I have eaten little since Friday, being in a state of keyed-up intensity where everything seemed to stick in my throat and my stomach, obligingly, looks flat and toned. I finally decide on a favourite sundress in tropical colours cut in a 50's style with full skirt and fitted bodice. Bright orange high heels complete the outfit; I give a few twirls in front of the mirror and then move on to focus on the make-up which must look understated but effective. I am proud of my long lashes, short nose and full lips and can make the most of them without it being obvious to the relatively untutored male eye.

After that there is little to do except pass the time which I do by pacing and fluttering; in and out of the garden for some foliage to go with Natasha's roses, checking the freezer for ice, putting on some soft music called, most appropriately, 'Music for a Summer's Evening', going to pee about fifty times. In between I clock watch and check the window with a view of the road. The hands on the clock creep round until finally they stand at 6. My eyes dart back to the window just in time to see the metallic blue Jeep pull up and park. My heart starts to beat violently; I put the curtain back in place as his shadow goes past the window and then the doorbell sings out its merry little chime. I open the door, he steps into the hall, and I am in his arms.

Each time it happens, I am amazed at the naturalness and easiness of my responses as I slide my arms round his neck and kiss him with increasing passion, even more so this time because I know it will have an outcome. His kisses trail down my throat to my breasts, and I lift his hand and hold it. 'Come upstairs,' I say throatily, but as we pass the kitchen I go in and take the champagne from the fridge and two flutes from the table. He comes up behind me and kisses the back of my neck as I take the strawberries out of the fridge; I laugh and give him the bowl to take upstairs while I carry the bottle and glasses. He looks me up and down and says, 'You look very pretty; and I love the orange shoes.'

'Enjoy the back view,' I say cheekily as I precede him up the staircase.

In the bedroom the shades are drawn against the harsh late-afternoon glare and I have put glasses of water on each of the two bedside tables and the aromatic candles are burning. I give him the champagne bottle for him to uncork and stand ready with the glasses; with a pop the cork explodes and, giggling, I catch the bubbling liquid neatly in the cut glass champagne flutes. We sip and kiss. Then he takes the glass out of my hand and puts it on the dressing table and, turning, begins to kiss me again but with an entirely different energy, as if this time it's serious. My hands slide up under his shirt and glory in the warmth and softness of his skin; I slide the T-shirt over his head and run my hands appreciatively down his lightly muscled torso, admiring the strength of muscle and the tanned taut skin. He turns me to face the mirror as he slides down my zipper and I step out of my dress and confront my own image in red silk bra and knickers; his body is behind me and I can feel his arousal, and my own is evident as he kisses my neck and I see the roseate flush creep up my throat. 'This is very pretty,' he murmurs between kisses, 'and quite my favourite colour, but it has to go.' He slips off my bra and his hands trace the curve of my thigh then slide upwards across my belly to cup my breasts softly.

I can see the pulse hammering madly in my throat; there is something immensely erotic in watching my own body being fondled, the physical response compounded by the visual. I turn back to him and slide my hands into his boxer shorts and encounter a wonderfully hard and muscled butt which, in contrast to my own, seems to have no soft flesh at all. 'Good lord,' I murmur, 'you're muscled like a porpoise.' This makes him laugh breathily in my ear as he responds, 'It gets better...' I am a little shy but determined not to show it; I hook my thumbs over the elastic of the boxers and ease them downwards, although they are somewhat stuck at the front which means I have to slide my hand around a very impressive and fully engorged penis and ease the shorts over it. 'Mmm,' say I in totally genuine appreciation, 'the Great Beast is unveiled at last!' It could be an awkward moment but, curiously, it is not; we move together so naturally and, although my pulse is pounding violently, there is no embarrassment, simply the slowly wrung out pleasure of violent physical attraction and shimmering sexual chemistry moving to a conclusion which is the most deeply satisfying I have ever experienced. We have all the time in the world for deep slow kisses and an erotic pas de deux of synchronized movement; Jason Knight is the lover that the Pointer Sisters sang about, the man with the slow hand, and I respond like an over-indulged cat, stretching and purring as he explores every inch of my body with hands and lips and tongue and, later, champagne slowly drizzled onto my belly and strawberries eaten off my throat. And through it all runs the golden thread of laughter and the security of a deep and natural intimacy that makes this lovemaking the most wonderful thing in the world. Later, when he goes and I lie lost in a golden dream of remembered pleasure, I think that this is love as I have never known it, the total absorption of one being into another, the truest and most magical experience of my lifetime.

And this is how it continues; we have four evenings of intimacy that are scorchingly sensual punctuated by periods of relaxation when we lie spread out, idly exploring each other's bodies with a lazy fingertip, and talking ... talking as if we have so much time to make up for. I learn and share so much in those precious minutes, as the bright glare of the afternoon falls into the sudden deep hush of evening as, in this desert city there is no twilight, no gloaming, just a sudden descent from light to darkness. The shadow of the trees creeps along the wall as we whisper and giggle and I learn about the life of this man who has come strangely into my life and who, already, I adore. He is 38 years old and has been married for seven years. He has not had an affair before. He married, as the old adage goes, in haste and now repents at leisure. His wife, Katie, is three years older than him and always said she never wanted children, an attitude which at the time, curiously, appealed to him. In the way of soft-hearted and naïve men who never really understand the devious machinations of women, she then went on to have their son, Jack, whom Jason adores, and he now sees what she probably had in mind all the time – that she now holds the trump card and, if he wants to keep Jack, he can never leave her. He expresses a curious kind of old-fashioned respect for Katie as a strong personality and the mother of his child, but several things are clear to my alert senses. He fears her and she dominates him. Jason Knight is the original hen-pecked husband and, in the interests of a quiet life and his inbuilt distaste for violent confrontation, he puts up with it. I can hear, in his quietly shared confidences as he lies facing me and I explore the smooth planes of his face, echoes of an obsessive and jealous woman. He knows he made a bad choice of marriage partner but, fatalistically, he accepts it. He has made his bed and he deserves to lie in it. And he has Jack and it is Jack who makes it all worthwhile.

I don't think I have ever been this happy. My feelings are impossible to analyse except that I am deeply fulfilled in every fibre, and rise every morning like the sun, full of a shimmering lightness of being. I hum with energy; my writing flows and I turn out several articles which are the best I have ever done. I am full of creativity and joy. I bubble like a brook and sing like a lark. I am ridiculously, foolishly and childishly in love and I would take the world to my bosom if I could. I scribble poetry in my spare time; I warble love songs and all my thoughts have just one focus – Jason Knight. Three days into my wonderful honeymoon, I go over to see Natasha. It is early afternoon and I leave the office because I am so far ahead of myself I have nothing left to do. Jason is not due until 6pm and it is only 3 o'clock. Natasha's curtains are open so I assume she is up and float over to see her.

She is in the garden, stretched out in the swing hammock, reading. A skein of smoke floats upwards, and she is clearly in relaxed mode, long legs stretched out and golden hair falling over the back of the swing. I come up beside her and kiss her cheek before she's even aware that I am there; then I fall into the chair facing her and beam at her. She looks at me and laughs out loud at my face.

'Have you any idea how foolish you look Sophie?' she says fondly.

I continue to beam. 'I know it,' I reply happily, 'but I'm in love with the world and I can't help myself!'

She shifts her weight over and lies facing me. 'Tell me,' she commands.

And I do. I tell her everything. I tell her that Jason Knight is the most wonderful lover in the world, passionate and inventive and controlled; and that our lovemaking sessions are beyond anything I've ever experienced where we draw so close to the moment and then flirt with it and draw away again, expanding sensation like ripples in a pool, so that when orgasm comes it is like exploding novae and orchestras and everything that the poets say that I never believed. I tell her that he makes me feel like the luckiest woman in the world, that I have never been so happy and that I am totally, deeply, ecstatically in love with him. And throughout the whole recitation her face grows more and more serious and finally, she stubs out her cigarette and looks at me with a frown.

'Oh Sophie, Sophie,' she says gently. 'You mustn't fall in love. He will break your heart.'

'Too late,' I say wistfully, 'I already have. And Natasha, I wanted to. I always dreamed of a lover like this and now I've found him and he's perfect.'

'Kester Woodseaves,' she murmurs.

'Yes,' I say happily, 'the storybook hero come to life and come to rescue me.'

She shakes her head and lights another cigarette while I lapse into reverie. 'What are you thinking of?' she demands, seeing my abstracted expression, and I giggle as I tell her, 'Jason says I have pale rose nipples. He says women with huge plum-coloured nipples freak him out …'

'Oh God,' she says with a laugh. 'I can see there's no use in expecting you to talk any sense. Sophie, what can I say … and why am I laughing? You are up to your neck in trouble.'

159

'No, no,' I say earnestly. 'I know it won't last forever, but at least I have what I want and it's even more perfect than I imagined. Natasha ...' I pause, because even now I'm not comfortable with asking her personal questions. 'Have you ever been in love like this? I hope so, because it's the most wonderful feeling in the world and every woman should know it at least once in their lives.'

She laughs shortly. 'As I've told you before, Sophie, I am not like you. I am a realist. I don't deal in soppy emotion; I am a business woman and I guard my emotions very carefully.'

'My kids used to call me Soppy Soapy,' I admit smiling. 'I am a creature of emotion, it's true. But you, my dearest friend, have you really never felt a special connection with someone?'

She exhales slowly and the smoke skeins into the golden air. 'My heart has never ruled my head,' she says softly, 'but, since you insist, once long ago I did meet someone who I think might have been special. It was on my journey to the West; I had no money but I needed a train ticket. I saw a man sitting at the station and I went up to him and asked him if he would buy me a ticket for Warsaw. He was young and smartly-dressed, a businessman. Why did I approach him? I have no idea. Perhaps it was like Prue Sarn says, that souls can be drawn to each other. Anyway, he asked no questions, asked nothing of me, just bought me a ticket and we talked through the night all the way to Warsaw. He was kind to me; he was married but offered me a hotel room for as many nights as I needed, no strings attached. I stayed there a week; one night I asked him to come back with me and he did and ...' she pauses, 'it was special, and for me too because he had asked nothing of me and I gave myself because I wanted to. He was such a one as your Mr Knight I think. Once, in a children's book, I read a rhyme about a child who is born on a Friday, and is "loving and giving" and I thought of him. He did not need a reason to be so, it was in his nature.'

I drink all this in. 'I'm so glad,' I say softly.

She pulls herself up sharply. 'Enough, Sophie, you are making me maudlin.'

'No,' I say dreamily, 'but you can appreciate what Shakespeare says, *for thy sweet love remembered such wealth brings/that then I scorn to change my state with kings.'*

She looks at me with a frown. 'Stop it,' she says, 'you are hopeless.' She stubs out the cigarette and asks, 'Is he coming tonight?'

'Yes,' I say, getting up. 'And it's our last night together because tomorrow the bunny boiler comes back.'

She cocks an eyebrow at me and asks, very seriously, but with the light of laughter at the back of her eyes. 'Would you like some advice on how to make it special? From an expert that is ...'

I look sharply at her but then see that she is laughing. 'No thank you!' I say with dignity. 'Boring old Sophie is managing just fine. I told you. We're *en rapport ...'*

She picks up her book. 'Well, remember variety is the spice of life. Have fun.'

I wander back home with a slightly strange feeling plucking at my heart. What will happen after tonight? The controlling Katie will return and Jason will be back on the short leash. I've been so immersed in my happiness that I haven't stopped to think what will happen when the four magical nights come to an end. I've been so lost in my sensual dream that I've forgotten that this is, essentially, an affair with a married man and is, under the laws of the country in which we live, forbidden. First the pleasure, then the pain.

Later, when I am lying in Jason's arms, satiated and replete with lovemaking, our bodies slick with oil and sweat and intertwined like mating pythons, I ask him when I will see him again. I hate myself for spoiling the moment but I must know. He doesn't say anything but I feel a little resistance creeping into his muscles, a little withdrawing as it were when I broach the subject. 'I don't know,' he says softly into the darkness. 'It won't be easy to get away and we can't have this ...' he kisses me softly, 'for a while.'

'I see,' I say, trying to keep it light.

He holds me closer. 'I wish it could be like this for ever,' he says and, as always, I believe him. Used as I am to a man who can spin words, still I always feel Jason is genuine. There's an honesty in him that makes me believe what he says.

I kiss him deeply and snuggle in closer. 'I'll settle for whatever you can give,' I say submissively. 'I love you but I understand the situation.' I may not consciously be trying to be completely the opposite of the control freak he lives with, but I also realise that this relationship has to be all on his terms. Like it or not.

'I've thought about you ever since we first met,' he says obliquely. 'And now I'll think about you every night ... and your gorgeous bum and amazing tits.' He strokes the parts of my body in question and says, meditatively, 'You've given me back my sanity I think. I was beginning to feel pretty down, depressed really, like I couldn't see the way out of the black hole I felt I was in. But these four nights have been amazing ... I didn't think I could still do half of the things we've done.'

Giggling, I say 'Yes, it's been pretty much wall to wall orgasms!'

He laughs. 'And fun ... I haven't had fun like this for years. I've forgotten what it was like to laugh I think, to share laughter like we do. Just to be with you has been ... amazing, rejuvenating.'

'You are my dream lover,' I say, and go on to tell him about Kester Woodseaves. He listens, lying back on his pillows in the half-darkness. I have this lovely feeling that I can *share* things with him; silly things, insignificant nonsense, the kind of light-hearted meaningless banter between lovers that I could never say to Rick. Now he listens as I prattle on and although he's laughing it's not at me. He flicks back a piece of hair; 'I love it when you're serious,' he says fondly. 'You look so earnest and intense. You'd make a good teacher.'

When he goes, in spite of my good intentions, it's hard not to cry. I cling to him for a last kiss at the door and he whispers, 'I won't forget to ring you and I'll come over when I can, but I can't promise anything. But I'll be thinking of you all the time. You're truly the best thing that ever happened to me.'

And with that I have to be content, and his words pretty much set the scene for the next months. He exists like a glorious and unexpected present which may, at any moment, arrive on my doorstep. He sends me brief text messages, full of innuendo to make me giggle, and shimmering with a transparent longing. But there are always the unspoken rules and I abide by them because I know that underneath that teddy-bear exterior, Jason Knight has one focus, his son, and he will never allow anyone to threaten that relationship. He may love me – and I have no doubt that he does – but probably only as much as he would love any woman who gives him what I do and, while Katie Knight holds him hostage, there is no chance of our relationship becoming anything other than it is.

Along with the pleasure, the nights in white satin and the stolen afternoons, there is a high price to be paid for loving a married man. Natasha knew it but, although I may weep with frustration and longing in the darkness of my room, I am not foolish enough to try for anything more. Sophie is learning caution and I never ask for more than I have, though there are times when I start to feel I deserve more and feel anger towards him because he treats me as a convenience. I want the things that lovers give such as flowers and perfume; I want to go out and buy him things, to lavish money on him to show him how much he means to me, to dine with him in a dimly-lit restaurant enjoying the presence of each other and heightening sensation and expectation with touching and kisses. But I can't. He could never wear anything I buy him; never use it without explaining its provenance. Sophie is learning discretion and how to live with the harshness of reality. And the short leash he spoke of is more of a choke chain. She checks his phone and his emails when she can and is constantly suspicious. Even at school parties she stays close to him and gives him hell on the way home if she thought he smiled more at one than another. Over the years his best friends have gradually been pruned away, as have the football dinners, the lads' nights out, a few beers with good mates. Only a minimum of social interaction remains and it is monitored closely. As we spend more time together, though, and I hear more about Katie Knight, I suppose it's no different from many men or women who find themselves in an abusive relationship and stay 'for the children' but it makes me hate her because I see her controlling a passive and loving man through fear and threat. He doesn't say much about her but one can glean it through small details or comments.

One time he asks me about Rick; I pour out the story readily enough but am shocked to find how little I feel it now; there is no pain in the retelling of it, rather a surprise that I haven't thought of Rick in months. Now I have the house and he is not required to pay anything to maintain me, he has disappeared almost entirely from my life and, immersed as I am in Jason, I have not bothered to pursue him. I have, of course, my own brand of psychological evaluation of Rick, which I share with Jason; he does not respond directly but says, 'Katie's father left her and her mother when she was a teenager. That's one of the reasons she's so obsessed with her fear of me cheating.'

I have a fleeting moment of sympathy and think of Tasha. 'That's tough. Girls have such a special relationship with their father that it probably hit her really hard.'

'She has so much anger, still, about it,' he says pensively. 'Sometimes I think she's transferred most of it to me.'

'That's entirely possible. He hurt her and she thinks you will do the same thing. You're a man after all.' I love playing psychologist and think I do it rather well.

We've been swimming naked in the pool in the dark (Katie's mother is in town and has been taken out to dinner and a show; Jason is ostensibly at football training) and now we're sitting on the wide shallow step, sipping cold drinks and fondling each other in the warm darkness. My pool is, most conveniently, surrounded by a thick hedge of bougainvillea, and is not overlooked by any of my neighbours. The water is warm with just a hint of chill in the depths and the night air is close and full of scent.

'She's so aggressive,' he continues softly. 'We had a dinner party a few weeks ago and she was pretty tense about all of it. I did the drinks and set the table and even offered to cook, but then I got a tirade about how dare I insult her cooking!' He takes the fallen bougainvillea blooms from the water and puts them in my hair, giving me a crown of flowers. 'Then all through the meal there was this undercurrent; she argued violently with me over one thing after another and I could sense the guests shifting in their seats with embarrassment. It was awful.'

There's nothing much I can say except softly kiss his fingers as he puts another fallen petal behind my ear.

'But it's when she's so aggressive with Jack that I really go to pieces,' he continues, 'she hits him, smacks him for the least little thing and, if I interfere, there's a full scale screaming row and he goes to ground, poor little bugger, under his bed.'

I am full of sympathy but don't know how to show it. I sense, however, that just being able to tell it is a relief. There aren't too many people he can open up to; similar to me really. We have each other's deepest confidences.

'And then she's angry with him for not loving her best,' he goes on. 'He always comes to me first if there's a choice and that upsets her. She doesn't realise how afraid she's made him.'

'That's both of you then,' I say softly.

He flicks me a look as he adds another blossom to my head-dress. 'I am afraid of her,' he admits, 'if she ever found out about you and me, she'd take Jack back to England and make damn sure I'd hardly ever see him. And she'd enjoy doing it.'

It's hard not to be persuaded by this picture of a deeply disturbed and unhappy woman. How sad, I think, to be so lucky as to have such a gentle and good-looking husband, a beautiful child, and to be so full of jealousy, anger and fear so as not to enjoy her blessings. But then I look at Jason's beloved face, lit by the soft light of the twinkling water, and I know that if I was ever able to have him I would cherish and love him; the fact that she doesn't makes me sad and angry with a dull ache.

'But surely,' I say, flicking water at Puss who has wandered out to see where his dinner is, 'you would not lose him. A court might well grant you custody if you could prove she is a bad mother.'

'Courts in England aren't very fair to fathers,' he says pensively, 'even if I could prove it, which I can't.'

'I don't see why not. She's an emotional bully – that's provable.'

'How?' he asks simply. 'It's just my word against hers.'

'It's against the law to hit your child, though.'

'But the only person who sees her do it is me and possibly her family. We don't see my parents very much and her mother isn't going to admit her daughter is an abusive parent. With other people she's pretty careful; she goes for overkill, fussing and spoiling him. Maybe they're convinced. But it's when she's unbalanced that I really get worried. You know she pulled a knife on me the other day?'

I gawp at him, one of the blossoms falling out of my wet hair and floating away on the water. 'What?'

'We were having a row in the kitchen, over nothing really; she was upset about school and I said something that she took as a criticism. Next minute she grabbed a knife from the bench and slashed at me with it. I didn't half jump!'

'Oh my God ...' I reach out and cuddle him close as if I can keep him safe.

'I just worry that one day she'll do something to Jack ... when she loses her head she goes absolutely berserk.'

I really don't know what to say. He makes these terrible statements so calmly but there's a wrinkle in that placid brow.

Next minute his phone, balanced nearby on a chair, starts ringing, startling us both. He leaps up immediately; even I jump and my heart starts racing because I know who it is. He doesn't answer it, of course, but the spell is broken and he's out of the pool and towelling himself while the phone continues to shriek and wobble. 'It's a bit like her, really,' I say on a laugh, albeit shakily, 'quite hysterical.' He's into his shorts and T-shirt in the blink of an eye, and would, I think, be out the door but he remembers me and comes over to kiss me briefly. 'Sorry, you know I have to go.'

'Of course,' I'm used to this now, but it never stops hurting that he goes from me to her almost without a backward glance and the power she has over him is evidenced in the panic with which is out of the pool and into his clothes like the guiltiest of husbands. 'Come again, handsome!' I say, determined to keep it light, even though when I hear his engine start and the car gun off down the road, I weep as I pull the petals out of my hair. I hate that phone and I hate Katie Knight. I hate the way that she breaks my dream and I hate her power. It makes me feel as if I am nothing and I have some work to convince myself that he loves me, needs me and will come again as soon as he is able. Sometimes the way that this relationship is all on his terms gnaws at me and makes me angry that I allow myself to be treated as second best. Then I remember that I have a choice: to play by the rules or to have nothing at all. And the thought of giving him up, of doing without him, of missing out on that amazing sex, is so daunting that it sets me back on the rails. Put up or shut up.

Following our exercise class the next evening, Natasha and I come back home and I fix us drinks in the garden. She listens to the latest instalment of Jason's life with a slight frown; 'So the bunny boiler is also a knife slasher. Be careful my Sophie; if she finds out about you I fear she will come and cut your ears off.' She wrinkles her nose delicately, and says, 'I hate crazy women.'

I stretch languidly and try to sound objective. 'Well she's certainly barking and I'm afraid he'll never be free of her. She has him by the balls, no doubt about that.'

Natasha laughs. 'I'm sorry, Sophie, because you love him, but really I cannot admire such a weak man.'

'It's in his nature,' I say excusingly, 'he's just a very gentle quiet type who loathes confrontations. But his caution does sometimes irritate me, I have to admit. You know, he never says my name ... even in bed, he never calls me Sophie. He never calls me anything, actually, not 'darling' or 'sweetheart' and certainly never by my name. Why do you suppose that is?'

She slants me a look. 'Ah,' she says, sipping her drink, 'a cautious man indeed. If he never says your name he can deny you exist, but more than that, he will never blunder into saying it to the bunny boiler. He will never say it because it is as if he doesn't know it.'

Curiously, this makes me feel like crying; names are, after all, who we are, the very essence of our personality and character. To have Jason deny me that, is to be faced with the knowledge of how peripheral I am to his life. He may love what we have but, by not naming me, he maintains the fiction that he is an honest husband. Natasha can see by my face, always transparent, how this is affecting me and she reaches over to touch my hand. 'This is why women are so superior,' she says softly, 'we can compartmentalise emotions. You could be with Jason one afternoon and with Rick the next and you would never confuse their names!'

'You make our sex sound like natural deceivers,' I say crossly.

'No, just more intelligent,' she says calmly. 'We can perform the feat of *legerdemain* with such flair! Sleight of hand,' she translates, seeing my ignorance.

My birthday, and curiously, Jason's also, is now approaching; separated by only a week, and a few years. I am not allowing myself to get too excited over it because I am aware that buying anything for me represents a special challenge as his credit card statements are gone through with a fine toothcomb by the witch indoors. I don't ever know when I will see him next, so I content myself with buying a humorous card and not hoping too much for anything, in the consoling belief that any outcome will be more than I expect. Natasha thinks we should eat at hers; she seldom goes out to the any of the city's excellent eateries, and Rosie is a wonderful cook, so to stay in is no hardship. Alexei is full of excitement and is clearly making something for me as there is a lot of flapping and laughter if I go over there unexpectedly.

I decide to give myself a birthday present, partly because it's been almost a year now since Rick left, and also because I'm desperate to have some resolution on at least one of the fronts in my life, I ring Rick and tell him I want to meet to discuss a divorce. It's quite amusing to hear the shock in his voice; he had me pegged as quietly contented and now, suddenly, here I am demanding closure. We meet at a discreetly-lit restaurant and I derive much amusement from watching my husband try and wriggle out of what, to him, represents a serious deviation from The Plan. My point is clearly made, however; we have now, to all intents and purposes, reached a point of 'irreconcilable differences' to quote the divorce attorneys. I see no point in trying to pretend otherwise, not even to humour him. I want out. I don't want money and I know there's not much of that anyway; in fact Rick represents a poor investment to me in terms of capital growth. I am not really sure what I got out of this marriage other than two wonderful children. He tries, desperately, to point out that he is happy to regard himself as separated from me; we don't need a Decree Absolute to confirm it. It's true that there is really no common property, as such; if I look at it in the cold hard light of day I have very little to my name but while I continue to live in Dubai I have all I need. Although I'm kidding myself that this desire for freedom has anything to do with my relationship with Jason, it is also true that I want to be free of Rick. It's funny, though, that he is not so keen to be free of me and then I suddenly see it; if Rick is a free man he would be able to marry Ophelia and maybe, just maybe, he doesn't want to or he doesn't want to be in a position where he could. His own nefarious purposes could be served by having a whining, demanding, estranged wife. But I'm tired of doing things to humour Rick. The magazine can sponsor me so I am no longer dependent on him for that; it is the practice that most husbands' employers sponsor the family's stay in Dubai but the magazine can sponsor me in my own right, as Sophie Haddon, journalist.

I leave Rick with lots to think about and tell him I want a resolution by Christmas. He is so surprised by sober passive Sophie suddenly turning into a Rottweiler that when I get up to leave he doesn't say a word. Walking out on him gives me a real buzz of joyous independence. I am no longer a trailing spouse but an independent woman and a divorce would be one hell of a birthday present. There's a little thought flicking away at me that perhaps if I am free Jason might be persuaded to leave Katie, but I crush it severely. I have enough rational sense to know that he will stay for Jack, no matter what, and I also recognise that for a gentle passive personality such as Jason, to leave a woman like her with all the associated traumas and drama would require an endurance and determination that I fear he does not possess. I think to myself, with a sardonic laugh, that all he can hope for is that one day she dies and makes him free. In the way of daydreaming I imagine how lovely it would be if he were mine and how much I would love him and spoil him. Perhaps this is the first time I think of her dying but only in the way that one might hope for something impossible, like winning the lottery. I imagine her as unbalanced and perhaps suicidal; I wonder, with a secret smile, what she would actually do if she found out about us and then the cold finger of fear pierces my heart as I imagine her turning on Jason with a knife and plunging it into his heart. *God, no*, I think with a shudder … and turn my thoughts away from it quickly. The status quo must remain for the time being. Beyond that I may dream, but I am perhaps more conscious of his obsessive security and forgive him for all the times he goes from me to her without a backward glance. He knows her best, after all, and what she is capable of.

My birthday is a week after Jason's and, although I send him a text and birthday wishes, I get only a quick line in return. The funny card sits unopened on the bench and he doesn't come. Then, the night before my birthday, there's a knock on the door and he's standing there with a bouquet of roses from the local supermarket and gives me the quickest quickie that ever was on the living room sofa. I am grateful, of course, but a little tearful too. To have the occasion acknowledged, but in a rather desperate way; is almost an apology, and there is the feeling that he is there because he has to be, because even he could not fail to see how hurt I would be if there were no visit at all. Natasha and Rosie do the celebrations in far greater style the following evening; the table is laid with pale linen and cut glass and my presents piled up by my plate. Earrings from Natasha, twinkling in their Tiffany box, a silk scarf from Rosie in my favourite colours of apricot and turquoise, and from Alexei and Hector a framed photograph of both, the frame decorated with tiny leaping dogs which Alexei has formed and painted himself. Rosie's salmon curry melts in the mouth, there is an exquisite chocolate cake to follow and a phone call from Nick and Tasha complete the happiness of my day. From Rick there is nothing at all, but to be honest I hardly notice the omission; I feel so loved and valued by the really important people in my life.

The year now begins its descent to Christmas and, curiously in a Muslim country, the shops are full of great bows and boxes wrapped in purple and red and there is a huge fake fir tree in the Mall, sparkling and decorated to within an inch of its life. The weather is cooler in the mornings and evenings, but the afternoons are as hot and blue as ever. Jason is to go skiing and grins with appreciation when I opine that Katie Knight deserves to be caught in an avalanche. For the rest of us non-teaching people, however, work goes on the same as ever with only Christmas Day itself off. Wayne is hosting his usual drunk and hilarious Christmas do which is worth going to just for the food as Bertie's cousin, a caterer, goes all out on the full Christmas dinner producing the tenderest of turkey and the yummiest of puddings, and the champagne flows like water and guarantees us all staggering headaches the following day. My Christmas present from Jason is perfume and I have bought him a rather stunning silk tie which he hopes he can smuggle under the tree and pass off as a gift from a favourite aunt. My big present, as it were, is a two-day visit from my son and heir, passing through Dubai on his way to a hike in Nepal. We fall into each other's arms at the airport, and talk frantically for two days and most of the nights; he says I look wonderful and, although I don't tell him about Jason, I admit to having a new man in my life and he says it clearly agrees with me. Rick doesn't ring or come round at all. Nick doesn't seem to care in the least ('we've got nothing to say to each other, mum'), but I am angry that he ignores his only son. But there is not much time, after all, and soon Nick is gone and the house seems empty once more. Natasha gives me a solid gold filigree heart-shaped locket for Christmas and says I should put a photo of Jason in it; instead I put a photograph of her and me facing each other across the hinge. BFF, Best Friends Forever, I tell her, and can see from her unusually soft smile that she is truly touched.

Work keeps me busy and I am writing and interviewing apace. There are a few celebrities in town and the Princess cannot interview them all; it's my least favourite occupation chatting to tinsel town babes and singers, but it's my bread and butter after all and the images dominate the text anyway. I do a big spread on the gold souks, old and new, which Shazza helps me with, and it's a well-researched piece which continues over two months and details the history of the gem trade in the Emirate. One of the smaller Indian dealers turns out to be the cousin of Mr Patel, the pet shop owner, in the perhaps not so curious way that many Indians are related in Dubai. He is just as charming as his cousin and I waste far too much time in the back of the shop sipping chai and listening to stories of the old days. He persuades me to buy a Sri Lankan sapphire too, a stone of amazing blue depths, and he promises to set it for me 'most superbly'. I look at my old engagement ring, the one that belonged to my mother, and agree. After all, it's a wonderful bargain and it will be my freedom ring. The solitaire diamond that Rick gave me has, I notice, departed with him. At least, the box has gone and I know that no one else would have taken it. I never liked it anyway, so it's no loss, but the diamonds in my mother's old ring do look small and tired and the setting old-fashioned. But it's a part of her and I love to wear it. I can simply move it to another finger. I haven't, of course, heard anything about my impending divorce and can guess that Rick has not had the promised legal interview. I send him a few messages reminding him that I'm expecting to be signing papers in the New Year, but hear nothing back. *Gone to ground*, I think savagely, but apart from the actual pleasure of being a divorced woman and free of him, there is no real reason why the whole process cannot wait a bit longer.

The New Year comes in and with it the best time to be living in the Emirate. There is a little rain, occasionally, and some cloud; the temperatures are delightful without the breath-taking heat of summer. Katie Knight is to take a party of primary school children up a wadi for two nights on some Desert Adventure and it means that Jason will be free to spend two nights in his mistress's arms. It is moments like these that I live for, when I have him all to myself and can pretend, for 48 hours, that he is mine. This time the nights fall over the weekend and, best of all, Jack is invited on a sleepover and dhow cruise for some small person's birthday and Jason can plan his own sleepover.

On the Friday morning we wake late, drink tea and make love in bed till midday, then cook a late lunch in the kitchen before retiring to the sofa with a soft porn movie which is constantly interrupted by a few soft porn moves of our own. In the late afternoon, however, things go horribly awry. Out of the blue, dropped into the conversation as it is, comes the news that Jason is applying for jobs in other international schools. It is not his idea; he is content where he is, likes the school, the people, his employment package and the quality of education that Jack is receiving. Katie, however, is not happy, and when Katie is not happy, things start to happen. Jason is chivvied and harassed until he begins sending out his CV and scanning the pages of the Times Educational Supplement to see which international schools might want a geographer and a primary school teacher. International schools tend to employ teacher couples; it's cheaper and easier for them, one house instead of two and probably more employee security. It is clear he's anxious; indeed, I think he lets it slip inadvertently, and then has to try and talk himself out of the blunder while my face gets longer and longer. I try not to wail, but it comes out like a child denied a stick of candy. 'But I can't let you go! What will happen to us if you leave Dubai?' He holds me tight and murmurs soothingly that it's very unlikely he'll find a job or a venue that will suit both him and Katie. But I refuse to be placated and struggle free of his grip.

'Why don't you leave yourself out of that equation?' I snap. 'If Katie wants it, I'm assuming Katie will get it!'

As always, at the mention of his wife, his face closes and he starts to withdraw and I understand well enough. He won't discuss her with me or, rather, he won't listen to me criticise his compliant attitude and complete inability to express his own wishes over those of his wife. But suddenly I have had enough; all my dislike of Katie Knight and her dominance comes out in a rush and I am determined that this is one time he will hear me out.

'Jason, for once let's face facts shall we? I love you but it doesn't blind me to the fact that you are weak and compliant when it comes to pleasing your wife; in fact you are absolutely terrified of her. I understand that well enough, and I forgive you, but this is *us* we're talking about here. You and I, and what we have and what we share. And suddenly, our relationship is in danger because she wants a change of scenery? No! You must fight it. You can't let this happen! You can't just walk away from me … you can't!'

And suddenly, in a striking contrast to my usual calm behaviour, I am in tears. Jason acts as awkwardly as any man confronted with a weeping female; he hands out tissues and is awkward and embarrassed. He looks as if he would like to flee the scene of the crime but can't. I try not to sob, but I am truly gutted by his supposed indifference to what could be, effectively, the end of this love affair. I love him, I believe in him, but now I can only hear Natasha's warning words 'used' and 'discarded' and remember my own dismissal of them, my firm belief that my gentle teddy-bear lover would never ever treat me that way. I feel like shaking him, demanding that he promise that he will never leave me. Suddenly all the losses of the last few years coalesce into a storm of near-hysteria and I demand, quaveringly, 'Don't I mean anything to you at all?'

I expect to be pulled into his arms and kissed and soothed but he doesn't. He looks awkward, shaken even by the depth of passion in my voice; without answering my question he says, almost sulkily, 'I don't do tears.'

In a minute I have gone from shock and betrayal to blazing anger. 'You don't do tears?' I almost scream at him, 'what the hell do you mean, *you don't do tears?* Have you any idea how many tears I've cried over you? All those times when you had to rush away, those times when you abandoned me without a backward glance? Whenever the phone rang, whenever *she* wanted you home? How *dare* you tell me *you* don't do tears!'

He is pale now and his mouth is set hard; I can see how this is upsetting him but for once I am impervious to his unhappiness. I feel the awful bubbling up of hysteria; I want to start screaming, or throwing something, or slapping him to make him see sense, to make him see how this is hurting me, tearing my heart out; all the anger and frustration created by all the times I have been delegated second best boiling up inside me. But something holds me back; something redirects my anger into saying, probably, the one thing that reminds him that I am not Katie Knight. 'Please,' I say pathetically, my voice breaking and tears streaming down my face, 'please don't leave me. I don't think I can bear it if you do.'

He looks up then and reaches to pull me into his arms. 'It's all right,' he says gently, into my hair. 'Nothing will happen. I won't leave you.'

I put my arms round his neck and sob on his chest; after a few minutes he grasps my arms and moves me away from him, handing me another tissue. 'Stop it now,' he says gently, with a smile. 'There's no reason to cry. Nothing's happened yet.'

I stare at him, almost willing him to say the words I want to hear but he doesn't. Instead, he reaches out to pour me a glass of wine and put it into my hand. 'Come on,' he says as to a child. 'Smile for me.'

I give him a watery smile and sip the wine but his eyes are guarded; he flicks an eye towards the clock and I know only too well what this means. He wants to go and sure enough, 'I should be going,' he says, 'Jack will be getting back from his sleep-over and I promised I'd cook him dinner. Something special. We love our boys' nights in,' he says appealingly, trying to win over my maternal heart, no doubt.

'Always Jack,' I say, and the words have a raw edge. 'Never me.'

He's already dressed and putting on his shoes and his scarcely-concealed desire to be gone grates at me. 'That's not fair,' he says now, 'I always made it clear that Jack comes first. Everything I do is for him. That's the reason I stay with her. You know that. I never promised you anything else.'

I pull my dress over my head. There seems to be something almost indecent in having this conversation naked. 'No,' I say, and even I can hear the bitterness in my voice. 'You never did. You never promised me anything at all. It was me who did all the imagining.'

'Sophie,' he says gently. 'I do love you but I love him more and I won't ever leave him. And she comes as part of the package. You – we – always knew this wouldn't last forever.'

'So I should thank you for giving me the bits that no one else wanted?'

He's genuinely upset at my distress, but he has absolutely no idea at the depths of my despair or, moreover, the self-anger at my own idiocy. In the face of all the warnings, in the knowledge of my own soft heart and deep desire to be loved and wanted, I have fallen into the oldest trap of all. I assumed that, because I loved Jason Knight with all of my being, he felt the same way about me; I presupposed love and commitment because I believed he was the flip side of my own psyche. *First the pleasure, then the pain ....*

'I have to go ...' he says again.

'Yes, please do,' I say crisply, sipping at my wine. 'I don't think we have anything more to say to each other.'

He looks at me for a moment then goes upstairs to collect his things. I sit, frozen, on the sofa, my finger running around the edge of the wine glass and making the crystal sing, its shrillness exactly echoing the state of my own nerves. I hear his footsteps; he puts his backpack near the door, and comes over to me, sitting down close and giving me his best dimpled smile. I look into those soft blue eyes, but with a difference because now I'm looking for something I've never looked for before, the ability to deceive. Jason reaches out and, with his thumb, erases the frown line between my brows.

'Do you forgive me?' he says softly.

I know my own eyes are cold. 'What for?' I ask and my voice is as brittle as the twanging crystal. 'For making me fall in love with you? For thinking that you could just walk out and no one would be hurt? For choosing her over me? Which of these should I forgive you for?'

'I'm sorry,' he says, 'that I've upset you. But, if you think about it, you'll realise I always told you it was Jack and that nothing, or no one, would ever change that. You're a mother, you must understand.'

He has got me there, of course, but I counter-attack. 'But you've never investigated whether you could have both Jack and me ... you'll never challenge her ... a court may award you custody, it's just that you'll never try!' Somewhere in my mind, I hear my daughter's voice: *'You're such a fucking doormat Mummy!'* And that's it, of course, what's really eating me is his passivity, his refusal to fight for the woman he loves. Unless he doesn't.

'Look,' he says now. 'This may yet all turn out to be immaterial. I may not be going anywhere.'

'Oh, of course. And we can just continue as we are until … what? The next time Katie decides she wants to leave? No, I'm sorry …' I'm aware of words coming out of my mouth, while my brain tries desperately to rationalise what I want. 'I think you've given away much more than you meant to this afternoon. I think you've told me very clearly that I *am* second best and I will never be any more than that. I will never be with you because you refuse to change the status quo.'

He looks pale and says quietly, 'So you're saying you don't want to see me again?'

God in Heaven, stop! What am I saying? Am I saying that? But my mouth continues to speak and my brain is so occupied with misery that it can't seem to make any contributory evaluation.

'What's the point?' I snap. 'You've told me quite clearly that this relationship has no future. So what are we wasting our time for?'

'We never had a future, Sophie,' he says quietly. 'I told you that right at the beginning. I thought you were content to be with me on those terms.'

Oh God, oh God! 'I was,' I say miserably. 'But now I want more. I love you Jason, and I want you to be with me. I want for us to be together. '

His blue eyes are very soft and gentle but with resolution in the depths. 'I'm sorry, I can't promise you that … not yet anyway.'

'But if you could?'

'Look,' he says gently, 'I can't make any promises. I'm not free to. If things were different … I would have left her years ago, and yes, if it helps, I would leave her for you. But I can't leave Jack. And I won't.'

'And you won't fight her for him? For me?'

'No,' he says, 'I won't jeopardise his happiness. You know how afraid I've been that she'd find out about us ... you know how unstable she is. I couldn't leave him with her; I don't trust her. If you think about it, you'll know I'm right. He's a child, he's my son, and I must look after him. I made the mistake; I married the wrong woman. But I won't let Jack pay the price.'

That's undeniable and, in a way, I honour him for it. He's doing the right thing even if the right thing is the hardest thing.

He draws me into his arms and I go willingly enough and relax against him. 'You are my beautiful lady,' he says gently. 'And I do love you. Think about what I've said and ... if you think you can't bear it, I won't come back. I'll understand.'

I feel tears welling up but try not to cry. 'Ok,' I murmur into his chest. 'I'll think about it.'

A last kiss, a last clinging of the lips, and he rises to go. My weekend in Paradise is finished, ruined yet again by the serpent in the Garden ... that snake of a woman I loathe and detest.

I do think about what he's said, though, and at bottom, I have to admit that it's true that he has made me no promises. The imagining has indeed been all on my part. Well, who could be surprised at that? I can imagine Rick roaring with laughter: *Oh Sophie! Face it, darling, you were a fuck buddy ... it's called lust, sweetie, not love...'* I think of my friends like Julia, bonking her banker at lunchtimes or Kirstie's words: '*All the available ass in this town!'* I think of all those light-hearted affairs that are as common as palm trees in this desert city. I told Jason my husband had left me; I virtually seduced him. If he knows Dubai at all, he would have thought it was par for the course; an amusing way for a desperate housewife to pass another afternoon.

I go upstairs slowly, my head pounding, and fall across the bed, sobbing into my pillow and overwhelmed with hopelessness. I know, at bottom, that of course I will go on seeing him, go on loving him and hope for redemption. And when he goes, as one day he will, the pain will be unbearable.

Would it be easier to stop it now? Of course it would. But the thought of not having him, being in the same city and yet not have the hope of seeing him, being with him, making love to him, albeit on his terms, would be impossible. I am not strong enough. The pain will happen, but it does not have to happen yet. I cling to that. After all, it's possible he won't leave.

Sometime later I get up for some water, and later still knock the empty glass off the table onto the floor along with the poetry anthology I had been reading earlier. The book falls open and the poem springs off the page at me.

In a mean abode on the Shankill Road
Lived a man named William Bloat
And he had a wife, the bane of his life
Who continually got his goat
And one day at dawn, with her nightdress on
He slit her bloody throat.

I stare at it and the words shimmer so that I have to say it out clearly, almost to understand what it's telling me, until the image they create swims into my mind and I think, again, how all our problems would be solved if only Katie Knight were dead. And, for the first time, I consciously wish she would die. I wish she would vanish from Jason's life and he and Jack (and I) can live happily.

Then I look at the words again and see a flaw in my neat conclusion. William Bloat may have murdered his wife but Jason Knight will not. She may murder him first. And I realise, with a strange feeling of displacement, that if there is to be any conclusion then I am the one who is going to have to make it. Jason Knight is a good man, a kind and loving father, but there are no circumstances under which he will leave his termagant of a wife. She holds him on an emotional slip-knot, for she knows that he will do anything rather than see that little boy suffer, and hence she holds the winning hand every time. I clench my fist and remember how I thought of myself as Jason Knight's shield maiden; well I am, and I will gird myself up for this fight and use everything in my power not to let that woman win. For the first time in my life I am going to have what I want and not let someone else walk away in triumph, not let Sophie become a victim yet again. I feel a burgeoning sense of resolution. It is not all over yet, not by a long shot. I have no idea of what I'm going to do, but that's immaterial at present. In the ridiculous way that the brain works a phrase leaps into my mind; my old school motto in fact. *Quod potes tenta.* Strive to your utmost. Well, I will.

I do eventually drift off to sleep but have a horrible dream where I am standing in the upstairs hallway of my own house with my hands covered in blood. I look at them in horror before I realise I'm in a play, and Lady Macbeth's words come out of my mouth: *'my hands are of your colour, but I shame to wear a heart so white.'* I awake with a pounding heart and lie in the darkness thinking; could I be a Lady Macbeth, could I actively bring about the death of another being because she stood in my way? Would it not drive one to madness, as it did the Lady? Anyway, I reason, it's an insane and illogical conundrum; Katie Knight is alive and well and living in Dubai. Although I firmly believe that she *deserves* an untimely death because of how unhappy she makes her hen-pecked husband, I cannot see how it will ever occur. Bunny boiler as she is, the thought of ever confronting her makes me go cold. Like Natasha, I hate crazy women. Any loss of complete order and sanity frightens me. I did, years ago, play Lady Macbeth in a school production but I could never kill a living thing. God help me, I couldn't even kill a cockroach; I used to jump shrieking onto chairs and Rick, who enjoyed my hysterics, would catch it and chase me with it. It was Tasha or Nick who used to flatten them. I caught them in jars and put them back in the garden. That's the killer instinct in me. But if I stood to lose Jason Knight, the one person in my life who gives me all the happiness I seek, and possibly deserve... what then? If it was she or I, two women fighting for one man? Would I stand back and let this woman take away my man, and watch him go because he cannot gainsay her? Now that, I do not know. The old Sophie would have stood back and effaced herself because she was a little coward; the new one may not, because the new Sophie has a sense of deserving a life of her choosing, of deserving love, of having sufficient self-esteem to fight for what she loves and to be her own woman, gratifying her own desires. I had told Natasha I was a tigress in defence of those I loved and in a way, it was true. The passive quality that Jason possesses, the quality that makes Natasha call him weak, is the quality that makes me love him most, which contributes to the little-boy-lost charm that wrings my heart. But it also means that I have to be strong for both of us.

The following afternoon I go and see Natasha. She is swinging outside and I pull up a chair. In spite of all my resolutions, I feel the tears well up in my eyes and she raises one perfectly groomed eyebrow as she looks at my woebegone face. 'Is it over?' she says calmly.

I shake my head. 'Not entirely.'

She calls for Rosie to bring tea and tissues and faces me; I see with concern that there is a pale blue bruise on the side of her jaw. 'What happened?' I ask.

'This?' she flicks it with her finger. 'I caught it on the edge of the car door.'

'My bruises are all inside,' I say tearfully. 'He told me that the Bunny Boiler wants to leave Dubai. Apparently she's sick of it, so she's made him apply to other international schools. If he gets a job and a school that she wants, they'll leave Dubai. Forever.'

Natasha lights a cigarette. 'Ah,' she says quietly.

'So we had a row and I accused him of not wanting to fight her for me and he didn't disagree. In fact he made it quite clear that Jack comes first and he and the Bunny Boiler are a job lot. You can't have one without the other.'

Natasha nods without comment. There is a short pause, during which time Rosie appears with tea and tissues and greets me with a smile and a word. When she has gone inside again, I continue.

'Anyway, he said he'd understand if I didn't want to see him again, but as for changing his mind, that's not going to happen. It's emotional blackmail; he won't leave Jack with her because he's afraid of how unstable she is. He seems to think he has to suffer; he won't even look at alternatives. Oh, it's a complete mess.' I stir my tea and mutter, 'I hate that bloody *bloody* wife of his. I wish she were dead.'

Natasha laughs shortly. 'Well this is Dubai. Hire a hit man.'

I grimace. 'If only …. She deserves to die, you know, not just for making a kind man miserable, but for making it impossible for him to be with me. He does love me, you know, he said if it weren't for Jack he would leave her for me, but words are easy to say …. Actions take more guts.'

Natasha reaches over and lights a cigarette. Alexei, presumably, has gathered frangipani into a garland for his mother and it lies, browning slightly round the edges, on the table beside the swing. In the warm air, the scent drifts upward. I pick it up and inhale the sweet perfume.

'It's funny you should say that,' I continue. 'Last night I had a dream I was Lady Macbeth and my hands were covered in blood … you know the play Macbeth?'

She nods, and I comment, 'How is it that you are *so* well read?'

She is in a relaxed mood and answers easily enough. 'In Poland I had a tutor that Babushka paid for to improve my English. He loved literature and he had me read widely and took me out to performances in English. I loved the Shakespeare and yes, I've seen *Macbeth*. Then, here, I had lots of time on my hands at the Palace in the early days, and I read through the library there. And then, you,' she smiles, 'introduced me to 'Precious Bane' and Prue Sarn. So continue, your hands were covered in blood … had you murdered the bunny boiler?'

'Chance'd be a fine thing,' I growl. 'No, but it made me think. You know I believe that Jason Knight is worth fighting for. He may not be prepared to fight for himself, but I am prepared to fight for him. I am *not* going to just stand back and let the Bunny Boiler have him!'

'Uh huh,' she says seriously, 'and what do you propose to do?'

I start trimming the browning frangipani petals in my lap and confess, 'Well you have me there. I don't know. He won't listen to reason about any legal solutions and he certainly won't fight her in a court of law for possession of Jack. He's terrified of confrontation. He stays quiet and hopes something will change. But I feel if he was a bit more proactive, he could get her on some sort of abusive behaviour charge. I've told him to keep a list of what she does, dates, times, and possibly even video evidence but he just looks at me as if I've been watching too many crime shows on TV. And what she does to him is emotional cruelty, no doubt about that.'

'So are you prepared to kill for him?' The question is typically Natasha; straight to the heart of the problem.

'I was asking myself that last night,' I say ruefully, 'and of course, in the cold light of day, I know I can't. I must let Fate take its course. I'm just kidding myself if I think any differently. Although I remember Shazza saying once that because CID is so hopeless in Dubai many murders do go unsolved, unreported and unsolved. I suppose in that way, it's a perfect place to commit a murder. But don't ask me how!'

Natasha muses. 'What if you let her find out about you?'

'Oh no,' I shudder, 'She'd go ballistic. Probably stab them both. And Jason would be furious with me so that would spell the end anyway. And it might precipitate what he fears, that she'd return to England and take Jack with her. Then he'd be stuck back there trying to get custody and tied up in court traumas. And it would be goodbye Sophie.'

She smokes and ponders, the skein of smoke drifting up into the magenta bougainvillea that pours over the wall above her head.

'I've agreed to carry on our affair, though, until he knows if he's going or staying but only because I can't give him up; I love him so much.' I feel my lip start to wobble but go on manfully. 'She organises him and he's sending out CVs and having phone interviews all over the place; the only thing that will save us is if the job is somewhere she doesn't want to be, like Mongolia, or the pay or accommodation isn't up to the present standard. But if he's offered something she likes, they'll go.'

Natasha says mischievously, 'I have to agree with her about Mongolia.'

I flick her a glance. 'My heart is breaking. Be serious.'

'Is he really worth all this heartache my Sophie? Really worth having? Surely there's another man out there, who is not in the thrall of a Bunny Boiler, who can provide all this?'

'No, there isn't,' I say sadly. 'I can't explain … I know you think he's weak and pathetic, but he's not. He's kind and gentle and the most wonderful lover in the world. And … I know you'll scoff at this … but he's doing all of this for the right reasons. He knows he made a mistake but he doesn't want Jack to suffer for it. He's honourable.'

The mobile eyebrow goes up again, and I know what she's thinking.

'Well,' she says, stubbing out the cigarette butt, 'I'm afraid I can't help. I said that you should not fall in love, and you did, and now you believe that this man, who will walk out on you, is honourable and, when he leaves you forever, you will still defend him. There is not much I can say, Sophie.'

'You think I'm stupid,' I mutter.

'Not at all,' she says, 'only indecisive. You know what you must do, so do it. Be your own woman. Fight for what you want.'

'What, by hiring a hit man? Oh, don't be ridiculous.'

'This is a world of winners and losers, Sophie,' she says softly, 'if you don't want her to win, you must not lose.'

The frangipani blossoms are now a heap of sweet-smelling debris in my lap; in my nervous state I've clawed them to bits. We sit in silence and my eye follows a little hoopoe bird as it hobbles its way across the piece of beautifully maintained lawn that joins the swimming pool. I simply don't know what to do. One may talk glibly, but the deed is a different matter; all I can hope for is that he doesn't go away – yet.

I sigh hugely and look at my friend, taking in her restful beauty; the pale golden hair spread out and the turquoise eyes reflective. 'Well, you look brighter,' I comment. 'Am I to understand that things are a little more settled at the Palace? You don't have the haunted look you wear sometimes. Is Alex looking after you?'

'Mmm … yes, there have been changes …' she looks across at me, and then flicks her gaze back to the bougainvillea. 'Alex is a strong man and helpful … we have a good relationship.'

'So you don't feel in danger any more?' I press.

'Oh no, there are still, how do you say, *fires within fires and wheels within wheels* … but, like I say, there are only winners and losers and … I don't intend to be a loser.'

'So you want all the stuff to stay in my safe?'

'Yes, for the time being. Thank you.'

'Good,' I get up to go. 'Is Alexei out?'

She looks round vaguely. 'It seems quiet. Yes, I think he went out with a boy who lives nearby.'

I give her a straight look and she laughs. 'Rosie knows where he is!'

I lean forward to kiss her and she turns her cheek to receive it. 'Do some serious thinking, Sophie,' she says and her eyes look into mine. 'We women have to fight for what we want.'

'I know. I'll go home and plan how to be as devious as Lady Macbeth. *'The raven himself is hoarse that croaks the fatal entrance of Katie Knight under my battlements!'*

She reaches for another cigarette. 'Let me know what you come up with.'

I do ponder all sorts of ridiculous possibilities in the small hours of the night, most of which are laughably improbable such as tinkering with brake cables – if I knew how, which I don't. But the next time Jason comes over and is taking a shower after a fabulously exciting session in my bedroom which involved the extensive use of mirrors, I take the photograph of Katie from his wallet, nip into the study to scan it, and then put it back before he gets out of the bathroom. I resist the temptation to draw a moustache and horns on her but it makes me giggle and Jason comes back to find me smiling. I love watching him walk naked around my room as though he lives there; for a few minutes he's mine and the pleasure of ownership makes me sparkle. 'Happy?' he asks, towelling himself.

'Come back to bed,' I say, snuggling down and peeping at him over the sheet.

He does for a few minutes, but not long enough; his eyes, as always, on the clock. As he pulls his T-shirt over his head and puts his shorts on, I lie odalisque-like on the heaped pillows, watching him. I have to ask him before he leaves, the question that's always on my mind, 'Is there any news about other schools?' He sits down on the bed to lace his trainers, his face averted. 'Not much,' he says briefly, 'a couple of schools she's quite interested in, but the pay is far less than we get here, so that's a negative.'

He comes up the bed to kiss me and, although I fall backwards on the pillow, pulling him down with me, he kisses me briefly and moves back. 'Don't worry,' he says, which is his mantra to defuse me. 'Nothing will probably happen.'

'But it's the possibility, not the probability, that disturbs me.'

'Goodbye gorgeous,' he says with a grin, throwing me a kiss from the doorway. His footsteps go off down the stairs, the door closes, and I hear the Jeep's engine start up and it moving away down the road. The room is suddenly very quiet; his presence seems still there in the wet towel slung over the rail in the bathroom but it fades as the shadows of evening creep up the wall and I lie alone, listening to the birds squabbling on the verandah. Not today, then, the threat of his leaving, but one day …. One day it will be so. And it is the thought of that day that makes me catch my breath. All I can do is to hope with all the passion of my soul that day never comes.

Part III

The Decision

There will be time, there will be time
To prepare a face to meet the faces that you meet
There will be time to murder and create ...

They say trouble often comes out of a clear sky.

A week or so later, as I bounce up the path with my groceries, I find a note from Rosie half-inserted through my letter box. I put everything away in the fridge and cupboards and change into shorts and T-shirt before I go next door. Letting myself in I call out cheerily 'hello!' and Rosie appears from the kitchen. She wears, much to my surprise, a worried frown on her face and she beckons me into the garden, shutting the ranch slider carefully behind her. I grin at her. 'What's up?'

She doesn't smile back. 'Madam, I am very worried. Madam Natasha has not come home.'

I purse my lips. 'What's unusual about that? You know she keeps very irregular hours.'

Rosie shakes her head. 'No Madam, she went out on Tuesday night and now it is Thursday afternoon and there has been no word.'

'Ah. Have you tried calling her?'

Rosie nods and I can see that she is really worried. She looks tired, like she hasn't slept well. 'Madam says I may not call her except in an emergency, but this morning I did call. But the phone just rang. No one picked up and it went to voice mail. I left a message but she has not rung me back.'

There is a little worm of unease now in my own stomach but I ignore it. 'I'm sure there's some explanation, Rosie,' I say cheerily. 'She'll probably be back any time now.'

Rosie shakes her head and looks at me very seriously. 'No Madam,' she goes on, dropping her voice. 'You don't understand. She told me that if she is ever gone for more than twenty four hours, and there is no word, then something has happened. She told me what I must do.'

I put a thumbnail up to my mouth and chew on it, an old die-hard habit from the Rick days when something bothered me. 'What you must do?' I repeat. 'What do you mean?'

Rosie is not a natural conspirator and she is not enjoying this. Her eyes are dark and anxious and she puts a hand on my arm. 'I must give her passport and Alexei's to you and also take what is in the safe and give that to you also. There must be nothing of value left in the house.'

The worm of unease is wriggling again as Rosie's fear communicates itself to me. 'Ok,' I say with a shrug. 'Of course we can do that. But,' I attempt to lift the atmosphere a little, 'I'm sure she'll be back tonight.'

Rosie does not look convinced. 'Madam, we will go upstairs, and you will take what is in the safe. I will get you a bag.' She disappears inside, and I follow her. Alexei and Hector are curled up on the sofa, watching cartoons; I throw them a quick greeting but they are engrossed. Rosie and I go upstairs and I open the safe. There is not much in it, surprisingly; the passports, a couple of files of paperwork and three of Natasha's stunning pieces of jewellery, the Star of the Sea (as I call it) with the matching earrings and a sapphire and diamond bracelet. I put them all into the bag and lock up the safe. Downstairs, Rosie opens the door for me and I hesitate on the doorstep. 'I'm sure we're over-reacting,' I say again, 'but ring me immediately if you hear anything. I'll come over later, before I go to bed.' She nods, and I go. Back home, I put the jewellery boxes on the bed and open Natasha's passport, the first time I have ever seen it. Her photograph gazes back and me, blank and cold, and I read her name, Natasha Anya

191

Svetlana Plisetskaya, her birth date, the 15th of May, and her place of birth: Novosibirsk. She is 32 years old. I touch the photograph gently. 'I didn't know when your birthday was,' I tell her softly; I realise I have not even known her for a year. I kiss my finger and put it gently on the photograph, then I pick everything up and cram it into the safe. I don't bother to look at the files, but slot them in at the top.

Downstairs I pour a glass of wine and put down a bowl of food for Puss. Ahmed is in the garden and his gentle knock reminds me that it is payday; I take his money and a Tupperware box full of chocolate brownies and pass these over to him. His smile is huge; he has a very sweet tooth has Ahmed. The evening passes but I can't settle; I have a feeling that something is wrong, but whether it actually is, or whether it is just a seed planted by Rosie's unease, I cannot be certain. I try and watch television but I can't concentrate; I flick the pages of a magazine without taking anything in.

Finally, I wander upstairs and sort out my clothes for tomorrow; that done, I sit down at my desk and do some quick research on the Internet. But my ears are ever on the prick for the soft purr of the Mercedes engine, or the tap of Natasha's heels on the path. The winter's evening drifts into an early darkness and I step out onto my verandah to breathe in the scent of the Rajasthani creeper that tumbles over the wall. I see Mrs Chokriti over the road watering the containers on her front steps; further down, two maids stand chatting on the kerb. I am just about to go in when something catches my eye; a black Mercedes is parked halfway down the road and, curiously, there appear to be two men in it. There is no movement that I can see, only the outline of their heads as they sit immobile. I stare at it, chewing my lip. There is something about their immobility that makes me uneasy. On an impulse I step back inside and rummage through the desk drawers for Nick's old bird-watching binoculars; I don't go back on the balcony but peep round the curtain instead, focusing on the two men in the car. I note the number plate first, not for any other reason other than that's what they do in the movies, and then move the binoculars up. Unfortunately at this point I'm stymied. The windows of the car are darkened and I can't see any features other than the shape of their heads. Two men, that's all I know. I shut the door and go back downstairs, putting on my shoes and stepping out on to the path ready to pop over to Rosie. On an impulse, I pause. If I go across the front I will be visible from the road; instead, I go into the house again and out the back door, creeping along the side of my own house and then stepping quickly over the tiny wall that divides the two properties. Natasha's house is dark except for the light in the kitchen/snug area; her door is unlocked and I slip in quietly. Rosie is at the kitchen table, alone; Hector is asleep at her feet and Alexei, presumably, is in bed. Hector raises his head as I come in, gives me a sleepy look, and drops his head again with a sigh.

She looks up when she hears the door and I whisper, 'Any news?' and she shakes her head. I sit down at the table wondering if I should mention the two men in the car and decide I should not. There is no point in upsetting Rosie further; I can tell by her face and the dark circles under her eyes that she is already disturbed enough. Now I myself begin to fear for Natasha but I remain stoical and believe that she may still walk in and laugh to find us all so stressed. 'I'm going to bed now,' I tell Rosie quietly. 'But I'll leave my phone on and I want you to ring me if you hear anything at all. Will you do that?'

'Of course madam,' she responds quietly.

'And Rosie,' I reach across the table to take her hand. 'I'm sure everything is fine but at least we've done what Natasha wants us to do. Now go to bed, and try to get some sleep. We mustn't worry Alexei, so keep everything normal in the morning and don't say anything to him.'

She gives me a slight smile. 'Of course, madam, I have already done so.'

'Yes, I know, you always put him first … sorry. And tomorrow, if there's still no sign of her, well … maybe, I should go to the police.'

Rosie's eyes fly up to mine. 'The police, madam? But why?'

I smile in what I imagine is a reassuring manner. 'To file a missing person's report of course. That's what you do when someone goes missing.'

Rosie stares at me, frowning, and I am reminded of Natasha's words about my safe English childhood of well-lit streets and warm safe houses. Rosie, like Natasha, does not come from that world. In her world, police equal danger. She does not associate them with help and security; she was not raised with the concept of the friendly local bobby as I was. 'It's all right,' I say gently, 'I'm sure they'll help us.'

She looks down for a moment and I know what she's thinking; maybe I know more and it is not her place to contradict me. She may disagree with my reasoning but she will not argue with me. She smiles bleakly. 'If you say so, madam. You don't want me to come with you do you?'

'Heavens no,' I say airily. 'Anyway, I'm sure it won't be necessary. She'll probably be home any time now.' I stand up to go. 'Don't worry,' I repeat, 'I'll see you in the morning.'

As I go home by the secret back route, though, and into my own house, I do wonder if my words are not just empty palliatives. There is a sneaking fear growing in me when I think of Natasha's own fears, her talk with Alex, and now her supposed disappearance. I think again of the dark car and its silent watchers and I go upstairs and peep out into the street but the car has gone. *There*, I think, to myself, *there's no relation between the two. It was just coincidence.* But the thought persists, as I get ready for bed, that perhaps I should talk to Alex. I feel the need for astute male advice. I pick up the phone and call him and, to my surprise, he answers.

'Yes, my sweet. What are you bothering Uncle Alex for at this hour?'

I laugh. 'I actually thought you'd be out. I'm amazed to find you in.'

'My dear child,' he says condescendingly, 'I am not in. The beauty of the mobile phone is that you can be in when you are out.'

'Oh,' I say defensively, 'all I meant was that there is no raucous background music. Where are you?'

'Just about to flag down a taxi,' he responds. 'What do you want?'

'Alex,' I say in a rush, 'Alex, Natasha is missing. She hasn't been home since Tuesday night and Rosie is very worried about her. She rang her phone, but there was no answer. And Natasha told Rosie if she was ever gone for more than twenty four hours, with no contact, then something was wrong and she should get rid of stuff. I don't know what to do.'

There is a silence at the other end of the phone; in the distance I hear sirens and the rush of cars.

'Alex?'

'Yes, wait, I'm going back indoors.' There is a pause and then he says, 'OK now I can hear you clearly. Natasha's gone, you say?'

I repeat what I said before adding, 'I think I should go to the police in the morning and report her missing. Do you think that would be the right thing to do?'

Alex sounds distant. 'Yes,' he says, and then, 'Look, I've got to speak to someone. I'll talk to you tomorrow. And yes, go to the police and report her missing. That's what you should do.'

'All right,' I say uncertainly, 'but Alex, do you think...?'

'No,' he says sharply. 'Look, Sophie, I can't talk now, go to bed, and in the morning, if she's not back, then you should go to the police. We'll talk tomorrow.' And he rings off.

I sit on the edge of the bed looking at the phone and feeling childishly rejected. I had meant to tell him about the car too, but there had been no time. But, as I plump up my pillows and turn out the light, snuggling down into bed, I think about his words and his tone. Alex was bothered, there is no doubt about that; he knows, better than anyone, what Natasha's disappearance might mean. What did he mean that he had to 'speak to someone'? As always, Alex's machinations are completely beyond my little brain to fathom. But as I drift into sleep, I say a silent and heartfelt prayer for her safety. And whereas usually I think of Jason's kisses as I snuffle into my pillow, tonight I think of Natasha's beautiful chill smile on the last morning I saw her. I feel my throat tightening and realise that I'm afraid for her survival in the dangerous world of make-believe that she inhabits. I remember her brave words that she did not intend to lose and I can only trust that she has not.

Next morning I am awake early and look first at my phone to make sure there are no calls or messages; on getting up I see Rosie walking Alexei out to the school bus and from the way he sings out goodbye to Hector, waiting at the window, it seems that he is not unduly disturbed. Rosie, however, looks tired and as she comes back up the path I knock on the window and beckon her in. She comes into the kitchen with me as I put on the kettle and I am concerned that she is so pale and tired-looking. There is still no news. In spite of my stiff British upper-lip, I am worried too. I take a quick shower and put on a very decorous outfit suitable for visiting police stations. I take a photocopy of Natasha's passport and also print out a copy of the only photograph I have of her; the one where we were all laughing at the dinner table. Walking into the police station, my outward confidence belies my jittery stomach. All expats hate dealing with the police, for this is a time when reality has to be encountered. The austere grimness of the police station is a reminder that we are nothing but insignificant functionaries living in a world which is kind to us only because we play by the rules and are useful. The moment either of those two factors cease to exist we become horribly dispensable and only our European qualifications and pale face can, perhaps, be briefly in our favour. The bubble is always on the point of bursting, but in any dealings with the law one is reminded of its extreme fragility. Now I am faced with officers dressed with military sharpness in khaki uniforms with a buzz of people and clerks rushing to and fro carrying files. Everyone is speaking Arabic. Usually my femininity is sufficient to ensure I don't have to wait too long; I aim for the queue marked 'Ladies Only' and, after only a few minutes' shuffling, am confronted by a smartly dressed young Emirati who eyes me coldly. I blunder out my request. He looks at me, then at the photograph, then the passport copy, then at me again.

'You have been to Embassy?' he inquires.

'The Russian Embassy?' I hazard. 'No, not yet.'

He hands everything back to me. 'Go there first,' he says briefly, and indicates for the next woman to come to the window. I step back, feeling slightly wrong-footed, and go back to the car. First I send a message to Wayne explaining that I've had to go to the police station, and then I look up how to get to the Russian Embassy. It's a round-about route, and traffic is heavy, but finally I get there, find a parking space and am inside before they close for lunch, which reminds me of how fruitless my morning has been. More queuing and the woman at the desk looks very severe and snaps out questions with all the charm of a barracuda. She takes a copy of Natasha's passport and I sit and fill in several forms before presenting myself once more at the desk and hand the forms to the barracuda. I add my business card to the pile and she staples it with great efficiency to the top form and gives me a look that indicates she'd as soon be stapling my hand. She slides back the pink copy of one of the forms which, I understand, I may now present to the police. Stage one has been completed. I find my way out of the Embassy, grimacing slightly at their artwork and cold interior design. It's pointless now to try and get back to the police station; the traffic will be murder and general inquiry hours will be over. I drive home instead, feeling nervous and pensive; my stomach is full of butterflies and on getting inside and changing out of my suit, I make a cup of tea and fall into a chair with puss on my knee. Stroking him is soothing and helps me think. No news yet from Alex; I know he will call me if he can help, so I restrain myself from bothering him again. Food seems strangely unappealing so I pour another cup and sit there thinking about what I should do next. There's a gentle tap at the door and Rosie puts her head in.

'Madam?' she calls softly. 'Are you in?'

'In here, Rosie,' I say and she comes into the living room.

'I wondered how you got on today, Madam?'

I sigh. 'Not as well as I'd hoped, but I went to the Russian Embassy and filled in paperwork which I now have to take back to the police. I'll do that tonight when they open. Have you heard anything?'

Looking at her now I realise she is pale and clearly very anxious. I put puss off my lap and stand up to hug her briefly. 'You look awful. Let me get you a cup of tea.'

She looks ready to sink onto the sofa so I give her a gentle push and go into the kitchen to squeeze the teapot yet again. Coming back she is still sitting and stroking Puss; she takes the tea and I go back to my end of the sofa where we regard each other with anxious frowns.

'I am worried, Madam', she begins, 'the phone has been ringing but there is never anyone there when I pick up.'

My thoughts flick immediately to that dark blacked-out Mercedes immobile in the street like a panther waiting in the shadows.

'Madam,' she continues, 'was there a note for you in the things from the safe? I am sure Ms Natasha said she had left you a note and I thought it might have explained what we are to do.'

'I didn't really look,' I confess. 'I just pushed everything into the safe; there were files and papers but I didn't look through them.'

Rosie clearly wants me to do so now so I go upstairs and open the safe; as I pull out the thin stack of files an envelope pokes it way out of the pile and I see my own name written on it. **'For Sophie.'** I sit down on the bed and open it. The note is very brief, undated, and written in Natasha's sprawling hand:

> **'Sophie, my friend, this is for you to know that the house is yours and you will find the deeds in my papers and see that it is in the name of a property company in London. They will tell you anything more you need to know. The jewellery is yours too, do what you want with it. Please give Rosie as much money as you can and thank her for her care of me. As to Alexei, I leave him to your discretion. You always loved him more than I did anyway. Forever your loving friend. Natasha.'**

I sit for a moment with aching throat and my hand across my mouth; then I get up and go downstairs and hand the note silently to Rosie. She reads it and her eyes fill, as mine have. We look at each other speechlessly; both of us thinking the same thing: this note reads like a last Will and Testament. In her own words Natasha seems to be telling us goodbye and making provision. For the first time I begin to wonder if it's true that she has gone, that she won't be coming back. It seems impossible. Rosie and I share the tissue box; not sobbing but both weeping quietly. Finally, I blow my nose and go to the sideboard and pour us both a small glass of brandy. It is almost time for Alexei's bus and he must not arrive to find us both in tears. Rosie wipes her eyes and we drink. Then she looks at me. 'What shall we do, Madam?' she says softly. 'What shall we tell Alexei?'

I bite my lip; I am not one of life's leaders or problem-solvers but I recognise that I must take charge here. 'I don't think we should say anything yet,' I say with more decisiveness than I'm feeling. 'Let's say that Natasha has had to go away – he's used to that after all – and as long as you and I and Hector are here he won't feel anything much has changed. Try and behave as if things are okay; I'll find out what else I can and we'll just play it by ear for the time being.'

Rosie's dark eyes are still full of trouble. 'All her beautiful clothes,' she says sadly, 'and her things … what do we do with those, Madam?'

I shake my head. 'I don't know. But look, I know someone who can help us …' I'm thinking of Alex, of course. 'You go home now, and I'll make some phone calls, and I'm sure we can sort things out. It might take time but …. Well, we mustn't give up hope. We may be over-reacting.'

Her glance flicks to the note but she doesn't gainsay me. 'Very well, madam,' she says, getting to her feet and automatically, as the good maid that she is, picking up the cups and glasses and taking them into the kitchen.

After she goes, I pick up my phone and ring Alex but there's no answer and it goes to voicemail. I leave a message for him to call me, and then I try to start thinking decisively. 'Where are you?' I ask Natasha, looking at the note again. 'Oh my dearest friend, where have you gone?' I remember when my mother died that I knew; even before the phone rang with the news, I knew she was dead. She had been ill, but was recovering, she said; but I remember so clearly the sudden coldness, a clawing in my belly, the way that time seemed to stop. Nick was a toddler and I'd been bathing him, sitting beside the bath and suddenly, from nowhere, it was as if a cold hand had clutched at my heart and, in a moment of shimmering light, I *knew*. I gasped and at that moment I heard her voice clear as day, the merest whisper of sound. *'Sophie…'* Later, I found that she had died at that exact time; worlds apart as we were, still our souls were twinned as if I had been there beside her.

Am I as close to Natasha as I was to my mother? I believe I am… and for that reason, too, I have faith that she is still alive, because I can't imagine her as dead. I don't *feel* that she's dead … I feel her presence, can see her slow smile and her chill turquoise eyes. No, I tell Puss, I won't give up yet. I feel she's still alive.

I'm waiting for Alex to ring me when Rosie comes in. Her face is as white as I've ever seen it and I look a question as she hands me a note. 'This was just put under the door,' she whispers. I unfold it and read the typewritten missive. It is short and to the point.

The house will be emptied tomorrow.

I look up at her. 'Oh my God, did you see anyone? Who delivered it?'

'I don't know madam,' she whispers and her eyes are huge with fear. 'I was making Alexei's supper, when Hector barked, and I went to the door. The note was underneath. What do I do madam?'

I bite my lip and stare at the note. Of course, I think, Natasha's house does not belong to her. It is rented, no doubt, along with the furniture, by the self-same prince who keeps her, or rather, by palace administration. I realise now that this would seem to confirm that she's gone and the cleaning up operation has begun, but I still refuse to believe that she's dead. Rosie, however, is not as sanguine. Tears are slipping silently down her cheeks as she looks to me for advice.

'Ok,' I say finally. 'You and Alexei and Hector must come here. You should pack up all your things, and Alexei's. Clothes, books, toys – anything that is yours or his. Don't worry about Natasha's stuff, I'll come over and help you with that. And tell Alexei – um – tell him that the house has to have repairs or something, and you're coming to live with me. Make it sound exciting, like a holiday.'

She nods and wipes her eyes. 'Yes, madam. But don't you think that …'

'No,' I say quickly. 'Let's not assume. Let's just do what we have to do. Just pack all your personal items, and leave all the rest. Oh and Rosie … I'll come over after he's asleep and help you. I don't want him to know we're packing up his mother's things.'

'Very well, madam,' she says quietly. 'I will phone you when he is asleep.'

When she's gone, for no good reason I go upstairs and look down the street. As I thought, the black Mercedes is still there, parked in the shadows, waiting. It is full of menace and I feel a chill run down my spine. We are being watched.

When Rosie rings, finally, it is past 9pm and I slip over. She has, in her own efficient style, got Alexei's things neatly packed and out into the hall. She whispers that he is excited, but has finally gone to sleep. We decide to take nothing from the kitchen or living room; the house was rented fully furnished and nothing other than the two photographs belong to Natasha. We go upstairs and I am confronted by the immense four-door wardrobe and Natasha's unimaginable collection of designer clothes and shoes. I sit on the bed and ponder how much money must be represented in these outfits that she ordered so readily and wore with such grace and beauty. Then I think perhaps they are not considered to be hers and, after all, what am I to do with them? It seems ridiculous but I decide to leave them as they are. The jewellery is hers, that is undeniable, but the clothes are a different matter. I open another cupboard and pull out one gorgeous gown after another; this, the gold tunic she wore on the night of the Ball, this, the green silk georgette that she was wearing when she told me she was not Alexei's mother. This, the black Givenchy that fitted her slim body like a glove; this, the red Vera Wang that was one of my favourites; this one, the blue lace and satin that she wore when she talked with Alex. I look through her stunning silk lingerie, much of it hand-made; scarves overflow from another drawer and there is a shelf full of handbags that would make Shazza weep with envy. There is nothing I want to take, nothing that would fit me, nothing that I would wear to remind me of her. Except one thing: hanging in the cupboard is her favourite dressing gown, the turquoise silk robe embroidered with flowers and birds. I pull it from the wardrobe and hold it close; there is the faintest smell of her and her favourite perfume, and some pale blonde hairs cling to the back of the collar. This I will take. I bundle it up and refuse to get emotional. One day she will be back and she will wear it again. She will. But the rest are worthless to her, and to me. Her prince can have them all back again; they are, after all, only so much cloth.

I explain my decision briefly to Rosie and start taking a few boxes of Alexei's things across. I know that we'll be visible to the black Mercedes but I don't care; I am angry and keyed up enough to march up to it, knock on the window and demand an explanation, but my more sensible side intervenes. Don't go looking for trouble, Sophie. There's more than enough around without you wanting more. Rosie can, of course, have Patti's old room which is as clean and plain as Patti left it. She and I go back and forth in the darkness, carrying box after box and, finally, around midnight, we are finished. Alexei has his books for school tomorrow, his clean clothes and his lunch box packed. Rosie will see him off to school and then bring Hector over and the rest of the food to be transferred to my fridge.

'Should I clean the house, madam, before we leave?' she asks anxiously and I look at her with affection. Poor Rosie, she looks all-in. There are great black shadows under her eyes, and she still looks scared to death.

'Of course not,' I say gently. 'I am sure they'll put in some sort of cleaning team. And you've done enough. Go to bed now and try and get some sleep. We've done all we can.' I don't elaborate on who 'they' are but Rosie is intelligent. She knows.

'Yes, madam,' she says obediently. 'Goodnight madam'.

I go back home and think that I too should go to bed, but the adrenaline is still running high in my veins and I know I won't sleep. I wish Alex would ring; I check my phone again but still no word from him. I take Puss and a drink of water up with me, and peep out at the road again from the top room. The black car has gone.

Regardless of events taking place next door, I leave everything in Rosie's capable hands and am back in the police station first thing, handing the pink Embassy form to the young man behind the counter. He takes it, and hands me more forms to fill in, which I do, adding the enlarged photograph of Natasha taken, so few weeks ago, at the party. How long, I ask, before they can give me some information? He looks down his nose. He cannot say. I should come back in a week. The Embassy will check their container and let me know. I look blank; what container? 'Ask the Embassy' he says, and I am dismissed. Puzzled, I wander outside and ring Rosie. Yes, she assures me, an unmarked removal van has come and everything is being taken out of the house. 'Who is doing the work?' I inquire, 'is it Indians or Arabs?'

'I have not spoken to them, Madam, I was here in your house when they came. Do you want me to go and ask?'

The journalist in me needs to know if my hunch is correct. 'Yes, Rosie, if you could. Just ask one of them a question, something vague, like if you can pop in and get something you forgot.'

'Very well, madam,' she says submissively.

I pop into the office, partly because I have work to do and partly because I'm trying to find Alex, but no one can throw any light of his whereabouts. He does this disappearing act every now and then, and it infuriates everyone. Shazza is usually pretty up to date with Dubai details so I ask her about the mysterious comment from the police regarding containers. She wrinkles her nose.

'Yeah, a revolting practise,' she says with distaste. 'You know how many of the poor fuckers die on the building sites … well, they don't send the bodies home one at a time. They put them into containers, cold-stored I suppose, and tagged, one marked 'India', one marked 'Pakistan' etc. and when they're full they get sent off.'

I stare at her with horror. I've never heard of anything so uncivilised. 'You're kidding, what, everyone? Even people who aren't construction workers?'

'Far as I know. Course that's people who don't have families to claim their bodies.'

I sit down hard on the chair behind me, feeling sick, to think that my beautiful Natasha might be in a cold storage container marked 'Russia'.

'If someone went missing, someone without family, how would you find out if they were in the container for their country?'

'Dunno. Embassy I suppose. There must be a list somewhere of who goes in. Why?'

'Oh … someone asked me, and I didn't know what they meant. Thanks.'

Fortunately she has questions about the piece we're doing on Gyms and Trainers in Dubai and has a list of things she wants checked out. I listen with half an ear, but when I'm finally handed a sheet of business names and addresses, I suddenly realise what I've agreed to. 'You want me to visit all these?'

'Yeah, awesome, thanks Sophie. I want two interviews at each and also two or three brief interviews with some of the clientele. Photos too if you can, or take Mohammed with you.'

I'm too preoccupied to argue, much to Shazza's surprise. I tell Mohammed I'd like him to come as his photography far excels mine; he also wants to drive, which suits me fine, although it can be a bit hair-raising. But when you're a rich lad with a job and a Lamborghini, as well as a number plate that tells the police to leave you alone, showing off is part of the territory. While Mohammed goes out to get lunch I pick up the phone to call the Russian Embassy; then, on a thought, I think that maybe my own Embassy may be more forthcoming so I dial the British Embassy instead. A crisp voice asks me who I want to speak to and I dither; then I think of the Press Officer.

'Catherine Mullins,' says a voice in my ear.

No matter how I phrase this, it is going to sound peculiar but I do my best. There's a pause and then Ms Mullins says yes, it's a practice she has heard of.

'But is the Embassy familiar with it?' I query. 'I mean have you had any British expatriates end up in these containers? How do you identify them?'

There's a pause and then Ms Mullins says, very carefully, 'Are you a journalist?'

'Not at all,' I say swiftly. 'I'm the friend of someone who's gone missing, and someone suggested that you would be able to help.'

'Is your friend British, madam? If so, you need to come in here and talk to us. There are certain regulations we have to observe.'

'I'm afraid not,' I respond. It won't help me if I lie; clearly she's not going to tell me any more. 'She's Russian.'

I can almost dictate her next sentence. 'Then I suggest you consult the Russian Embassy, madam.'

I thank her and ring off. But in a way she has told me what I need to know. She's virtually admitted the horrible container story is true and that the Russian Embassy will have some knowledge if any of their expatriates have ended up there. It seems I will have to go back there and inquire further, but the thought makes me feel sick. I pour a coffee and ponder and, on thinking it through, I see an inconsistency. Very few people die with their passport on them, although it is the law that everyone must carry their UAE identity card at all times. It seems obvious that there must be a morgue where bodies lie to be claimed or identified, and that should be my next port of call. And it is only unidentified bodies that end up being shipped home in such a medieval Black Death kind of anonymity; if I can find Natasha, and identify her, then I can arrange a proper coffin and cremation. I can't send her body home, after all, I have no one to send it to, although I think she would want to lie in Russian soil.

Mohammed comes back upstairs to find me pale and shaking; he looks at me with some concern as I down my coffee and two Panadol. 'Are you okay to go?' he asks.

'Yes,' I say getting my bag, 'and look, on the way, I have some questions to ask you. We might have to make a detour. Would that be all right?'

If there's one thing Mohammed doesn't mind it's being asked to drive around town. He struts a little as we go downstairs and swings his keys with éclat. His answers to my inquiries are not, however, particularly helpful and, as the Lamborghini growls its macho way through Dubai traffic, scorching across lanes and making light of the freeway restrictions, I hesitate to break his concentration. Mohammed is not one of life's natural multi-taskers. It does appear, however, that any visit to any morgue must be authorised by the police so it's Mohammed's firm belief that we should go back to the police station. He has a cousin, he says, a police captain who will help us. Whether from apprehension or exhaustion, however, I cannot face the police again so soon, and one must at least give them a day or two to pursue their own inquiries. I thank him for his offer and we arrange to go together the following morning. After that, I try and do my job; we tick four gyms off the list and Mohammed and I prove to be a competent team.

Arriving home I find Rosie, Alexei and Hector already established and Alexei greets me with a hug and a full-on chattering excitement that clearly indicates that Rosie, bless her, has done a wonderful job as always and he is unperturbed by and unaware of the traumas she and I have been going through. Hector has already dug a hole in my garden; Alexei reports with glee that puss has gone to ground under my bed and Alexei himself is a little concerned to find my swimming pool so small. But, these insignificant issues aside, all is well. Rosie, whom I am glad to see is looking less drawn, makes me tea and I sit down at the table while Alexei goes back to the task of sorting out my snug to his satisfaction.

I ask her if she had got any answers from the removal team earlier and she answers quietly, 'Yes, madam, they were not Indian. I asked them where they were from and they did not answer. There was a team of four with a man in charge; I tried to speak to him but he told me to go away. But they were speaking Arabic, not Hindi.'

I take my tea upstairs to change and also to placate Puss, who is doing a fine impression of betrayed and terrified under my bed. I manage to get him out and soothe him; he is just relaxing in my arms when a volley of barking from downstairs sends him clawing off my lap and back under the bed. I sigh. Puss's trauma is a casualty I didn't think about and his reaction parallels my own; I want to hide and ignore all the horrible imaginings but I can't. Natasha has gone and I must find out where. I sigh, and as I hear Alexei call shrilly downstairs to Rosie, I have a moment of regret for my quiet house, now given over to one small excited boy and dog. I think of Jason, too, of course and recognise that from now on those delicious sexual liaisons will be difficult; no more mid-afternoon trysts up against the kitchen bench or skinny dipping in the pool. I change into jeans and T-shirt, thinking that, curiously, at present Jason is the least of my worries.

Next morning I go into work because I can't think of anything else to do, but also because I hope I can catch up with Alex and, mid-morning, he wanders in. He sees me and does a smooth by-pass where he comes past my desk, scoops me up and whisks me off "for coffee." He calls to Shazza as we go downstairs, all the way to the basement as it happens, and into Alex's car. Then he turns to me and his face is serious.

'Tell me what you know,' he says simply.

I do. He frowns and says 'Mmm' occasionally but, apart from that, lets me get it all off my chest.

'Good,' he says finally, 'I think you've done everything just right.'

Well that's a relief. I continue and tell him about the blacked out Mercedes and the removal men being Arabic. He nods as if it's entirely what he expected. I tell him I will go back to the police station tomorrow and take Mohammed who must have some serious *wasta*; perhaps his cousin will get some answers for me. I ask him about the mortuary and the containers and he frowns. 'I doubt that you'll find her,' he says gently. 'If it happened as she thought it would, it would be a hit killing. Her body would be taken out into the desert or tossed overboard from a boat. She'd never be found.'

I stare at him blankly. 'I don't feel she's dead,' I say stoutly. 'I just can't believe it.'

'Good girl, Sophie,' he says and squeezes my hands. 'That's exactly what we must do, keep hoping.'

I'm trying to be rational and not give in to emotion. 'But if that's the case,' I say uncertainly, 'then there's no use going to the police, filing a missing person's report etc. So why am I doing it?'

'Oh no, we must follow protocol,' he says surprisingly. 'We can't seem to know about any other possibility,' he adds, seeing my puzzled face.

'I see. So you think the car in the street and the house clearance was *them?*

'Of course.'

'It seems strange, though, that it should happen now. She seemed so much happier, more relaxed; I thought all the troubles were behind her. Obviously not.'

Alex looks sage as I continue, 'She said you had made it easier … was it just the writing, knowing that the story would come out, no matter what?'

'Maybe. She needed someone to talk to, to confide in. I helped. A trouble shared is a trouble halved, or so the adage says.'

I digest this. 'But that might mean we'll never know what happened to her. Isn't there some way we can find out? Surely you would be able to? You have so many underworld connections, isn't there a chance you could ask around? I don't think I could bear never to know what happened.'

Alex looks at me with a strangely considering expression, starts to say something and then changes his mind. 'Maybe,' he says finally, 'the underworld is the place to start. But I can't take you with me, Sophie,' he holds up a finger as I start to protest. 'No, no, it's no place for a woman. It's a different city, one of shadows and darkness and danger.'

I stare back at him mulishly. 'I want to go. I'm not afraid. I want to find out what happened and if there's someone there who can tell me, I want to meet them. Alex … don't think you can fob me off. I'll do what you tell me, dammit, but I am coming with you!'

He looks at me and recognises determination. 'All right' he says grudgingly, 'well, maybe there's a way around it. But listen … don't ring me and don't say anything about any of it on your phone. I'm not sure it's safe. We'll have to meet somewhere. Ok … tomorrow night, we'll meet here and go in my car. Around 11pm here in the car park. If there's any change of plan I'll text you saying the tennis game is off. Ok?'

'Ok,' I am terrified but triumphant at the same time.

The next morning Mohammed confidently collects me and whisks me into the police station. His cousin, a good looking young man with a very grown-up moustache and trouser creases you could cut your finger on, greets him with a kiss on both cheeks in the Emirati fashion and deigns to shake my hand as we are introduced. We are taken into his office; coffee is served by a thin and elderly Indian, and the conversation switches entirely to Arabic as Mohammed explains the situation which I have so carefully outlined to him in the car on the way over. His cousin listens, scribbles a few notes and then pulls up something on the computer screen, tapping the keyboard occasionally. He seems puzzled at what he's reading; he goes out and comes back and then the whole timbre of the meeting suddenly changes. The pitch of voices goes higher and Mohammed seems to be being told something he doesn't like; he snaps back a retort and there is an exchange of words that sounds almost like a minor quarrel. The cousin draws himself up with military precision and says something very clearly, which stops Mohammed in his tracks. Both have completely forgotten me, sitting silently but watching the interplay between them and trying to guess what is going on. The captain turns to me and waves me to my feet. 'I am sorry, Mrs Sophie, but we cannot help you.'

I look from him to Mohammed and back. There is tension in the air you could cut with a knife. 'Excuse me?' I say, politely, 'I don't understand. Do you mean you have no record of my friend missing?'

'I am sorry,' he repeats. 'There is nothing.'

I glance at Mohammed who is clearly furious but also, puzzlingly, afraid. He doesn't look at me.

'But maybe tomorrow ...' I begin.

He gives a polite and dismissive smile and hands over his card. 'Of course,' he says, 'please to call tomorrow. I will do what I can.'

'Thank you,' I say uncertainly as Mohammed grudgingly shakes hands and we go out; he marches through the police station and out to the car without another word while I run behind like a good Emirati wife. His manners, usually so impeccable, fail him too, and I am left to open my own door and scramble in while he guns the motor and the Lamborghini swings out of the car park with a squeal.

'Um,' I begin, 'can you tell me what happened back there?'

Mohammed stares straight ahead. 'He did not know anything,' he says, almost rudely. 'There was nothing.'

I hate this feeling of pacifying-the-little-woman, and anyway, in the magazine world, he's just a junior, so I don't back down. 'It didn't sound like there was nothing,' I say. 'There was clearly something. What did he see on the screen? What made you so angry?'

I can see the muscles in his jaw clench and I am suddenly afraid too. 'It was nothing,' he mutters, 'he thought it was, but it was another woman.'

'But you argued with him ... why?'

'I did not understand,' he growls, and races the Lamborghini through the traffic on a rising snarl. He is desperate to get back to the office, obviously, and me out of the car and out of his hair, so I don't press him any further. After all, the police can clearly do little to help me if, as Alex opines, Natasha's disappearance is not within their jurisdiction. I am just puzzled and curious as to what happened back there. Alex, when we meet tonight, might be able to throw some light on it.

Going downtown at midnight is quite a departure for me with my staid lifestyle, so, when I get home, I tell Rosie I'm going to have a power nap as I'll be going out later. I get up around 9pm feeling very drowsy and quite unprepared for any late night revelations, but after a shower and some dinner, I'm ready to go, although my stomach is tight with tension. As instructed, I'm dressed in dark t-shirt and jeans with flat shoes. As I drive into the car park, I see Alex's Audi and, parking my own car, I slip into the seat beside him. I look up at him and smile and he must think I look excited because he says, severely, 'This is not a pleasure jaunt, Sophie. This is deadly serious and you must do exactly what I say. '

'I know,' I say, as we set off. Of course, I've been downtown before but never off the beaten track. Alex winds in and out of small roads and smaller lanes; I think we must be near the Creek but I'm missing most of my regular landmarks and it takes me a while to get my bearings. I'm very quiet, concentrating on where we're going. In spite of the serious nature of our quest, there's an unwitting sense of excitement in me too; this was what I used to dream of being, a real undercover journalist on a desperate and dangerous assignment. Weaving through the dark alleys, slashed by the occasional dimly lit street with passers-by, this is what Sophie Haddon used to fantasise she would do one day; be a fearless, prize-winning journalist, leaving no stone unturned in her search for the truth. Then I shake myself out of my Walter Mitty illusion and concentrate on what Alex is saying.

'I've arranged to meet someone,' he says quietly. 'He's a contact, a sort of go-between, who's arranged for us to meet a man he knows, a hit man, a paid assassin. Do you have Natasha's photo that I told you to bring?'

'Of course,' I say with tension spiralling in the depths of my stomach. Alex pulls in and parks; he locks the car, and looks across at me. 'We walk from here,' he says. 'And Sophie … I've told him that it's you who wants to know, and why, so he can see we have a genuine reason to meet, but its best that we keep it simple. He'll tell us what we want to know, if he can. Otherwise, he won't.'

We walk on and I can hear the wash of the Creek away on my left and the distant voices of stevedores working the docks where the dhows bring in contraband from Iraq and Iran, and where a fast boat or two can be across the Gulf to a rendezvous and back by daybreak. The street is a dark alleyway with an uneven surface of sand and rock with potholes that are hard to avoid; a little breeze blows the dust up into my eyes. At the end we turn sharply away from the Creek and see, across from us, a darkened shop front with its grill windows pulled and locked and, half hidden, by a semi-dead neon sign, two men are standing, discernible only by the glow of the cigarette one is smoking. 'There they are,' says Alex quietly. We come up and he nods to them; 'It was good of you to agree to meet.'

Both men are foreign; it's impossible to tell their nationality but the dark hair and eyes and swarthy skin could belong to any Mediterranean country. The younger man indicates the older. 'My contact,' he says briefly. Alex turns to me. 'This is the woman whose friend has gone missing,' he says, and to me, he adds, 'Sophie, show him the photograph.' I do so, handing the print over to the older man. He looks at me and then at the photograph; he studies it for a few seconds and then hands it back. 'No,' he says briefly.

'You don't recognise her?' I ask. He shakes his head. 'But what if it was another assassin? Someone you don't know about?'

He looks at me again, but it is not a cold look; rather it has a brief feeling of sympathy. Alex starts to speak, but the man holds up his hand, and addresses me again. 'You are worried for your friend,' he says, his English harsh and guttural. 'I understand. But among ourselves we know what is happening. And there have been no instructions about … her.' He indicates the photograph.

I look at him for a moment longer and I think I understand; there is clearly a kind of cartel among these men of death and shadows, and he speaks for them all when he denies all knowledge of Natasha. I believe him. I hold out my hand and, surprised, he takes it. 'Thank you,' I say. 'You are kind to tell me the truth.'

Alex says something quietly to his contact; I turn away with the photograph still in my hand and my eyes blurry with tears. I feel Alex slip his hand quietly under my elbow and we cross the road and walk back to the car. Inside we sit for a moment. 'That was well done, Sophie,' he says at last, 'and you were right. He does not know anything.'

We stop for hot coffee and sit quietly, talking, arguing possibilities backwards and forwards; he is intrigued to hear of the incident at the police station. 'It sounds like the palace has put a ban on Natasha's story,' he says. 'That would explain why Mohammed was obviously told not to ask anything else and why he wouldn't discuss it with you. The police captain was clever to give you his card. You can ring and ring and he will either never take your calls or the answer will be the same: no news. Sophie,' he says carefully, 'I think we must face the fact that she is gone and we may never know where. I'll be leaving Dubai soon myself; I've got a desk for six months on the New York Times and I'll be publishing Natasha's story when it's complete. That way, at least, the world will know and she will rest in peace.'

I look up at his kind, clever face watching mine in the half-darkness. 'You don't think we should go to the Morgue?' I ask. 'Just to be sure?'

'If you want to set your mind at rest, Sophie, then go, of course,' he says, patting my hand. 'But I suspect an instruction to have her disappear would mean just that. There would be no body left in Dubai to confuse issues and bring possible embarrassment upon the Palace.'

'I just want to be sure there's no chance of her being there … unidentified,' I say, blowing my nose.

'I doubt it very much,' he says gently. 'She would have been taken a long way from here. We must hope that she lies under friendly stars …'

'I want you to make this the best exposé you've ever written,' I say with bitterness. 'It has to be a Pulitzer Prize winner to make up for whatever they've done to her. But who are the villains, Alex? The fanatic in whose eyes she said she could see her own death? Will they ever pay for what they've done?'

'If you believe in karma, Sophie, then yes, they will,' he says with a rueful smile.

'That man tonight,' I continue, with a sigh, 'a paid assassin and yet there was a kind of honesty about him. I really felt he … understood.'

Alex sips his coffee; 'You should not doubt their honour,' he says seriously. 'I believe they hold themselves and their reputation in high regard. You pay your money and you get a very professional service, I believe.'

'A paid assassin,' I say reflectively. 'What would one pay for a hit in Dubai these days?' I recall the conversation I had with Natasha such a short time before and I ponder the irony.

'I believe ten grand is the basic, American dollars that is. Paid in cash of course.'

'But who would employ them?' I ask, 'How would they advertise?'

'It's hierarchical,' Alex explains. 'You may just want to frighten your creditor, or threaten a business rival; that's just small scale thug stuff. These guys are the professionals; you won't read about someone being murdered because it's done so discreetly. And they have a hundred choices at their disposal. My contact is a barman in one of the hotels; an almost invisible observer of what goes on which is what makes him so valuable to me. If someone wants to meet a hit man, they discreetly drop the word and in a few days they'd receive an invitation to a meeting. All very well ordered.'

'That was your contact tonight?' I query. 'Where does he work?'

'The Fantasia,' says Alex and then laughs. 'Why do you want to know that?'

'I don't know,' I sigh. 'It seems so odd that the two worlds mix; from the bar of the Fantasia to the back streets of Dubai. Crime and conventionality hand in hand.'

Alex smiles and crushes his coffee cup. *'And nothing is,'* he quotes 'Macbeth' reflectively, *'but what is not.'*

As he drops me off back at my car, he says, holding my hand, 'I'm glad you came. I think it will help you find what our American cousins call 'closure'. Natasha is gone, but life goes on. You are stronger than you think, Sophie, and all will be well, I promise.'

'She taught me to be strong,' I say. 'I'll get on with life, Alex, but I'll never forget her. And it helps to know that you will avenge her. Thank you for taking me tonight.'

Any sense of peace I might have found from my strange late night assignation fades abruptly the next morning as my phone rings and I hear my husband (in name still, anyway) almost shrieking at me from the other end. It is several seconds before I can work out what he wants because of the unusual amount of invective. Rick is usually so composed and self-aware that it's bizarre to hear him almost hysterical. 'You stupid fucking bitch ... what the hell have you been doing? Sophie? Sophie!'

'What on earth is the matter?' I ask calmly.

He takes a deep breath and is obviously pulling himself together. 'I've had a phone call,' he says, 'from the police. They asked me why we're not living together ... who did you tell?'

'I've told no one,' I say truthfully, 'What on earth would they ring you for? What else did they say?'

'They said,' he grinds out, 'that you are causing trouble and they wanted to know why I am not living with you. What the fuck have you been doing? What trouble are they talking about?'

'I have no idea,' I say, 'I went to the police station to file a missing person's report because my neighbour, the blonde Russian Natasha, has disappeared. That's all the dealings I've had with the police.'

He's a little calmer now but obviously still deeply shaken; Rick has any number of good reasons for not wanting any kind of police investigation. 'Why the *fuck* do you have to get involved?' he asks. 'That's so fucking *typical*. She's probably gone on holiday or something and not told you. But look … police means trouble and I can't afford that at the moment. Just forgot the silly bitch and stay out of it. It's nothing to do with you anyway.'

'Rick,' I say clearly, 'there's no problem and please don't feel you have to move back here! I've filed the report but I won't be going back to the police anyway. They're of very limited assistance.' Mindful of Alex's suggestion not to trust the security of my phone too implicitly I'm being very cautious of what I say. Rick, however, is not privy to the same self-control.

'All right,' he says sulkily, 'but take my advice and stay the *fuck* out of any trouble. I don't want anybody ringing me up again to complain about you. You know what it's like here. My visa could be revoked at the drop of a hat and I'd be out of here on the next plane. And yours too, come to that. So whatever you're doing to cause trouble, stop it. Is that clear?'

'Actually you're not quite correct,' I can't resist the opportunity to add, 'I'm living in my own house, and I'm no longer sponsored by you but by the magazine direct which is, of course, the Princess. So if it comes to staying here, I think I have a little more clout than you.'

There's a frustrated growl at the other end of the phone which makes me grin; it's such a pleasure to hoist Rick by his own petard that I can't resist another jibe. 'Which brings me to the point that if you got on with that divorce, as I suggested, you and I would be separate entities and no one would be ringing you in the first place!'

He clearly can't think of a retort, so contents himself with, 'Just stay the fuck out of trouble, Sophie. You were always a stupid bitch but I'm warning you, this time be a bit smarter – if you can.'

'Do my best,' I respond with waspish charm, and hang up. *Wanker.* It's interesting, though, that the police think it's necessary to get Rick to warn off his errant wife. I ponder as I shower and get ready for work. The long arm, not of the law but the Palace – which, in this police state, is the law – is clearly working to eliminate all mention of the disappearance of a beautiful Russian girl who used to work for them and it seems that I am in the frame. Not that I'm surprised; the watching Mercedes and the phone bug – although not proven – would seem to confirm that. But they must be convinced by now that I know nothing and am helpless to find out more. Warning Rick to rein me in just makes it clear that they're serious, and will 'scare' me off pursuing any inquiries of my own. I won't be bothering the police any more except a cursory phone call just to make it seem that I am still anxious about Natasha's whereabouts, enough to throw them off the scent, so to speak, by convincing them that I know nothing. God forbid that Rick should feel it necessary to chastise his nosy wife or possibly move back in, temporarily, to alleviate suspicion. Fortunately, men in this country have such a poor opinion of female intellect, or tenacity, that *they* will presume that I will scuttle back into my burrow and lie low. That is, after all, what expats do here; they only have to have the admonitory finger of the law pointed at them briefly and they suddenly bethink themselves of all that could go wrong with the dream lifestyle and hastily retreat. And thus is the status quo retained. Yes, in this case I can most adequately follow Natasha's advice and turn a man's weakness to my advantage. I wonder, idly, if the house will still be watched; I doubt it somehow. But it might be wise to be vigilant. If Jason does come over – and I still have to work out how that will be possible with Rosie and Alexei in residence – I will have to make sure there are no mysterious watchers. We are, after all, breaking the law of the country in having an adulterous affair, and what Rick said was true – people are deported for less. It might, after all, suit the Watchers to get rid of me, but only if I'm an irritant. If I get back into my hole and behave, they will forget all about me. I haven't yet sent Jason a message about the events of the past week; I've been too engrossed in living them. I'm nervous about texting now too, but finally I send a very innocuous message saying that I have people staying and why don't we meet somewhere for coffee.

Rosie and I sit a little longer over breakfast than normal, as Alexei has already gone on the school bus and Hector is snoring in his corner of the snug. She seems to have settled in with a minimum amount of disruption; she has already made up Alexei's room as much as possible as it used to be, with his favourite pictures on the walls, his Footballer Trophy on prominent display, and all the paraphernalia of his young boyhood scattered around. Hector has been restrained from digging further holes, and Rosie has, it seems, already imposed her authority on old Ahmed so that he is now hoeing and clipping with more energy than he has shown for years, with the odd backward glance to see if he is being observed. Although there is a quiet air of melancholy between us still because of recent events, like a transient dust mars a mirrored surface, Rosie is one of the world's natural survivors and she accepts, probably even better than I, that life must go on. But her self-control is fragile and, when I ask her about the money that Natasha wanted her to have, she looks as if she might cry. 'No, no, madam,' she says earnestly. 'I couldn't take any money; besides I don't want it. Just pay me for what I do here and that will be enough. I loved Madam Natasha, and I love Alexei. It is my pleasure to be here.' I look at her with affection; she really is a lovely woman. 'Well as long as I am here, Rosie, you and Alexei are here too, and we are family. But, actually, Rosie, we must talk about finances. I will need money for Alexei's school fees and other expenses, and I don't earn enough for that, so some of what is in the safe will have to be cashed in. The gold bars, for example. The problem is that I don't know how to do this. Do I take them to a bank or the gold souk?'

She smiles at my ignorance and pours me another cup of tea. Rosie, like so many of her race, knows all the myriad ways to get the most for her dirham. 'You could, madam,' she says, putting sugar in her tea, 'but, if you will trust me, I think I can get us a better rate of exchange for them.'

'Dear Rosie,' I say with feeling, 'I would trust you with my life! Well, take two or three of the bars and see what we can get for them. Where are you thinking of taking them?'

She taps the side of her nose and twinkles at me. 'I have an Indian contact,' she says, 'he will give me the best price and not cheat me.'

'Okay, that sounds wonderful. Do it as soon as you can, then. I'll have to look through the paperwork and see when Alexei's school fees are due, and there will be expenses on the house too. Power, water, things like that.'

She rises and takes the things to the sink. 'Very well, madam.'

There's a wonderful feeling of absolute confidence when dealing with Rosie. When she says she will do something it will be done, and efficiently. I sally forth to work secure in the knowledge that, as long as the gold bars and the jewellery last, we will be well provided for. The Star of the Sea, as I call it, I should be loath to sell, so that will stay at the bottom of the safe until we have no more options. There is, also, of course, the London property company that Natasha mentioned but I put that on the back burner mentally. When the summer comes round again, Alexei and I, and maybe even Rosie, will go to England for a holiday and I will check it out then. In the meantime, I think I should write them a brief note explaining events, and that I will now be responsible for any expenses on the property.

I have been so occupied with events that I have hardly had time to wonder why Jason is so quiet. My response for a meeting has been ignored, it seems, so I send an email to our private account and tell him what's happened and how Alexei and Rosie are now living with me. The knot of tension in my stomach which, latterly, seems to have eased not at all, becomes a little more kinked when I think how long it is since I've seen or heard from him. No news is good news, the adage says, but I have a feeling that in this case no news is just the opposite. Finally I get a text message; he'll meet me this evening on the strip of desert where we used to walk the dog. I drive over there as the sun is going down and have a moment of panicked symbolic awareness; if Jason is going then the sun is indeed sinking in my life. I am the first one there and I sit watching the sun sink and sipping my takeaway coffee, which does nothing to ease my dry mouth. Presently the blue Jeep swings in beside me and Jason climbs into the front of my own vehicle. We kiss for a few minutes; as always, his presence calms me and I feel all the tensions draining away at his touch. For the first time in this whole horrible week I feel the knot uncoiling in my stomach and my body relaxing. In his arms I feel safe and guarded from the exigencies of the world. Finally he releases me and I hand over the coffee I have bought him. I love the way he looks at me sometimes, like now, his blue eyes very soft but with a hint of lust in the depths.

'I'm sorry,' he says now. 'About Natasha. Tell me what's happened.'

I give him a quick summary, watching the play of expression across his face at my words, like sunlight moving across water. 'So,' I conclude finally, 'I guess life goes on. I can't understand why I'm not more upset and angry except I think that it hasn't quite sunk in yet that she's dead. I don't feel she is, you see, I feel she's still alive.'

Jason wipes a dab of coffee off my lip with a handkerchief. 'I don't know what to make of it,' he says gently.

'Although now her house has been emptied, and it's almost as if she was never there, I have no idea if it's all over. I haven't seen anyone, and as far as the phone was concerned, I was never sure if that was tapped or not. It was just Alex being his usual paranoid self probably.'

A slight frown brings Jason's eyebrows together. I know what he's thinking; like Rick, he stands to lose everything if we should ever be discovered. It was dangerous enough before, heaven knows, marginalise it though we did, but now it is doubly dangerous. The idea of the house being watched and comings and goings recorded is enough to make a far less sensitive lover than Jason Knight head for the hills. I have a feeling I have just ensured the end of those idyllic trysts that have been the breath of life for me these past months.

He takes a last mouthful of coffee and turns to me. 'Sophie,' he begins gently, and I have a horrible presentiment of what is coming, turning my head almost as if to avert a blow. He reaches over to take my hand, and holds it pressed against his heart. I look at him, my eyes swimming with tears; I would do anything to stop him saying the next words but he says them nevertheless. 'It's over, anyway. We're leaving. I've accepted a job abroad and we'll begin there next September.'

I stare at him speechlessly. This is the blow I've dreaded for so long but now it's fallen I can hardly register it.

I say, stupidly, inconsequentially, 'Where?'

'Moscow. We've signed a two year contract.'

That awful pronoun reminds me that he's part of a couple that is not he and I, and the loss hits me like a sledgehammer. Coupled with the loss of Natasha I do not know how I will bear it. I sit there speechlessly, shaking my head, tears pouring down my face. And Jason is not insensitive; there are tears too in his blue eyes as he reaches over and tries to dry my tears. 'I'm sorry,' he whispers now, 'You know I wish it could be different.'

He pulls me into his arms and lets me sob on his chest; maybe indulging me because he knows that he can't be harsh at this time of parting. He's saying things, which I hear only partially; his voice is broken and I know that, for this moment anyway, he feels the pain of separation as I do. And the thought hits me, then, suddenly, that Katie Knight has won. In this desperate unspoken battle between two women for one man, she has played the final hand and she has triumphed. Jason will leave and she will go with him. Not I. I will be left behind. I have lost. I have lost him and I have lost the game. And, suddenly, I am furious. I will not let her win, I will not! I pull myself out of his arms and, grabbing his handkerchief, wipe my own eyes. 'No,' I say, 'I'm not going to let her win. I'm not going to let her take you away from me.'

He smiles at me gently. 'Sophie, if it means anything I'll always love you. She will never have my heart. Only you and Jack have that. But you know I have to go; you know why.'

I look at him, words bubbling up, but words that I do not say. For maybe the first time in my life I don't blurt out what I'm thinking. But there is resolution in my breast; I take a deep breath to calm my wildly beating heart. 'There's a long time between now and July,' I say shakily.

He shakes his head, the blue eyes still swimming with unshed tears. 'No,' he says softly, 'I mustn't see you again. It's too dangerous. You know what it would mean if we got caught.'

Strangely, the sight of the tears welling up in his eyes makes me even more resolute. I am his shield maiden and I will protect him. I will let him go now, but this is not over. I feel steel licking through the fire in my blood and I welcome it. Battle has been joined and I will fight with all my women's intuition and deviousness. And he must never know it. I remember Natasha's words about *legerdemain* and now I look at him very straightly so that he laughs. 'What?' he says, cocking his head. 'Suddenly your eyes are like green swords.'

'Yes,' I say, and it is, perhaps, the first time I have not told him what is in my heart. 'Because I would fight for you if I could. But I know it's hopeless. I can fight her, but not you. And you want to go.'

'No,' he says on a sigh. 'I don't. God knows I don't. But there is no alternative. I have to go.'

I look at this man, this man who I love so dearly, and realise that Natasha has been right all along. Jason Knight is weak and lacks courage. For whatever his reasons, even given that they are honourable, he is not a fighter. Lady Macbeth's words march through my consciousness. *'Yet do I fear thy nature; it is too full of the milk of human kindness to catch the nearest way.'* I take his hand and kiss it and although the pact is unspoken, and he not an active part of it, it is nevertheless a resolution. Whatever it takes to keep him, I will do it. Because I love him, and because he will do nothing, I will. On a breath I echo Lady Macbeth's lines; her determined nature juxtaposed with her husband's passive one; *'unsex me here and fill me from the toe to the crown top full of direst cruelty'.*

When the blue Jeep drives away I sit in the dark, in my own car, contemplating the twinkling lights across the small dunes. There is a full moon tonight, swimming clear in a sky the colour of sapphires. I look down at my sapphire ring, my ring of freedom, and place the cold gem to my lips.

'I swear,' I say softly, to the moon, 'that I will do whatever it takes to make Jason Knight my own. I will risk any danger, overcome any obstacle and forfeit any conscience in this objective.' I have a feeling that Natasha is listening to me and I smile. 'To the one who taught me to be strong,' I say to the stars, as I turn on the engine.

I go home and walk resolutely upstairs to the study and lift the lid of the printer. The enlarged image of Katie Knight looks back at me. She is not a pretty woman. The eyes are small and cold, the lips thin. Her only beauty is the short thick blonde hair that is tucked behind her ears. 'Know thy enemy,' I say to her, as I put the lid back down like a guillotine.

Two nights later I find myself sitting at the bar of the 'Fantasia.' It is late for me, but not, it seems, for everyone else. There are two barmen serving drinks but neither of them is the one I seek. I wait 'til one comes to take my order and I ask him, 'I was talking to a young man here the other night. The barman. But I can't see him tonight. Is he here?'

'That would be Ravi,' he says, wiping the counter and putting a new bright pink coaster in front of me with a small dish of peanuts. 'He's off having a break, but he'll be back in about half an hour.'

I thank him and sit sipping the vodka and tonic he brings me, not even glancing around the room. It is full of dark corners and dimly lit tables, but I stay where I am, solitary above the buzz of conversation and soft music. For the first time in ages I feel relaxed; having made up my mind I am acting on my decision.

I see Ravi come back and, with a wave, the young barman indicates me sitting on my stool; Ravi comes over to me. I say nothing, just look at him, and see recognition dawn in his eyes. He takes the empty nut dish and fills it; putting it down beside me once more he says quietly, 'How can I help you?'

'Your contact,' I say, 'I want to meet him again.'

He takes an ice bucket and adds a few more blocks to the dregs of my drink. 'Why?' he says, 'he cannot help you any more. You agreed.'

'No,' I shake my head. 'It's not about her. It's about something else. A job.'

His dark eyes flick to mine and I hold the glance. I don't know how these things are done but I hand him my card and he pockets it in a smooth, hardly perceptible, gesture. 'He will be in touch,' he says softly, and moves away. I finish my drink and slip off my stool; as I walk through the jostling lobby of the Fantasia I feel invisible, unnoticed. In the throng of brightly-dressed people I am as insubstantial but as implacable as a drifting shadow of death in the midst of a crowded celebration of life.

The next thing that I have to think about is money and the next night I sit down with Rosie. She has good news. Her contact is more than ready to give us cash for the gold bars and the price of gold, saints be praised, is high at present. But my plan to give Rosie the diamond and sapphire bracelet to take to her contact and get cash for dies, stillborn. I may be limited in my knowledge of the byways of murder, but I have enough sense to know that I must cover my tracks and act alone. Fortunately, thanks to Natasha, I have what amounts, essentially, to disposable and untraceable income. But I cannot involve Rosie. Besides, the danger of it – an Indian maid selling an employer's bracelet – might alarm even the most supportive expatriate; the sheer audacity of involving this intensely moral woman in a grossly immoral deed cannot be even contemplated. I can damn my own soul to hell for all eternity, but not Rosie's. Not Rosie's and not Jason's. No matter how this concludes, he will never know anything. They are both innocent parties and that is how it will remain.

Morning brings counsel, it is said, and sure enough, driving to work next morning I bethink myself of dear Mr Patel, he of the gold souk and the sapphire ring. The next day I take the bracelet from the safe and call on him in the late afternoon, carefully timed between the end of his siesta and the reopening of the shop for the evening trade. He is, predictably, delighted to see me and sends the elderly servant running to make me strong sweet tea with sterilised milk as he welcomes me into the backroom. We chat, over tea and biscuits, as of one expatriate to another, about the building of so many new roads, the traffic jams and how the high price of gold is affecting Mr Patel's business. Finally I cut to the chase, producing the sapphire and diamond bracelet with a facile story about why I want to sell it. Mr Patel's eyes gleam with the acquisitive glint of a master craftsman presented with flawless gems in a classical setting. 'Madam,' he says with genuine feeling, 'I am a very bad businessman to be telling you, but this is a beautiful workmanship and very pure gems. Where did you get it?'

I trot out my story; my neighbour, a Russian girl, was given this by a friend (Mr Patel understands the sub-text of 'friend' and twinkles obligingly at me) and now her son is ill and she needs money very badly. But she is afraid to take the bracelet to a jeweller because she may not be believed and she does not want to get into trouble. He nods as he gets out his jeweller's eyepiece and examines the bracelet through it. 'How much does she need?' he queries.

'How much is it worth?' I counter. I know this little pirouette of steps in a pre-arranged ballet of getting to a price that satisfies everybody. I accept another cup of creamy tea and choose another biscuit. This could take some time.

'You have taken it elsewhere for appraisal, madam?' he asks me.

I give him a straight look. 'Mr Patel,' I answer. 'You are an honest man and my friend. Of course I would only bring it to you.'

He twinkles again. 'Well,' he says reflectively. 'How much does your friend think it is worth?'

I start high. 'Thirty thousand US dollars.'

Mr Patel does an artistic recoil and plumps himself onto his working stool, turning on his little light and examining the bracelet closely again, turning and twisting it so the light refracts off the cut surfaces into a myriad of flashes. 'No, no, madam,' he mutters, 'now I look more closely, the gems are a little flawed. I could not offer you more than ten thousand.'

This little play goes on for another ten minutes or so as both of us get closer to the price we want in the classic bargaining technique. The bracelet could be worth fifty thousand, I have no idea, and judging from Mr Patel's grin, I feel he is probably very aware that I have no idea of its real value. I am putty in his hands, but then I only need ten thousand dollars. Finally we compromise at fifteen thousand and, notwithstanding his protests that his kindness to me will be the death of him and the ruination of his business, I can tell he is well pleased. As am I. We part on the best of terms; I with five thousand dollars from his safe, and another ten thousand to be handed over the following week.

I have taken to wearing the gold filigree heart that Natasha gave me for Christmas; her photo in it makes her feel closer to me and I find myself talking to her occasionally; now as I drive home I thank her for the gift of the bracelet which makes it possible for me to win Jason. It is almost as if she is there beside me in the car; I tell her my fears and concerns but also my determination that I will not lose him to Katie Knight, that I possess the resolution that she has given me; the surety that I, myself, and myself alone, will have the courage to change my destiny.

Truth be told, I am no Lady Macbeth, but now that my decision is in the lap of the gods, I do not lie awake at night pondering whether it is right or wrong. I sleep without dreams in my grey and purple bedroom; I do not pine for Jason, for I feel secure that, at some time to be specified, he will be mine. He and Jack and Alexei and I will live together, and I will have my heart's desire and so will he. Beyond that, I do not allow my thoughts to go.

The message comes on the third day. It is a simple text message on my phone, a model of brevity, a simple one line statement; 'Midnight tonight, Fantasia car park, F16'. My mouth feels dry and my heart is beating in thick strong strokes as I drive through the glittering night-time city to my rendezvous. I have the gold heart round my neck, and I talk to Natasha as I go; in my mind I can hear her replies, her encouragement. 'Be strong, Sophie,' I hear her say, 'I am with you.'

The Fantasia car park is large and dimly lit as well as sparsely occupied; F16 is a well-chosen space as it is in a far corner, hemmed on two sides by shrubs and facing a busy road across a large strip of grass. As I swing round into the space, a man steps smoothly out of the bushes and opens the car door to slip into the seat beside me. In the sharp yellow light that pours down from the streetlight above, I recognise my contact of the other night. He expresses no surprise at seeing me; his eyes are cold and focused; he is here to do business.

I kill the engine and start to speak and I feel a curious sensation as if Natasha, lying above my heart as she is, is doing the talking. This clear sharp voice, bargaining for a woman's life, is not mine. I pass him the photograph and he hardly looks at it; the phone in his hand is recording everything I say.

He starts to speak, laying out the terms of the contract as it were. I will pay him $5,000 to do what he refers to as 'research.' If a resolution is possible it will be achieved at a time and date of his choosing. There will be no further discussion; one further message only will indicate where the remaining money will be paid. I hear my own voice, chill as his own, giving him the details he requires, and stressing above all else, that the child must not be involved, must not be touched. He growls assent; his professionalism perhaps insulted by my persistence on this point. He watches as I take the money out of the glove box, but I sit for a moment holding it to my breast, unable to bring myself to hand it over, to complete the transaction.

The minutes pass leaden-footed. The bright lights of the night time traffic flicker by; outside the closed container of the car, life goes on: trapped in this little metal box, this time capsule, there are just two of us. Two people who last week had no idea of the other's existence. The sound of waiting is palpable; my heart beats with thick strong strokes. There is no comprehension in my brain, only a beat like a ticking clock; a death watch beetle – but not for me. No comprehension of what this might mean and still yet everything it would mean if I bring myself to say the word. He waits and, in the harsh yellow light, his face is cold. He is a man of shadows and he hides from the light; he glances away and shifts in his seat. His coat smells of stale smoke; the leather squeaks uneasily under his weight. 'Well?' he asks, and his voice is dark, accented, redolent of the restless streets that are his territory.

And still I cannot speak. The breath sticks in my throat.

'Khelaas,' he says bluntly. The single word in Arabic is familiar: *enough.* He has had enough, he is making ready to go; his hand reaches for the door handle. The moment is here; it stands on tiptoe waiting to see what I will do.

'And there will be time, time to murder and create …'

I give him the money, the door opens and he is gone. It is done.

I drive home slowly, my mind numb. I cannot think of anything except what I have set in motion and how my whole upbringing, my moral character, the lessons in humanism taught at my mother's knee have just been overturned by a love that I cannot put aside, a pride that will not let another woman take from me what is mine. I hear Natasha's counsel and realise what I must do now. What I have done I have done, and I will never speak or think of it again. What is decreed will happen, and I must pretend a disinterest in it, distance it as an event not connected with me at all. That way I will be able to maintain the illusion that it is none of my doing. *Insh'allah*, as they say here, God willing. She will live or she will die. The matter is out of my hands.

Life goes on. The days unwind like orange peel in a continuous motion and fall every evening into oblivion. I am getting used, once again, to living with a young child and I am more proactive than Natasha ever was. I go into school and talk to his teachers; I supervise his homework and take him to football practice. I think that in the summer when we go to England I will draw up papers and adopt him legally. We are a close-knit family now, a curious unit brought together, an unholy alliance of a boy, a dog, a maid, and a woman who is contemplating murder. Maybe I am trying to atone for that sin by my love for Alexei; I know only that my resolution is that Alexei will become a man to be proud of, and one who will validate what those other women have given up for him. And he is changing. The irresolute, passionate child is giving way to a boy of sensitive charm, but with intelligent and measured focus. Alexei is growing up.

And I am organising my own life too. I consult a divorce attorney and serve papers on Rick. If I am to be with Jason then I must be free of Rick. On the evening of the day the papers are served, I take Rosie and Alexei out to dinner and a movie. It is a celebration of sorts and we have a marvellous time eating at Alexei's favourite restaurant and stuffing our faces with popcorn and soda as we giggle through a Pixar movie. We are a mismatched trio but united in love and adversity. They are my moral compass, these two.

And, suddenly, we are back into the summer months; Alexei does brilliantly in his exams and more celebrations are in order. He is particularly strong in Maths and the Sciences although the languages teacher says he has a wonderful ear and can pick up the rudiments of any language in a very brief space of time. I book our holiday in England and buy tickets for Rosie to go home to India for three weeks – her preference. 'Madam,' she says glowingly, 'to see my children and my friends. And to take presents! I will be so popular!' Alexei goes online and books himself into the English sports camp for two more weeks and is thrilled to receive an email from blonde Katrina saying she can't wait to have him back. Life is good. The only one who is miserable will be Hector, and he is booked into a boarding kennels recommended by my Pet's Parlour contact. Puss is going too but fortunately the kennels are segregated and Puss will be in the felines section.

And what of Jason? We communicate on our secret email account; he tells me that he misses me, that in spite of the excitement and stress of packing up and moving to another country, he thinks of me constantly. He asks to meet one more time. I decline. I have it in mind that he will be with me for the rest of my life; I can do without him for a few months.

Every morning I wake and wonder if it will be today that I hear. I think I am foolish not to have asked how long this would take; does *he* remember, I wonder, that Jason and Katie are moving on and there is a time restraint? I want to go back to the Fantasia and ask for another meeting, but I restrain myself. Sophie is learning patience. He is a professional and biding his time, waiting for the right moment, and I must do the same. I sleep with Natasha's turquoise silk robe across the bottom of my bed; it gives me comfort and makes me feel as if she's close by, supporting me.

A new family has moved in next door and it seems strange to see Natasha's house come to life again with kids swimming in the pool, the maid hanging out the washing on the roof and a pleasant looking family of unknown origin hosting BBQs in the evening. But I am like Natasha; I keep myself to myself and have very little interaction with them beyond the occasional friendly wave if we see each other in the street.

The days go by. We have a final edition of the magazine and start to pack up the office for the summer vacation. And still there is no news of the kind I want; my divorce papers come back signed and uncontested by Rick so I am three-quarters of the way to being a free woman but, curiously, this makes me more fretful than ever. I leave the matter with the divorce attorney who is, of course, also away for a few weeks over the summer. I don't know what to do. Alexei is in his final two weeks of school; Rosie is packing and buying presents for family in India and I am biting my nails in a fret. What has happened? Each time my phone buzzes with a message I nearly jump out of my skin; Shazza remarks that I look 'stressed'. I have no one to confide in, no one to talk to; I am sleeping badly, the slightest noise wakes me and food sticks in my throat. I think of Lady Macbeth's words: *'these things cannot be thought of, it will make us mad'.*

Then I begin to wonder if something happens, when something happens, if he will tell me. Perhaps he wouldn't. I think of Rick, so anxious not to have Ophelia know that he is divorced in case it should change the nature of their relationship. With a sick feeling at the pit of my stomach, I wonder if this is also true of Jason Knight. When Katie Knight dies, *what if he does not tell me?* What if he should just take his freedom and move on? He has, after all, finished with Dubai; he has signed a contract with an international school in Moscow. He is on the way out of the country and, without his wife, he is free. For the first time I wonder how much he does love me; is it possible that he would move on without telling me what has happened? Is it possible that he would relish the chance to start again; to create a new life that does not include me? At bottom how much do I really know of Jason Knight? How much do I really trust him?

I am sitting at my desk one morning, chewing my nails and drinking coffee; there is a summer sandstorm blowing and the windows are shrouded with dust. Shazza and I are alone in the office; Alex's desk, abandoned now for some six weeks, looks like it has become a dumping ground for other people's coffee cups. Alex has sent me an email from New York; a facetious little scribbling in his inimitable style, saying no one understands either his accent or his British sense of humour but, in spite of that, he's imposing a degree of order on the office and his article is shaping up nicely. He has a few last facts to confirm and then, come mid-summer, it will be published.

Shazza is sitting at her desk, coffee in hand, flicking through the pages of the local daily paper; every now and then she laughs at something or snorts with derision at some badly written piece. 'Then suddenly, she says, 'Fucking hell, Sophie,' and I look up sharply at the note in her voice. 'Listen!' And she begins reading:

'A British woman who was yesterday killed in her car by a hornet sting has now been identified as Katie Knight, a teacher at a leading international school here in Dubai. Mrs Knight, aged 41, is thought to have suffered from anaphylactic shock after the sting and died in the car within minutes. Her husband, Jason Knight, a teacher at the same school, was not available for comment.'

I feel as if I have turned to stone. 'Fuck!' says Shazza, with feeling. 'Can you believe it? That cute guy … and now he's lost his wife. Well, you never do know, do you? Allergic to a hornet sting. Well, it happens, and people just don't know they're allergic. And those hornets are nasty fuckers.'

I sit there; I feel the blood drain from my face and my limbs feel heavy as lead. Shazza looks up. 'Sophie? Christ, you look terrible. Here …' she fills a paper cup of water from the cooler and brings it over to me. 'Oh, sorry love … I shouldn't have jumped it on you like that. Drink this …' she holds the water to my lips and I gulp it obediently. I feel deathly sick; I think I am going to faint or cry, I am not sure which. It turns out be the latter, and I burst into tears and sob hysterically, exhausted with relief that it has finally happened and the waiting is over. Shazza applies tissues and sympathy, but clearly has no idea in the world why I am carrying on in this way. Finally, I quieten down and look at her; she cocks an eyebrow at me and I say, muzzily, 'Sorry. That was ridiculous. I have no idea where that came from.'

Shazza gives me a pat, then goes back to her own desk and sips her coffee. 'Weird,' she comments, and I have no idea whether she's referring to my behaviour or to Katie Knight's death.

'You look awful,' she says now. 'I think this divorce business has hit you harder than you let on.' I had told Shazza about my divorce from Rick as an excuse for my 'stressed' appearance of last week. At least that gives me a semi-genuine excuse for my hysteria and I grasp it eagerly. I take myself off to the Ladies and fix my face and swollen red eyes; back at my desk Shazza makes me a fresh cup of coffee and, sensibly, changes the subject away from either accident or divorce.

I take myself off home presently; the office is a week away from closing entirely for the summer and there is only filing and tidying up to do. I can't settle, though, even at home; Alexei is out to an end of term party so, although the evening is exhaustingly hot, I take Hector round the block. He seems almost as lethargic as me; the summer heat is sapping and I can do no more than totter. Hector is a shadow of his winter-time self; he even ignores a cat sleeping under a bush which is totally uncharacteristic. My mind is going round in circles like a scrambling mouse in a wheel; she is dead and Jason is free. I have won. She is dead because of my planning. What to do now occupies me for the remainder of the walk; when I get in I send Jason an innocuous text message: '*Read the tragic news in the paper. Deepest sympathy. Sophie'.* Now at the least the ball is in his court and I wait, chewing my nails, for his reply. It takes a day but finally I get a text message back. *'Jack and I are going to England. Get in touch with you there?'* I send a message back with my UK phone number and wait and wait for any further response. There is none. Finally, desperate, I dial his number but the phone just rings. The schools are finished and he has a body to take back to England and a funeral to arrange. He has gone.

The holiday season is upon us once again; Hector and Puss are taken off to the pet hotel, Rosie to the airport and Alexei and I find ourselves alone for a few days before we too are on our way home to England. I have been watching my phone waiting for a message from *l'assassin* but, curiously, there is nothing. His further $5000 sits unclaimed in the safe. I have no way to contact him, so I can do nothing but shrug and decide to ignore it until I get back. He will, obviously, assume that I have, like the rest of the expats here, gone home, and will no doubt wait until the end of the summer holidays and my return. Maybe June is a busy month for contract killings.

I think about it when I close up the house and Alexei and I set off for the airport; I think about it as the plane rises smoothly into the cloudless sky and sets a course for England; I think about it as I drink a couple of stiff vodka and tonics and bless the entertainment system for keeping Alexei blissfully quiet, headphones clamped to his ears. Finally I can't think about it any more. *These things cannot be thought of; it will make us mad.* My stupid brain doesn't understand though; it changes tack and now I am bedevilled with thoughts of *what will he do now*? Will he go to Moscow as planned? His job in Dubai has finished. What will he do? What will he do about me? What will I do? Finally, worn out, I fall asleep and minutes later, it seems, we are on the ground. A chill breeze and heavily overcast sky publishes the fact that we are home.

We settle back into my aunt's house in Worcestershire with the accustomed ease of homing pigeons returning to the roost, and within the week Alexei is off to camp and I have time for leisurely strolls in the woods or across the fields or a gentle afternoon's weeding of the herbaceous borders.

One warm summer's morning I suddenly bethink myself of the trip I had intended to make to London to speak to Natasha's property company. I ring to book an appointment and the next day sees me at the station early and childishly excited to be going on the train to London. I walk from the

Underground up Regent Street, enjoying the crowds of tourists and the shop windows; London has a wonderful summertime buzz which makes me feel free, for the first time in ages, and I feel youthful and sexy in my summer dress and high pink shoes. I feel like a new Sophie, bouncy and curiously excited, as if something wonderful is going to happen. Then, like a creeping cloud obscures the face of the sun, the feeling comes that I shouldn't be happy; I push it aside and think instead of him for whom I have done this thing, and wish that he could be with me now. But my head is high as I push through the crowds and, when I see a man turn his head and look after me, I flash him a dazzling smile and feel a resurgence of positivity. I clasp my gold heart and think how proud Natasha would be of me.

The property company offices are very minimalist and smart; I am offered coffee by a receptionist with perfect red talons and a smile to match. After a while a rather svelte-looking young man appears and introduces himself as 'Angus'. 'Welcome to London Ms Haddon. Please come this way.' I follow him down a corridor and take a seat in a chrome and black leather office that feels both cold and prosperous. He has a desk full of files and starts talking as I frown and try to follow.

'So the property our client has left you is the property you currently occupy in Dubai, free of all debt or charges. We have here your letter dated some months back, wherein you offered to take over the costs of maintaining this property and also the school fees of our client's son, Alexei. However,' I sip my coffee, 'you will recall that I wrote to you explaining that none of this was necessary as there is more than enough money in our client's account to pay for all maintenance on the property and to support Alexei.'

'Yes,' I say helpfully.

He continues in this vein, while I listen attentively and try not to focus on the sharply pointed toes of Angus's shoes, pondering their shine. Finally he pauses and I put my empty coffee cup on the desk. We look at each other, smiling. 'Well,' he says, 'I think that about sums it up. Is there anything you'd like me to explain?'

'No,' I say, 'you've been very thorough. Thank you.'

'Oh,' he says, with a start, 'You must think I'm very remiss. Of course you have my sincere condolences for the loss of your friend. It was a tragedy. She was such a very charismatic person.'

That makes me smile; I think how Natasha would fix him with a cold eye if she were here. For charismatic, read intimidating.

'Yes,' I say again, 'thank you. She certainly was.' A sudden thought makes me frown. 'But how did you know she was dead?' I ask him, 'who told you? What did they say?' For it suddenly occurs to me that this property holding company of Natasha's, secret as it is, could hardly have known of her death through the ordinary channels. After all, there was no one to tell them, no death certificate. So how did they know? I, her closest friend, was not even sure of it.

He flicks through the file. 'Yes,' he says, 'here is the death certificate ... issued by the UAE authority.' He extracts it from the file and hands it to me. Here, at last then is the proof; the whys and wherefores remain unanswered but this stark piece of paper is a pronouncement of what, up 'til now, I have feared but also tried to deny: confirmation of her death. But it does not answer the question and I ask him again, 'But who sent it? I never knew that her death had been confirmed and I was her closest friend.' I am about to add that I never saw her body, but keep silent. There is something going on here that I don't understand.

He looks again at the paperwork. 'I'm sorry,' he says finally. 'There's no indication – just the death certificate, but that was all we needed of course to make it official. And everything is very straightforward,' he continues. 'There was just the bequest to you and the bulk of the property left to Mrs Prue Sarn.'

'What?' The word bursts out of me, so that he looks up at my tone.

'Mrs Prue Sarn, did you say?' I query.

'That is correct,' he looks down at the file to check, 'yes. She was the main beneficiary.'

I stare at him, mouth open, brain reeling. Prue Sarn! Prue Sarn, the fictional heroine from 'Precious Bane', a name that only Natasha and I would know!

'Ms Haddon?'

'Sorry,' I say feebly, 'um, I think I might know her. Could you, um, give me her address?'

'Yes, of course,' he takes a card and scribbles an address on it. 'There you are. And thanks for calling in, Ms Haddon. If you need anything else, please don't hesitate to call.'

I hardly hear him, and I wander out of his office in a daze, shaking hands at the lift, his card held tight in my hand. As the lift descends, I look at it and my breath is coming fast. *Could it be ... could it be?* ... I never felt she was dead. I clench the locket and feel my heart beating with great hammer strokes of happiness. Who is Mrs Prue Sarn? I look at the card now; 'The Old Barn, Rectory Lane, Tillingham.' I frown as I walk out into the sunshine. Tillingham? A village in the Cotswolds, if I'm not mistaken. I stand amid the bustling crowds on the pavement, my eyes glistening with tears in the sun. Natasha, Natasha ... are you still alive and waiting for me to find you?

Back on the train I realise that, idiot that I am, I did not ask for the phone number. But then he did not offer it. Maybe they communicate in some other way. In Worcester my aunt is waiting for me and I choke out the story in excitement. She smiles in her vague way as she navigates us home through the market day crowds. 'How wonderful for you, dear,' she says, 'but if she is alive, it would mean, surely, that she faked her own death. Why would she do that?'

I try and explain without it sounding too much like a John Le Carré novel; once home I rush indoors and find an Atlas, tracing the route through Cotswold villages to the tiny dot that is Tillingham. It should of course be Shropshire, I muse. My aunt agrees I can have the car the next day, and I spend the evening in a buzz of excitement, hardly able to sleep for wondering what the morrow will bring. Late in the evening there is a text on my phone with Jason's number; finally all my ducks are lining up in a row. I ring him, and my stomach nosedives at his voice; my heart beating so hard I can almost not speak.

'Darling.' I say softly. 'How are you?'

'Fine,' he says. He sounds tired. 'How are you?'

'Is everything … finished? I've been thinking about you such a lot. It must have been awful.'

'Yes,' he says, 'it was. But Katie's parents were very good and organised everything. I was in a bit of a state and of course I wanted to keep it together for Jack.'

'Yes, of course.' I ignore the little frisson of irritation – Jack, always Jack first. 'How's he bearing up?'

'Quite well, actually. He misses her but I think he appreciates the peace and quiet. Like I do. And England is always good for him, constant entertainment by grandparents, outings, that sort of thing. And he's getting used to her not being here; some days he hardly mentions her at all.'

He sounds so calm, so resigned, I start to feel more relaxed myself; everything, it seems, has indeed worked out for the best. 'So,' I say softly, 'can we meet? When can I see you? I miss you so much.'

He sounds vaguely distracted. 'We're off to Cornwall tomorrow for ten days, to see some friends. They have kids of Jack's age and a house near the beach. But that's a bit far from you.'

'Oh,' I say feebly. 'Ten days. But after that?'

'Yes, perhaps, after that. We will be in London for a few days. Maybe you could come down?'

'Of course, you only have to let me know when and where and I'll be there.' There's a pause, 'Yes,' he says, finally, 'brilliant.' A longer pause. 'I miss you, gorgeous,' he says.

My stomach contracts with joy. This is the old Jason speaking, his voice soft and tender. We speak for a long while then he rings off. I hug myself and feel thrills of anticipation coursing up my spine. He loves me still and now we can be together – the last bar to our relationship is gone and we have years of happiness to look forward to.

It is in this mood of joyful anticipation, therefore, that I set off in the morning to find Natasha. The day is fresh and beautiful; great trees arch over the green byways of the shires as I drive through, wending my way through tranquil chocolate box villages, their peace disturbed only by the tourist buses that occasionally draw up to disgorge a group of chattering visitors. Tillingham lies at the bottom of a valley and is very remote; in the winter it must be nigh-on inaccessible. But it is charming on this sparkling summer's day, the golden stone cottages wreathed with roses and fronted by gardens full of wildflowers. Rectory Lane winds down behind the church and I am upon it so suddenly I overshoot the gate of a small converted barn tucked in off the road and almost hidden by a high stone wall. I back up and see the sign on the letterbox – The Old Barn. I pull in off the side of the road, and walk back; there is a high wrought-iron gate in the stone wall and, through this, I can see the house. The countryside is hot and silent and nothing moves in the well-tended garden; there are roses and flowers in abundance but all is quiet with no car in the driveway, no sign of life at all. I am trembling with excitement but also with a sense of fear; I have been so buoyed up with hope and now this silent welcome betokens disappointment. Nevertheless I ring the bell with energy, and wait. Nothing. I ring again, and now the front door opens and an elderly woman looks out. I feel a stabbing moment of despair, but I wave and she comes slowly along the path to the gate. She is tall and elderly, but well-dressed in the style known as 'county'; dark green trousers with a silk shirt and scarf and her hair is fair rather than white. She comes up to the gate and looks at me through it. 'Yes?' she says.

'I'm looking for Mrs Prue Sarn,' I say, 'are you she?'

'Yes,' she says, and I hear the hint of an accent in her voice. 'Who are you?'

'I'm Sophie Haddon. I'm a friend of Natasha.' I look closely at her, hoping to see some emotion register in her face but there is nothing.

'Who?'

Now this will not do at all; I have come too far to be disappointed now. 'Natasha,' I say firmly. 'The property company in London told me you were the main beneficiary of Natasha's will, so it's pointless to pretend that you don't know her. I'm Sophie Haddon from Dubai. Can I come in? I need to talk to you.'

She looks at me for a long minute and then reaches up to unlock the gate. 'Thank you,' I say as I walk through. She locks the gate again and precedes me up the path into the house. It is small and light with sunlight streaming in from windows high in the walls, a charming open-plan conversion. On one side a large stone-flagged kitchen, on the other a sitting room looks out onto a well-stocked orchard. 'Please go into the sitting room,' she says, closing the front door, 'I will bring coffee.'

I do so, choosing a large wing chair near the window; the room is furnished in a comfortable Laura Ashley style that is elegant without being chintzy. The woman re-enters with a tray and suddenly, on a flash, I know who she is. 'Babushka?' I query, and she nods with a slight smile. 'Alexei is with me,' I say, 'he's well, and happy, and … he's a great kid. You would be proud.' She smiles again as I hunt in my wallet for his photo and hold it out to her. She studies it intently. 'He has changed,' she says, 'but I see something of his mother in him.' She gives me a straight look as she hands me a cup of coffee. 'Thank you,' she says.

As I put the coffee on a side table there is a stir of movement behind me and a voice says, mockingly, 'I always said you would be a better mother than I was, Sophie.'

I swing around and there she is, standing in a beam of sunlight, laughing at me; Natasha, as real and beautiful as she ever was, the turquoise eyes softer but mocking still … Natasha alive, and as I leap up to hug her, holds me closely for a moment and then puts me gently aside.

She goes to sit in another wing chair and takes the cup that Babushka holds out to her. 'So you found me, Sophie,' she says. 'That must be the journalist in you.'

I am still breathless from shock and excitement. 'I knew it!' I blurt out. 'I just knew you weren't dead!' My eyes take in her beloved features; she looks well, happy and relaxed. 'Tell me, tell me everything,' I command.

She tosses back the thick blonde hair and twinkles across at Babushka. 'You have guessed who this is, Sophie, my dearest Babushka, now become Mrs Prue Sarn, and the owner of this charming cottage. We are now country-dwellers, Babushka and I. As to the story, it is quite a simple one. Dear Alex was the answer to my problem as you believed he would be. He introduced me to the right people – people who were prepared to rescue me in return for the very valuable information I gave them. So I came here, with Babushka, and now Mrs Prue Sarn and her daughter live in this little village. The people here are friendly and kind especially to a mother and daughter from Poland who want only a quiet existence.'

'You mean MI5?' I query, 'you're on the witness protection programme? And the death certificate? I suppose they faked it?'

She smiles at my wide-eyed excitement. 'I'm sorry I couldn't tell you, Sophie,' she says. 'I was sworn to secrecy but it was to protect you and Rosie and Alexei. To vanish as I did was the way that my mentors thought most appropriate; I believed, as I told Alex, that my life was in danger. We were running out of time. I was flown out secretly on a private plane and given a new life here. My choice. And Babushka of course came to join me. And for you not to know what was happening was essential because you did everything you would do if you had believed me to be dead and that was enough to convince the watchers that I had gone. The Palace might suspect outside intervention but nothing was provable. They cleared the house, I imagine, as they always do and proceeded to forget about a certain Russian girl who knew too much.'

'I've kept the Star of the Sea safe for you,' I say, and then I remember that the bracelet has been sold, and for what purpose and reach for my coffee to cover my blunder. 'But they took everything else.' She shrugs in the fatalistic way she has. 'I am happy to be out of that place,' she says, 'away from those people. The clothes were only trappings. As to the jewellery, as I told you, sell it or keep it for Alexei.'

'Can I tell him? Can I tell Rosie? She was desperately upset when you went missing.'

Even before she answers I know what she will say. 'No, no one must know; Rosie and Alexei will forget me soon enough. I knew you would find me eventually; I guessed that once you heard of Mrs Prue Sarn you would put the rest together. Angus deals with Babushka of course; no one knows about me.'

We talk on and the long afternoon fades to golden twilight. Babushka goes to prepare dinner and Natasha and I walk around the orchard and the garden, picking vegetables and herbs for a salad, admiring her roses, me trying to fill her in on everything that has happened in her absence. Well, almost everything. I haven't mentioned Jason yet, or Katie Knight's death. I am to stay the night and I text a message to my aunt, telling her I'll be back in the morning. Natasha is just the same – except perhaps more tranquil than before. She has given up smoking; she works online for the Russian language service of the BBC and spends a lot of time preparing her broadcasts. How else does she fill her days? I ask. She smiles pensively as Babushka serves us some marvellous vegetarian goulash with baked potatoes and salad. 'I have lived such a life, my Sophie, such a rushed, desperate life that, for me, this is the childhood I lost. This quiet country cottage with my Babushka, our little pursuits, the hens, the roses, making elderflower cordial … one day, perhaps, I may tire of it, but for now it is so restful. For the first time in my life I am relaxed, I wake up in the morning and I am happy to be alive. We walk, we talk, we are the best of companions …' here she says something in Polish to Babushka who smiles. 'For Babushka too, this is heaven on earth, something she never dreamed she could ever have. How strange it is, Sophie, that out of all that darkness could come so much light.'

I am so happy to see her like this that my eyes fill with tears, blurring the candlelight. 'I sometimes wish,' she goes on, 'that Alex would never publish his exposé. I would so like just to forget it all.'

'It should be very soon,' I say, 'he did promise the beginning of August. And after that, it will all truly be over. But you should be proud of the role you played; it was through your information, as I understand, that Alex's story could come together. It will be sensational.'

'Maybe,' she says tiredly, 'but I know politics and I know the Palace. There will be spin and cover-ups, and, when the dust settles, life will go on. The evil will continue, perhaps worsen, but at least the eye of the world will be on Dubai, so in that way, I have achieved a small outcome. And those who are fighting against such terrorism know the truth. I have told my story, given names and dates, hard evidence against those who kill in the name of religion and the princes who support them. At least I have done that much.'

I raise my glass to her. 'To the bravest woman I know,' I say and Babushka raises her glass too and we drink the toast. Babushka collects up our plates and bustles into the kitchen, taking something that smells wonderful from the oven. Natasha laughs. 'Babushka is loving having her own kitchen, and time to cook in it! She is feeding me up; I will get fat.'

'It's her therapy,' I say wisely. 'You are both relaxing, recovering from the hurricane years. Time for you both to just enjoy every day.'

'And you Sophie?' she asks. 'What of you? What of Jason Knight? I have often wondered.'

I don't want to say anything about Jason yet, and fortunately the re-entrance of Babushka with a marvellous cooked cheesecake ('a genuine Polish recipe I had from my mother' she tells me) provides me with a genuine distraction. We drink wine, eat amazing food, gossip and laugh for the remainder of the evening. The windows stand open to the garden, and the air is full of scent.

Later Babushka goes to bed, leaving Natasha and I alone. 'I love these cool English summer evenings,' she says, 'they remind me I'm a long, long way from the heat of the desert. It's gentle too, not like the heat of a Russian summer. And the winters are such fun … we tucked ourselves up with lots of food and the Aga and were as happy as two squirrels.' Her pronunciation is more 'squillels' and makes me giggle.

There is a wonderful sense of déjà vu; a reminder of the nights we spent in Dubai, lying on two separate sofas, talking about life, Natasha's hard-headedness remoulding my soft and trusting nature, her cynical heart disciplining my own overtly-sensitive organ. She is softer now, less hard on herself and others, but no less of a mystery to me really than she had been all those months ago. Still unhappy to talk about herself, guarding her secrecy, uncomfortable to share her closest feelings, even with me. What had she really done? I am sure I will never hear the full story from her lips; I will have to wait until Alex's story is published and then piece two and two together. Whether she is silent from necessity or caution or just plain modesty I do not know. The truth about her involvement may never be known; like her, it is secretive, filed away by the democratic powers that are in league against Islamic fundamentalism, kept in a locked filing cabinet, visible to only those who dwell in the ivory powerhouses. And guarded by them until the day it should be needed.

'So tell me now,' she says softly. 'Has he left Dubai? Did you win or did you lose the battle for Jason Knight?'

It's a hard question to answer, I realise. Katie Knight may be dead but her husband is still an uncontrollable factor in my present happiness; apart from a lustful date in London I have no idea what he will do. He may go to Moscow but he may not. Katie's inheritance, a considerable sum of money, has been left to him by her; her father had been a rich man and Katie his only child. Ironically, Jason is far better off financially without Katie than he ever was with her. He may decide that Jack needs to be close to his grandparents and remain in England for that reason. Whatever else he does, however, it is almost certain that he will never return to Dubai. I will have to cross that bridge when I come to it.

And so I tell her. I begin at the beginning, how Alex and I went looking for an assassin who could have had her own name on his hit list and how, later, I went back and recruited him myself. How I sold the bracelet and paid the man for a hit of my choosing, and how he had carried out his commitment. I tell it all, and sit watching her face as she slowly nods with approval as I come to the end of my tale. 'You were with me, all the time,' I say, holding the gold heart that hangs over my breast and which I never leave off wearing. 'I talked to you, and you told me what to do. You never left me and for that reason I always knew that you weren't dead.'

'What a good student you are, Sophie,' she says finally. 'Look how strong and self-determined you have become.'

I look down at my hands, spreading them wide so the cool blue sapphire glows in the lamplight. 'I keep thinking of Lady Macbeth: *these things cannot be thought of, it will make us mad'*. So I don't think about it. And I don't have him yet anyway. Whatever happens he will never return to Dubai; he may stay here or go to Moscow – whichever way I have to be prepared to move, to change my life, to give up everything from Dubai and make a new life. And there's Jack; I don't know how he would respond to a stepmother. So it's not a done deal, not by any stretch of the imagination.'

She maintains that level look over her coffee cup. 'How practical you are,' she says coolly. 'Well, we shall see. And at least you won the war.'

'No,' I say slowly, 'only one battle. The war for hearts and minds is still to be fought.'

'Que sera sera,' she says lightly, 'so I can have my house back?'

We sit up and chat into the small hours; there are so many things to discuss. She is more than happy that I should adopt Alexei and, indeed, both of us regard him as mine already. She agrees he may come and visit Babushka but as for Natasha, she has gone from his life and will never return. She shows no signs of wanting any particular information on him even; I try and excuse her coldness to myself by arguing that he was never hers, merely a child left on her hands and for whom, in all fairness, she did the best she could and will continue to support, albeit silently. She does not indulge in idle speculation about Jason Knight and where he will go but she laughs at me when I wonder if I could ever get a job in England. There is no newspaper or magazine, I believe, that would employ me. I suddenly realise I have nothing here, no assets, no friend to buy me a house, no job and very few prospects. Loving Jason Knight and leaving Dubai to be with him may prove to be an expensive exercise for me and something that I never considered; I always imagined any future with him as a kind of perpetual golden domestic dream, where we drifted through love-filled days and jasmine-scented nights. The cold truth is that I may end up giving up all I have for love. Foolish Sophie.

Over a last Baileys over ice before bed, I change the subject. 'I would love to know what happened,' I say quietly. 'What was the connection between the man you spoke of – the fanatic in whose eyes you saw death – and Alex's story?'

She sighs deeply. 'It is such a long story, Sophie, and I don't have the heart to tell it. But I will give you a brief outline and when you read Alex's story you will understand the whole thing.' The ice clinks gently in her glass as she lies back on the cushions. 'I always knew that the palace was a hotbed of intrigue and secrets and, most of the time, I stayed out of it on the premise that none of it concerned me. But I am ... intelligent ... and I began to pick up scraps of information, overheard comments, and of course I read too, especially the news about the UAE and I began to see there was a link ... not just the old news that everyone guessed that Dubai was paying Al Qaeda to stay out, but something darker and more sinister. In spite of the apparent political will to be part of the West, the presence of the Americans and the British intelligence services, the control at airports and the port, the apparent transparency of motive, there was something that didn't fit. I began to suspect that the palace was doing a separate deal; at first I thought it was Al Qaeda again, but then, on the summer trip, I began to understand that Al Qaeda was just small fry. The real enemy was Al Shabbab. They were the ones that Dubai feared. Men came on board the yacht; I was confined to my cabin but I talked to the Filipino crew and found out who was there and pretty much what was said.'

She laughs softly. 'It's always fascinating, to see Arab contempt for their servants and to turn the tables on such ignorance. Several of the Filipino boys spoke good Arabic, enough to understand what was being said, and who would suspect them? They came and went like shadows, serving the food, filling up the water jugs, invisible and all-seeing. And then they came to me and told me what they had heard ... it was a challenging project for a bored woman, and good exercise for my brain. And then ... one day, quite by accident, I saw ... him. I had been diving, and I came back onto the yacht at the same time as he came on deck. We stood, maybe two metres apart, and looked at each other and, in his eyes, I saw it all. They were the eyes of a fanatic; if looks could kill I would not be standing here now. He was African, pure black, and his robes were of purest white. And I realised, suddenly, how much he hated them too, not just me, a rich man's plaything, I was nothing, but the princes that he did business with, how he must have despised them.

I knew then that I was in danger too, I had seen him, and I knew who he was. It was not so difficult to guess he was Al

Shabbab and my laptop was full of evidence of my searches into Al Qaeda in Arabia; if any of the Filipinos betrayed me it would confirm that I was, essentially, spying. For a while I was safe because of the contempt they had for me; a woman and therefore a fool, but I knew it could not be forever. And there was something else. I knew of the demands of Saudi and others who were funding Dubai, that there was to be an end to their dissolute lifestyle; the Muslim faith was under scrutiny and if they wanted to run with the hounds, they had to be pure. And they were far from that. I knew my time there was limited, so I redoubled my efforts to find out as much as I could. I got names and dates, hard facts; to what end I wasn't quite sure, only that it was a quest, a fulfilment of personal curiosity perhaps, a determination to understand it all. And although I was desperate, I was never careless. And then I spoke to Alex and it was like a trouble halved. He had friends in high places, and they wanted the information I had. So we did a deal. My safety and a new life in exchange for everything I had on the Dubai-Al Shabbab link. I went back to the palace and this time I was fitted with all the technical wizardry that was essential; I was wired, I took photographs, copied computer files. And the strange part was that I loved every minute of it. I forgot about its being dangerous, and I enjoyed it all the more because it was my revenge; the perfect revenge too, on all those who treated women as objects and mocked their intelligence. And then, it was done. And now ... here I am.' She indicates the room with a wave of her hand. 'And I am happy. I am ... vindicated. I have made this long journey, Sophie, which often seemed without purpose. And I am now, at last, one of life's winners. I have my work with the BBC which occupies my brain, and I have this life, this house, with the one woman who always loved me.'

I have been sitting, fascinated by this tale, completely absorbed in her telling of it. 'Wow,' I say finally. 'I stick to what I said before – you are truly the bravest woman I know! And, you don't have only one woman who loves you ... you have two!'

She smiles, and gets up, stretching her long body, she leans and kisses me on the forehead. 'I know. Dormez bien, my Sophie.'

My bedroom is under the eaves; the window is open and there is the intermittent call of an owl, but it cannot keep me awake. Lulled by the scents of roses and honeysuckle, as well as the sweet peas Babushka has put on the chest of drawers, I sleep like a baby. My world is restored, and for this night I sleep the sleep of the righteous.

Back in Worcestershire, my extraordinary lightness of being continues. The low-key sense of loss I have laboured under for so long has disappeared; Natasha is alive and well and my world is once more joyful and full of promise. Tasha comes to stay for a week, and I am amazed at the pleasure I experience in my daughter's presence. We have fun. We share things, and laugh; she is lovely with Alexei whom she teaches to play tennis on the neighbour's court and there is real companionship in the way we chat as we prepare dinner, giggle over television dramas and kiss each other goodnight with genuine affection. Tasha has changed; she is not the expat brat she once was; gone are her spoilt ways and airs and graces. She brings flowers and chocolates for Jessie; she is quiet and polite, does her share of chores and is, in every way, delightful. I am proud that she is my daughter. I am sad when I have to take her to the station and wave goodbye as she departs for a week with her boyfriend's family in the Lake District. But my sorrow is tinged with happiness that Tasha is clearly so relaxed and has really, as the saying goes, grown into herself. The beauty and charm flow now from a much softer and giving source than the intense preoccupation with self that Tasha inherited from Rick and which was honed in the instant-gratification world of Dubai. She has also grown closer to her brother, a fact which makes me very happy, and their long conversations and mutual support seem to have moved Nick into the place that Rick once occupied. We don't speak of Rick very much. She has heard little from him since, as he perceives it, she has moved into my orbit. As to the divorce, both she and Nick see it as a positive move on my part and are only angry that I get so little out of it; it takes a great deal of talking by me to get them to see that there is very little to be had. We are all on our own; once they leave university they understand I cannot help them further and they have only themselves to depend upon. Maybe it is this new focus and reality that has brought out the best in Tasha. Whatever the reason is I know, as I wave her goodbye, that she will be all right. There is steel in Tasha, and now it will work for her good.

The days fly past and Jason sends me a message to say he's going to be staying at a cheap but comfortable hotel in London for two days, while Jack goes off with some cousins. If I can arrange to get myself to London, then we can spend two days together. The idea makes me almost sick with delight. Two whole days on my own with Jason ... no wife, no child, just us and the delights of a hotel room and the lure of London on the doorstep. Could anything be more exciting? Jessie, who knows nothing of Jason, comments that I am 'glowing' but suspects only that I am excited about two days' shopping and meeting friends in London. She and Alexei are to indulge in various local pastimes, a flower show and the village cricket match, and Alexei seems quite happy to hang out in the garden, weeding the odd border which he does with surprising care, and taking the neighbour's dog out for long walks, a task which he adores. It is a large and boisterous young Labrador, and Alexei loves playing dog trainer, putting into practice all the lessons he learnt with Hector. The neighbours think he is tremendous, and have already sent over various platters of cakes and goodies as solid proof of their appreciation. Alexei, who lately has an ever-increasing pre-teenage appetite, considers being paid in consumables to be a very civilised practice!

I pack my sexiest outfits, including a new set of lingerie which was an early birthday present to myself. I travel up to London on the train and make my way across town; the hotel is one of a major chain but is well-priced and comfortable as well as being centrally situated. The lift carries me up to the sixth floor; there is a long quiet corridor to navigate and then I press the doorbell. My heart is beating like a drum with anticipation; the door opens and we are in each other's arms.

After such a long separation, the magic of union is more glorious than ever. There is such joy in the sensation of being kissed and held and loved by this man I so adore that it really is the most perfect feeling life can provide. Finally, we move apart and he looks at me with a long look, his fingers lifting the hair off my face; 'The magic of holding you after so long,' he says finally. I kiss him again, lightly, and move into the room; 'Tea!' I say, dumping my bag, and filling the small kettle. He comes up behind me, kissing the back of my neck in a way that makes me shudder with anticipation, and says, 'Tea? Not champagne?'

'We have all the time in the world,' I say, 'tea now, and then champagne later. Are we going out for dinner?'

He lies back on the bed but with such an alluring smile that I go and join him, kneeling over him and kissing him deeply. The kettle rises to a little singing shriek so that I have to go and make the tea, bringing two cups back to the bed, and settling beside him on heaped up pillows.

'You do look pretty,' he says, turning on one elbow to face me.

'You think?'

'I thought that I'd never see you again,' he says softly, running his finger round the outlines of my face.

'Me too! But just look how everything has worked out,' I say with a smile; looking into his blue eyes makes me want to kiss him again, so I do. But he doesn't pull me down on top of him for more kissing as I expect; he turns away and picks up his teacup and for a moment there is an unspoken distance between us.

'I'm sorry,' I say, sipping my own tea. 'I didn't mean to be insensitive. No matter how much you wanted her out of your life, her…' I pause, 'death, must have come as a shock.' He continues to face away from me, 'do you want to talk about it?' I query. God knows I don't want to talk about Katie Knight but I must be aware that she still, ghostlike, stands between us in a small way and her shade must be expunged before we can be free of her.

He falls back on the pillows, his profile silhouetted against the slanting light of early afternoon. 'I did hate her,' he says slowly, 'but not for any of the reasons you might think; not that she ruined my life or anything like that. But simply because of Jack. She had the most wonderful kid alive and she could never see it. She was a cold-hearted bitch to him, and that was what got to me in the end... Sophie,' he says, turning his head on the pillow towards me, 'why didn't I marry you? Then none of this would have happened.'

I smile softly. 'Many people make mistakes in their choice of partners,' I say, 'I did, you did ... fortunately we live in a time when it's possible to get out of a bad marriage.' I want to go on to say it's not too late, he can marry me now if he likes, but it seems pushy and I am trying hard not to be that. But I feel we are moving in the right direction and it thrills me. 'But you were ... dare I say ... lucky? You didn't have to divorce her, you were spared that trauma ... and Jack too. And now you are free, and you can do anything you like.'

He says nothing, just gazes at the ceiling again. I've got plenty to say, however, and I babble on happily for several minutes, telling him about Natasha (having first sworn him to secrecy), my thrill at finding her alive, the happiest resolution of my fears for her. He listens carefully to my story and raises his eyebrows at my hints of what Alex's story will expose.

'Wow,' he says, 'it's like something out of Frederick Forsyth.'

I go on chattering about Alexei, about Tasha, until at last he's up to date with all the unimportant events which constitute my life. He listens attentively enough, smiling at me in the way that I know means that he's amused by my earnestness.

'Sophie ...' he says softly. I reach over and smooth the hair off his forehead and he turns to me; there is a moment of silence while we gaze at each other. 'Sophie ...' he says again, and I smilingly respond, 'What?' while smoothing away the faint frown lines between his eyes.

'Nothing,' he turns away and finishes his tea; turning back to me he takes me in his arms and we snuggle down into the bed. The luxurious quality of his kisses and the rising tide of passion stems any further thought of what he clearly decided not to share with me.

The evening is memorable; after an afternoon of glorious and abandoned lovemaking we go out and get tickets to a show, a musical (his choice) rather than a play (my choice) because, as he says, we have enough drama in our lives without paying money for more. I tease him that now he has so much money it doesn't matter; he looks angry for a moment and I apologise for making such a poor joke and in such bad taste. Clearly I have to guard my unruly tongue and remain sensitive to the fact that this man is bereaved and no matter how much he wanted her dead, the fact that she is must still be something he is coming to terms with. But it is hard for me not to be dizzy with happiness and the thought that, finally, everything I want is going to fall into my lap. Every event is charged with a special pleasure; the domestic quality of drying my hair in the bathroom while he showers, the light-hearted conversation punctuated with touching and kisses and giggles as we both dress. He has bought me perfume and insists on spraying it on what he refers to as my 'naked curves'.

It is like a honeymoon, a shimmering golden afternoon shot through with a delicious anticipation of what the evening will bring, recently recharged memories and the sheer unadulterated precious pleasure of being together at last with no barriers to the future.

The show is wonderful London entertainment at its best; during the interval Jason gets ice-creams and we sit and chat. When I enthuse over the singing and dancing; he says slowly, 'I can't comment, really. I've never been to a London show before.'

I gawp at him in surprise; he takes advantage of the moment to say with a gleam of humour in his blue eyes, 'Can I have your ice cream if you're not going to finish it?'

'Of course,' I hand it over meekly, still shocked by his revelation. 'Really? You've never been to a show before?'

'Not like this,' he says, spooning up ice cream. 'Oh pop concerts and that sort of thing, obviously, but not a show on the London stage.'

It reminds me that there is so much about this man I don't know, but also the fact that there is so much that we can share together; I see a glorious vista of cultural discovery ahead and smile with pleasure. 'I never grew up in London like you did,' he goes on, 'and we didn't have much money. I've got a lot of catching up to do!' I lick my finger and wipe a suspicion of ice cream off his mouth, more for the pleasure of touching him than any other reason; were it not for the seats behind us filling up rapidly I would have kissed it off but for some quiet reminder in my head that, although I may feel like a teenager, I am not one.

And London is *en fete* for us. We wander back to the hotel, stopping at an elegant hamburger joint, where we sit on barstools in a shining black and white American 50's diner, complete with Elvis guitars and an Oldsmobile parked in the corner. Later we walk, hand in hand, through the still-busy streets, thronged with young people on their way to clubs or bars. We stop in at a wonderful old Pub for a late night drink before heading back to the hotel. After all those years in Dubai the cultural kick of London is almost palpable; the eclectic charm of this older, sophisticated city so much at odds with its brash young cousin. For both of us it is the thrill of the homecoming expat – the never-forgotten heartbeat of one's own culture and one's own town. There is something in the air which correlates with my own sense of excitement and positivity.

I comment on this as we sit out on the square, sipping our drinks and people-watching. Jason says after the alcohol deprivation of Dubai, he can't get enough of good English beer and never passes up the opportunity to order an ale. 'One has to agree with Dr Johnson,' I say, 'when a man is tired of London he is tired of life.' He is busy concentrating on his beer, so I go on, 'I wonder what Moscow will be like?'

He flicks me a glance, 'No idea', he says briefly.

I wasn't really intending a fishing expedition, but I go on, neutrally, 'Are you looking forward to it?'

He looks down at his beer. 'Not sure,' he says laconically.

'But you will go?' I persevere. 'I thought perhaps you might decide to stay in England … for Jack. Grandparents and that sort of thing.'

He sips his beer. 'I'm committed to Moscow,' he says, 'I've signed a two year contract. Pulling out of that would be a bad career move.'

'But surely things have changed now… you signed up as a couple, with Katie. Are they still prepared to take you as a single man with a dependent child?'

He smiles at me over his beer. 'It was me they wanted, Sophie; Katie came as part of the deal. Primary school teachers are easy enough to find whereas secondary geographers are harder to come by.'

I twinkle at him over my glass. 'Well you won't find me disagreeing with them that you're exceptional!'

'To my biggest fan,' he says, raising his glass in a mock salute.

'Goodness,' I muse, 'how different Moscow will be after Dubai. Imagine all the wonderful things to see. I suppose you'll be in an apartment?'

'Yes, there are details somewhere. I've rather ignored it all I'm afraid. But I'll have to get on with reading it. And what about you? Will you stay in Dubai?'

I stare at him, trying to work out what's behind the question. It certainly isn't the one I was wanting to hear. And he says it so coolly, as if I'm a distant acquaintance he's politely chatting to over a drink.

'I don't know,' I answer slowly. 'I don't have anything here, whereas there I have a house, and of course there's Alexei to consider. He needs the continuity of school and friends. And I have my job too, such as it is. But I don't really want to be in Dubai without you. I don't actually want to be anywhere without you.' There, now I've said I and a little *frisson* of fear flickers through my heart as he looks down into his beer.

'Sophie,' he says on a sigh. 'I can't include you in my plans because ... I have no plans. Well not yet. I have to make decisions about what's best for Jack and ... I haven't made them yet.'

I feel as if the world is falling in on me; the street scene, so merry and bustling seconds before, has suddenly become a place of darkness and menace, reminding me of the dark streets where I had once sought an assassin. I grasp at words. 'But,' I begin, 'I thought that now she was gone, we could be together. I've always thought that. You told me she was all that was keeping us apart.'

He looks at me and the teddy-bear-soft blue-eyed lover seems to have vanished now in the man who looks back at me across the table. 'I did think that,' he says coolly, 'but now I'm on my own, well, I don't want to rush into another relationship. I think Jack and I need a little time to adjust.'

I'm struggling to process his words, but there is a terrible sense of my whole world unravelling as I see him moving on, without me. Everything I fought so hard to have happen has occurred but now the object of all this planning has just punctured my future with a few succinct phrases. My face must reflect my inner turmoil because he finishes his beer and, rising, takes my hand. 'Don't look so despairing,' he says, hugging me to him. 'I'll always love you, but just now I can't make too many rash decisions, too many changes. Jack and I are newly bereaved; I don't think he'd take kindly to a stepmother. We both need time to come to terms with what's happened.'

I shrug away from his hand; I'm having difficulty finding the words to say because they threaten to come out in a semi-hysterical rush of pleading and I'm afraid of losing him completely if I say what I think. Our relationship seems poised on a knife edge and one wrong word will send it hurtling into the abyss. I am truly shocked at what he's said. In my fairy-tale ending Jason and I, Jack and Alexei, would ride off into the sunset and live happily ever after. I see now how foolish I have been.

We walk back silently to the hotel; me trying not to cry and tense with fear, he, knowing he's upset me, fearing perhaps a tirade when we get indoors. I realise, dimly, that his wife's death has brought Jason Knight to a sense of self-determination that he never possessed before. He has a newly positive look about him that conveys a quiet steely strength; his speech is that of a man who has found the courage to act on his own initiative and needs no one to validate his sense of self. As Shazza would say, and Natasha would endorse, he has grown a pair of balls at last.

In our room, we look at one another; somehow the champagne cooling in the ice bucket and the bowl of red roses now exude a sense of failure, a stage set for a play that will never be acted out. I don't know what to do. I am afraid of pushing him for an answer, and I am afraid of letting him go to Moscow alone. I do not want to return to my lonely house in Dubai, with only a maid and a child who is not mine for company, no supportive Natasha next door to pop over and talk with, and to fill my days with a foolish job on a foolish magazine that is merely the plaything of a spoilt princess. My world seems, in a few hours, to have crumbled into sawdust. I had thought I held a winning hand but now, when the cards are on the table, I realise I have been deceived, trumped by a false belief that love would save me.

Perhaps to avoid further discussion and subsequent confrontation, he pulls me onto the sofa and kisses me. In the past I have melted into his kisses, unable to think coherently or even focus beyond the passionate response that flickers through my body, melting my bones, but now I am thinking ... thinking ... and the real Sophie seems to have withdrawn, despairingly, into a corner. My body goes through the motions but there is a sense of distance between us; I make love to him but almost warily, knowing how much he can hurt me if he wants to. There is no way I can be sure of which way he will leap ... I realise now I have absolutely no hold over this man other than the claims of a pretty face, a good body and a liking for inventive sex. It is a huge shock to my always-fragile sense of self-esteem that I have fallen into the oldest trap of all. I believed and trusted a man on the flimsiest of evidence – and in the teeth of all the warnings – a pair of soft blue eyes, a blinding sexual chemistry and a teddy-bear charm.

Later, I lie on the pillows and watch the lights of London flicker across the blinds and listen to the distant hum of the traffic while, beside me, Jason sleeps. My thoughts scuttle like cockroaches across my consciousness, randomly obtrusive; I get up finally to pull the shades so the room will be darker. I am tired, I want to sleep, but my brain is dully unsparing; I think of the long road I have taken to arrive at this place and how it has been all for nothing. I look at the sleeping form of my lover and know that all I ever want is to be beside him. I feel I should be planning how to persuade him, how to be sure of him but I feel empty of all imagination; used up, dried up, unable to fight any more. The Sophie who believed was a creation of Natasha's; this miserable, timid Sophie is one I recognise. This is the Sophie who doesn't believe in her own value.

Perhaps the movement of the curtain disturbs him; he mutters in his sleep and turns restlessly. 'Katie,' he says, and her name turns my blood to ice. I feel her presence, suddenly, in that quiet room and it makes me shiver as I slip back into bed. 'Katie,' he says again, and then clearly, 'Stop! Leave him alone!' I freeze; he is clearly in the grip of nightmare as his arm stretches out, the hand turned upwards, the thumb working up and down. I watch, puzzled, as he mutters 'no, no, no' and then, the merest whisper which sends chills up my spine – 'she's dead', followed by a softly-spoken, 'don't let Jack see'.

He sighs and suddenly, in the absurd way that the unconscious mind works, I see a scene in my mind's eye, *Macbeth,* as the doctor says, *"Heavens, what a sigh is here."* And I remember that Lady Macbeth spoke; sleepwalking she told the truth about those events which had led to her present madness. Will Jason also speak to me, lost as he is in the grip of unconsciousness? I moisten my lips and say, softly, authoritatively, 'Jason Knight, tell me … how did your wife die?'

There is a moment of silence and then he says, so clearly that I am sure he is awake, 'I killed her.'

The breath leaves my throat in a stunned half gasp; I lean over to look at him, but his eyes are shut. He is asleep. My head is reeling but I go on in the same quiet tone. 'How did you kill her?'

He says, quietly, almost conversationally, 'There was a hornet. I locked her in the car and it stung her. I knew she would die.' He pauses, and then goes on, dropping his voice a tone, but still clearly, 'She deserved to die.'

He sighs again, and turns over; in a moment his breathing becomes calm and regular and I know he is sound asleep. I lie there, thinking, and rubbing my aching forehead with my fingers. *God in Heaven, what a turnaround.* I think of the torment I have gone through that Katie Knight had died because of the actions of the assassin that I had bought and instead now I learn that her gentle husband had finally turned on her and killed her. I find I am shaking as the adrenalin licks through my blood. He must have known of her allergy; the thought of him planning such a murder makes my blood run cold. And Jack? What had he seen; how much did he understand? A child, only 8 years old, but perceptive enough to realise, not now perhaps, but later, that his father had stood by and watched his mother die. It is horrible, and it makes me feel sick; I sip water and try and reason it out but to very little avail. But I am determined now to know the whole story. I slide into an uneasy sleep, troubled by dreams; when I awake the sun is shining into the room, the curtains are drawn and

Jason is standing, naked, by a singing kettle and greeting me with a smile. I swim up out of sleep, and then suddenly, I remember, and sit up in bed with a frown on my face.

He brings me a cup of tea, kissing me and saying, 'Morning, gorgeous,' as he puts the cup into my hand. I stare at him and he laughs. 'Why the frown? You should be happy! It's a beautiful day in London.'

He walks around the other side of the bed and gets in. I turn to him and say, baldly, before I've even had a chance to phrase the words.

'You talked in your sleep. You said you'd killed your wife. Jason, what happened?'

His face loses all colour and he looks, for a moment, terrified. 'What did I say?' he asks eventually.

I repeat it all and watch his face, now curiously impassive, his mouth set in a hard line. 'Well,' he says finally, 'I suppose I had better tell you the whole story. But it doesn't make good hearing, I warn you.'

'I don't care about that. I want to hear the truth.'

He sighs deeply as though unearthing memories from a deep well.

'We were packing to leave Dubai,' he says slowly. 'She'd been super-stressed all morning and suddenly she just flipped, screaming at Jack because he'd left stuff in the car that she'd told him to bring in. I was in the hall, packing a box, and he started screaming. I went in and she was holding him by the hair, just shouting into his face. I pushed her away and grabbed him … she started hitting at me and then she whirled around and went storming downstairs and out to the car. The maid was in the kitchen, so I ran downstairs and pushed Jack in there with her. I was beside myself with anger. She was in the car, muttering or sobbing … I'm not quite sure which … kneeling on the seat, looking for his hat or whatever it was; I started to say something, but then I saw, crawling along the seat towards her bare leg, was a massive yellow and brown striped hornet. I just stood there, watching it getting closer and closer. I knew what it would mean of course, if it stung her, I knew about the allergy. But the Epi-pen was inside, upstairs, locked away, and without it I knew what would happen … she started to back out of the door, and … her thigh went down right on top of it.

And then, I'm not sure what happened. I know that I pushed her and slammed the door shut, and I know that I had the remote in my hand and I just kept my thumb down on the lock button. And I watched her die … right in front of me, and all I could think was that it was Fate. She had hurt Jack and she deserved to suffer. And …' he heaves a trembling sigh, but his face is pale and hard as though sculpted in marble. 'It didn't take long. I suppose that she was so strung up that her heart was beating very fast … she was scrabbling at the door with her hands and gasping for air … she sort of slid down into the seat and then Jack came belting out of the front door and I grabbed him and held him against me so he couldn't see anything. Then I think I took him inside then and gave him to Delia and said, 'Don't let him outside, I'm calling the police.' And he was crying 'Mummy! Mummy!' His voice falters slightly, but he goes on.

'And I rang the police and said my wife had died from a hornet sting, from anaphylactic shock, and by the time they came I'd got the story straight, and I told them that she'd gone to the car and shut the door, that she must have been stung, that she couldn't get out because of the child-locks … that she must have, in panic, locked herself in. They took it very much at face value. The Embassy doctor came and I told him the same story; I was in the house, by the time I got to the car it was too late. And he was like the police, took it as a tragic accident, gave me lots of sympathy and a sedative, and went away. Jack was my main concern; he was hysterical for a while so I gave him half the sedative and he went to sleep. I stayed awake all night, watching him, and thinking … thinking how easy it all was. There must be a catch somewhere, I kept waiting for something to happen, for the police to come back and arrest me … but there was nothing. The school made sure that everything went smoothly and did all the paperwork to spare me the trauma; I stood in the church on the day of the funeral and I knew then that I'd gotten away with it; I knew that I could start over and it would be just me and Jack, like I'd always wanted. It was a heady feeling, being alone, just the two of us and gradually he stopped missing her; he'd talk about her sometimes but he hardly ever cried. I guess the peace and quiet was soothing in itself. And now he hardly mentions her at all. I used to wonder if he saw anything but I don't think he did. I didn't want him to see but I forced myself to watch. It was a punishment, really, I think, for letting her make us suffer for so long … a punishment to myself for allowing it to go on and not do anything to stop it.'

There's nothing to say. I sip tea to moisten my dry lips.

He heaves a sigh. 'So now you see Sophie, why I have to go away, just me and Jack, for a while anyway, just us two. Besides, technically …' he grimaces, 'I'm a murderer. You deserve better than that.'

What is there to say? I shake my head, and think if only he knew. Maybe we all have the seeds of violent resolution within us … who can say? Driven far enough, who amongst us may not resort to the final and most dreadful solution? I myself could only do it second-hand, but I did it nonetheless.

'I'm sorry,' I say finally. 'I think she must have been a little bit mad, not entirely responsible for her actions. But I understand why you did it. And I don't think any the worse of you … I guess none of us knows how far we will go given desperate circumstances.' I mock the irony of my remark, but it is apparent only to me, of course.

His blue eyes are harder than I've ever seen them. 'I'm not sorry,' he says, 'a little bit guilty of course, but she doesn't haunt me.'

'She haunts your dreams,' I say, giving him a straight look.

He shrugs. 'Not for long,' he says. 'I am determined to get over it. As far as anyone knows my wife was the victim of a tragic accident. And that's the story … some days I almost believe it myself.'

I'm looking at him and seeing, not the gentle teddy-bear lover of my dreams, not the golden-haired Kester Woodseaves, but a new man, one I don't know very well, a man who took destiny into his hands and will live, not unhappily, with the consequences. 'You've changed,' I say reflectively, 'but I don't see why we can't be together. I don't believe you'd ever be tempted to murder me.'

He gives a rather grim smile. 'I love you, Sophie, I haven't lied about that. I haven't told anyone what I just told you and I never will. But I need to go away on my own, with Jack, for a while. I have changed and I have to get used to this new Jason. I quite like him, you know. He has *cojones.*'

Morning brings counsel, so they say, and while we eat breakfast, enjoying orange juice and croissants and hot coffee, I find myself yielding. Notwithstanding the events of last night, I do understand him. In the same way as, months before, I understood why he could never leave Katie because Jack came first; I understand why he has to be free now to find himself. I am selfish, I suppose, in that I want to be sure, to know that he loves me and will come back. I don't want to press for an answer, still less for any type of commitment because I feel instinctively that none will be forthcoming. I have to trust him, trust to the love that he says he has for me, and believe that when he comes to terms with this resolute confident new Jason, he will come back to me. I can only trust that time will purge the last ten years of misery and submission and allow him once more to trust himself to a woman. It will be a test for me too, a test of patience and trust and the healing passage of time, but I feel my heart rising to the challenge as the warm summer sun streams through the windows and a finger of golden light points straight at Jason's head, so similar to the artist's rendition of Kester Woodseaves. I take it as a sign.

'What's the date?' I ask suddenly.

'The first of August, fair lady,' he responds with a smile.

'It's today,' I say, 'oh my God, it's today! Turn on the TV!'

He does so, but with a puzzled look. 'What's special about today?'

I grab the remote from him and switch to the news channel. It's just on the hour and the newsreader is already into the first item. I shush him and listen with attention.

'... *An expose by British journalist Alex Lyngate, writing for the New York Times. The article, spread over three pages of the American broadsheet, gives a graphic and detailed description of an alleged fundamentalist coup by Al Qaeda affiliate Al Shabaab, aimed at toppling Dubai's ruler, Sheikh Mohammed bin Rashid al Maktoum.*

Mr Lyngate, who spent more than two years living in Dubai and doing extensive research, has an astonishing breadth of material which appears to prove a link between the renegade Prince Faisal, the Sheikh's youngest brother, and a plot to bring down the present administration and install the young prince in his place at the head of a fundamentalist Islamic state.

The Ambassador for the UAE in London commented this morning that it was a nonsensical allegation, but the news has been taken seriously across the Arab world, with the UAE stock exchange falling three points on its opening this morning. Sheikh Mohammed himself has declined to speak to the press, and the American ambassador in Dubai has commented that the Sheikh has the full backing of the American people for his recent and sustained efforts to combat terrorism in the area. The piece has been widely published by most of the leading newspapers of both the Arab and the Western world and featured on the controversial Middle East based broadcaster, Al Jazeera.

I mute the sound and stare at Jason with shining eyes. 'He did it, oh my God, he and Natasha – finally,' I punch the air, 'Alex gets his great moment and, God willing, his Pulitzer Prize! We have to go out right now and buy The Times. I can't wait to read the whole thing!'

Jason comes over and sits down on the bed, his hand on the side of my head. 'Sophie,' he says softly, 'will you wait for me? I don't know how long it will take, but I believe if I know I have you at the end, it will come right.'

I lean forward and kiss him and, in that moment, I have all I ever want. 'Will you wait for *me?*' I respond. 'All those gorgeous Russian girls ... and I should know!'

He smiles that soft Kester smile that makes me catch my breath at the depth of my love for him. 'What is it that my lookalike, your hero, says to Prue Sarn?' He cocks his head and says, *'I've chosen my bit of Paradise. Tis on your breast my dear acquaintance.'*

I clasp the golden heart at my throat, my Natasha talisman, with pleasure at, first his having remembered the quotation, and second, the aptness of it.

'How good you are for me, Sophie,' he says, with something of my earnestness and I get the feeling that he's totally serious. 'Will you live up to your name and be wise? Will you make the world the sane sweet place it used to be?'

We seal the bond with a deep kiss that both obscures the past and welcomes the future; apart for a while, perhaps, but with the promise of things to come. And like Pip and Estella, I can say, with confidence, *I saw no shadow of another parting.*